QUICK BRIGHT THINGS

By the same author

The Greatest Sorrow

QUICK BRIGHT THINGS

Keith Ovenden

HAMISH HAMILTON · LONDON

HAMISH HAMILTON LTD
Published by the Penguin Group
Penguin Books Ltd, 27 Wrights Lane, London W8 5TZ, England
Penguin Putnam Inc., 375 Hudson Street, New York, New York 10014, USA
Penguin Books Australia Ltd, Ringwood, Victoria, Australia
Penguin Books Canada Ltd, 10 Alcorn Avenue, Toronto, Ontario, Canada M4V 3B2
Penguin Books (NZ) Ltd, Private Bag 102902, NSMC, Auckland, New Zealand

Penguin Books Ltd, Registered Offices: Harmondsworth, Middlesex, England

First published 2000
1 3 5 7 9 10 8 6 4 2

Copyright © Keith Ovenden, 2000

Set in 10/14pt Meridian
Phototypeset by Intype London Ltd
Printed in Great Britain by Clays Ltd, St Ives plc

A CIP catalogue record for this book is available from the British Library

ISBN 0–241–140 870

For Crispin

If there were a sympathy in choice,
War, death or sickness did lay siege to it,
Making it momentary as a sound,
Swift as a shadow, short as any dream,
Brief as the lightning in the collied night,
That, in a spleen, unfolds both heaven and earth,
And ere a man hath power to say, 'Behold!'
The jaws of darkness do devour it up:
So quick bright things come to confusion.

Shakespeare,
A Midsummer Night's Dream, I, i, 141

CONTENTS

1

Dear Felix

1

2

The Worst Five Weeks

175

3

Sympathy in Choice

227

1

Dear Felix

CLÉMONT

Friday 13 June   *Morning*

Dear Felix,

You were absolutely right about Boswell. When I woke up this morning he was sitting on the bed, just inside the crook of my arm, giving me a deep, steady stare. I think we are already friends. At any rate we rubbed legs down the stairs, and then he sat and waited for the fridge door to open. After milk he instructed me to clear the kitchen windowsill so that he could sit and watch the Sauldre for a while. When I looked round a few minutes later, he had disappeared. Does he really remember everything he's told and sees? Such creatures of instinct, aren't they?

I got here a little before ten last night. Dark just about, and raining, but a sort of warm fug among the trees. The drive down was pretty easy, and the road from Châteauneuf through Tigy and Isdes, even though wet, was rather better than I'd anticipated from your description. It was still light most of the way and not much traffic. Madame Morisot hadn't left the keys in the box, but the driveway gate was open and she was waiting for me in the porch, drying her hands on a pinny, yellow kitchen light spilling out behind her through the door. She reminded me rather of Philip's mother, Doris, whom you met at the funeral. A younger version of course, because I don't suppose she's much older than me – forty-something maybe – but very like her in the set of her face, her pink elbows, and the hair clip she was wearing behind her ear. You don't see many of those these days. She said I must call her Madame Jeanne, just as you said she would. It had also been her mother's name. 'Not uncommon around Orléans!' She has a lovely smile. She gave me a quick tour of the house, helped me to bring in the boxes, and chattered along about '*le professeur*'. I couldn't understand all of it, but the outline was clear: she thinks you are a god. I quite like this idea, so we sang your praises together.

The first thing I want to do, before anything more important, or at any rate pressing, gets in the way, is to tell you something about Philip's funeral. The boxes reminded me, and once I started thinking about it, it wouldn't go away. By funeral I don't mean the ceremony bit, because of course you were there. You'll remember that it was the Master's idea to have the service in the college chapel, even though Philip wasn't religious, because the crematorium chapel was fully booked for days. Apparently they always have an early-January rush, and this year was especially cold. Anyway, after the reception, or function, or whatever you call it, I went to the crematorium with Philip on my own. I didn't want to have anybody else there. I just wanted, I suppose it sounds silly, I just wanted to be with him one last time, and to see him off, say goodbye. I even had a few things ready to think about as he, well, as he went through the fire.

We got there quite late in the evening, around eight o'clock if I remember, and it wasn't until after the undertaker's men had left that I discovered that there was a queue. Really. Philip was eleventh and last in line for the day, and the man who operated the equipment on the late shift had gone for his tea break. So we had to wait, Philip and me. Somehow it seemed prosaic and special at one and the same time. The industrialization of death, with tea breaks and shift work, routine maintenance, capacity constraints and supply bottlenecks. I sat there trying to think about Philip, and the things I wanted to say to him, but all that would come to mind was how he hated waiting in queues, and how frustrated he would become. He particularly detested immigration and customs formalities. He said it was an inflexible rule that whichever passport queue he joined would immediately stop, and wouldn't start again until all other queues had cleared. And now here he was, at the ultimate immigration post, once again stuck at the end of a completely static queue. It made me very sad for him at the time because it was like a cruel endorsement of his view of things and events, the last and

4

deliberate revenge of circumstance on a life that had been defeated by it, and lost.

Then it occurred to me that if there was a bit of a queue on this side of things, then God alone knew what it must be like on the other. The queue of queues. Poor old St Peter, or Michael, or whoever, with lines millions long, almost no one with the right documentation, moral passports mostly expired or forged, and an awkward cuss like Philip right at the back making clever but ill-judged remarks about celestial administration, inadequate staffing, bureaucratic obstructionism and fascist officials.

He used to get into trouble for this sort of thing. That story he told of our visit to Herzen's tomb in Nice is a case in point. His description of what happened that day is quite good as far as it goes, though he leaves out how hard I tried to talk to him about it afterwards, in the afternoon, and how uncooperative his silence was. But never mind about that. The real trouble is that it doesn't go far enough. In particular he omitted an incident in the morning which coloured everything that followed. We had been staying in an hotel along the coast somewhere, Sainte-Maxime perhaps, and got up early to drive into Nice. As we came into the old town, Philip made a mistake and found himself, very briefly, driving us the wrong way up a one-way street. There wasn't much traffic, and he quickly turned round, but of course there would have to be a couple of gendarmes sitting in a patrol car under a tree watching this whole manoeuvre, and when it was finished they pulled us over. They gave the car and Philip's documents a thorough examination, and then said that they intended to issue him with a ticket for 200 French francs, payable immediately.

Philip's French, as you know, was fluent – both formal and colloquial kinds – and throughout the inquiry bit he had kept up a stream of explanation and apology: all a mistake, terribly sorry, moment's inattention, but little traffic and no harm done, etc. This made no difference of course. They simply told him what the penalty was, and started to fill in the ticket. As I'm sure you know, these sorts of fines are not really for offences committed. They're a tax on foreign tourists, and the assessment can't even be discussed. You just keep a straight face, say as little as possible, and pay up.

I was trying to get Philip to stop talking – eye contact, nudges and winks sort of stuff – and I even had my bag open, and was looking for my wallet to pay the fine when Philip, at the mention of 200 francs, suddenly flipped and went on the offensive. He produced his own notebook and Biro and made a show of writing down the patrol car registration number. He asked to see the *flics'* ID, and when they refused to show any he ostentatiously looked at his watch, wrote down the time, and took down verbatim what the officers had just said. Then he began expanding on the general theme of letters to the editor, the British Embassy and his Member of Parliament. He had never had much time for Mrs Thatcher, but her opinion of Mitterrand was beginning to make sense to him now, and more besides. The cops watched and listened to all this for a while, and then one of them got out another pad of tickets and wrote one out for 500 francs. As he did so, he pointed out that this was the maximum but normal fine for driving the wrong way up a one-way street, and that this was now the sum that Philip would have to pay.

Philip then said, very quietly but very deliberately: 'Fuck you.'

Now it's true, as he pointed out to me later, that Philip didn't say this in a belligerent way, and that he used a tone of voice that actually means something along the lines of 'Oh, come on. I'm not out of my tree, you know. You can't possibly want to charge me as much as that for something that wasn't even deliberate.' But the policemen, who gave every sign of knowing no other English, certainly knew the word fuck, and within seconds Philip found himself handcuffed in the back of the patrol car and being driven to the police station, while a policeman wagged a finger in his face saying, 'No fuck you.' 'No fuck you.' It took him two hours and 2,000 francs to extricate himself from this situation, and then only by making a full, frank and shamefaced apology to someone senior.

Eventually, when they had let him go – I had followed in the car and ended up waiting for him in a pavement café outside the gendarmerie – he said that it had been worth it, because one always learned something from these sorts of experiences. But he was pretty sheepish about it, and a bit shaken, I think. And anyway, there are lots of things that I don't think one does want to learn all that much. One of my tutors – Ricketts in Nuffield, you may know him, genial Canadian with a good TV manner on Budget Day, or when there's a crash on the capital markets – would sometimes preface the answer to a question with, 'I'm now going to tell you rather more than you want to know.' And generally he was right.

Still, the important point is that our visit to Herzen's tomb in the old graveyard in Nice came right on the heels of this experience, which really coloured it for him without his wanting to admit it. Philip was a bit careless, I think, about the fact that one inevitably carries forward into whatever setting feelings and emotions that arose in an earlier or preceding one. He was so preoccupied with the idea of feelings being continuously lost that he failed to recognize their continuity in some instances, even through sleep. Anyway, to go back a page or two, Philip was cremated in the end, and I collected his ashes a couple of days later. I didn't know what to do with them, of course. Still don't, six months on. I've brought them down here to Clémont with me, and they're in their box in front of me at the kitchen table. When I looked inside they were a sort of grey colour. Philip was never grey.

I didn't tell you, I think, but a week or two before I came away I had a letter from the Master, Sir Philip. He wanted to know if I could remind him who the 'aristocratic French gentleman' at Philip's funeral was. I had to smile because I remember your telling me that the Master had been quite exercised afterwards, at

dinner, and had commented on 'the unusual range of mourners –
very gratifying, and flattering for the college' – who'd turned
out for Philip's obsequies. Former students, many of whom are
now quite eminent in various walks of life; those two very
polished men from the Russian embassy; Mullens and that extraordinary mistress of his – the one who writes an astrology column
somewhere; my 'supporters' from the Bank, who all parked
their Rollers out the front; that American couple with the baby,
who may or may not have been with the philosophy faculty, who
all talked so loudly and drank so much afterwards; and the
couple who came from Paris. 'Very distinguished chap' who
spoke perfect English, and said that he and Philip had 'spent a
lot of time together when we were younger'. I think the Master
would have liked to snuggle (or is it wriggle?) a bit closer to him,
but of course he had his 'duties' – mainly Philip's poor parents.
I mustn't be horrid, because Sir Philip did do awfully well with
Doris and Stanley, and took such a weight off my hands and
mind.

Anyway, I wrote to the Master about this Frenchman. His
name's Roland Beaumanière, and his wife, the stunning brunette
who was wearing a Louis Féraud suit and the most beautiful
gold bracelet I think I have ever seen, her name's Florence, and
she's (or was, until she married) a Sobieski – one of the French
ones, like the Poniatowskis. Actually, I seem to remember your
telling me that you talked to them yourself, and that you had
something in common. This part of the country, perhaps? I can't
remember. Anyway, I didn't feel that I could really write and tell
the Master about him without letting Monsieur Beaumanière
know that I had, and since I was visiting here I also told him this
address. And when I came down for breakfast with Boswell
this morning, there was a letter for me from him. Very friendly,
asking if we might meet. He wants to talk a little about Philip,
he said. And he has always regretted that, at least until Philip's
funeral, he and I had never met. He says he and his wife have
connections in this area, and will be coming down for the

weekend. Apparently there's some function or the other that they're committed to. Afterwards they will stay somewhere locally overnight, and then hope to see me on the Sunday, before returning to Paris. I feel I ought to invite them here. I hope you don't mind. It's a bit awkward having guests when it isn't my place, and you've been so generous already, just letting me be here. I sent Roland B. the phone numbers, yours and mine.

—

Early evening

'Oh joy,' as Philip would say, in that flat, emotionless voice that he used to put on. You know the one: pleasure, indifference and condemnation all at once. Well: 'Oh joy.' There's another English woman here in the village. Did you know this? Well, she's just *outside* the village, really: first house on the right, set back, on the road south, just after the bridge. She's a fair bit older than me, but she seemed familiar somehow, though this afternoon she was drunk. This was how I met her. After lunch I drove over to Argent to buy some groceries and to look around, and on the way home, just outside the village, she was coming towards me on her bike. That bit where the road narrows and there's a sharp turning, and a little lane goes off to the right. She was coming towards me going very slowly, a bit wobbly, and just as we were passing she raised a hand to give me a wave, lost control and toppled into the ditch. I stopped to fish her out and took her home, which is the house down the lane. It was still raining, so she was pretty muddy, and we had the devil's own job getting the bike in the back. She said she always waved to cars with English number-plates in the village.

'And do you always fall off?'

'Only when drunk.'

'Ah.'

'Which is quite a lot, I suppose.' She sighed. 'Though I don't usually try to bike on the bottle. But today I had to send a

9

telegram because the phone's been cut off again. Come in if you like.'

I did. A big farmhouse, stone and ivy, with flagstone floors, set in a huge garden right down on the river bank. Someone had scrawled the name 'Favelas' in chalk on a wonky board at the top of the drive. Looked and sounded rather unpleasant. The garden showed signs of having been in good order once but now reverting to water meadow and forest. At the house, I only went in the kitchen, which is where Beatrix – ' with an X please. Adults only' – clearly lives, if that's the right word, most of the time. It was a terrible mess. There was about six months' worth of washing-up; quite a lot of underwear, perhaps not all of it dirty; magazines and paperbacks; tins of snails, catfood, beans, olives, all open, some for quite a while, I should think; about 30,000 pounds' worth of CDs spread around like rice at a wedding; some old, some newish furniture, some broken, some not; shelves of books, spices and herbs suggestive of someone who was once interested in cooking but had lost her nerve. Huge fireplace with a motorbike in it, though the front wheel was missing. 'Johan took it,' she said, noticing my expression. 'Bastard!' I could go on, but you probably get the picture. The smell I couldn't begin to describe, but there was some pot in it, overlaid with a number of other stale substances more legal but less attractive, like Turkish tobacco and rotten meat. The fridge door was open.

Beatrix went somewhere and had a wash, then poured herself a gin, cleared some space on a sofa, sat down and promptly went to sleep, snoring. I think I've seen her before. Indeed, I think she might be someone I know and have stupidly forgotten. Perhaps she and I were at the same school but a few years apart. One always has this uneasy feeling about people who were a number of years ahead of you at school. You knew their reputations, but you couldn't get to know them personally, and they always seemed terribly knowing, and on the verge of something brilliant. I wondered whether I shouldn't do some washing-up or housework, but decided that the neighbourly thing would be to rescue the gin from her fingers and slip away. She woke up briefly as I was doing this.

'You just passing? Or staying somewhere nearby?'

'Staying. For a week or two. Felix Cunningham's place in the village. Do you know . . .?' But she had shut her eyes again.

'Come again if you want,' she mumbled.

I went out through the hall, where the front door seems to stand permanently open. The hall was dominated, I almost said overshadowed but that would be quite wrong, illuminated perhaps, by a huge photograph, six feet by four at least (perhaps bigger), of a very beautiful young woman wearing not much at all, her large mouth glistening with wet lipstick.

I spent the rest of the afternoon with Boswell, going through the first box. He came and sat right in front of me on the desk, exactly where I wanted to work, purring very loudly, and keen to rub noses. Eventually I managed to get him settled in my lap. The box turned out to contain mainly photographs, and it was a melancholy business sorting through them. Some of them I knew, of course – ones of him and me over the years, though it's odd, isn't it, now that I'm looking at them like this, with Philip gone, how it's only in very few of them that we're actually together? One or other of us was usually behind the lens, so it's him plus view, or me plus view, or me with his parents, or him with mine. We are coupled here and there, especially in the ones taken on our occasional visits to Bué with Moser and Vita. It's funny to think of Bué being nearby here, of our going there over the years, yet never knowing this sort of 'next door' region existed. Lots of France is like this, isn't it? The little regions have their backs to each other, and knowing one you don't even notice the next. I'd never even heard of the Sologne until you mentioned it, and yet now I'm here it reminds me of somewhere. Maybe it was just something we had to read when I was at school. When the weather's like this – and it's still raining, not hard but with a sort of steady relentlessness, as it used to at the farm in Suffolk sometimes – well, then the countryside becomes all misty and dripping and wet, and there's a lovely feeling of nostalgia and, well, loss. Is that why you bought this place? Why you come here? It helps me to understand why you hesitated when I asked if I might come down on my own for a while. You probably thought I ought to go somewhere light and bright, like Rhodes or San Sepolcro, and that coming to the banks of the Sauldre to think about Philip would be a recipe for misery.

So don't worry. I like willows, and oaks, and beech trees, and the feeling of there being a sort of *Wind in the Willows à la française* going on along the river banks, and I like the muddy lanes strewn with leaves even though it's supposed to be summer, and the sounds of woodpeckers and cuckoos and owls, and the whizzing kingfishers over the water. Swallows in abundance – you know, they nest under the stable eaves – with, oh dear, a harvest of midges and mosquitoes for them to feed on. 'If there is a paradise,' Philip used to say, 'it'll have mosquitoes.' Actually my brother-in-law Robin, the one who works on *Bagehot's*, Tanny's husband, he warned me about the mosquitoes. They have a house much further south, in the Dordogne, and he was sniffy about this part of France. Tanny said it was nice, but it wasn't a good place to be alone because it was too much weeping willows and sad sunsets and melancholy mists. But I think women are better adapted to solitude than men are. Not that we always like to be alone, but we know the difference between solitude and loneliness, and we can be content with our own company when we have to be. *Rebecca Crusoe* would be a quite different story from *Robinson*. We don't count the days because they're not really our sort of measure of time. We have our own clock somewhere, internal and unthreatening. Also I think we're better at fantasy, which is what preserves sanity in isolation. I feel quite sure of these things, though Philip would have wanted to know how I *know* them to be true. But I don't think it's really a question of truth. Some knowledge simply is, and doesn't have to be proven.

Like my relationship with Philip. This was so strong, had endured so many difficulties, that I have this feeling that he's still part of my life, even though he's dead. And I don't mean that I have the sensation that he's in the room, or that I can talk to him – those sorts of I think rather silly things. I mean that our lives had become so intertwined that I felt able to explain as well as understand him, and this very special sort of knowledge will go on influencing and shaping me for the rest of my life. It's as if even things that happened to him, or that he did, and which I knew nothing about, can still affect my own life. As if he can still touch me, and influence things, in ways that I might never know about. And I don't mean it's ghostly or ghoulish or anything like that. The feeling is very real to me. And I like it.

I'm rambling, aren't I? I'm sorry. I think of it as settling in. Also, to be honest, I'm procrastinating. Those few thousand words you want me to write about Philip are a bit of a millstone. It wasn't hard to agree to do it, because I know there has to be some sort of appreciation in the Harcourt College *Chronicle*, and I'm relieved that it's you who will write it. I do want to help. But now I'm here I can see how hard it's going to be. And I haven't even started yet.

But it was a good idea to bring Philip's papers. Also rather fun. That scout of his, Mrs Wharton, packed the boxes terribly neatly, but in the pursuit of order she completely obliterated any other organizing principle. Apart from the photographs, which were all together in one box, everything else seems to be muddled up: lecture notes with family letters; book reviews he did for *Mind* and *Ethics* jumbled up with credit card receipts and those circular letters people write at Christmas; longer manuscripts, including early drafts of *The Politics of Eden* and *Alexander Herzen*, along with the references he wrote for his former pupils, advertisements for all sorts of things, though mainly books and magazines; even a file labelled 'The ironies of fate', which I peeped in, that seems to consist of the sorts of things that always gave Philip pleasure: a Frenchman employed to write a cover-up of the Rainbow

13

Warrior affair who really was called Tricot; and another to head the European Bank called Trichet; private companies that call themselves Mercury, who is the patron saint of thieves; and so on. He loved things like this. He said it was evidence that humour, like the rest of life, was present in nature, and would still be there even if mankind disappeared, or forgot how to laugh.

I'm not sure whether to go through the boxes first and write the piece for you after I've finished, or the other way round. These sorts of choices are so difficult. I had half expected to have my mind made up for me by finding earlier volumes of diaries and journals – earlier than *The Greatest Sorrow*, that's to say. But there don't appear to be any, at least not on a first quick look. I suppose it's just as well. Philip could be so terribly convincing, and yet unutterably wrong. Quite unlike most philosophers, who may well be right about lots of things but never persuade anyone. So if Philip had left any more journals, they'd just as likely be misleading.

I'm sure this is true of *The Greatest Sorrow*. I know you were surprised when I agreed to let HH go ahead and publish. (Was there some reason you wouldn't offer it to Mullens?) But the thing is that even though it seems to be a journal, and will probably get reviewed as one when it comes out in the autumn, it isn't really a documentary at all. Really, it's fiction. Oh I know some of the events actually happened, but it was all fiction in the sense that poor Philip was *in extremis*, and quite unable to tell the difference between fact and fantasy, truth and falsehood. And he knew this himself. He says as much. He must have suffered very badly. You said, after you read it the first time, that I didn't come out of it very well. 'Very cold, his portrayal of you,' you said. 'He should have warmed you up a bit.' But I don't see how he could. It's Philip's confessional, not mine. And all that stuff about my infidelities – well, it was wounding, of course – but Philip knew with at least some part of his being that it wasn't true, even when he was at his worst. And I think he came to see that much, perhaps all of it, was projection. The ghost of Vita, perhaps. I don't know. Philip loved to quote Anthony Powell: 'One passes through the world knowing few, if any, of the important things about even the people with whom one has been from time to time in the closest intimacy.' He said it so often, even I can remember it. It was something he really believed. Other people were just about unknowable, not only because of the impossibility of empathy but because of the shortage of data. This was, I think, why writing the life of Herzen turned into such a terrible paradox, expanding and shrivelling him simultaneously. He knew so much but counted it worthless because, in the end, the man eluded him. And he came to see that this was inevitable. Perhaps if he'd been able to say, I can't catch Herzen because I'm not talented/knowledgeable/hard-working/whatever enough, that would have made it somehow OK. But having to say, I can't catch Herzen because no one can ever catch, in that sense, another; the whole project is doomed; the task is hopeless – well, this put him in the position of Sisyphus, and it destroyed his self-confidence. It also tainted so much else that previously he had valued and enjoyed.

And it wasn't just the sexual infidelities that weren't true. All that stuff about me and Marxism isn't true either. Really, it started as a joke between us but evolved over the years into a standing reference. Most of the time I don't think he believed it any more than I did. It was an old boot that we kicked around the attic of our memories, and when he was in a good mood Philip could be very funny about it. 'And with reason' – as he would say, letting the double meaning hang for a moment – because when I was twenty, and Philip and I met for the first time, I *did* imagine myself a romantic revolutionary, putting the world to rights. But we all change an awful lot between the ages of thirteen and twenty-five. The important thing, Moser used to say, is not to get stuck, or to allow your own judgement of others to get stuck and assume them to be unchanging. Everybody evolves. This was one reason why it was so awful when Philip fell into one of his mixed states, depressed but sort of manically

15

angry at the same time. Somehow he was projected into another way of being, where everything was logical, but all the axioms were wrong. I tried to point this out to him once, but he said that I was confusing him with economics, and that I should make up my mind which one I was married to. Pretty wounding stuff.

Well, I think the tone of this sort of thing comes through in *The Greatest Sorrow*. He makes accusations, but you can tell they don't ring true, even to him. He acknowledges that they come from somewhere that's in him but not of him – his Furies – and once he'd got them back on the leash, or in the kennel or wherever, he would be terribly ashamed and remorseful. I imagine that reading it, for someone who didn't know Philip, must be a bit like being a magistrate – one of those French *juges d'instruction* – confronted with a witness whose accusations are, simultaneously, very logical but quite unreliable. As a result, deciding what to believe just comes down to a question of personality.

Philip would have hated this. Perhaps this is why he felt so defeated after the gaudy affair, because, what with all the publicity, those dreadful pieces in the *Guardian* diary and the *Sun*, and the item in the *Telegraph* that had obviously been inspired by Conrad Jesty, he believed everyone was saying that he had an unstable personality, was a nasty character, or whatever. But Philip didn't believe there was any such thing as personality. He called it – this was one of his phrases, usually produced in a stagey voice, crisp and mock upper class – 'a fiction to grease the gears of intercourse'. Most people, he said, even if they didn't like their own fictions, settled into them and played along. But you don't have to do very much, or go very far, to acquire a new one, if that's what you want. Learn a foreign language and you get a new personality. Take up a sport you've never played before, with people you've never previously met, and you can make an entirely new start. Even tiny things can go a long way. If you change your hat, or the way you walk, or the beer you drink, or the music you listen to, or how you have your hair cut, you'll get some aspects of a new personality right away. People judge us on these sorts of trivialities, and out of their judgements they erect models of what we are like. But they're quite empty and meaningless, really.

I never agreed with this, but I think it's the kind of argument that men make. It fits their view of life as something that can be manipulated and conquered. But women see through it. I think this is because women are quite content pursuing two different things simultaneously: we want to be fashionable (which is to conform), but we also want to be different, if not unique. As a result, we are constantly discovering how robust a personality really is. No matter how hard we try to change, with this year's clothes, or a new hairstyle, or the very latest in make-up or hair colour, or by diet and exercise, personality keeps on peeping back, the same, ineradicable.

The thing is, surely, that even if, like me, you believe in personality, you can still be quite wrong about it. I knew Philip well. Better than anyone, probably. But I may not have got him right. I've been worrying about this today because among the photographs there were some I'd not seen before, pictures that date from at a guess about twenty-five years ago. Several rolled-up ones of what look like school outings, in which Philip is always standing apart and looking bored, or detached, or sheepish, or something. Perhaps just pensive, with his tongue between his teeth. And then there are a lot more that must come from holidays: young people, beach scenes, café tables presumably in France. One of these, of Philip on his own, is stunning. From the look of it he must have been about sixteen or seventeen. He's crouched down on his haunches, those long, thin hands of his folded across one another, his arms on his knees. Actually he's holding a bit of string, or fishing line, or something. Behind him there's a sign, partly obscured, that says, I think, 'orge'. But it's not the posture, or the place, or any of those things. It's the look. He's staring straight into the camera, and yet it's as if he isn't

17

there. The face is empty, like a mask from behind which he has fled, leaving a void. And the eyes are so deep set, and so dark, that they exist only as black ovals on the pale plate of his face. Where is he? Where has he gone?

—

Saturday 14 June   *Morning*

It stopped raining in the early evening, and there was one of those pale blue and white washed skies, like something off a jigsaw puzzle. A flock of blackbirds, starlings and thrushes came tap-tapping on the lawn. Madame Jeanne looked in with some fresh bread and a goat's cheese that she said was made by her neighbour. She's awfully kind, isn't she? She had her daughter with her, a beautiful young woman called Micheline, who works as a nurse in a hospital just this side of Orléans, between the town and the university. She doesn't get home to Clémont very often because either she's working or she has to go to Paris for weekends. You probably know all this already. Micheline has the most lovely deep brown eyes, quite unlike her mother's, which are that startling blue colour that one always associates with heroes and film stars. They didn't stay long, and when they left Micheline slipped her arm through Jeanne's as they went up the drive.

I wanted a walk, so I took the bread and cheese and went down to pay Beatrix a visit, see if she was all right. She was standing by the river when I arrived, watching a couple of swans shepherding a clutch of cygnets about. She had a big goblet of wine in her hand and didn't recognize me at first.

'Alice. Alice Crighton. We met earlier today . . .'

'Christ, yes. I remember. Sorry. Specs.' She indicated the bridge of her nose. 'Put them down somewhere and can't find the bloody things. Want a drink?'

We went inside where the mess, if anything, was worse than it had been before lunch.

'It's probably in the fridge.' She waved at it, indicating I might help myself, and then hunted down some CDs which she poked into a player. Some very loud, unrecognizable music filled the room. Bending over to investigate the contents of the fridge, some of which were identifiable but none of which was white wine, I suddenly remembered who she was, and where I'd seen her before.

'You're a quarter of Nix! I'm sorry, that's very rude of me . . .'

''S all right.'

'I should have . . .'

'It's not the first time.'

'It's simply that I knew I knew you when I was here this morning. Or rather, knew you were familiar. Of course, I don't know you, or didn't, and . . .'

'Do you gabble a lot?'

'Ah.'

'Look, er, Alice. And it's over there' – she pointed at the fireplace, where I spotted a wine bottle next to the motorbike – 'glasses on the shelf over the what-not. This used to happen all the time. But not any more. It's over. I'm finished. Nix hasn't been together for nineteen years and six months almost to the day – *Top of the Pops*, Christmas 1977 – and yes, I am, or was, the one they called Bix Nix. I sang on my own after, but I haven't worked now for about ten years and my voice's shot.' She flung herself on to a sofa, dislodging various items. 'Those were the days, eh!' And she drank a long draught of wine.

You won't know this, Felix, because, well, because you won't. But Nix were a fantastically popular rock group in the early and mid seventies. Three boys and a girl – this very same Bix. Her real name's Beatrix Stapleton, incidentally. I was about twelve when they came on the scene, and they were it, or IT, for four or five years. They started off with some stuff that was a bit political. Nixon was skidding out of office, and Nix made something of that, but their *real* music was a blend of sex and blues, and she did most of the singing. She could sing gravel like Janis

Joplin, and shout like Grace Slick, or be smooth and polished like Christine McVie. I don't suppose any of this means anything to you at all, but she really was terrific. And of course the picture in the hallway is her. Or was her.

'What do you do?'

'Me? Oh, I, er, I'm an economist. Pretty dull, really. With Blount Brothers, the merchant bank.'

'Blunt with an O? Or Blunt without an O?'

'With an O.'

'Blount with an O. Beatrix with an X. Gotta get our words right. Are you going to drink that, or are you just warming it up? And for Chrissake find somewhere to sit. I'm getting a crick in my neck.'

I sat down on a stool next to a big, complicated-looking exercise machine that was being used as a clothes line. 'Have you lived here long, Beatrix?'

'About eight years. First, you know, after Nix broke up, I was in Amsterdam. I did shows and night clubs and stuff, work that Johan found me. He's my manager. Or was. Well, still is, really, 'cept there's nothin' left to manage. Bastard. He said I had a great future after Nix, and I was the silly cow who listened to him.'

'Did you come here to get away?'

'From Johan? You don't get away from Johan. He's my manager, right? A real Dutch treat.'

'You mean he . . .'

'Fuck knows. Look, forget it. Have another drink. It's always nice to have visitors.' She dragged her legs up on to the sofa, and settled some pullovers on top of her.

'I wondered if you were going to eat this evening. Whether we might do something together?'

'Do what?'

'Well, eat. Have dinner. Go out, perhaps. There must be somewhere in the village, or in Argent, even Tigy. Or else you could come to Felix's place, where I'm staying. Or I'd put something together here. I don't know.' I trailed off into silence. She turned

20

off the music with a remote control and then looked at me as if I was mad.

'Have you seen this place?'

'I could clear up a bit.'

'Are you out of your head? Why'd you want to do that?'

I shrugged.

'Suit yourself.' She drained her glass and closed her eyes, and seemed to fall asleep immediately.

So I did clear up a bit. I found something to wash up with, made some space on a drainer, stacked a load of crockery and pans, and got started. Beatrix snored on the sofa. It was all pretty hideous, and the more I did the more gruesome the things I uncovered, but it can be quite soothing to bring order out of chaos, and anyway Beatrix interests me. She was such a star when I was a girl. The ones at school who were potty about pop music used to dress like her, and there were crazes for the things she did, like putting lipstick on her ears, or carrying a riding crop everywhere she went, and wearing men's trousers back to front. She called them her 'Greers' after Germaine and *The Female Eunuch*. And the songs, you know how music does, painted, illustrated, accompanied everything, especially boys and parents, and hope and love, and anger and that feeling of unfairness that we all have when we're young. 'He'll never ask me,/ I know he won't./ He just goes on past me/ I'm only smoke to blow away' is a party at Amy Jeffries' house, I expect it was her fourteenth birthday or whatever, though the occasion doesn't matter because what's preserved is a boy called Eric something-or-the-other, Blackmore? Brentley? Never mind. The point is that that song is him, my memory of that evening and all my feelings of hopelessness and incompetence, and they're all summed up in it and stored away complete. So that any time the song is played there's me, and there's funny little Eric, and he's all indifference and superior knowledge, and I'm shy and helpless and full of hope and unutterable sadness. It'd be hard not to be intrigued by someone who had organized your memories in this sort of

21

way. Music as the filing cabinet of the mind. 'Shut your mouth, Mr Moon,/ Don't you yawn at me./ I'm too alive for you to sleep/ So don't go down,/ And don't ride on,/ And don't you dawn at me.' A family beach holiday in Spain, 1975. I knew you'd be interested! Tanny and Vi and I used to lie on the edge of the wet sand after dark looking up at the stars. It's funny now, all these years later, to think of Philip that same summer, under the same stars, hitch-hiking round France with Moser, Vita putting in her mysterious appearances beneath the same black sky, and the selfsame song probably echoing in his own head. And now here's the very Bix herself, singer and so author of it all, in a sense.

And in one way she doesn't seem to have changed all that much. Not her appearance or any of that, which is a disaster and makes her quite unrecognizable, really. But she does still have the sort of childish quality that she had then, and that was a big part of her appeal, especially to people older than me. It's a sort of endearing childishness, and makes her a waif. And she's still beautiful in certain lights, though horribly diminished. Also she walks in an odd way, stiff, as though her ankles and knees and hips were mechanisms worked by stretch-string or elastic. Even so, there's still something of the charisma that she had as a star. It's silly, but she makes me feel hopeful. Do you know what I mean?

Eventually I'd done enough to bring an electric stove to light, and with a bit of scouring I got it clean enough to use. I found some eggs in the fridge, and a scrap of lettuce recent enough to eat, and with these and a few other odds and ends I was able to put together an omelette with salad, and then the bread and cheese. Then I made some space at the table and woke Beatrix up.

'Dinner.' She blinked at me and groaned. 'Come on. I've made us an omelette. On the table.' She swung her legs round and got unsteadily to her feet.

'Table. Jesus. Didn't know we had a table.' And she padded

out of the room. A few minutes later she came back, having aimed some mascara and lipstick at different parts of her face and carrying a bottle of vodka. 'Better drink to this,' she said, twisting the cap off the bottle. 'Not every day I find the table.' She flopped into a chair and squinted at the place settings, the food. 'And a clean glass. What are you? My fairy godmother?' She swigged from the bottle, then filled her tumbler. 'Help yourself.' She passed me the bottle. 'Go on. Don't be shy. Plenty more in the cellar.'

Then we ate, which I was really glad about because she's obviously got a serious alcohol problem, and they don't usually, do they? Eat. Alcoholics. Afterwards she went over to the dresser, fished a plastic bag out of a drawer and rolled herself a reefer.

'You?' I shook my head. ''S good for you, you know.' But she didn't press the way people used to, as though getting you to do it too made it all right for them. The addict's article of faith. She was looking for something, and eventually found a bottle of gin down the back of the sofa, poured herself one, and added a little tap water to it. Then she lay down on the sofa and closed her eyes. It had started to rain again, and the last of the evening light was fading rapidly through the open door. A standard lamp by the chimney switched on automatically.

'Reminds me of Sim,' said Beatrix.

'Sim?'

'Yeah. Samuel Ian Morris. Sim. Sim Nix. The only Jewish drummer ever to come out of Scarborough. We were lovers about a hundred and ninety years ago. He liked everything automatic. Cars, CD players, computer composition software, guns . . .'

'Do you still see him? Others from the group?'

'Sim's dead. Fo's in California counting his investments. I've lost track of that shit Rod. When the Nix split, it was nuclear fission, not a tear in a seam. That's *Time Out*, not me. Good hash, this. You should try it. All the best Turkish comes from Holland.

Would you mind?' She was holding out her glass, indicating the gin bottle on the draining board.

'You seem to . . .'

'Drink too much. Yeah. Before, I was only an amateur. Rock musicians are. It's what makes them interesting. When they become professionals they're boring. The Rolling Crones . . . Anyway, retirement's boring, so when I retired I became a boring professional drinker.'

I poured her another gin. 'Don't you think it would make sense . . .'

'Yeah, yeah. It's nice of you to show an interest. Thanks.' She took the drink and lapsed into silence.

'Who is Johan?'

'I told you. Dutch guy. My agent. He owns this place. That's his writing on the name plate up the drive. "Favelas" was his idea. He said it suited. Johan's one of the great twentieth-century bastards. But don't take my word for it. He's coming down in a couple of days. You can meet him then.' She looked at me seriously over the top of her drink, like someone trying to keep a grip on something but knowing she was about to fall off. 'You will come again, won't you? I'd, well, I'd really like it.'

I said I would, but she just gave a sniff and didn't say anything more. Soon after this she fell asleep again, so I did the washing-up and left shortly afterwards. It's not true about her becoming boring. I'm rather intrigued by her, and I certainly want to meet this Johan character. But I'd like to get to know her better first. Anyway, it was getting dark, and I wanted to get home to the boxes.

———

Early afternoon

OK. Here it is. When you write your piece for the *Harcourt Chronicle*, you can put any or none of this in, as you choose.

Philip was born on 3 April 1956. His people lived – still do, for that matter – in Finchley, and that's where he grew up in a neighbourhood of Victorian and Edwardian brick villas peppered here and there with council flats, which Philip called 'Hitler's town planning'. Stanley, his father, was an actuary in an insurance company in the City (he retired a year or two ago), and his mother, Doris, was a primary school teacher. She gave it up when Philip was born, but took it up again when he was in the sixth form. Philip was an only child. I don't think there was anything particularly interesting or special about the name Leroux. It was just one of those names with Norman or French connections, like Hainault and Rivault, or Ashby-de-la-Zouch and Theydon Bois, that had been assimilated into English. Doris's maiden name was Smith. There was no family history to speak of. Philip said he'd never known his grandparents, and his own parents never talked about them much. Actually Philip said his parents never really talked about anything, and I have to say that on the occasions when I visited it was always very quiet. Or, to be honest, dull.

Philip told me that his parents met when Stanley was at Manchester University. Doris's background was unclear, but there was a story that she was working as a cleaner in the student hostel where Stanley lived in his first year. This would account for how they met. I do know, however, that Doris eventually got into a training college to qualify as a teacher, and I think it was Stanley who helped and encouraged her in this. Philip said he couldn't imagine how his parents had fallen in love, or had an affair, or managed to get married. He thought sex was beyond them, literally, something that was 'out there', on the other side of a window, like moorland, or a plane passing over. Something that sort of was, without there being any explanation for it. He used to say that his own existence from a conception initiated by two consenting adults was implausible. There had to be another way. He had quite a funny party piece imitating his parents as young people and going out together for the first time. This was mainly mime and gesture, so I can't get it down on paper, but little bits of this performance stuck to both of us as a sort of ready reference, a private sign language for discussing other people without having to speak.

Stanley was a mathematician, and took his degree in about 1950, I think. I may be wrong, but my impression – surely I got this from Philip – is that he was a disappointed man. He had wanted to do research in a lab at Manchester where there was pioneering work going on with computers, but he wasn't quite good enough. He got a first but wasn't Wrangler class, something like that, and the postgrad slot went to someone else. Anyway, the point was that Philip felt there was a lot of disappointment in the air at home. Pessimism and defeat.

Of course, Philip was in revolt against his parents, and Finchley, and suburban life, and boredom, and all those things, but it was a funny kind of revolt because there was so little to react against. Stanley and Doris aren't forceful. I suppose they're conservative in the sense of being quiet and retiring, never shoving themselves forward, but it's as if there isn't really anything there to get hold of at all. 'Maddeningly English', Philip called it. 'You know, if you hit it, it sort of sags.' So his revolt took the form of being intellectually aggressive against their timidity; three-dimensional against their sort of cut-out quality; opinionated against their void. His early interest in Sartre was largely, or so he used to say, the result of an intense interest in the idea of nothingness, because he had encountered it from earliest infancy at his parents' knee.

It was a solitary life the three of them led. Philip told me that the only occasion when he and his father went somewhere together, just the two of them, was sometime in the early or mid seventies, I think after Philip had done A-levels, and before he went up to Oxford. I was still a schoolgirl, dancing to the Nix. They went to the Oval one Sunday to see England play a test match, but his father's presence was the kiss of death. All they saw was someone Philip called the Gnome of Chelmsford make the slowest test match century ever scored. It was 'the most boring day's cricket ever played', and this from Philip, who liked cricket a lot. Well, there was that hat, wasn't there? Like an object out of what's-his-name, that American writer, or Edith Wharton, who took after him. The only interesting thing that happened all day was some barracking from a couple of Australians in the stand behind them, which Stanley characterized as 'uncouth', but afterwards he told Doris that he and Philip had had 'a really nice day', and Philip was quite sure that he meant it. When he was a boy the Leroux used to take Philip to places like Torquay, Newquay and Paignton for holidays. Ideal locations for a budding existentialist, Philip said, because there was nothing to do, nothing to see, and nothing ever happened. Eventually he saw that there was nothing much in Sartre either, and used to quote Lear about him – 'Nothing will come of nothing.' But that was later.

I think his adolescent decision to become a philosopher may have been the most important part of his revolt against home. He thought of it as revolt because when his father went through university the fashion was all for applied mathematics – maths as the handmaiden of atomic physics and so on – and Stanley always talked of what he'd done as 'science'. Philip grew up to think that taking up the heartland humanities subject of philosophy, quite abstract, and not really much attached to any practical matters at all, represented a complete break with everything his father stood for. This appealed, naturally, so he gave up maths along with all the other sciences in the sixth form. It was only when he got to Oxford that he discovered – probably, and like so much else, from Moser – that maths was one form, perhaps even the form, of pure philosophy. He used to say, wryly I think, that he should have realized that his father, who was generally wrong about most things, would be quite likely to be wrong even about his own profession. From this he derived one of his general principles: that it is unhelpful to assume that other people either know or understand what it is they are doing. He used to pretend that his becoming a philosopher had been a

mistake, even a defeat, certainly an accident. He had a horror of
being thought dull himself, but, perhaps paradoxically, didn't
think he had much choice in the matter. Philip never really
believed in choice. 'A chimera,' he said. 'People do what they
must, and justify it afterwards.' And he used to quote something
from Shakespeare.

This is one version of how he came to read philosophy, and
it's the one I heard first. It's also the funnier one. Philip told it to
me, complete with imitations of his father, whom he could
mimic with devastating accuracy, the very first time we went
out together. We had an Indian meal and he kept me in stitches,
so that I got indigestion. He used to say that this was a metaphor
for something. The other version of why he took up philosophy
I only learned later on. It's a little bit about his grammar school
– and I don't know anything about that at all. He never went
back there, and he barely talked about it either – and a lot about
France, and the holidays that he used to spend there – here –
when he was a schoolboy. He did an exchange, organized
through his school, with a French boy his own age – the Roland
Beaumanière the Master was so struck with at the funeral. The
Beaumanières turned out to be very well-off, and rather upper
in the French manner. *BCBG*, I suppose we'd call it these days.
The father was some sort of a banker who Philip said probably
lived in Pompidou's pocket. Through Roland, Philip met lots of
other young French people, and he learned to speak the language. But the main thing was, he said, that being with them
made him think. They gave him a sense of his individuality –
the business of having a different personality when he was 'in
French', perhaps – so that he developed an idea of himself as a
separate entity, someone who could be contemplated by himself
as if from the outside – I'm not putting this very well – someone,
he said to me once, that he could know although not necessarily
understand. As a result, he kept tripping over interesting but
possibly insoluble problems, like: how can I know that the things
that I believe to be true are so? And: what does it mean to

say that any act of mine is authentic? Or: are feelings expressions of inchoate ideas? Or: can an act be random if I will it? At one time in his life, pretty early on, I think, he said he wanted to experiment with these and similar questions by acting them out. A sort of practical approach to moral dilemmas, setting up real situations with people (who of course didn't know) and then going through with them. The idea was to see what would happen. For various reasons he came to see that it was best to keep the experiments between the covers of books. Hence philosophy.

There may have been other reasons, for his being a philosopher, that I don't know about or have forgotten. And of course Philip was very good at finding intellectual reasons for things being one way rather than another. I think that a lot of this was justification after the event, and that he became a philosopher because that was his temperament. We do what we have to do. As you know, or at any rate as I've said, he wasn't terribly good at living in the real world of things and places and people. He was easily irritated, and often frustrated. Philosophy, however, gave him safety and security because it conformed to rules. There were properly defined 'approaches' to questions. 'Topics' were delineated by 'boundaries'. 'Principles' might be 'deduced' so long as 'axioms' were 'defined' 'correctly'. 'Proof' was a 'function' of 'evidence' supported by 'logic'. And so on. This was why he was such a marvellous teacher. In philosophy you – or I, really, since I was, after all, one of his pupils – always knew where you were with him. And he was wonderfully entertaining. Very good at inventing those problems and paradoxes that undergraduates are supposed to wrestle with. Is this a good question? Did you hear the cat bark last night? Does nature abhor a circle? If unicorns didn't exist, would philosophers have to invent them? (That was my favourite!)

Was he a good philosopher in other ways? Is a wife, widow, competent to say? Moser certainly thought that he was, and Moser (at least according to Vintner in Wadham) was the cleverest man of his generation. But then you know how Oxford people talk. Philip said that philosophy was the only subject left in which teaching and research were the same thing, and since I believe him to have been a great teacher, ergo . . . (as Philip would have said). I know that other philosophers at Oxford felt that he ought to have been writing 'a great book', and that his book on anarchism, and the biography of Herzen, were of secondary importance. But Philip believed that outside of the sphere of political philosophy, which he thought still in its adolescence, there were probably no 'great books' left to write in philosophy proper, and that works of synthesis were a waste of time. He had a profound distaste for general histories of philosophy. He took the view that philosophy was culture specific: that it had to do with thought, the meaning of thought, and the precision – or otherwise – of thought. It was, therefore, inseparable from the language in which the thoughts were being had, or expressed. Translations were no substitute for the originals because all translation is approximate. What is lost in translation is precision, and yet it is exactly this which is essential to the business of philosophy. This explained why philosophers – Greeks, Germans, French and English, say – argued past each other all the time. They were, Philip said, never really aiming at, let alone ever hitting, the same targets. They weren't talking about the same things.

This also explained why questions simply fell out of philosophy from time to time. He said that, once upon a time, philosophers were very interested in the dimensions of eternity. But not any more. 'How many angels can dance on the head of a pin?' is a question that has become synonymous with pointlessness, and philosophers, though they pretend otherwise, are acutely sensitive to accusations of pointlessness. Philip thought it was because they had so little influence despite being generally so very bright. They were sort of living proof that the meritocratic society, whatever else it valued, didn't value pure brain power. So philosophers were always trying to insist that their concerns were thoroughly practical 'really,' and would desert one the instant it was shown to be of no practical importance whatsoever.

'But the interesting thing is,' he used to say, 'that the dimensions of alternative spaces – or the spaces envisaged as alternative dimensions – might actually be terribly important, if only we knew how to get at them.' I was never really sure what he meant by this.

I think this explains why his own best contributions to philosophy were what he called his miniatures: for instance, the article he wrote on 'precepts and concepts in the subjective', and that essay on 'Hume and cultural relativism'. These were the things of which he was really proud. I found a letter yesterday from Brian Barry – Philip had clipped it to an offprint of his Hume article – saying how much he, Barry, admired it. Philip must have been thrilled with this. He thought Barry's *Political Argument* the great neglected masterpiece of twentieth-century English political thought.

These things certainly singled him out of the dull ruck of Oxford philosophy. Philip used to do an imitation of Jeremy McGlashan in Jesus discussing the philosophical basis of rationality. In the course of this, Philip's McGlashan would fall asleep, but without its making the slightest difference either to what he was saying, or to what his audience understood. But they weren't the only things that made Philip unusual. It's true that he got a reputation as a Russianist, almost a Slavophile, but I don't think that Russian was ever anything more than a means to an end for Philip. He had a deep interest in Herzen, and wanted to know more. Learning Russian was essential to develop the interest. So he learned Russian. But this never turned into a general interest in things, or philosophies, Russian. The only other Russian philosopher I ever heard him refer to with any warmth at all was Chaadayev, and he only read his little book, *Eight Philosophical Letters*, because Herzen had read it and been influenced by it. Philip told me that Chaadayev held that Russia (this was in the 1830s) was a backward country with no history – 'We are a blank on the universal landscape', Philip told me he said – and that it should modernize its government, and abandon Orthodoxy for Catholicism. The Tsar was so shocked that he declared Chaadayev insane, and he was forbidden to publish anything further. Philip said this mightn't be a bad precedent. Every philosopher should be permitted to publish one book, after which he or she would be declared insane and restricted to oral pronouncements.

No, what really interested him outside of Herzen, or the thing that drew him to Herzen in the first place perhaps, was not Russia, but the mid-nineteenth century. He was fascinated by this period. Perhaps even obsessed by it. In addition to his anarchists, and then to Herzen and his circle, there was also the literature, and the music. He particularly loved Schumann and Brahms, and whatever it was that had drawn them together towards the end of Schumann's life. He was preoccupied with this during those last terrible five weeks before the accident, but I don't want to think about all that for another few days.

—

Night

Before I sat down to write about Philip, Madame Jeanne and Micheline looked in. This time they brought me some eggs, an absolutely delicious *tarte aux fraises* from the patisserie in the village, and an invitation! Apparently next Saturday, the 21st, which I think of as the longest day of the year, but which Madame Jeanne kept calling the first day of summer, is also Micheline's birthday. And she's going to be getting married on the same day to a surgeon – I think that's what she said (I didn't follow this bit so well) – from the same hospital where she works. The ceremony is in Orléans, and there's a reception afterwards at a nearby hotel, and would I please come? They really would like it. I felt very touched. When I said surely this was a family occasion, and they wouldn't want an outsider like me, Madame

Jeanne said she felt I was family because I was the professor's guest, and he had said that they were to look after me, and he had been so good to her in the last however many years, and she and Micheline would have been so very proud, '*n'est-ce pas, Micheline?*', if he could have been there too, and more besides that would make you blush. And so of course in the end I said yes. I felt apprehensive about this at the time, but now I'm really looking forward to it, provided I can lay my hands on something to wear. It's so nice to get integrated into a place like this, where you feel that people belong in the way that no one seems to any more in England. You know, to have roots, and allegiances, and to know the history of a place not out of books but from what they've been told, and have seen and heard. This village really is its people. Its history is their history. I shall have to find something really nice for a wedding present.

Perhaps it was feeling buoyed up about this that enabled me to break my duck – as Philip used to say – and actually sit down and write something about him for you. I've just read it through, and doing so has made me realize that perhaps the stress is a bit wrong. Somehow there's too much rationality. This is a trick of philosophy, isn't it? The philosopher's touchstone. Because they put rational discourse at the very centre of their discipline – both its method and its purpose – there is a tendency for the rest of us to treat philosophers as people whose discourse is always, or at any rate generally, rational. My experience of Philip and his colleagues over the years was that this is a mistake. Some of them seemed to me quite irrational a lot of the time, some others eccentric in the most bizarre ways, and others again quite dotty, not to say crazed. Wittgenstein shaking a poker at Popper and Russell is well known – Philip used to do an imitation of this, including a heavy Viennese accent. Once he broke off at the end, saying, 'Did you know that Brahms knew Wittgenstein's father? Amazing, isn't it, how close we are to greatness?' – but there were lots of other examples much closer to home. Philip and I came across Pinkney one day when we were out for a walk. He was standing on a ladder at the gate of Queen's, his back to the High, stretching up the wall as far as he could go with his head, and reading a copy of *Mind*, which he held at an awkward angle that made him look as though he might fall off the ladder at any moment. People were having to squeeze past him to get into college, and the general situation was providing fairly good entertainment value for a longish queue at a bus stop. 'Are you all right, Ralph?' said Philip, looking up at him on his perch. 'Mmm?' said Pinkney, surprised and a bit nettled at being interrupted. 'All right? Yes, of course. Why?' 'Well, you just looked a bit odd, we thought . . .' 'Odd? Oh. Oh really? Well, it's perfectly simple. I just washed my hair and this is the last little bit of sunshine I could find.' He waved his hand at it. 'Soon be gone, too.' And he resumed his position.

Some parts of Philip would say that this was rational behaviour: wet hair, patch of sunshine, convenient ladder, bring them together, Bob's your uncle. But other parts of him knew what the rest of us know with our whole being: that Pinkney is a nutter. Did you know (I expect you saw. Philip told me about it) that Pinkney went to the gaudy, *the* gaudy, Philip's nemesis, wearing evening dress over a pair of roman sandals, no socks. Odd enough in the summer, but on the coldest night of the year, and with three feet of snow on the ground, positively, well, what do you think?

So perhaps I've painted Philip in a few too many of the colours of rationality. For one thing, he suffered a great deal from the frustrations of everyday life. Things – literally, objects – got on his nerves. They weren't inanimate to him, but forces with motivations, mainly malign. He could joke about it sometimes. He used to say, only a little grimly, that when you weren't waiting at the traffic lights you were fighting the packaging: especially yoghurt pots, biscuit packets, the cellophane round new CDs, anything in clingfilm, the seals on medicine bottles, and so on. Even so, I don't think that Paul Jennings's theory of resistentialism – which Philip used to say was first published on the day he was born – ever struck him as being particularly funny. Philip used to say that though heavily disguised as humour, it was a serious contribution to contemporary thought because it emphasized and clarified the true sources of the alienation experienced by the great majority of people. Abstruse analysis of the nausea and deformity of experience *à la* Jean-Paul Sartre or Herbert Marcuse, or the Frankfurt School, was all very well for one in a hundred thousand, but the truth for Jo Bloggs was that his bus had left three minutes early, he had a corn on the outside of the little toe on his right foot, he couldn't get the watch-strap prong through its hole, his shoe lace had broken just as he was about to go out of the front door, and the cardboard milk carton wouldn't open properly (as usual) and had deposited milk on his trousers, the tablecloth and the newspaper, but not on his cornflakes.

Philip believed that you could be betrayed by objects. I don't mean he believed it the way some people believe in God or reincarnation, but that sometimes he behaved towards inanimate things as though they were malevolent. Once he told me that he occasionally punished things. Sometimes this was in anger – say, flinging a pot of yoghurt in the bin after it spurted on his tie when he was taking the top off – but more generally in calm and judicious deliberation. A coat hanger that he had trouble extracting from inside a shirt, or a cake box whose lid wouldn't go back on. He would set them aside and then take revenge later, twisting the hanger into a tangled mess, stamping on the box before screwing it into a ball and shoving it on the fire. 'There. That'll bloody teach you.' He said he understood Basil Fawlty perfectly. 'He's an adult version of me,' he said. Though Philip constantly poured scorn on the idea of empathy, secretly he believed that lots of other people felt the way he did.

His saving grace was that he knew that his relationship with objects was potentially – assuming the right mood – funny. He told me once of an incident in an hotel when he'd gone away to a conference. He'd been on the platform at a plenary session in the late afternoon – suit and tie, all that – and afterwards he thought he just had time for a bath before the official dinner. He went in his bathroom, and turned the taps full on over the bath. The water pressure was very great and someone, a cleaner perhaps, or the previous occupant, had left the little pull-plug that selects bath or shower in the shower position. The shower hose was one of those articulated metal ones with a heavy rose head that sits in a cradle above the taps. Maybe it hadn't been put back properly. Anyway, the force of the water lifted the head out of its cradle, and the hose started to writhe like an angry snake – whizzing about the bath, clattering on the enamel, bashing into the tiling on the walls, and of course showering water everywhere: ceiling, Philip, floors, towels, lavatory, Philip, lavatory paper, mirrors, Philip again, and so on. Within seconds everything was soaked. And there was Philip, philosopher and rational man, trying his damnedest to catch hold of the shower as it flew past instead of – 'as a moment of sober reflection might have recommended' (Philip's account) – turning off the taps, or pushing the pull-plug down. 'By the time I'd caught the thing the bathroom looked as though it might recently have been occupied by a demented Japanese tour party. And,' he added, wagging a finger in mock seriousness, 'none of this was my fault. Simply the animosity of things. Furthermore, this was my only suit, so that I made an unusual sight at the dinner, providing an opening for various of the weak jokes that philosophers sink to on occasions of this sort.'

When it wasn't funny, however, it was bathetic, occasionally alarming. But there was also something mysterious about it, which Philip once described to me. It happened when he was a boy, ten or twelve years old. In those days, apparently, there was a bookshop in Baker Street called Bumpus, where Philip used to go with a friend whenever he got a book token at Christmas, or for a birthday. This happened when he was on his way there one half-term break, a mid-week afternoon. There were a lot of people about, the pavements very crowded, and he'd just turned into Baker Street from the Marylebone Road. Traffic was heavy, and he remembered a swirling breeze that was putting grit in the air. Among the people walking towards him down the pavement was a biggish man, podgy, going bald, with a fawn raincoat over a shabby suit. The raincoat was unbuttoned, and billowed out behind him. He appeared to be one of a knot of people all coming along quite fast, but he wasn't with the others, merely among them. Also, although he was on his own, he was talking out loud, almost shouting, and his words were a stream of complaint about his problems, mainly, it seemed, impediments placed in his way by a variety of enemies. He was being ignored by everyone, the usual English embarrassment. All this happened very quickly, and Philip said that afterwards he could only remember the sort of detail that sometimes got left over in dreams when the main substance had vanished, like having only peripheral vision, or something. But anyway, the man's eyes fell on Philip, and as he bore down on him he released a bellow of pain and rage, saying, 'Oh, no. You're not going to get in my way as well, are you?' and he reached forward with an arm, brushing from side to side like a blind man with a long cane, as if to knock Philip out of his way. 'For God's sake,' he said, as Philip half-floundered, was half-pushed to one side. It was over in a second. The man was gone. Philip found himself suddenly, mysteriously, almost all alone on what had just before been a crowded pavement, the grit still swirling around him. He felt himself being overwhelmed by a sense of disquiet, a feeling almost of dread. What he feared he had seen was a premonition, himself at a future time, mad in a crowd of bystanders pretending not to notice, defeated and ruined by frustration, and unable to express it in any other way than by bellowing at a frightened child on a pavement. Philip said, 'Of all the countless thousands of pavements on which I've walked since, and the millions of strangers whom I've encountered for a moment, never to see again, this one has remained with me. He still gives me an agony of recognition. But I do not know whether he is humanity, or evil, or both, or neither.'

It was no help to Philip to say, about an event of this sort, well it wasn't any of those things. It was just a bloke on the street who was in a hurry, and behaving badly. It didn't mean anything. It's just something you happen to remember. Maybe the fact of your remembering is interesting, but that doesn't mean the chap was of any importance. None of this helped, because Philip took the view that the self barely existed in isolation, and only came to life 'so to speak' when engaged with others. It was the engagement that gave meaning to life. Because of this, the man's eruption in his young life meant something, and because he was blessed with inexhaustible curiosity he needed to know what it was. The trouble was that there was no means of finding out other than by introspection. And by this route he came to maudlin conclusions, which further added to his frustration. 'Variations on a theme,' he would say.

I tried to get him to take things less seriously, to see that everyone was tempted from time to time by these sorts of feelings, and that they were only important if we allowed them to be so. But he didn't agree with this. As you know, he clung with great determination to the view that it was impossible to know other people's feelings, and it was an opinion ('more than that, far more than that') that was hard to disagree with, I think because he was so opaque himself a lot of the time. For instance, no one would have known how much he suffered from these agonies of frustration, because he managed to keep up such a good appearance of being calm. He gave every impression of being the intellectual equivalent of those men who build dry-stone walls across vast distances of hillside and mountain. The task must appear interminable, yet they just keep going, implacable and uncompromising. And you wonder how they can do it. How can they be so patient and so durable?

The only time I ever made any chink in the armour of this argument of his (about the isolated nature of our feelings) was once when we dropped in on a friend of mine at Univ. one afternoon. We had something exciting to tell him, though I can't now remember what, and it doesn't matter because what was important was that Philip knocked on Misha's door and opened it simultaneously, and we were just in time to catch Misha and a girl – I think one of his students – standing a little bit apart, and looking a bit awkward. They weren't actually *doing* anything, but there was this tremendous, well, *feeling*, somehow. Do you know what I mean? As though they would have been in the middle of something compromising if we'd come thirty seconds earlier or thirty seconds later, and so were feeling guilty about the possibility of its being seen, even though it wasn't. We didn't stay long because this sort of situation kills off conversation, doesn't it? When we left, and I said something about cutting the atmosphere with a knife, Philip said: 'An axe, more like. Atmospheres don't come much thicker than that.'

'So where does it come from?'

'The axe? Search me.'

'No, silly. The atmosphere. It was charged, right? They were feeling something – guilt and embarrassment probably – and we apprehended it. Now how did we do that?'

'Ah,' said Philip. But that was all he said.

You had to be very careful with Philip's silences. Sometimes he used them as a weapon. He'd just stop participating in some discussion or the other, saying, 'There's no point,' or 'It's not going to make any difference what I think, anyway.' And then you were stuck, because if it (what you were discussing) was something that might require his agreement, like where to spend Christmas, or which carpet to buy, or whether to invite Jessie Bierhof – you know, that linguist, who's so deadly dull but is lonely, and badly wants company – to dinner or not, then his silence basically meant non-compliance. The marital equivalent of civil disobedience. If you went ahead, and it turned out to have been the wrong thing to have done, then he'd be vindicated.

I think at least some of the time he felt vulnerable in arguments.

They were all right in tutorials and seminars because there were rules, then, and people usually adhered to them. But in conversation he could feel threatened. 'I can't handle this,' he'd say. And then there'd be silence, like in a Beckett or a Pinter play. In fact, he liked Beckett and Pinter a lot, and often said how strange it was that people thought their plays difficult or strange. Philip thought them exactly like everyday life. He sympathized terribly with Vivien Merchant.

But not all of his silences were like this. Sometimes he really was thinking, and not just stone-walling. The incident with Misha and the girl turned out to be one of these occasions. It was several days later, and we'd been to a concert in the Sheldonian and were walking home down St Giles'. I was talking about something, probably the music – Bach, I think, which I really like but which Philip used to call 'tolerable', as though it were a modest country hotel where, to his surprise, the hot water actually worked – when he suddenly said, apropos of nothing that had gone before, 'People share situations, and situations have certain qualities, of exuberance say, like a party, or restraint, like a lecture or a funeral, and in sharing them they adopt various socially agreed, or encouraged, patterns of behaviour. These are learned, and by means of practice they become what we call "second nature" . . .'

'One of those sloppy, meaningless terms that we employ to disguise the poverty of our pathetic . . .'

'Yes, dear, but I do the funnies. Please don't interrupt. Some situations, however, are new, or at any rate extremely rare, so that when we find ourselves in one we don't quite know how to behave, what's expected of us. The period of maximum occurrence of this kind of thing is adolescence, which is what makes it so excruciatingly painful a lot of the time. Generally, in adult life, when it happens we have enough time to feel our way, so to speak. But occasionally, as with our visit to Misha's rooms the other day, we are thrown into the situation quite abruptly, and have to react at very short notice. No notice at all, really. *Our* immediate response, because we're inexperienced, was embarrassment, a sort of emotional way of saying, "Oh dear, I do wish I wasn't here." This feeling of embarrassment is so strong that we project it on to others, also present. Sometimes we may be right to do this. Misha's mouth was wide open. The girl was smoothing her skirt down . . .'

'I missed that.'

'Perhaps I'm making it up. Perhaps it was unnecessary if she was. An involuntary movement? Anyway, perhaps, though only perhaps, we were all feeling the same or similar emotions, and we aggregated these into "an atmosphere you could have cut with a knife". But you can't *know* that this was the case. They *might* have been feeling something quite different. And the "atmosphere" of which we speak is really a fiction. The barometric pressure did not change, there was no increase in humidity, the physical environment remained the same. What we call the atmosphere is really each of us giving external representation to our own internal sensations. But these may be quite inappropriate. If I told this story to Ben Gould, or indeed if Ben had been there instead of us, he'd pounce on it as evidence of Misha having a liaison with this girl, and in no time it'd be all over the university. But it might not be true.'

He stopped talking at this point, and stopped walking too, and stood looking across the great wide avenue of St Giles' as though something outside the Eagle and Child had caught his attention and was holding him enthralled. 'In a small way,' he went on, 'this experience of ours in Misha's rooms, with Misha and the girl – and that could be a pub, couldn't it? Misha and the Girl, the Eagle and the Child, with the two of them posed on the sign, mouth open, skirt being smoothed – illustrates everything that's wrong, and immoral, with the idea of empathy. Its bastard offspring is gossip, which begets reputation. Ignorance masquerading as knowledge.'

This was, I'm sure, a cornerstone of his sorrow about Moser and Moser's death: that poor Moser, his closest friend – deprived of children, robbed by cancer of his wife Vita, horribly treated in his scientific career – had somehow become trapped in a web of gossip and innuendo that labelled him with a reputation for cussedness from which he was powerless to free himself. But then Philip's depression wasn't just about this. It was mixed up with all the other things too. With Vita and so on.

I've been thinking about this all afternoon, sitting in your study with the boxes open around me, and the rain tapping on the slate roof. It's a terrible puzzle, isn't it, Philip's death? That he should have had a car accident is understandable in a way. The conditions were poor, and he often drove a bit fast, and on that particular evening I expect he was running late. He was meeting me in town for a concert at the Barbican – but you know all that already. If it weren't for the fact that January 10th was the same day that Herzen died, I think I'd be reasonably sure that it was just a stupid accident: a patch of ice, a car travelling too fast, loss of control, a concrete motorway bridge buttress . . .

I talked to Peter Kahn about it. You know he's the therapist Philip was seeing in that last month, after the gaudy and before his death. Actually I should really call him Dr Kahn because he's a clinical psychiatrist, not one of those 'amateur alchemists of the soul', as Philip used to call them. But he's very approachable, and I felt at ease with him, and you can imagine how deeply upset he was about Philip's death. I suppose if it had been suicide it would be a bit like a surgeon losing a patient on the operating table. He asked me if Philip was wearing a seat belt. Apparently they have lots of these accidents on the German autobahns, depressed middle-aged men driving high-speed into reinforced concrete. And the tell-tale sign is the seat belt. If he was wearing one, it was an accident. Philip, of course, had to have things both ways. The police accident report stated that 'the victim' had a seat belt across his shoulder and lap, but that it was not fastened. One possibility is that it was dislodged on impact, but I'm told this is a chance in several million. Another is that he was changing the CD on the player. He had complained about not being quite able to reach it when strapped in. This could also explain how he lost control. Anyway, the belt certainly hadn't protected him, and he was horribly broken up. I think it would have pleased him, though, to be known in the end as 'the victim'. That really was how he thought of himself in those last five weeks. A victim whose wounds had all been self-inflicted.

—

Sunday 15th   *Morning*

Something rather wonderful has happened. I went straight to bed after I'd finished writing to you about Philip last night, and then found that I couldn't sleep. A result of thinking about the accident, I suppose, because I hadn't wanted to do that yet, although it is something that I planned to do while I'm here – write about Philip's last five weeks of life. But I hadn't meant to start remaking it in my mind (which is how I think of it) until I'd done the piece for you and finished going through Philip's papers. So instead of lying there torturing myself – or at any rate being tortured by recollections of how Philip died – I got up and went back to Philip's papers. Right at the bottom of a box, one that was otherwise full of the most dreary and uninteresting stuff – Court G.B. agendas and minutes, I'm afraid – was another manuscript by Philip. Not an article, or anything like that, but another real, whole manuscript. A book almost. And there's no doubt that it's his. It's typed, so I'm not recognizing his handwriting, but it's definitely in his style. And anyway, it's about himself, written in the third person. It's very finished and polished, but there's no sign of earlier drafts, or notes even. It's dated 1980, which is just after he and I met, but I'd never heard about it before. My heart just about stopped when I pulled it out and saw what it was. A bit like finding a wallet full of banknotes in a deserted street. You feel there ought to be some collateral evidence to show how it got there. But there isn't. And there it is, rich and marvellous. And you look through it rather furtively, already beginning to feel guilty, because you just want to keep it for yourself, but you know that you can't, and that somehow you've got to return it.

I took it back to bed with me. It made me feel quite wild. The manuscript reads like a novel, but it's really a documentary account of something that actually happened when he was seventeen or so. Genuine autobiography. Philip obviously couldn't find a name for it: the file it was in had a whole lot of titles scribbled on the inside, but they were all crossed out: 'On the Edge', 'The Windmill', 'Free Passage', 'Only Testing', 'A Secret Mind', and another one I can't quite read, 'Acting the Part', perhaps. I haven't read it all yet – it's quite long – but it's a very good likeness of Philip. I didn't know him when he was that age, but the Philip in this story is definitely the precursor of the Philip I *did* know. And a brutally honest one too. He was funny, and clever, and precocious, and a good mimic. And he had terrible mood swings, and other periods when his emotional state was mixed up, happy and elated, but also biting and hyper-critical; or dark with melancholy, yet loving and tender. The awful sorrow of affection, he called it. It's a cliché that, when he wasn't being a philosopher, you never knew where you were with him, and it's not entirely true either because I did learn how to interpret and understand the signs. But in general, and certainly for people reasonably well acquainted with him – colleagues, I suppose: people who are neither family nor strangers – he must have been a frightful enigma. His account here of his love affair with the Danielle figure is exactly like him: trying to uncover the truth by saying and doing.

Also, the characters in this 'story' are real people. I wrote about Roland Beaumanière the other day, how the Master wanted to know his address and so on. Well, he and Philip had gone on being friends, and Roland was, I know, genuinely and deeply attached to Philip, though I imagine they were quite different types. He told me at the funeral that the last time he saw Philip had been two years before. He was in London briefly on business, and he and Philip had dinner together. Then there was another boy very close to both of them who was called Michel, just like in the story. The three of them – Philip, Roland and Michel – even when they were teenagers, used to call each other *l'Académicien, l'Homme d'Affaires* and *le Militaire*; later Sphynx, Mynx and Lynx; and sometimes *Lui-Même, Moi-Même* and *Quand-Même*. I imagine when they were together they were a riot, but this was years ago now, and I never saw it. Roland asked me, at the funeral, whether I realized how close they had been, how they would have done absolutely anything for each other. Anything. '*N'importe quoi.*'

The *Militaire* one, Michel – I don't even know his surname – came from one of those pukka French families where the great-great-grandfather fought at Austerlitz, Jena and Waterloo; and there was a great-uncle on Joffre's staff at Verdun. His father had been a subaltern in a tank squadron in Leclerc's division at the liberation of Paris. Michel really did go into the army, and went through Saint-Cyr, but he was killed quite soon afterwards in a terrorist bombing in Beirut in the late 70s, when the French were still trying to do their interventionist bit in the Middle East. This was a little before I met Philip, and he only told me later, when we got to know each other, how terribly upset he'd been about it. The Danielle figure is presumably the girl he once described to me, a French girlfriend he'd had years ago, but broken up with. The story here is a pretty faithful account, I shouldn't wonder, though I haven't finished reading it yet. I was loving it so much I didn't want it to stop, so deliberately kept half back for today and put the light out feeling ridiculously happy. I'm going back to it just as soon as I've had some breakfast.

(The manuscript just said 'Philip Leroux: 1980' at the top, and then started. If 'On the Edge' – one of its titles – doesn't quite work, I'm going to call it 'The Portrait of a Philosopher as a Young Man'.)

———————

Yvette sent a car to meet the children at the railway station. Six of them were coming for the weekend, friends of Mireille from high summer and the beaches of Brittany, kids she had taken up with perhaps only from boredom. *Les gosses*, she called them. Mireille went along in a state of great excitement, the black DS swishing through the narrow country lanes that glistened from a fine early-autumn rain. She perched rather than sat next to the driver, twisting the belt of her raincoat between her fingers, ignoring the fields, hedgerows and farms as they vanished behind her in the dripping mist. Was it thought she was lost in?

Les gosses were filing out of the station as the sedan crunched across the gravel forecourt, where Mireille flung herself into the embraces and chatter of reunion. All present and correct: le Matelot, Roland, la Grande Berthe, DD, l'Angleterre and Michel, coats and ties awry, travel bags scattered at their feet, a confusing array of styles and postures. Roland, for instance, who had turned seventeen, was aristocratic, tall and slim, impeccable in an English tweed suit still, even then, thought 'correct' for the country in certain small but influential French circles. Roland walked with his feet splayed ever so slightly outwards, but it wasn't obviously an affectation. He kissed Mireille with far more interest than the normal French pecks of salutation required, held her hand behind her back, and went on holding it as she swung away from him, beaming with pleasure.

'And you, England? Still the same?'

She was addressing herself to another young man, to a French eye unmistakably Anglo-Saxon in his lack of style, as though he might have been thrown together very quickly as he got out of bed, gawky and cheerful.

'As you see,' he said, his face breaking into a grin. 'Perfidious Albion, always at your service.' He made a stiff mock-etiquette bow, then brushed a shock of unruly, long brown hair from his eyes.

46

'The enemy within,' shouted Madeleine, starting to do a jig in front of the surprised driver, who had been trying to get bags into the boot but was now hemmed in by the substantial bulk of a reeling teenager. Madeleine Suresnes was known to her friends as la Grande Berthe, a nickname in which she revelled.

'Shut up, Berthe,' intervened Mireille. 'And leave off seducing old Alphonse.' She heaved Roland's bag into the boot. 'Careful of his pyjamas,' said England. Mireille gave a giggle. 'It's her rite of spring,' she explained. 'We all learned how to do it at Tréveneuc. But now' – and she turned to the corpulent woman/child beside her – 'is the wrong time of year.'

'Yes, come on, Berthe,' said le Matelot, 'nearly time for lunch. Trotters to the fore.' And the two of them lurched into the back seat of the car, she with her arms around his neck.

'Ah, love at last. How long it has eluded me.' Everyone collapsed into laughter as they packed into the car.

'To the windmill, then, miss?' inquired Alphonse.

'Yes, yes. To the windmill.'

The station-master, who had watched these proceedings from the entrance to his empire, arms folded across his chest, stayed to see the vehicle off his premises. 'Kids!' he muttered to himself. 'Kids!'

As if in reply, a chant struck up from the receding car, first in one unnaturally powerful female voice, then taken up by all the others. '*Qu'il est beau le matelot, qu'il est beau le matelot, qu'il est beau le matelot, qu'il est beau . . .*'

—

Two days in the country. At sixteen and a half, as all the world of sixteen-and-a-half-year-olds knows, two days forwards is an eternity of opportunity, carries the prospect of complete mastery, while two days backwards is a blink of the eyes, a glance at a wristwatch, a spin of a coin.

'*Pile ou face?*'

'*Face.*'

'I win. You go.' Mireille smiled at England in her most seductive manner. Cruel, he thought to himself as he slid down the ladder. Cruelty to dumb animals. The drizzle had yielded to a warm and gentle sun in the early afternoon, and he picked his way across the puddles of the cobbled yard, steering his feet into the patches of sunlight, heading for the kitchen door. Yvette was there, along with a *femme de ménage* up to her elbows in vegetables at a sink.

'And how is the barn lunch?' asked Yvette, smiling. '*Les gosses* well fed?'

'A bit short of *saucisson*, I'm afraid. And bread. And beer. I am the messenger sent at the bidding of the gods.'

'Ah. And how are the gods deified in this barnly paradise?'

'Actually we spun a coin.'

Yvette went to a large walk-in larder, disappearing inside and rummaging for more provisions. Philip followed to the door and looked in behind her. She had bread and a bottle of beer in one hand, and was reaching up into the ceiling to unhook a sausage from where it hung on a beam. Sunshine, falling across her white dress from a high skylight, laid clear the rise and fall of her breasts, perfect in silhouette. Philip, who had read a lot of books, and who until the summer had been anxious to make some sort of a start on sex, now regarded himself as something of a professional. 'Eight hundred and fifty-five,' he said out loud to himself as he walked back across the yard under the shadow of the stationary arms. I would have expected a little more from a star of stage and screen.

'Here, catch.' DD was sitting with her legs dangling beside the ladder, and Philip threw her the bread, so that by tucking the beer under his arm he had a free hand to hold the rails as he climbed up.

'Is that England?' asked Mireille from somewhere among

the gloomy recesses of the hay-bales. 'And about time. Been making a pass at Mamette, I suppose.'

'On the contrary,' said Philip, holding the sausage high in the air, and blowing a silent fanfare on the trumpet of the beer bottle. '*Apollon le Prisunic*, fleet of foot, with daring in his heart and loyalty in his loins, has returned with the treasure. Mamette means nothing to us English. Her wiles and charms are as naught. We are, how shall I say? . . . too phlegmatic.'

'Too loquacious, rather,' said DD, swinging her knees up from the trap-door hole, and starting to break the bread. Philip tapped her lightly on the head with the sausage.

'With this scroll I thee bless. Go forth and multiply.'

He sat cross-legged and started cutting thick wedges off the *saussisson*, peeling it as he went. 'Anyway, Mamette, who I take it is the delightful *femme de ménage* I encountered wrestling with a basin full of snakes that she plans to stew for dinner, is as nothing beside the beauty of your remarkable mother, Mireille. In my childish way I have awarded her a score of 855. What do you say, Roland?'

'A bit on the low side, England. You don't appreciate French beauty.'

'Not so,' interposed DD.

Madeleine, who was guzzling beer straight from the freshly opened bottle, gurgled something, at which Marin nodded wisely, removing his glasses, and polishing them on his shirt-tail. 'Very true, Berthe. I noticed it in Brittany: you really speak best under water.'

'I think you're blinded by love and self-interest,' said Philip to Roland, biting a hunk from the bread in his hand. 'A recurrent feature of French history. Here you are, utterly besotted with this wench, this temptress, this seducer, this goddess Mireille. So how can you be expected to give a reliable judgement about her mum? Obviously your own circumstances dictate that she should get a score only slightly less

49

than your paramour. That's bound to mean nine-eightyish. But your judgement is worthless. Am I not right, Marin?'

'Yes, yes, yes. The eight-fifties are far too generous these days. Personally I wouldn't give any film star more than about 700 anyway, simply on principle. No one who sells herself to the celluloid can be truly beautiful. Only the live theatre allows true inner beauty to shine through with all its intoxicating force. Eh Berthe? You're a great intoxicated force, so you should know.'

'Piss off, maggot.'

'Ah, such tenderness. Her love knew no bounds.'

'You all speak of love too easily,' said Danielle, turning her dark, almost black eyes sharply on Roland. 'Michel makes it a tragedy he can star in. England only believes it if it's in a book. Marin and Berthe see the whole of life as music-hall, with love a rough-and-tumble act after the crooner. Roland and Mireille here are infatuated with each other's bodies.' She got to her feet and went back to the trap door. 'I'd rather go for a walk.'

'Me too,' said Philip, and scuttled after her on hands and feet. 'Wait, Persephone. Never go to pick flowers alone.'

—

Danielle Dublinot waited for Philip in the yard. He smiled at her, crinkling his eyes against the sun as he emerged from the shadow of the barn. She put her head on one side slightly – a familiar gesture, simple but somehow intimate.

'We might as well go this way, I think,' said Philip, pointing through an archway to the right of the windmill itself, and diametrically opposite the kitchen door on the far side of the rectangular cobbled yard. 'There's some sort of a formal garden through there, with a gate out into what looked like a wood.' He anticipated her question. 'My room looks down on it: that's how I know.'

Danielle still said nothing, but made her way towards the arch. They went through it, crossed a small lawn, and then through a white gate on to a path that, like a tongue, quickly swallowed them into a wood. They walked in single file for some minutes. The path joined forces with a stream, and together they ambled gently downhill for several hundred metres, the little river silent in its muddy bed beside them. DD walked ahead. She was slightly older than Philip, nearly seventeen, slim but with none of the awkward angularity of childhood. Her dark brown hair was cut very short, and swept backwards on either side of her head into a sort of low ridge at the back that ran down to her blouse collar. She always dressed simply and conventionally. Her father, who had liked to joke with his little daughter that he came from a long line of French Irishmen, was actually from Reims, and, as he would explain with a twinkle in his eye, 'travelled in Champagne'. She could only just remember this. He was killed in a train crash when she was seven, and for the past ten years she and her mother had lived in a tidy little apartment on the Boulevard de Montparnasse. Her mother worked nearby – one of those formidable women who guard the *caisses* in the brasseries along the boulevard. Philip had learned recently that such women were not interested in books and were best not joked about. Danielle had some of the same traits, and they showed in her face, a topic on which Philip reflected as he walked through the wood behind her. Her eyes were very round and very dark, almost black, but they were not large, not doe-like, not cherries, none of those clichés, soft and melting. They flared occasionally, and could have a gimlet-like penetration if she was, as was common enough, roused. Beneath them her nose ran straight and clean-edged, almost to a point in profile, while on either side her cheeks made almost perfect ovals. Philip had once, when they were in bed together one afternoon in Tréveneuc, compared the shape to an almond, and she had been pleased. She'd smiled up at him, one brown

51

downy arm coiled around his neck, her small even white teeth suddenly bright in the half-light that seeped through the closed wooden shutters.

'Do you love me, England?'

'Of course I do. Would I be here otherwise? Besides, when I say I have never loved anyone else, it is literally true.'

She broadened her grin, and made faces like Jean-Paul Belmondo grimacing at Jean Seberg in *A Bout de souffle*, which they had all just been to see at the cinema in Saint-Quay-Portrieux. '*Prochainement sur cet écran, le spectacle que vous attendiez tous.*' She pulled his head down on to her shoulder. He liked the feel of her naked breast on his.

He wondered now, as they walked through the wood, what had happened to this past. They had seemed to him so completely happy throughout the month of July in Brittany. Inseparable. Now everything was different, and he had no idea why. Yet it was only two months ago, and now he was on the verge of leaving, still not knowing what, if anything, had gone wrong.

'Couldn't we stop somewhere? Sit down for a while?'

'It's awfully wet.'

'Surely we could find somewhere.'

They came out into a little clearing, but Danielle did not pause, even when he reached forward to take her hand. She let him hold it, however, though without really responding to his pressure. They both plunged on through the wood, still going downhill, until suddenly the sky was light above them, and they were standing at the trees' edge, the wood stretching away in formation on either side of them, and the little stream now in a ditch that followed a line of poplars splitting the field in front of them in half. The hillside continued to fall away into a shallow valley, no doubt with another, larger river winding through it. The fields had grown wheat, recently harvested, and the golden stubble, still wet from the drizzle, gleamed and winked in the afternoon sunshine. The air was warm. Philip peeled off his pullover, threw it down at the base of a tree and did a head-stand on it, resting his feet above him on the bark, gazing upside-down at Danielle.

'Will you kiss me ever again?' he said.

She leaned down on both hands, and gave him a peck on his inverted nose.

'Won't you join me?'

'No thanks. Wouldn't be decorous in this skirt.'

'I wasn't thinking of decorum. It was intimacy I had in mind.'

'Standing on our heads?'

'Oh, all right then, sex.'

'Do you ever think of anything else?'

'*C'est ainsi que ma Muse, aux bords d'une onde pure,*
Traduisoit en langue des Dieux . . . la voix de la nature.'

'One of ours?'

'La Fontaine, slightly abridged, with apologies to. Please talk to me.'

'You're impossible to talk to. I can't understand you. My past is quite unlike yours. We met because of Mireille and Roland. If I hadn't known Mireille from art school, you and I would never have met. Marin and Berthe, they are my people.'

'Well, I know that. But they're my people too. This summer belonged to all of us. No divisions. Roland is my brother, well, sort of. We love and hate like brothers anyway. And Michel is his oldest friend, from long before I turned up on the school exchange, so he is my friend too. I inherited him. Roland and Mireille are in love, I agree, although I don't know how it happened, and I don't think it will last.'

'True. And me and Marin and Berthe, we are appendages to that temporary love affair, and without it you will forget us.'

'And our love?'

'Happened in July.'

Philip tumbled out of his head-stand and sprang to his feet.

'Past tense?'

'I imagine so.'

'Then future imperfect.' Philip pulled a long piece of string out of his trouser pocket and began winding it around the tree, binding himself to the trunk as he went. 'I shall be found here dead of exposure in the morning. The newspapers will say that I was killed by a heartless woman, left to freeze in the first frosts of autumn. This scene' – and he waved his free arm with its coils of string towards the slope of the bare field in front of them – 'will be the last thing that I shall see. You will be dubbed "the heartless gamine of the Grande Chaumière" and questions will be asked in the House of Commons. I don't suppose that had occurred to you, had it? Questions in the House? Ah, this will teach you to trifle with the love of England.'

Philip concluded this surprising speech by tucking the end of the spent string through itself, and stuffing a handkerchief in his mouth. Danielle, who had begun by smiling, and continued via giggles to full laughter, first reeled away from him, then came up close and put her hands behind his head, pressing her body against his.

'Oh, poor old England,' she said, still laughing, while he pulled the handkerchief from his bulging cheeks, and mysteriously freed both arms from their binding. 'I am quite helpless before you, really.'

'That's what I wanted to hear,' said Philip, gently pushing her away while he loosened the string enough to escape. Then he spread his pullover for them both to sit on, but Danielle lay back in the damp grass, pulling him down on top of her.

———

Roland Beaumanière was sitting at the head of his bed, leaning against the whitewashed wall behind him. He was a fastidious young man, having learned that scrupulous care about one's appearance was one effective way of gaining acceptance in the large world of grown-ups. Currently he was using an elegant little ebony-handled device to press the cuticles of his fingernails into perfect half-moons.

Outside, a light wind had got up in the late afternoon, so that the sails of the mill, mere skeletons now, but directly outside his attic bedroom window, creaked gently and made a low whistling sound. The sails were bolted to a concealed system of iron braces, themselves sealed into the concrete of the new foundations. One of these braces ran vertically and invisibly down the inside of the wall at exactly the place where Roland leaned against it, his legs drawn up so that he could rest a hand on his knees for manicure.

Michel was sitting opposite him, on a chair beside the door. He had propped the chair up on its back legs, managing somehow to lean backwards against the wall while simultaneously appearing to sprawl casually. He cupped an ashtray over his tummy and blew smoke rings towards the white ceiling.

'She's a lovely woman. You have the luck of the devil.'

'The gods,' Roland replied, without lifting his head.

'Very well, the gods. Anyway, whichever, I ought to be dying of jealousy.'

'That doesn't surprise me.'

Roland always affected nonchalance. Indifference, even. It was his 'preferred style', as he liked to put it. It served, in particular, to emphasize the distance that separated him from Michel because Michel, although only a month or two younger than Roland, was thought by most grown-ups to be the baby of the group. This was not because of his physical development, which if anything was relatively advanced for his nearly seventeen years, but because his natural enthusiasm for life seemed, to adults wearied by time and experience, to be positively, perhaps even admirably, childish. Roland, on the other hand, had early noticed that in the world of adult discourse a relaxed and faintly cynical approach to life might attract admiration, and in imitation of it he had successfully adopted many of its visual characteristics. He would smoke a cigarette right down in the corner of his mouth, speaking from the other side of his jaw, and cocking his head to one side so that the smoke curled just out of contact with his eye, held half closed. He had copied this from Jean Gabin. Similarly he could shrug, either one or both of his hands extended, the gesture accompanied with a down-turning of the mouth and a slight drooping of the eyelids. Expressive, relaxed, indifferent. He had absorbed these gestures into his character. 'Roland? He's a smart one, he is.'

Michel sensed otherwise, but he could not articulate it. He suspected – they had been friends for ten years – that Roland was tense, nervous, acutely competitive. The remote, aloof, superior spirit was surely a façade, one increasingly difficult to crack, it was true, and smooth enough to make Michel doubt his better intuitions. Anything the least bit 'difficult' about other people was a problem for Michel. This was because he was involved in life, not separated from it by speculation, and brought a simple enthusiasm to whatever project was to hand. He had yet to lose his schoolboy enthusiasm for railway engines and model fighter planes, and he brought these inter-ests with him to the conquest of girls – an activity for which he felt a similar passion. He discovered that girls found this distasteful. They did not want to be wooed with descriptions of the gear ratios of Facel Vega motorcars, and seemed unable to indulge, even for the briefest of moments, his own strong interest in the engineering characteristics of nuclear submar-ines, detailed scale models of which were at that time just beginning to reach the better class of Parisian toy-shop. Michel could not understand their reluctance, but thought that it must be his fault, and that therefore he was to blame. All the girls he had attempted to, well, conquer in the last two Breton summers were noticeably drawn to him, were playfully friendly even, but since he couldn't set eyes on a band in the park without starting a description of differences in French regimental uniforms – he was the owner of a substantial collection of toy soldiers and other authentic-looking mini-ature military equipment with which he could re-enact the battles of Austerlitz or Jena – these tempting young women drifted away, bored. These sorts of disappointments never happened to Roland, who as a result now exercised a sort of hypnotic superiority over his friend.

Michel was, however, largely correct in his intuitions about Roland. The marvellous air of superiority, of mature accom-plishment, which Roland carried so easily into adult company, seemed to him, peering out from behind the mask, to be the flimsiest of veils. Tension was far too weak a word to describe the extent of his terror at the thought of being exposed as a sham, and it was a matter of acute discomfort to him, some-thing which made him squirm with apprehension whenever he reflected on it – which was nearly all the time – that he was still a virgin.

Michel would have found this hard to believe, even if Roland himself had sworn that it was true, because from his vantage point Roland seemed to have been striding from conquest to conquest for about as long as he could remember. In July, at Tréveneuc, Roland often stayed out all night, disappearing through the window at midnight, returning in the early dawn. Véronique, Antoinette, Sylvie – these were just the names from the summer before last, before Mireille came on the scene. Each of them had passed, or perhaps failed, the test of Roland's charms, while expanding the catalogue of his reputation. Roland valued the admiration that it brought him, particularly from Michel, because it was indispensable to his self-esteem. And Michel did not doubt his friend's reputation, because he had so often been witness to it. How often had he walked home alone from the '*soirée des jeunes*' at the local casino while Roland escorted Véronique to her hostel, and then appeared at their bedroom window at three in the morning, grinning, carrying his jacket and tie? Every day for a week one year they had sailed their dinghy to the islands that lay scattered in the bay, and while Michel hunted for gulls' nests, and climbed the rocky cliffs, Roland and Monique would settle in a sandy cove for the afternoon, and then sail home in silence, smiling, occasionally caressing each other. Fours at tennis were as likely as not to end in Roland and Marcelle – this was two years ago – wandering off on the common, and not being seen again until dinner. The evidence, accumulated over the years, was endorsed by Roland's mannerisms.

'Women.' And he would give Michel one of his expressive shrugs. 'It's a question of taste.'

Michel lowered his chair on to all four legs, sauntered over to the bedroom window, and flicked his cigarette butt out into the courtyard below.

'Our tastes must be similar, because every single one of the girls you've been with this past year or so has seemed to me like one out of the box.'

Roland smiled, stretched out on the bed, and dropped his little instrument on to the marble top of the bedside cabinet.

'What time's dinner?'

'Seven-thirty. Yvette said that we had to be absolutely on time because Patrick would throw a rage over punctuality. Something about the film industry, apparently. And anyway, he likes a little formality at dinner.'

'Don't we all?'

'And there'll be aperitifs in the living room from seven onwards.'

At this point Philip arrived. They heard him bounding up the wooden stairs. Michel positioned himself at the door, and when Philip came in he threw himself on him from behind, pinning him with his arms. They struggled and heaved together, panting and laughing, Philip cursing fiercely in a mixture of English and French, Michel just managing to keep his balance, squeezing the trap of his arms tighter.

'Beg forgiveness, England. Beg it for Trafalgar, for Waterloo, for Fashoda. Above all, beg it for Joan of Arc.'

Philip managed to fall forward on to the bed and then rolled over, so that he was on top of Michel, who still gripped him from behind. Roland drew his knees up to his chin, then jumped off the bed and leaned against the window frame to light a cigarette.

'Ah,' he said, looking down on the courtyard. 'There goes the charming Danielle Dublinot. Her skirt is a trifle creased. What have you been up to, England?'

'We were discussing the philosophical basis of La Fontaine's fables,' said Philip, manoeuvring on the bed as Michel released his grip to scramble to the window and look out over Roland's shoulder. 'I was advancing the view' – and he paused to take several deep panting breaths – 'that La Fontaine was in reality a philosopher of the new age of science who wrapped his empiricism in the familiar ribbons of morality and antiquity. I further suggested that, since this made him a modern philosopher, there was surely at least the possibility of a serious philosophical manuscript still to be found, and that a proper search should be made for it.'

'And DD? In agreement?'

'Not really. Bit hard to understand. I think what she said was that he was just an entertainer. "A sort of eighteenth-century Georges Brassens" was the expression she used.'

'Sensible girl,' said Roland.

'Not really,' said Philip again, standing up and starting to do toe-touching exercises. 'Wrong century.' Down, up, breath. 'La Fontaine was born in 1621.' Down, up, breath. 'Still.' Down, up, breath. 'What's a hundred years between friends?'

'Or a wrinkled skirt, for that matter,' said Roland.

'Ah, there you're wrong,' said Philip, sitting down again. 'That's your department. We intellectuals: minds on higher things. Actually we had a jolly good walk through a nice wood, and came back by a long way round on the road. Have I missed anything?'

'Yvette Delachêne entertained us with a few songs by Jacques Prévert, then we did a screen test for Patrick's new film, and then . . .'

'Really?'

'Ah, England, if only. No, you missed nothing. Mireille and I fell asleep on the hay. Berthe got drunk and went off to dance for Alphonse, so Marin thought he'd better go too, although to protect whom was never entirely clear. Michel here has just been mooning about.'

'Actually,' said Michel, 'I spent a couple of hours talking to Yvette in the kitchen. You were quite wrong about her, England. She's stunning. Think of having a mother like that.'

'Think of having a mistress with a mother like that,' said Roland very softly, almost under his breath.

'Can't bear to,' said Philip.

Michel said nothing. Or at any rate nothing more. What had actually happened was that he had told Yvette about a number of important matters in his life, notably his collection of *outre-mer* stamps, the difficulties of painting detail correctly on pewter model soldiers, and the differences between pre- and postwar editions of Tintin comic books. And not only had Yvette listened to what he said, but she'd actually been interested, asked some sensible questions. No woman had ever done this before, except of course his aunties, and they didn't count. Now he thought he was in love. Hopelessly in love. Aching with it. And there was no one he could explain it to, no one who would listen and sympathize. No one who would understand and comfort him. For it went without saying that this new love couldn't be declared or realized. Yvette was Mireille's mother. She belonged to another world: the great world of grown-ups, where the future stopped moving, and there were cheque books and driving licences, lawyers and garden parties, christenings and theatre critics. Not only that, but in this other world she was famous. The great Yvette Delachêne, actress, star, remote and glamorous on the front cover of *Paris Match*, smiling and *décolletée* on the inside pages of *France-Soir*. Merely to have stood in the kitchen of her country house was an honour. And to have done it for two hours, with her, to have been able to talk to her quite naturally about, well, OK, about stamps and toy soldiers. But she's human too. She really was interested. And to have done this all alone, except for Mamette, of course, but she doesn't really count. And to have been asked to help with the sauce for dinner. To have stirred the syrup with her wooden spoon. To have, just once, felt her fingers on his shoulder as she leaned past him at the stove to reach for an apron which she then tied, and with such care and tenderness, around his waist. Oh heaven . . .

'He's gone stiff. Perhaps we'd better put him in a bath of warm water.'

'What's that, Philip?'

'You, Michel, old chap. You, the heart-throb of the Saint-Quay clay-court junior open. Are you still with us, or have you deserted for a better place? The land of *petit-suisse*-with-too-much-sugar, or the Renault works team at Le Mans, or a bottle of Uncle William's *premier cru*? Speak to us. You have lapsed into a mysterious trance, and we fear for your sanity. Is it love? Tell us. Your friends deserve an answer. No, no, let me guess. Yes, I have it. It's la Grande Berthe. Her subtle features and gentle tongue have finally wormed their way into that cold warrior heart of yours. You have caught a glimpse of a delicate thigh, seen the gently rounded soft breast of the girl-woman lift in your direction, and you have been melted. The icy cold of your stern indifference has turned to a racing torrent of desire, even as the cold snows of winter melt in the warm winds of spring's affection. Now you are blind to all but her beauty, and your longing is an ache that burns . . .'

'Shut up.'

Philip had delivered this speech for the most part with his eyes closed, standing in a mock dramatic posture on the bed. He opened them to find Michel white with fury, his fists clenched, his face a blank sheet of hatred, the eyes round.

'Shut up.'

This second time he shouted it. The three young men stood, silent, just for a second, each at a corner of their triangle. Then Michel abruptly turned away, flung open the door and slammed it shut behind him. Roland and Philip looked at each other for a moment, hearing the thunder of Michel's feet on the stairs. Silence felt again, but for the creaking of the mill.

'Shit,' said Roland, very gently, blowing air out through rounded lips and shaking his right hand at the wrist as though it had recently been close to getting burned. 'I think you just stepped on a mine.'

'Something certainly went off,' said Philip. 'You don't think it's true, do you? That he really does love Berthe.'

'Don't be silly. Nobody could love Berthe. She's just a mascot.'

—

Philip didn't see Michel again before dinner. He left Roland's room after a few minutes, went down the corridor, ran himself a bath, and soaked in it for ninety minutes, chain-smoking Gauloises. He tried to think about the immediate future. Tomorrow, last Sunday in September, they'd all go back to Paris. Then he had one day, Monday, in Paris before leaving on the hated boat train on Tuesday morning. On Wednesday he'd be back in school, his first day in the sixth form, though he was three weeks late for the start of term. Special permission granted for acceptable extra-curricular activities, to wit, attendance at preparatory college in Paris. Philip grinned inwardly. Preparatory to or for what? Every day he'd been going along to the Grande Chaumière near the Luxembourg Gardens and signing in for the life class in which Danielle, Marin and Berthe were struggling to get enough technique together somehow to scrape through the *bac* at the second attempt – having failed last June – and thus keep alive their diminishing hopes of getting into the *École des Beaux-Arts*. In the end, just last week, only Marin had made it, placed next to bottom of the pass list. Berthe said he'd clearly overworked. DD had just missed, coming twelfth on the fail list. Berthe seemed to have disappeared altogether, because they couldn't find her name anywhere at all. She said she had not so much chosen obscurity as had it thrust upon her.

Philip lay back in the water and blew smoke into the steam. In six months you will be seventeen, and three months or so after that it will be time to return to Brittany for July. I wonder if you can wait that long. He added up the days to the first of July and made it two hundred and seventy-five. He multiplied this in his head by twenty-four and got a total of six thousand six hundred. He liked the roundness of the number, but groaned inwardly at the eternity it embodied. He thought of going on to multiply by another sixty to see how many minutes it came to, but shied away from what would only cause pain.

[He did the sum in bed at home three days later and made the answer 391,680, and it did cause him pain, a pain that was not eased in the slightest by a subsequent calculation that those three elapsed days had accounted for 4,320 miserable minutes that would otherwise have had to be added to the grand total. After all, one doesn't have to be a French intellectual to know that future time moves at quite a different speed from past time, and anyway a substantial proportion of those past minutes had been spent in the company of Danielle, whom he would now never hear of again. Or so it seemed from a dark suburban bedroom in north London.]

Instead Philip thought about Marin, and his chances of a career as a theatre designer, which is where he had set his heart. Le Matelot was the same age as Danielle: lived with his parents somewhere out near the Porte d'Italie, where Philip had never been. Philip believed, with the familiar frisson of jealousy from which he absentmindedly sought to distract himself, this time by adding more hot water to the bath, that Marin loved Danielle, and would make tracks for her during the winter. He had wanted to question Danielle closely about this possibility under the trees this afternoon, but the moment was ill-chosen because Danielle was absorbed in him, then, and refused to talk about anyone else.

You were unprepared for the egotism of a woman in love, before July you were at any rate, but it pleased you enormously at first.

Now it worried him, particularly in the light of those thousands of lonely hours strung out between here and next July. Could Danielle get through them on egotism and love letters alone? No wonder the good, the anarchic, the talented Marin kept coming back into ever more unpleasant focus. He's an old friend of hers. He'll stand by her. She'll tell him everything. When she starts work he'll be her link back to the models, the *ateliers*, the good and the mad times. She'll live in him vicariously. He'll be her line, my God, her only line now that Berthe's flunked too, to the old *demi-monde* of art, art students, Rabelais, Baudelaire and the mess, the marvellous eternal bloody mess of shabby Parisian bohemian hopes. He's bound to win. Philip stood up in the bath and scratched his bottom. Then he sat down again, moving backwards and forwards slowly to coax a steady wave pattern, and then lying down to let it flow over him with a slosh.

And it's not as if one afternoon under the trees on the edge of a sunny cornfield makes you feel all that secure anyway. After Brittany he hadn't seen Danielle for a month. She had been promised as a summer housemaid to a friend of her mother's who kept a guest-house in Chamonix, and she couldn't, or wouldn't, cry off. Philip, back with Roland in the

Beaumanières' apartment in Paris, had filled the lonely month with a stream of letters. When she returned to Paris at the beginning of September, Danielle had been different. She slipped back into *les gosses* but seemed to treat him as just one of the group. They had not slept together again. Come to think of it, she hadn't written to him all that much from Chamonix either, one letter a week, half a dozen postcards, pleading long hours and tiredness. Philip, you are authentically perplexed, just as you are sincerely in love. But what can you do?

Philip often lapsed into the third person about himself. He felt that if he could distance his consciousness from his immediate problems he might somehow be able to solve them, or at any rate work on them, more easily. He added some more water, worked up another wave sequence, and lay back in the bath again.

Roland never thought about himself in the third person. I and he looked pretty solidly like one and the same thing to Roland, and with not much you in between. Indeed Roland, who was specializing in mathematics and was a Beaumanière, which meant that he was expected to place in the top fifty for entrance to the *Polytechnique* (and did, in due course), never showed the slightest interest in any philosophical question. He was happy to assume that what other people detected as his particularly well-integrated personality was indeed the person he was. And Roland was pretty confident, even from the uncertain position of his attic guest room, and all the anxieties associated with his virginity, that most of life's problems were the product of thinking too much, and that there were not many difficulties that couldn't be solved by the steady application of reasonably large sums of money. The only big thing that was troubling him right now was the question of why Mireille, like all of his former apparent 'conquests', still refused to allow him, despite all the petting, the kissing and caressing, despite, even, having spent several afternoons and two almost-complete nights in bed together, still wouldn't allow him actually to penetrate her. He had gone to some trouble over the past two years to keep a supply of contraceptives available; he enjoyed ample opportunity in the summer when freed of parental restraint; he talked to girls, he coaxed, he was considerate, gallant even. Yet as with all the others, so now with Mireille; he had still not had the ultimate success so eagerly and earnestly sought, and which his friends all assumed he had long since achieved.

He had not achieved it again this afternoon in the hay, a painful fact that kept him morose in his bedroom until almost seven o'clock, fiddling with his cuff-links, adjusting his tie, praying that dinner would be over and the parents out of the way early enough for him to return to his task. He was still thinking about this as he made his way down the stairs and across the cobbled courtyard, swept in the dusk by fallen leaves harried this way and that in the rising wind, towards the warm glow of the lighted windows of the living room.

—

'Left to themselves, first strong wind that comes along, they blow over. Used to happen all the time. If you build something to catch the wind, you mustn't complain if it behaves like a yacht.' Patrick was speaking with his back to the company, pouring drinks at a dresser – big, black and heavily carved – that ran half the length of one wall of the living room. His remarks were addressed to something that Danielle had said, but she was not paying very much attention. She was a little tired and dreamy, and the large whitewashed room, with its polished wooden floor, its Turkish carpets, the indirect lighting from table and floor lamps, and the blazing wood fire in the huge brick grate, had warmed and lulled her into a state of abstraction. 'This is why Quixote's tilting at the windmill is especially poignant, because not only can he not bring it down, but nature can, just like that.' And Patrick snapped his fingers, then picked up a tray and started passing it round.

These actions brought Philip back from a reverie. He was perched on the arm of Danielle's chair, where he could maintain contact with his lover's person – her hair at this precise moment – rather than suffer the far more exquisite pain of having to sit and look at her. They had been in a patisserie in Saint-Quay, eating brioches and raspberry tarts, and Danielle was telling him about the summer when she was six and she stayed with her parents in a little valley near Reims, and how her father used to ride a bicycle to the village to buy wine and cigarettes and the evening paper, and would come home whistling with his shirt open to the waist. The story meant nothing to Philip, but as she talked Danielle stirred her hot chocolate and gazed down into the cup without once looking up at him, and he knew that she was giving him a part of herself, something that she had probably never given to anybody else, in that first slow telling of intimacies that might end our isolation. So much for individualism, thought Philip, reflecting on his own reflections, and snapped out of them by the click of fingers. Over the fireplace was an oil painting, a beautiful landscape that seemed to Philip to be a seasonal pair with *Little Spring Meadows* by Sisley, which he had seen in the Tate Gallery, only this one had no figures in it. The picture shone, somehow: the trees, the grass, the hedges and fields, the same washed sky, all just as they had been this afternoon. Surely this couldn't be a Sisley too. Not a real one. But how could you tell? And whose judgement could you trust?

'They tell me you're the intellectual, young England. Have you read Cervantes?'

'Not yet,' said Philip, who was acutely conscious of the gaps in his literary education and tried his best to disguise them, or, failing that, not to let others dwell on them. 'Is what you're saying that the mill sails used to be on the outside wall, at the far end of the courtyard, and that you had it all changed?'

'Well, it all looked quite wrong when we bought it, eh Yvette . . .?'

'Fakers,' said Mireille. 'It wasn't really a windmill ever. It was a watermill, drawing water from the stream that runs through the wood over there' – and she waved vaguely towards the windows. 'The old race is still there. I'll show you in the morning when it's light. My parents are just romantics.'

Roland came into the room at this moment. 'So am I,' he said, smiling at the faces turned towards him and closing the door gently behind his back.

'Twaddle,' said Berthe, from the sofa where she was sitting next to Yvette. 'You're about as romantic as the thing from outer space. Roland is to sentiment and fine feeling what I am to Leslie Caron.' She slurped her drink. 'Good piss, this, Mireille's father.' She held the glass away from her towards the fire light. 'Pity about the scum on the glass.' Yvette laughed. Roland, deeply embarrassed by Madeleine's astonishing outbursts, tut-tutted his way to the fire.

'Berthe, you have all the quiet sophistication of a regiment of Napoleonic . . .' said Roland, though he got no further.

'Napoleon, my arse,' said Berthe, launching into one of her favourite quotations from *Zazie*, but herself cut short by Marin.

'Eh oh, eh oh, eh oh, enough, Berthe. You're already French heavyweight champion clown: no need to try out for the world title tonight. Concentrate on the booze.'

Madeleine threw him a scowl. Yvette put her arm through hers and held her hand. Michel, who had not heard much for the past ten minutes, and had barely noticed Roland's arrival, imagined to himself the ecstasy of being Madeleine's hand. He sighed, twirling his empty glass in his fingers. He was finding it difficult not to gaze at Yvette's knees, which were exquisitely round. Also, pointing directly at him.

'But you are, aren't you?' said Mireille, reverting. 'Romantics. I mean you, Mummy, "the meaning of life" being recreated on the stage, you called it once. Acting. And that's a romantic idea because you can't really do it. It's a trick. And you too, Daddy. I know they call it New Wave, but your films are romantic too, not really slices of life but full of illusion and trickery.' She turned to Roland as if to confide a secret, a gesture observed from the sofa by Yvette with a distinct feeling of distaste. 'I'm in one of them, you know. Dressed up as an urchin, no shoes, torn dress, very grubby. I was eight. I had to steal an apple from a market stall, and in the film I'm right in the corner of the picture, almost off camera, and so quick that you could easily miss it.'

'Which film is it in?' said Roland.

'*The Fountain*. My favourite. Yvette thinks not, eh my dear?'

Yvette smiled at Patrick. 'I can't be objective,' she replied, and shook her head. 'But don't be sidetracked. You were telling these young people about the mill.'

'Right,' said Patrick, and he sat down on the floor to one side of the fire, hoping no doubt to establish the right kind of intimacy with his juvenile audience.

'Mireille is absolutely right. Though this was a windmill at one time, centuries ago, they installed a water wheel later, and part of the dug-out mill race is still there. We have a little sheltered vegetable garden in it now. When it stopped being operated, actually grinding wheat for flour, we don't know. Probably before the First World War, because no one in the village has any recollection of it. The last owner died in 1922, and by all accounts he was as derelict as the property. There was no electricity here. No mains water. Very primitive drainage. Windmills, after all, predate the industrial revolution.'

'But did you have to change it all so much?' asked Philip. 'Couldn't it have been restored just the way it once was?'

'And how was it, young England?'

'Well, I mean, with the mill sails in the proper place, and the old house more or less as it was. That sort of thing.'

'No, no,' said Patrick, smiling expansively. 'This is what I was saying to Danielle at the start. Left to themselves, mills blow over in the first strong wind that comes along. Like tonight,' he said, cocking his head to one side, and they all listened to hear the still rising wind sweeping through the courtyard outside. 'And anyway, we think it feels more like an old mill the way it now is, so in a sense it's closer to the truth of what it once was for us than if we'd rebuilt it exactly as it had been – with all its draughts, and inconveniences, and discomforts.'

'Fascinating,' said Roland.

'I'm starving,' said Berthe. 'If I don't get in the trough soon I'll fade away.'

'Yes, come on,' said Yvette. 'Let's give these young people their dinner. They must be hungry.' And she led the way to the dining room. This was dominated by a long, highly polished oval table, set with silver and cut glass. There were candles alight in a silver candelabra, and soft indirect light from various corners. Yvette sat down and tapped the seat next to her.

'Michel, you come and sit here by me, please.' His heart was pounding hard, but he had the presence of mind to feel glad that Patrick, busying himself with bottles at a table in the corner, was unaware of his progress. 'Roland, you sit opposite me, please, with Berthe, that's right, on one side of you and Danielle on the other. L'Angleterre next to me here. Mireille next to Michel, I think, with our Matelot at the head there. Good. Patrick will be near the wine.'

She touched the floor button with her foot and Mamette came in with a steaming tureen of soup, which she put down in front of her. Behind her, the soup bowls were carried by a girl in a black dress with a white apron and a circle of decorative white lace at her throat. Philip noticed that she had very slim wrists and very long dark eyelashes, features that seemed somehow to be related. She was exquisitely well built, slender at the waist, what one class would call '*mince*' and another '*svelte*', Philip thought. Delicate but well-formed, firm breasts. Narrow thighs. The girl kept her eyes down as she distributed each bowl filled by Yvette and then turned on her heels to leave the room under the watchful gaze of Mamette, who followed her out.

There was silence during this ritual, but as soon as it was over a babble broke out, with bread-passing and -breaking, butter-asking-for and spoon-rattling, until Berthe quelled the general noise by pronouncing sonorously, and between two loud sips of soup, 'Nine hundred and ninety-five.'

Philip smiled. No doubt about it.

'Shut up, Berthe,' said Marin. 'That's enough.'

'Enough what?' she replied. 'It's a compliment. And it's only what the Beaumanière here is thinking, eh king lover?' And she gave Roland a hefty dig in the side with her elbow. 'Too polite to own up, you see,' she added, leaning forward across the table to address Yvette as if in a secret conspiracy of understanding.

'Nine hundred and ninety-five what?' asked Patrick, getting up from his seat and setting out round the table to pour *aligoté*. There was a brief awkward silence.

'Come on, England, speak up,' said Madeleine, grinning mischievously. 'Let's all throw Roland in the soup here, in front of his girlfriend's dad' – and she laughed.

'Now, now, don't be unfair,' said Yvette, reluctant to rescue Roland, but a hostess has duties . . . 'It would be fun to know, England. What's it all about? Come to think of it, didn't I hear you airing some sort of number out loud earlier today? What do these numbers mean?'

'Well,' said Philip, only too aware that every eye was on him, and profoundly conscious of the unfortunate fact that the table would not turn into a deep trench into which he might jump and disappear. 'It's a kind of joke. An English joke, really.'

'Rare enough already,' said Michel.

'Hush,' said Yvette. 'Let the boy speak.'

'Well, in an English play, by a man called Marlowe whom I

71

don't suppose you've heard of much in France, well, Helen of Troy is described as the face that launched a thousand ships, and, well, we sort of allocate scores to girls with a thousand as the Hellenic possible maximum. So nine hundred and ninety-five is the sort of score that might start a war, and . . .'

Philip's confusion and regret might have overwhelmed him at this juncture, but Yvette had already pressed the floor button, and Mamette came to the door.

'Jeannette, please, Mamette.'

The serving girl appeared almost immediately, and Yvette stood up and walked towards her round the table. The girl stood absolutely still, a light in the corner behind the door casting one side of her beautiful face deep in shadow. Yvette approached her with her arms outstretched, and then began to speak in an almost faultless English accent.

'"And burnt the topless towers of Ilium?
Sweet Helen make me immortal with a kiss!"'

She pulled the girl's mouth towards her own, caressing the high cheekbones on either side, light and dark, of the angular face, running the palms of her hands up by the eyes to bury her fingers in the piled black bun of hair on the oval crown, and then stroking downwards again to run her fingertips and nails the length of the long white neck until she could push the still form away gently by the shoulders, holding it there, and then looking intently at the perfect forehead.

'"Her lips suck forth my soul: see, where it flies!
Come Helen, come give me my soul again.
Here will I dwell, for heaven be in these lips,
And all is dross that is not Helena."'

Yvette let her arms drop but continued to look at the girl,

72

who returned her gaze, watchful but as if unmoved. The room was in complete silence, a silence which Yvette broke eventually.

'Is that right, England?'

Philip could only swallow and nod. Yvette motioned Jeannette from the room.

'I agree, she is a very beautiful girl.' Yvette returned to her seat. 'We all love her dearly, don't we, Mireille?'

'Mummy, you are awful,' said Mireille. 'Poor Jeannette. Being made to act like that.' And she put her hand over her mouth, though it was patently obvious to Philip that she'd loved every second of it.

'She doesn't mind,' said Patrick, sipping his wine. 'We had the Lascombes over for dinner a couple of weeks ago, and Yvette got her in to show a bit of that Pirandello thing about six characters in search of an author. Jeannette told me the next day it had been a lot of fun. She likes it. *Voilà!*'

General hubbub broke out again. Michel declared himself completely bowled over, and that if he hadn't been sitting next to her in her own dining room, he would have asked Madame Delachêne for her autograph. Berthe told him not to be such a booby.

Marin began telling Roland about the sort of set required for the last act of *Faustus*, a subject of technical complexity which Roland couldn't grasp. This was because he had no idea who Faustus was or what had happened to him, *and* he'd been perplexed by the drama that had been enacted in front of his eyes. He was feeling simultaneously annoyed that no one found it necessary to explain it to him, and anxious in case, detecting his ignorance, someone did. Also he had fallen completely in love with the serving girl, what was she called?, ah yes, Jeannette, and he wanted to be alone to think about her without Marin boring him to death with trap doors and hell fire. Mireille's future, he realized through the haze of other people's conversation, would also have to be dealt with. There was something else to think about. Marin was not exactly helping with this.

Philip complimented Yvette on her English, but she brushed this aside. It was 'stage English', a 'form of mimicry', 'something one learned at drama school', 'part of the illusion of theatre', and not really anything to do with language at all.

Danielle wondered how nice it would be to be kissed like that by Yvette, and since she was sometimes given to asking outspoken questions of men with whom she felt safe – a trick she had learned from watching her mother in the brasserie – she asked Patrick what Yvette's kisses were like. Patrick, who was a modern man, and also very wealthy, believed that children should be raised 'honestly' by having all of their questions answered. This particular one tested him a bit, however, because if there was one person in the room with whom it would unquestionably be enjoyable to demonstrate one of Yvette's kisses, it was young Danielle here on his right, and if she had just been a bit older – well, perhaps not even that – but if she had just not happened to be one of his daughter's friends, and if his daughter hadn't also happened to be sitting in the same room at the same time, well, then maybe he would have tried.

Danielle, whose thoughts were far too complicated about everything at the moment, and who could still feel something like the memory of the warm afternoon sun on her legs, was quite unaware of the turbulent thoughts in motion in her host's mind in the second or two that followed her question. She finished her soup and put down the spoon, looking to him for a reply.

'Oh well,' he said lamely, 'her lips suck forth the soul. Didn't you understand the English?'

Danielle shrugged. She hadn't understood a thing, but it didn't matter, and she imagined that only Philip, damn his eyes, and Yvette had fully understood what was going on. Here she felt a stab of pure distilled jealousy, and quite liked

74

it. Look at them now, with their heads bowed together in concentrated, private talk. It's so unfair.

This was true: it was unfair, but not to Danielle. For Yvette was indulging in that most unfair of all adult ploys, questioning Philip 'in confidence' about Roland, and what Roland's friendship with her daughter 'amounted to'. She and Patrick had been in Greece in July, happy to let Mireille have her own holiday in Brittany, joining forces with some friends she had made at her Wednesday art classes on the Left Bank. Some of these friends Yvette had already met. Madeleine, for instance, whom she rather liked. True, she was a crazy, but Yvette and Patrick both worked with actors, and were accustomed to the mad, the zany, the improbable and the dubious. And besides, Marin was quite different, a serious boy with some talent for the theatre, perhaps a future protégé, and as long as he was involved – and it was his parents who had invited them all – there seemed no harm. But Mireille had returned with a fund of stories about a trio of boys who had 'captivated' her: a strong arm called Michel, an aristocrat called Roland, and an English intellectual in tow called England. When the friendships didn't blow over at the *rentrée*, she and Patrick decided that it would be for the best to get *les gosses* to the windmill, and see what they were like.

Madeleine Suresnes and Marin had been there before, and Yvette had already developed a strong sympathy for Berthe. She wasn't quite sure why. Perhaps it was because she liked her improbable *obiter dicta*, the wild obscenities that flowed from her, and which, although they lacked charm, implied some sort of aesthetic code, parallel with but indifferent to the rest of society. Her physique worried Yvette as well. Berthe wasn't just big, she was gross, and as she went from child to woman she was not shedding the load. Puppy fat was giving way to Amazonian muscle, making her look a big, tough, hard street girl. Yvette would refer to her as a *jolie laide*, but it wasn't really true. With her close-cropped hair, round and slightly ruddy face and mud-grey eyes, the fact was that she was not *jolie* at all, merely *laide*. The saving grace, Yvette thought, was her gift for living the life that she had. She had no real artistic talent, no literary insight, no abilities in science or logic. She had grown up in one of those dismal Parisian suburbs, one of which she even carried with her as her name, where there was little of physical beauty and few social opportunities. Yet somehow, in the markets and streets, she had acquired a prodigious command of language, and great fearlessness. Patrick had toyed with the idea of making Berthe a star, if only he could find a suitable script. He would see. Meanwhile, Yvette was trying to be more practical. She had found Berthe a position in a theatrical wardrobe company. It wasn't stardom, and it wasn't even close to any particular small centre of affairs, since it was stuck out in a warehouse in Bagnolet. But it was a start in the trade, and, in the few days since the art examination results had been published, she and Marin had been putting Berthe under pressure to take the offer. Berthe herself, who never expected to have any prospects and had no family in particular to turn to – no one had ever heard her talk about her parents, and she lived in a hostel for single girls in Paris – seemed reluctant to commit herself.

Philip knew all these things – they were much dicussed among *les gosses* – and they made him wary of Yvette. Also, he was used to being cross-questioned about Roland, mainly by his father, who had formed a confused and ambiguous set of views about his son's pursuit of French language and culture. He had sensed readily enough that anyone with the name Beaumanière must be reasonably acceptable, and was gratified to discover, in due course, that his son had indeed forged a personal link with someone in France who was wealthy, well connected, and in possession of a good name. So good that it was amenable, in that glorious English inversion, to being dropped. Against this, Mr Leroux was far from happy with the effects Philip's French experience appeared to be having on what he thought of as the boy's prospects. True, he did appear to have become fluent in the language – itself a matter for public gratification – but he also now seemed to be only very rarely at home during the holidays. No sooner was school over than Philip was away, and if the dribble of information from his occasional correspondence was anything to go by, he had gone where parental authority could not follow. Torn between the pleasure of not having to pay much attention to his son's doings and annoyance at the loss of a portion of desirable domestic power, Mr Leroux would try to slake the thirst of curiosity by pumping Philip about the Beaumanières. Philip devised a number of responses to these inquisitions, which normally occurred at a Sunday lunchtime. Sometimes he would turn them aside with what appeared to be a joke which no one could believe, though it was true; sometimes with half-truths that had a ring, however false, of the truth about them; and sometimes with quite improbable lies that were always accepted by a father who, mortgage holder that he was, was more than ready to tolerate inflation.

Practised at fielding Beaumanière questions, Philip paused for a moment over Yvette's inquiry, chased a last drop of liquid around his tilted soup bowl, and then settled on a suitable reply.

'Roland and I are very close,' he said, dipping his head, and speaking confidentially. 'Normally we don't talk about each other to outsiders because friendship of our sort is like I imagine a marriage to be – a mystery to all but those who live it. I am tempted to make an exception now because I sense that you are still able to think and to feel as we children do, simply and truthfully, but there is little that I can say even so. One problem is that all of Roland's strengths are my weaknesses, so that to praise him would be to condemn myself, while those few weaknesses that he has are trivial, and not worth the attention of people who, like yourself, have their minds on higher things.' He spread his hands, palms upwards, in imitation of a massive Gallic shrug. 'No one should fear Roland Beaumanière. He threatens only himself.'

These sentiments, rendered ludicrous in the English language, carried tremendous authority in French. Philip had noticed how French adults, unlike the English, thought it a compliment to be compared with children, and he took it as a general rule that to touch on this, then couple it with an inversion or two before adding a suggestion of philosophical intimacy, could generally be relied upon to persuade the average French bourgeois audience that it was present at a moment of profound discourse, as a result of which its understanding had been immeasurably deepened. Yvette Delachêne was no exception to this general rule. Expressing herself impressed with the strength and honesty of Philip's feelings, she sank back into what would have become a reverential hush had it not been for the return of Mamette, accompanied by the shadow of Jeannette, and the business-like termination of one course in anticipation of another.

Matters now arranged themselves far more into the normal pattern of a family dinner. A lavish, bleeding gigot, rich with rosemary and garlic, was dissected, physically first, and orally second. The sauce was much admired, its strength attributed to Michel, and it subtlety, by him, to Yvette. Patrick poured a generous burgundy, and invited Roland, and then Marin and Michel, to discuss its qualities. The women were excluded from this exercise, as was Philip, who knew that when it came to the appreciation of red wine, foreigners were regarded as women. Opinion having been sought from the places where it might be thought to be of interest, Patrick then embarked on a brisk speech on the topic of French geography and viticulture, advancing the now commonplace view that wine, like beautiful women, has to suffer in order to be truly great.

When Philip pretended to take this preposterous remark seriously, Patrick asked him if he had perhaps thought of making a career in the wine industry. English attitudes in need of correction, expansion of future prospects, possibilities of eminence in his chosen field, indeed all remarkably like Mr Leroux at his most tiresome. Philip responded by saying that he had no idea what he wanted to be, although he had once considered becoming a music-hall magician. Yvette said 'Bravo! Why not?' 'Ah,' said Philip. 'Parental pessimism. My father took the view that I might be better advised to become a bomb disposal officer, or to join the parachute regiment, than try to earn a living by disguising my intentions from a discerning audience.'

Philip was gratified to see, or at any rate glimpse, because he didn't like to look too hard, that Patrick didn't know how to take this joke, and was possibly wondering whether he might be being sent up. Marin, a great frequenter of music-halls, saved all potential embarrassment, however, by giving an account of magicians that he had seen, and stories of this kind occupied the salad, after which attention shifted to cheese, and from there by easy stages to politics, coffee, and a return to the living-room fireside.

Patrick, perhaps encouraged by the attention he imagined himself to have secured from Danielle, settled comfortably into a monologue on the future triumph of French socialism, which led him, by way of various well-signposted landmarks, to a proof of the weakness of the Fifth Republic, and the reasons why it could not survive, plus a number of other related topics on which, in some Parisian circles, he was recognized as an expert.

His audience drowsed behind its coffee cups, interest barely awake. What we are really interested in, thought Philip, particularly when passing through this moment in life, the very one we are all, more or less, negotiating right now, is to preserve the appearance of childhood innocence at the same time as we seize adult opportunities. We have learned that the grown-ups' world is a world of appearances, a land of actors and actresses, a *mise-en-scène* devised by and in the great world of directors, touts, producers, walk-on bit-part performers, great tragedians, impresarios, lighting experts, floor sweepers, supporting roles, clowns and ticket salesmen. Truth, which is what we had been confidently led to expect would be the logical outcome of the sufferings of childhood, we can see is in retreat, ever less tangible, increasingly remote. The image, the appearance, make-up and make-believe, the great false world of celluloid and stage, expands to fill the space of ever-widening perceptions, the enormous press of the theatrical crowd closes around us, the confident assumption of childhood that all would be well when, when only, once we are, after we have become, all that turns cloudy, and is lost eventually in the need to put on a costume, answer a curtain call, fix the make-up, usher the crowd, man the crush bar, tune the instrument. As for truth and knowledge, those fresh, once vivid expectations of an adult future, well, really!

From somewhere out of the gloom of the sofa Madeleine Suresnes released a belch.

'I think you may lose your audience altogether for a while, *chéri*,' said Yvette. 'They want to run along and talk for a bit. Off you go, *les gosses*. But remember. Only half an hour more and then it's bed. It's half-past ten already.'

—

The wind strengthened in the early part of the night: a southerly that blew an unseasonal warmth. As it grew stronger, the creaking of the stationary mill sails was married to a gentle whistle, like air sucked through gap-teeth, but intermittent, and as if in imitation of a distant and incomprehensible Morse code.

Parts of the old buildings rattled and shook. Fallen leaves were stirred into heaps, and then redistributed from corner to corner of the cobbled yard. The confusion of shapes was lit from time to time by a harvest moon, which occasionally erupted from behind black, racing clouds. The buildings them-selves, so white and clean-lined inside, were dark in the night, mere lumpish shapes, ill-formed in outline, and clustered about the courtyard so that they hemmed it in, giving it definition. A few spots of particularly intense blackness marked the places on the walls where doors and archways gave access to the wings beyond.

In one corner, close to a shuttered kitchen window, a char-acter leaned in silence, her back against the wall, a grey shawl gathered around her shoulders. Beneath, a dark blue nightdress fell full-length to her bare feet. This was Jeannette, the serving girl. All summer she had been unable to sleep in the early night, and regularly took up station here in this dark corner, visible to no one, barely moving, but watching, waiting, tempted and tempting. She knew the sounds of the night by heart: the rustle of the trees by the stream that Philip and Danielle had followed in the afternoon; the strange, hunted call of an owl in the woods beyond the kitchen garden; the whistle and creak of the mill sails caught in perpetual stasis as the wind licked past. Sometimes a nocturnal bird or animal would penetrate the yard, a pheasant, or a moorhen, once a baby fox. The house cats then would see them off, pelting through the archway, returning moments later on silent paws, their dark tails raised high. Jeannette observed all this closely, not moving, content to be a part, ignored and accepted, of this unthinking world. The loneliness of her vigil was, she sensed, its central purpose, the reason for her standing in wait of something else.

Tonight, however, she was not alone. A little after twelve some dark figures flitted silently across the yard and climbed the ladder into the loft of the barn. After a minute or two a soft light shone down through the open trap door, illuminating Mireille and Madeleine, who arrived, breathless and giggling, their eyes shining as they followed their friends. A few moments later Michel, Roland and Philip arrived, each carrying a bag which was passed up ahead before each then disappeared through the square of light. Then the trap door was closed, sealing the darkness behind them.

Inside the loft Marin had lit two spirit lamps that hung in opposite corners of the roof and threw a gentle white light towards the centre of the room. Now he was busy with a trestle table on which Roland had set up a portable record player. DD started making sandwiches, Michel pulled corks and set out glasses, Mireille put on some music. Philip sat down on a stool and counted the petals on the flowers on Danielle's pyjama bottom.

'A hundred and twenty-three,' he said eventually. 'And the peculiar nature of the number is due to the asymmetrical sewing. The seam is very carelessly in quite the wrong place. You will have to change your lingerie supplier, DD. These pyjamas are quite unsuitable for public occasions.'

The idea of a pyjama party was Mireille's. Indeed, her invitation to *les gosses* to come to the mill was specifically for this purpose, the secret and central focus of the whole weekend. In the event, perhaps typically, Mireille had come in a night-dress, not pyjamas, a long, white gown, prettily *décolletée*, and, as Philip noticed, marvellously revealing when in front of a light. He could also sense, though there was no obvious empirical evidence for it, that Danielle disapproved of Mireille's attire. Her own stout winceyette was almost an accusation.

Roland had come in a flowing velvet dressing gown with a gold cord at the waist and a matching gold cravat at the throat. He had little leather pumps on his feet, and it was possible that he wasn't wearing any pyjamas at all. Philip liked to say that Roland wore only perfume in bed, but declined to explain how he knew. 'All the Beaumanières always smell divine,' he would say. Now that there was music Roland took Mireille in his arms and began to dance. She pressed close against him and laid her head on his shoulder. The embrace deprived Philip of his former focus of attention, but he was distracted anyway by Danielle, who, having finished with the sandwiches, came over and held out her fingers for him to lick.

'And you shouldn't be unkind about my practical night attire,' she said. 'Your own makes you look like a convict.' This was welcome news to Philip, who had deliberately brought with him a pair of striped English cotton pyjamas that he thought approximated Kansas State Penitentiary standard issue, *circa* 1910. His mother had bought them for him, thinking them 'smart', and he regarded them as one of the few novelties of his small wardrobe. An opportunity to wear them, so to speak, in public had never before arisen. Pleased with Danielle's remark, he took her fingers out of his mouth, and pulled her down on to his lap to whisper in her ear.

'Anyway, I'm nothing compared to Marin. You have to admit that.'

'Incontrovertible,' said Danielle softly, her hand over her mouth. The word was one of Roland's favourites, in imitation of his father. Marin had chosen to come in a pair of shorty pyjamas, the bottoms very ragged and in a pale blue colour, the top a brilliant red open-necked shirt, collarless, with long sleeves that widened hugely towards the wrists. The garments gave him the air of a stage Chinaman above the waist and of a 1920s athlete below it, an anomaly that his physique did nothing to resolve since his remarkable thinness seemed wonderfully appropriate at the top and wildly incongruous at the bottom, particularly about the knees. The oddness of it was endorsed by the quizzical air of his expression, emphasized by his round rimless glasses, so that despite the care with which he had planned his striking appearance, he managed to convey the impression of being haphazard, a truly accidental man. Marin made a deep bow, Berthe closed in on him with an all-engulfing hug, and they embarked slowly on an improvised, almost motionless dance.

Berthe, discarding all restraining undergarments, had come

in a pair of grey sailor's pyjamas, gathered at the ankle, wrist and waist, shapelessly ample everywhere else. Michel, turning over record sleeves at the table, shuddered at the thought of all that flesh moving, like a great underground current. His own pyjamas, blue with a red flash down the sleeves and trouser legs, had a military cut, adorned with a row of medal ribbons above the breast pocket. Perhaps he looked officer-like, but what he felt was a mixture of revulsion and sorrow at the fact of Berthe's physique, nakedly unattractive, interfering with his thoughts of the divine Yvette. He went to sit in a chair next to Philip and Danielle, tilted it against the wall and lit a cigarette. Danielle brought them each a glass of wine, and they sipped in silence for a while.

'Nothing like a party for good conversation,' said Philip, breaking into the what seemed to him like gloom. 'Tell me, Michel, do you believe in God?'

'What sort of a gambit is that supposed to be?'

'Standard. All young people sit up late discussing God, politics and sex. It's one of the rules of adolescence. And here we are up late at night, clearly keeping the rules, downing the booze, and I just thought a hardy tussle with one of the required topics would sort of round things off. But I'm easy-going. It doesn't have to be God. What do you think are the chances of a nuclear war over Berlin? Or, do you think sexual gratification is an essential part of loving or can there be Platonic love, pure and undefiled by the sweat of ardour? Or, . . .'

'Shut up,' said Michel.

Philip turned to Danielle and began to talk to her in mock whispers, loud enough for everyone to hear.

'Michel's upset about something. It must be God because he's a Gaullist through-and-through, and everyone knows they never think about politics. And as for sex, well, unless model soldiers can do it, which I don't discount because after all American dolls can wet themselves, I'm sure he never thinks about that either.' He turned back to Michel and raised his voice slightly. 'Danielle believes firmly in a loving God, Michel. You shouldn't let it get you down.'

Michel hadn't stirred from his chair, still propped up against the wall, but now he drained his glass before fishing with a circular motion of his right hand to set it down on the floor beside him. The four shadowy dancers, attracted by the sound of conversation, came out of the background, Madeleine bearing the wine. She refilled Michel's glass, plumped herself down on the floor and started to drink from the bottle. Roland, settling into a small cane sofa next to Mireille, gave la Grande Berthe a withering look of disapproval.

'You don't drink enough,' said Marin, holding his glass out to Madeleine. 'Let me help you dispose of that.'

'Michel was leading us in conversation about divinity,' said Philip, 'and as the company's leading agnostic I thought it only right that I should put the conversation into some sort of perspective. My point is that since there is absolutely no evidence one way or the other for the existence of God, we are entitled, when confronted with the debate about His existence, merely to shrug. We cannot say that He does not exist, since to negate is also to affirm. This is why it is essential for us Anglo-Saxons to acquire the veneer of French culture, because only the French know how to shrug in such a way as to give the right kind of weight to the issue.' And he gave an illustration as best he could, which was not entirely a success because Danielle had resettled herself on his knee.

Madeleine dealt with this extemporary opening by belching loudly from the floor and then smiling broadly up at Philip.

'So bloody clever, aren't you, England? But it's obvious for anyone to see that if there is a God, He is certainly not a loving one, but violent, destructive and hateful, and that therefore it's a matter of principle to insist that He doesn't exist.'

'You don't think, do you,' put in Marin, 'that that mightn't make him even madder?'

'Of course. But so what? All we've got is our pride, and so

long as that's not defeated we can face anything. Even this God-awful plonk' – and she upended the bottle to show that it was empty. Marin fetched her another from the table.

'Steady on, Berthe,' said Mireille quietly.

'Balls,' said Madeleine.

'Well, loving, or destructive, or not,' said Roland, 'I take the view that gods are not to be mocked. I mean, why shouldn't a god be both loving and wrathful at one and the same time?' He looked at Philip for confirmation, but got another shrug instead. 'After all, there has to be some explanation for the mystery of life. Surely no one seriously believes that the universe is just a great big accident, or that the feelings that we have aren't . . .'

'Ah. The great mechanic in the sky,' said Marin, raising a finger to indicate that here was an argument he'd heard before, and which he already knew how to dispatch.

'Well, you can mock it like that if you want, Mr Clever-clever,' said Roland. 'But really, how else are we to explain the incredible sophistication of, of . . . a blade of grass, or a spider's web, or a snowflake. And they are nothing compared to the organs of the human body.'

'Ah yes,' said Berthe, swigging on the new bottle. 'You should see my liver. Now that really is evidence for the existence of a vengeful God.' She raised the bottle again. 'And I spit in his eye.'

'Why is God always a man?' said Danielle.

'Because He's such a beast,' said Madeleine.

'Because,' Michel broke in, 'men are stronger and more dominant. And since God is clearly strong and dominant, He has to be masculine. Eh, Philip?'

Philip gave another of his shrugs, which Marin applauded lightly.

'Michel is right,' said Roland.

'You'll tell me next that woman was conceived from man's ribs,' said Mireille, unwinding Roland's arm from around her shoulder, 'when it seems to me that women are the really indispensable part of the universe, and ought to count for more.'

'But you are already on a pedestal,' said Michel.

'Ah,' said Philip. 'Does this mean that we've finished with you-know-who, what's-his-name, thing, and have now got on to sex? I have quite strong views about sex, and wouldn't like to have to sit here shrugging away just because no one was really sure whether the last topic was open or shut.'

'Come outside and show me your strong views,' said Berthe, 'and I'll show you mine.'

'A fate worse than death,' said Marin.

'Well, you should know,' said Berthe, digging him in the ribs with her finger. 'You've been dead for long enough. The rest of us have no basis for comparison.'

'The difference between God and sex,' said Philip, adopting a lecturing style, 'is that whereas we must insist that the former is beyond discourse, with the latter we are required to admit its universality.' There was a round of ooh-la-las and applause at this point, which Philip, grinning, pretended to ignore. Madeleine got ponderously to her feet and crossed to the table, where she eased the caps off a couple of bottles of beer, and then returned to her place on the floor, one bottle in each fist. 'To put it another way,' said Philip, 'we can say nothing about God, but we must say everything about sex. This I now propose to do.'

'Then I think I'll go for a walk.' Michel lowered his chair on to all four legs, got to his feet and went over to the trap door.

'Do you want company, my love?' Berthe called after him. He paused at the top of the ladder, half his body framed in the trap door, a wan smile on his face. The lights picked out his boyish features in hard planes.

'Sincerely, I think not,' he said, and disappeared downwards, lowering the trap above him with the flat of his hand.

'And Marshall Ney set off to review his troops on the eve of Austerlitz,' said Berthe, and she took a long draught from one of her bottles of beer.

At the foot of the ladder Michel lit another cigarette and breathed the smoke in deeply. A sensation of melancholy settled on him, so that he felt weary without being tired, unhappy with no immediately obvious cause, isolated in the company of his friends.

—

The mood of the party changed once Michel had left. Without his presence to give it focus, Philip's banter was no match for Roland's anxiety, Madeleine's debauchery, or Marin's seriousness. If he ever went permanently, Philip thought, we would all just drift apart, because we are held together by our differences, which Michel makes compatible. Once he's gone our differences will divide us. Perhaps this is what it means to be mature. Once you have come across somebody who simply does not like you, not because of anything you have said or done, but simply because you are not liked, then you have no option but to adjust to the world of people as it is. The first compromises lie in the affections, and maturity is the discovery that it is neither possible nor desirable to be liked by everyone. The stale taste of this insight is what makes us feel that maturity is to be regretted, while childhood was a state of grace. Having been allowed to love spontaneously, we find the necessity to dissemble hard. Affection by arrangement.

'Speak, sphinx,' said Marin.

Philip gave him a weak smile, but said nothing. Roland and Mireille had chosen some new music, and gone back to dancing. Madeleine, still with two large bottles of beer, had wandered off to the straw bales under the sloping roof at the far end of the barn, and was stretched out on her back, occasionally guzzling. Danielle got down from Philip's knee and sat on the floor with Marin, who asked her to tell him something about her life. Philip drifted again.

The worst temptation is the belief in permanence, to think that things can always go on as they are. Evil, for instance, constantly takes new forms, and is unpredictable. So we are bound to be at a moral disadvantage. Perhaps Michel senses this, but can't articulate it. Maybe what he sees is the great adult world of contradictions, which they all think we are only too anxious to join, but which we see as madness. When you grow up, they say, you become realistic in your ambitions and desires. What this really means is that you agree to compromise in the face of failure and defeat. We are all, ultimately, to be defeated, and will be qualified grown-ups when we come to terms with this fact. That's one side of it anyway. On the other side is another code of behaviour that sounds quite different, but whose difference, for some reason, adults don't notice. Here it says that to face disappointment and actually be disappointed is to be defeatist, and we should beware of anything so 'childish' or 'immature'. Such is the great adult world of contradictions. Anyone who is not a pragmatist by forty has not matured. Anyone who surrenders his ideals in the face of history is unworthy of the name of man. And so on. What *are* we to do with this adult world?

Philip didn't know the answer to this question, from which something apparently was missing: something, or somewhere, a space of some sort that lay between the passionate instincts of childhood and the naive irrational objectivity of the adult world. But he was jolted from these reflections by a commotion. Madeleine had slipped off the hay bale on which she had been lying, and was wriggling on the floor like a beetle. Roland and Mireille had gone to her aid, Mireille suggesting that perhaps it was time for her to go to bed. Berthe rejected this idea with a stream of colourful oaths, during which they got her into a sitting position where she took another long pull on a bottle of beer. Roland bent to put his hands under her arms, hoping presumably to help her back on to a hay bale, but his efforts were forestalled by Madeleine vomiting all over him.

Various things then happened all at once. Danielle jumped up to fetch a cloth, knocking over and breaking a glass that had been beside her on the floor. Marin, slightly slower getting to his feet, and only doing that because, on balance, this was evolving into one of those situations when it was probably better to be on your feet than not, promptly trod on a jagged sliver of glass and cut his foot. This began to bleed profusely. Roland, whose situation was unenviable, to say the least, swore violently, freed himself from the clutch and stench of la Grande Berthe, and peeled off his dressing gown. This revealed a pair of yellow silk pyjamas, the family crest and an RB monogram stitched on to the breast-pocket.

'I knew he wore the fucking things, really,' squealed Madeleine, who had started to laugh, coarsely and with tremendous force, and was once again rolling from side to side on the floor, in and out of a puddle of sick, yellow, Philip noticed, and horribly flecked with red.

Mireille, who had a background of her parents' artistic friends, and so was not entirely unfamiliar with scenes such as this, tried to hold Berthe still, then to get her on to her feet so that she could lie down properly on the hay. She combined this with various anodyne words about her old friend needing a good night's sleep. Berthe rose slowly and unsteadily, her face covered in sweat. Then, with what had all the appearance of deliberation, she very carefully crossed the line that separates moderation from hysteria.

With a deep animal growl of what Philip thought was 'Fuck off', she hit Mireille in the eye, intending to use her fist but, since it still contained a beer bottle, using that instead. Mireille fell back against the wall, her head in her hands. 'You bastards, you cunts, leave me alone.' She confronted all of them, still laughing horribly. 'Leave me alone, you sods. Think I need help from you pathetic lot? I'd rather have smallpox. Look at that creep over there' – and she pointed a half-empty beer bottle at Roland, sloshing some of its contents on the floor. 'Silk-perfumed namby-pamby with his head in a bucket of shit. Fine adornments to a dull fart.' She was still laughing, more horribly than ever, a feral noise that filled the barn with fear.

'Oh do calm down, Berthe,' said Marin, hopping about on one foot trying to look at the other one, which was streaming blood. 'You're drunk.'

In the circumstances this was an unhelpful observation, and it attracted Madeleine's attention. She lurched towards Marin with a fighting glare. Philip could see that she intended to fall on the luckless Marin and that, given his lack of mobility, she might do him some serious damage. He jumped between them, whereupon, still three metres or so distant, Berthe flung her two beer bottles at him with tremendous force. The first, empty, struck him on the shoulder, and bounced harmlessly away into a corner. The second, half full and gushing, whistled past his left ear and shattered against the wall. Broken glass and splatters of beer showered across the room. Philip closed on the screaming figure of Madeleine.

'Bloody England,' she was shouting. 'What do you know about love?'

Philip hit her in the face with the flat of his right hand, once and very hard, so that the slap was like the crack of a whip, and his palm went numb for a second before starting to sting painfully. Philip had seen this done in plays and films. Apparently it was what one did with hysterics. After it, there was a moment of complete silence, and then Berthe slumped in a heap at his feet, whimpering like a dog, and saying over and over again, 'Oh England, can't you see that I love you? I love you. Can't you see? Can't you see?' And she lowered her head to the dirty floor and beat a soft accompaniment to her words with her fists.

Marin, still hopping around the table spilling blood, suggested that they get Madeleine out into the fresh air where, as he put it, she might cool down 'and recover some of her normal calm'. Roland, trying to comfort the wounded Mireille, but finding it difficult with vomit in his hair, thought this was a good idea. He could use the chance to get his head under a tap. He opened the trap door, and together with Philip they half-lifted the slumped Madeleine and guided her as far as the top of the ladder. Here they encountered a problem. La Berthe had no strength in her knees, so would have to be lowered down. Marin, leaning on Danielle's shoulder, hopped over to offer advice.

Eventually they decided that Philip should go down first and guide Madeleine's feet on to each rung, while Roland and Danielle took her weight from above, and lowered her as gently as they could through the hole. This worked reasonably well until they had their cargo just over halfway down, but from that point Roland and Danielle were progressively and rapidly unable to support Madeleine's considerable weight. Four rungs from the bottom they let go altogether, and Philip and Madeleine fell in an untidy heap on the cobblestones. Philip scrambled to his feet as Roland came down, but Berthe lay on the ground where she was, groaning and noisily sucking in the air. Then she was sick again, and this time the mess engulfed her. After this she appeared to go to sleep.

Danielle came down the ladder.

'I think if you two can manage to carry her, we should get her to bed,' she said. 'It's not far.' Philip and Roland bent to pick her up, but she was slippery, and seemed heavier than ever.

'A hundred and twenty kilos of trouble,' said Philip, letting out a gasp as he tried to get one of Berthe's arms round his neck. 'They never seem to have any trouble removing the dead and wounded in the movies, do they, Roland. Just goes to show.'

'What does it go to show?' They half-dragged, half-carried their load across the courtyard, and followed Danielle through a door into what might be a store room. Danielle found a light switch. Along one wall was a couch with a blanket.

'That you can't believe what you see at the cinema.'

'I'll believe anything now.'

'We'll never get her up the stairs,' said Danielle. She indicated the couch. 'Berthe can sleep here. Put her down, would you?' She went out and then came back with a cloth and a bowl of water. Roland disappeared. Philip sat down on the doorstep, the light from the room behind him spreading like a white sheet at his feet. He started to tremble, and the trembling spread to every part of his body. For some reason he felt himself absent from this strange and uncontrollable motion. Or rather, although he realized that he was part of it, was, so to speak, sitting inside it, he was not being touched by it. It was somehow other. He let his head fall forward, limp, into his hands. His teeth chattered, and he could feel his shoulders heaving and his knees shaking, as in descriptions in boys' comics and adventure stories. Then he found that he was weeping, and a moment or two later he understood why.

The light went out and Danielle sidled past him, went down the yard a few paces to a tap, and rinsed her hands. She cupped a hand for water and brought it back to put on Philip's forehead. Then she sat beside him and put her arm through his, taking one of his sweating, trembling hands in her own cold, wet palm.

'It's a touch of shock, my love,' she said softly. 'You ought really to go in to the warm.'

Philip shook his head and made a sort of gurgling sound of disagreement which Danielle interpreted correctly, and they stayed where they were. Slowly his trembling subsided. Everything was quiet about them. He put his head on her shoulder, still shedding quiet tears.

'Is it true?' he asked.

'Is what true?'

'What she said, upstairs.'

'About loving you? Yes, I expect it is.'

'But why?'

'Why not?'

'Because I haven't done anything.'

'But you don't have to do anything to get someone to love you.' There was musical phrasing to this statement. 'All you have to do is to be.'

'But that's my point.' Philip sounded very miserable. 'Everything I am is foreign to her. In my being there is no point of contact with her world. She is one of a group, and I am another. Sometimes she made me laugh. Tonight she is making me cry. But we were just friends, and now she's being untrue to that, and spoiling it.'

'You sound as though you want it all to be rational.'

'No, of course I don't. But I think it should be fair.'

'Fair? What on earth can be fair about love? Madeleine thinks she loves you, and has probably done so all summer. She wouldn't tell anyone because everyone she knows treats her like an outrageous bogus boy, not entitled to normal female emotions. Everyone may discuss whether Mireille loves Roland, or I love you, but no one's to discuss whether la Grande Berthe loves anyone at all because after all she's just a clown. The mascot of Tréveneuc. What she's discovered this summer is the first glimpse of her future, what her life is going to be like permanently, for ever and ever. And she knows that for her this summer of laughter and games, the days of *les gosses*, the fun and excitement that have brought us here to the mill, all of this is not the beginning. For her, it's the end.'

—

Michel stood at the foot of the ladder, pulling on his cigarette, uncertain what to do. Jeannette, still in her dark corner,

94

watched him with a sudden feeling of wretched happiness, hopeful and fearful together, the simultaneity of these emotions freezing her with an exquisite pain. Like a girl at a school dance backed up against the wall as a saxophone begins to wail in the darkening hall, accompanied by the skitter and brush of a snare, she felt the agony of hope of being asked to dance, and the delicious terror of its actually happening.

Michel was thinking about Yvette, a companion to his melancholy. Oh, how miserable I am, he thought. The prospect of going up to bed was unbearable, but the alternative of returning to the party, like a schoolboy who has slipped out of the dance for an illicit smoke, was distasteful. Philip's corrosive chatter, Berthe's obscenities, all that lovey-dovey cooing from Roland and Mireille, Marin's sorrowful jealousy of Philip's success with Danielle, it was a world in a crystal snowstorm, fascinating for a while, but as insignificant as a paper weight. He flicked a tiny speck of tobacco from the end of his tongue with a thread of dry air through his teeth, and walked through the archway into the little garden.

The air was warmer than ever, the stones of the yard dry on his bare feet. He followed the path across the garden, curling his toes slightly at the bite of the gravel. When he reached the far side he went through the gate, but instead of following the path down through the wood, he turned to the right, and followed the line of the garden fence. A little wooden bridge over the mill-race stream took him into a thinly wooded area of undulating country that ran, in humps and hollows, towards a shallow ridge clearly outlined in the moonlight. Michel felt like a soldier returning from night patrol. He had successfully negotiated the enemy lines but wouldn't be safe until he reached the ridge and could give the password to the sentries. Confident of their duty, they would be sure to challenge as he approached. All the greater need for silence. He went up on his toes and relaxed slightly at the knees, deadening his step, holding his breath in the dark. Tense now, he leaned against a tree, extinguishing his cigarette on its bark. The moon lit up the clearings on either side of him, a shallow depression ahead, and beyond that the little ridge whose summit was his initial objective. He strained his eyes and waited, listening for the sounds of men in the undergrowth, of soft boots on dead leaves and epaulettes tugging at low-hanging branches.

Nothing. He steadied himself for the sprint to the lines. No, wait. Something. A crackle in the undergrowth, the snap of a twig, perhaps a shuffle. Then silence again, complete and weighty, a silence so profound that it filled his head. Surely he hadn't imagined it. He tried to listen harder, but the silence prevented it. I can't have imagined it. Michel's heart began to pound beneath the medal ribbons of his pyjama tunic. No, it can't be true. I'm alone here, and always was. But he stayed crouching all the same. And then the noises started again, this time definitely feet rustling through the leaves, and coming towards him. His heart beat harder, audibly it seemed, and he imagined spirits and ghosts, enemies real and impossible. Without thinking he cleared his throat gently and called out.

'Philip? Philip, is that you?' There was complete silence, the noises stopped.

'Is it you, Philip? Or Roland? Don't muck about.' He whispered these questions, hoping that the distortion might conceal his location. Fear made him want to urinate, and he had a rash of sharp pinpricks in the backs of his knees. His neck was cold. These discomforts turned fearful paralysis to fearful action. Suddenly he rose and ran, a flight of terror during which he saw nothing, and which lasted approximately three seconds. This was how long it took him to cover the twenty metres or so of the slight declivity between his tree and the little ridge.

Down through the dip he went, and up on to the little knife-edge, and there, with a crunch and a couple of almost disembodied gasps, he ran full speed into Jeannette. The violence of their collision locked them together, and they fell, clinging to each other, rolling over and over as they crashed from the top of the ridge, slithered something like five metres through soft ground, and came to rest in a wind-blown bank of flowers and fallen leaves.

Neither of them moved for several seconds.

'Are you all right?' Jeannette asked eventually. 'It's Michel, isn't it? I'm so sorry I startled you.'

Michel didn't understand any of this. He had never met this person before. She was a stranger to him. Also his shoulder hurt, and the dryness in his mouth had given way to a saliva flood, the taste of which was sickening. His fear, however, was completely gone. Perhaps this was because of the calmness of the voice, or the softness of the arms around his neck.

'I'm sorry,' he said, shifting his weight so that she moved off his shoulder and unwound her arms, enabling him to sit up. 'I didn't see you.'

She began to laugh. 'The understatement of the year.'

'But true, though.' He grunted quietly, massaging and flexing his shoulder. 'Why didn't you answer who you were when I called out? Come to that, who are you anyway?'

'I'm Jeannette,' she replied, lying back in the leaves. 'I work in the kitchen. And I've hurt my shin.'

'Pretty amazing either of us survived at all,' said Michel. 'Do you want me to have a look?' He felt in his breast-pocket for his lighter, and was relieved that it was still there. He struck it, and then let it go out just as suddenly.

'What's the matter?'

'My pyjamas.'

'So?'

'It's all I've got on.'

Jeannette started to giggle. 'That's all any of you were wearing. Are you telling me that they're all right for partying with Monsieur Delachêne's daughter, and rushing round the *domaine* in the dead of night, but not for talking to the servants?' She was laughing a lot by the time she finished this question. 'Oh God. Too good. Too rich. Too funny. You people really are the end.' By this time she was rocking backwards and forwards on the ground, hugging herself in her arms.

Michel was a bit crestfallen at this. It hadn't occurred to him before now that he might be undressed in his pyjamas, especially not these ones, which were the definition of elegance. But for some reason the situation he was now in was different. All of a sudden he felt naked. He sat on the ground in silence, feeling ashamed. After a while Jeannette stopped laughing. Then she sat up and put out her hand to find his.

'Look,' she said. 'If it's any consolation to you, I know how you feel. I followed you out here tonight, but lost you when you stood still for some reason. When you called out I could tell that you might be frightened . . .'

'It wasn't that . . .'

'No, listen, please. I knew I must have alarmed you by creeping about out here, but I didn't dare to speak back because I was ashamed. Ashamed of following you, of seeming to pry. I didn't mean to. I don't really know what I meant. But I couldn't sleep, and when I saw you set off from the house I just followed. I didn't mean any harm. I'm sorry.' She knelt up in front of him. 'Friends now?'

He could just make out her face in the dark, a white oval, deep pools of black for eyes, sudden touches of white where her teeth shone in the shadow of her lips. She leaned forward and kissed him on the cheek. Then very deliberately, moving her shawl slightly to accommodate the gesture, she raised his left hand and placed it firmly on her right breast. In the darkness he reached up to the kneeling figure and kissed her on the mouth. This kiss lasted a few seconds. Full and bold it was also chaste, cool, and slightly tense. Both participants, examining the record in silence, agreed about the result without having to compare notes. Jeannette sat down again on a mound, holding Michel's hand for a second longer before releasing it. Michel's heart was pounding again.

'Will you please,' said Jeannette, 'now take a look at my shin?'

Michel obliged, holding the flame well away from himself. Two deep-brown bruises were rising in unison on Jeannette's leg, but the skin wasn't broken.

'Thank goodness,' she said, in a practical, matter-of-fact voice. 'I hate those tetanus injections.'

The lighter went out, and they sat side by side in the dark again. Neither spoke until their eyes had readjusted.

'What were you doing anyway, wandering about out here in the middle of the night?'

'Oh nothing. Thinking. I don't know. I got bored with the party. Anyway, how did you know about our party? It was supposed to be a secret, especially from Mireille's parents. You look as though you'd dressed to come. Did Mireille invite you?'

'No such luck. I was just hanging about in the courtyard because I couldn't sleep. It often happens. When I saw you come down the ladder and walk off into the garden I thought I'd follow. I didn't expect to be hit by a runaway express.'

'Sorry,' said Michel. He used the opportunity afforded by this apology to search for Jeannette's hand. He located it about one centimetre from his own, and squeezed it gently. It replied. Both hearts bounded again, and there was another dark, silent pause while they measured the bounce.

'How old are you, Jeannette?'

'Seventeen. And you?'

'Nearly. Sixteen, still.'

'Do you mind?'

'Not at all. Should it matter?'

'I can't see any reason.'

'Shall we walk for a bit?'

'Yes, let's. I can show you a favourite place.'

Michel stood up and, holding out both hands, he pulled Jeannette up too. His shoulder was all right now. They kissed again because, having changed position, it seemed the right thing to do, then threaded their way through the sparse trees in a downhill direction. Soon they were walking across a field of grass that flowed away from them like silver water in the moonlight. On the far side of this field they climbed over a low dry-stone wall and sat down again, their backs against it. In front of them was another field which sloped away a little more steeply into a river valley, the course of the river marked by lines and clumps of trees, black shading in the night.

'Over there,' said Jeannette, pointing, 'is my village. It's beautiful from here. Spire, rooftops, stone walls, grey-green shades and the colours of the light.'

'Lovely,' said Michel in sympathy.

'What's Paris like?' asked Jeannette in the tones of one who, having shown you her village, now asks to see yours.

'You've never been?'

'Nope.'

Michel took a while to absorb this. The idea that there were people in France who had never been to Paris was a new and difficult one, and he was conscious suddenly of swampy territory where one might slip, and mud start to fly. Jeannette stepped in to save him.

'Don't be surprised,' she said. 'It's normal here in the country. How would I go? I don't think I've any relatives in Paris, and since my mother died and I finished school, I have to work.'

Michel thought of something stupendous.

'Would you like to come? Visit Paris, I mean. You could stay, well, we'd find you somewhere, and there's masses to do and see, like the Invalides, and the museums in the Palais de Chaillot, and the Palais Royal, and the Odéon . . .'

'Is that where Madame Delachêne acts?' Jeannette interrupted him. Michel had forgotten about Yvette. Being reminded of her now surprised and faintly annoyed him.

'No, she's with the TNP,' he replied eventually.

'Oh!' said Jeannette, to whom the initials meant nothing. She had an instinct for symmetry, however, and sensing the conversation drifting in a decidedly asymmetrical direction she thought it best to leave this fiddly problem of Madame Delachêne's theatrical whereabouts up in the air. As with most questions of fact, the answer would be revealed when it was good and ready. Instead she said, 'I'd love to come.'

Michel and Jeannette understood at this moment that they had struck their first contract, and that contracts, being serious matters, required evidence of commitment. Michel put his arm around her and drew her towards him. Then he kissed her on the lips again, though not in an exploratory way this time, but with a heat dictated by impulse that filled him with happiness, making him larger than himself, giving him a heroism that was altogether new. This embrace lasted until their physical positions became profoundly uncomfortable. Eventually Jeannette detached herself.

'Just a minute,' she whispered, rustling in the moonlight. When she returned to his arms a moment later, she was naked.

—

Roland may have gone to treat the walking wounded, but Marin, who seemed most obviously in need of treatment, was incapable of walking. The wound to his foot was ugly and painful. The sliver of glass had made a curved incision in the sole of his foot, and then broken off at the surface of the skin. The cut was long as well as deep, and a piece of glass was buried in the flesh.

Roland examined this by the light of the oil lamps. He found it profoundly distasteful. Marin's foot, like the rest of him, was disagreeably thin, so that having it cupped in his hand was like holding the remains of a foot that was fast decomposing into a skeleton. This, coupled with the stink of Madeleine's vomit, was making him feel sick. Marin felt much the same. He lay back on the hay and swore at the ceiling.

'Quite so,' said Roland.

Mireille suggested that they go and look for Danielle. 'She's good at this sort of thing, and she might have Berthe settled by now.'

Roland put his head and shoulders through the trap door and peered into the courtyard. He dropped an arm and waved it at what looked like a couple sitting on a step. They got up and sauntered over.

'Danielle, can you come up and take a look at our Matelot. His foot's a bit of a mess, Mireille can't see too well because of her eye, and I do stink, rather. Wouldn't mind putting my head under a tap.'

'Why does everyone talk to me upside-down today?' said Danielle, climbing the ladder.

'What's that?' said Mireille.

'Nothing.'

Roland joined Philip in the yard.

'Great party,' said Philip dryly.

'One of the best. Cigarette?'

Philip took one, examined it carefully, and then dropped it on the ground, where he crushed it with his foot. 'No thanks. I'm going to give up.' Roland puffed away, looking up at the sky.

'Lovely night,' he said eventually. 'Look, if it's all the same with you, I think I'd better go and have a bit of a rub down, get this muck off my hair. Then I'll come back. We might have a chat. Get things straight.' He walked off in the direction of his bedroom, and shortly Philip saw a light come on, heard the sound of running water.

Mireille came down the ladder, using one hand, holding a cloth to her damaged eye.

'How is it? asked Philip.

'Pretty bloody awful. Has Roland gone?'

'Only to wash. He said he'll be back.'

'Tell him I've gone to bed,' she ordered. 'Good night.' And she marched off, swinging one arm, away from the guest rooms and into the main house. Philip thought she shut the door a bit over-firmly. Well, he thought to himself, uttering a little sigh, what a performance! And he began to sing, quietly, a snatch from one of the old LPs his parents had in a cupboard at home: 'For you and I have a guardian angel on high, with nothing to do . . .' Still humming to himself, he ambled over to the deeper darkness of the archway and leaned against the wall, looking at the moonlit scene beyond, still, dense with shadows, filled with the smells of autumn which were strangely out of place on this inexplicably warm night. He was relieved to be alone, and toyed with the idea of sneaking off to bed himself, leaving the rest of them to get on with it. But then he remembered Danielle, and thought how unfair it would be. He knew that she loved him, but he sensed now that the physical side of their relationship, so recently revived, also accounted for her occasional estrangements. By loving me physically, he thought, she's impeding, perhaps denying, her love for the others. She wants to love us all, but when I'm there I exclude the others because I make claims on her which all the others are denied. I suppose, to be honest, she surrendered to me much as she might have surrendered to any of them. It could have been Roland or Michel, even Mireille or Berthe – why not? It probably will be Marin, once my back is turned. He felt a twinge of jealousy again, stronger than the one he'd had in the bath. Perhaps that's why she didn't mind Berthe's outburst of devotion to me. Drunk or not, competition was a welcome relief. Well, there wasn't going to be a war to the death over Marin, or any romantic nonsense of that sort, because he hadn't the energy or the desire to fight. Even so, the jealousy gripped him. It was a torment, and strangely enjoyable.

'Perhaps it will be for the best if I never see her again,' he said to himself out loud.

One of Roland Beaumanière's natural assets, inherited no doubt, was timing. That he should arrive at Philip's shoulder, smelling freshly of eau-de-Cologne, dressed in polo-neck sweater and slacks, at the very moment when Philip was fantasizing about a crude and painful liberation, was no real surprise. Philip had noted this kind of thing before. 'You know,' he said, without turning round to look at Roland, 'you remind me of Miss Pagnall, a teacher at my school. Extraordinary woman. She has a sixth sense for disorder. If you are ever doing anything silly, or foolish, or frightful, like fighting in the coal bunkers, or shouting in the library, or playing cricket in the corridor outside the chemistry labs, then sure as hell is hot Miss Pagnall will prowl round the corner just as you begin, and give you one of her looks. She can stop a herd of galloping fourth-formers dead in their tracks at thirty metres, and have them falling over each other to get in line and doff caps without uttering a word. It's a great gift. I sense you may have it too.'

'I have no desire to be a school teacher. Tell me, whose permanent departure are you plotting?'

'My own. Today is already Sunday. I leave on Tuesday.'

'Don't remind me. We are all appalled at your leaving us, as usual. But you will be back, perhaps even at Christmas if I can persuade my mother. I take it that it is the delicious Berthe, who is your latest and I must say most stunning conquest, whom you are planning never to see again?'

'Please don't joke about it, Roland. It's not amusing.'

'Oh, I don't know. She didn't actually kill anybody tonight. It will be best to laugh over it in due course. Besides, the kernel of the incident is very funny. Huge Parisian girl declares love for thin Englishman in traditional way, attempting to drop him stone dead with a couple of Belgian beer bottles.'

'Across a crowded room.'

'Exactly.'

'We could set it to music. Get Mireille's dad to run it up into a film. Win an Oscar.'

'With Berthe as herself?'

'Who else?'

'Roland, you really are a shit at heart. She's suffering . . .'

'Let me remind you that it was me she was sick on, and the only suffering she'll do is tomorrow morning when she wakes up with the most colossal headache. And serve her damned well right.'

'Which reminds me,' said Philip. 'Mireille said to tell you that she's gone to bed. I'm afraid she didn't say it in the tone of voice that would have encouraged you to follow her either.'

'No matter,' said Roland, yawning noisily. 'Come on, let's go and sit down in the yard. I'm tired of standing about in this tunnel.'

They were just in time to meet Danielle and Marin coming away from the barn. Marin, his foot bandaged neatly, limped heavily, walking on the heel of his damaged foot. Danielle was holding him by the elbow, though more for comfort than support. The four friends stopped to exchange words. Danielle explained that she had removed a piece of glass from Marin's sole. Philip said that if she had done this in English, it would have made a pun with symbolic potential. Roland said, rather tediously, that you could only get a similar effect in French if your listener was one of those extraordinary people who believed that vegetation could feel pain. Marin said thank you for the linguistic instruction, but thought he'd better turn in. Danielle said that she hoped the bleeding had stopped, but that it would probably be for the best if he kept his foot outside the bedclothes overnight. The two of them went on their way together without Philip and Danielle exchanging words. Roland sat down with his back against the ladder, and rubbed the side of his face, appearing to think.

'Funny things, women,' he said. 'Do everything for them and they bugger off. Treat them like dirt and they beg for more. Nothing straightforward if they can possibly bend it.'

'You sound like my father talking about trade unions,' said Philip.

'Trade unions are to the English what women are to the French. Half of them belong to them, and the other half lies awake at night worrying about them. Everybody agrees they're necessary, but nobody understands them.'

'Are you trying to tell me, through these *bons mots*, as we say in English, that the English understand and appreciate women, while the French bourgeoisie has a spiritual relationship with its own working class? I am bowled over.'

'I never know what I'm trying to say,' said Roland candidly. 'But I know when I'm muddled, even if I don't know exactly what to do about it. Tell me, did you see that young woman Jeannette this evening, at dinner?'

'I could hardly have missed her.'

'Quite. Well? What do you think?'

'Very interesting performance. Yvette should have kissed her a second time, of course, to bring out the full force of the lines from Marlowe. I told her this after . . .'

'Oh damn Marlowe. What's the matter with you, England? Don't you people appreciate beauty? Didn't you look at her at all, at her face, at her figure, at the way she moved? Didn't you see her wrists and fingers as she gathered the plates? Her thighs as she went through the door? Her profile as she brought the cheeseboard from the dresser? How can you be so blind? Sometimes I think we could erect the eighth wonder of the world in Hyde Park and no one in your country would take the slightest notice.'

'Not for the first century or so, no,' said Philip. 'Only old things have merit in England. Things that are young are regarded as unsafe. Anyway, I thought you were concentrating all your energies on Mireille. I'll tell you this, her mother was certainly concentrating all of hers on you. Fair gave me a grilling at dinner, she did. Wanted to know all about you, what I thought, whether you were reliable, all that sort of thing.'

'And?'

'Well, I told her everything of course. About your mental illness, and the syphilis in the family, and your father's weekends at the chateau filling the parterre with naked seven-year-old boys. Yvette was impressed. These bohemian, arty types like to hear about the decadence of the aristocracy. It makes them feel more mainstream than they really are.'

'Thanks for nothing.'

'Anyway, what is all this about Jeannette? Are Mireille's sands of time running out? It seems only yesterday – indeed it *was* only yesterday – when you were telling us about eternal affection, the strength of bonds formed in physical compatibility, the fidelity of your intentions, et cetera, et cetera, et cetera. Now here you are telling me that your eye has wandered from the daughter of the house to the serving wench.'

'Well, I'm no snob,' said Roland, stretching his legs and straightening the creases in each trouser leg. 'I simply want to be a connoisseur of beautiful women. It is of no concern to me whether they are high, low, or in-between born.'

'And?'

'Well, and nothing. Or nothing new, anyway. Jeannette's beautiful. And if there's some way of getting close, it would be nice to try. I thought I might, that's if you don't mind, get you to sound out Patrick about her tomorrow. Would you? It's the sort of thing you could do. Find out where she lives, that sort of thing.'

'Do your own dirty work.'

Roland ignored this. 'I think it's so important at our stage in life to maintain a flow of experience, don't you? Never to rest for too long. Of course, later, once one's grown up, taken one's place and so on, then stability's everything, security really matters. In one sense it will be really pleasant to be married, a home organized, the rhythm of the day, the week, the year. I look forward to that.'

'You're making me feel old.'

Roland still ignored him. 'But we're not ready for it yet, are we? There's this gap, don't you see, between childhood and grown-upness, which is where we are now. And it's the very best bit of life, and it stretches ahead of us for years and years.' Roland let out a sigh of contentment and searched his pockets for another cigarette.

'I think I'll be a disappointment to you,' said Philip. 'I can't see any gaps in the fabric of daily life at all. And as for your maintaining a flow of experience, frankly it all looks rather repetitive to me, the same thing done over and over again. And the prospect of endless domesticity, which you claim to look forward to in some adult nirvana, I find profoundly depressing, but unlike you I . . .'

Jeannette entered the courtyard at this point, interrupting the conversation. Light step and quick gait, the moon throwing a dark shadow in front of her as she came out of the archway from the garden. She ignored Philip and Roland, and headed for the kitchen door. Roland sprang to his feet.

'Excuse me, miss.'

She turned. Philip couldn't see her face, but he readily identified the stance of the patient servant, the hands folded in front of her, body ever-so-slightly to attention, head forward. 'Sir?' she said.

'Where are you going?' asked Roland.

'To my room.'

'You are up very late.' Roland leaned his back against the ladder, one foot up behind him on the bottom rung.

'I'm sorry, sir. I couldn't sleep, and so went for a walk. It was such a beautiful night.'

There was a silence between them. Philip could almost hear Roland searching for a gambit. She gave it to him.

'Is there something you require?'

'Well, yes, there is,' said Roland, clearing his throat. 'This room of ours, up here in the loft, is a bit of a mess.' He smiled.

'One of our friends was taken ill, and as a result things became a bit of a shambles.'

'Understatement,' chipped in Philip.

'We wouldn't want Monsieur or Madame Delachêne put out in any way, and if they saw the room as it is at present, they might get the wrong idea. I wonder if you wouldn't mind perhaps getting a bucket of water and a couple of brooms. I'm sure we could get it cleaned up in no time. I'll gladly give you a hand.'

'Yes, me too,' said Philip unhelpfully.

Jeannette gave a tiny bob of a curtsy and went in through the kitchen door, leaving it open behind her.

'You stay out of this,' said Roland to Philip, an edge in his voice. Jeannette came out of the black hole of the kitchen door, broom and mop in one hand, bucket in the other. She filled the bucket at a tap in the yard, then crossed to the barn.

'Perhaps,' she said to Roland, 'you wouldn't mind carrying the bucket up for me. It's a bit heavy.' Then she gathered her nightdress about her knees, climbed the ladder, and disappeared into the loft. Roland gave Philip a quick grimace in the half-light that fell through the trap door above him – lips pursed, eyebrows raised, head tilted to one side – and then picked up the bucket and followed Jeannette up the ladder. Philip stayed below, listening to the low voices that came out of the loft. After a few minutes, and interrupting briefly the scratch and paddle of broom and mop, a rather smelly dressing gown flopped down into the yard. It was followed by some bits of rag covered in blood. Philip listened to the water being sloshed around above him. What next? he thought.

Next, on cue, came Michel, striding purposefully into the yard through the archway. Philip felt uncomfortable and realized that the wind had dropped, and that the temperature was dropping too. He felt a shiver of cold. Michel looked ridiculous, marching across the yard like a military figure, but dressed in pyjamas. You can't be a marshal without boots. And look at those pyjamas! They're filthy!

'You can't come on parade looking, arf, arf, like a bear just out of winter hibernation,' he barked, as Michel marched up to him. 'Look at you, arf, arf, arf, you shabby specimen, you look as though you've been after rabbits, you nasty little weasel. How many, arf, arf, times 'ave I told you never to come on parade, arf, arf, looking like a pregnant fairy.'

Michel grinned and gave Philip a mock salute. Then he dropped into a sparring posture and danced around him, throwing imitation punches, ducking and weaving.

'Well, we have changed our tune,' said Philip, abandoning the drill sergeant for a high-pitched mocking tone. 'Last time we spoke it was Michel Kreisler, the sullen romantic, declining to chat with his friends, too overwhelmed with angst and the cosmic *Zeitgeist* to share in the chit-chat of idle wotsits. Oh how he yearned to be alone in nature, to repudiate society and all its sordid trivialities. Armed only with his sad heart, he set off into the night, mirror to darkness and despair.' Philip gave up the declamatory manner at this point, but continued talking. 'Now here you are, popping up a couple of hours later, all frisky and lamb-like, full of *joie de vivre*, wanting us all to dance round the maypole like a load of skittish yokels. Meanwhile' – and Michel slowed his boxer's dance at this point, coming to a grinning stop in front of Philip – 'meanwhile, *we* have been through the mill-race of experience.'

'What happened?'

'Oh, just la Berthe,' said Philip, running his fingers through his hair, sounding nonchalant. 'Threw a bloody great wobbly that scared everybody witless, then threw up and passed out. Quite a scene.' Philip indicated the barn loft with his head. 'Roland's up there now, helping to clear up.'

'Roland? Roland's never cleared up a thing in his life.'

'Well, he has now,' said Philip. 'Although' – and he leaned close to Michel, as though entering into deepest secrecy – 'it

110

might possibly have something to do with the fact that he's managed to get Mireille to go to bed, and has cornered that pretty serving girl, Jeannette, up there in the loft with him.'

Philip wasn't sure afterwards, but he thought he saw Michel's eyes flash in the night. Then he was gone. He launched himself at the ladder and tore up it, disappearing from Philip's view at the bottom and appearing into Roland's view at the top, a jack-in-the-box released by its spring. What he saw did not slow him down. Roland had his arms round Jeannette from behind, his hands overlapping at her waist, and was kissing her rapidly just below and behind her right ear. Jeannette was wriggling from the hips, trying, with this unselfconsciously seductive movement and with the prising of her fingers, to unlock Roland's grip. In the glow of the lamps Michel saw that she was red in the face, her eyes combining disgust and panic together. She was saying nothing, but she did not need to speak.

As soon as he saw Michel, Roland knew that he was in trouble. He didn't understand it, but he knew it. Michel hurled himself across the room. Roland let go of Jeannette, who slipped to one side. Michel hit the momentarily defenceless Roland hard in the stomach with his fist, winding him, and as he fell to the floor flung himself on top of the gasping figure. Locked together, they rolled over several times, Roland hugging Michel tight to prevent further blows. They were brought up short by crashing into a pile of hay bales, the top one of which, dislodged, toppled on to them, splitting open and engulfing them both in the clinging, spiky, dry straw. Michel and Roland stood up from this dried-grass storm, Michel slightly ahead of his slimmer opponent, and, while the dust and grit blew around them, traded blows. Roland tried to speak, intending to ask 'why?', but the word was stopped in his mouth by a left jab from Michel that turned his upper lip numb. Moments later he tasted blood warm in his mouth.

Roland was not a coward. Nor was he weak. He was a bit

underweight for his height, but he was well enough built, had quick reflexes, and had done a bit of judo. Swearing out of the one side of his mouth that he could still feel, he aimed a sharp kick at Michel's shins and then waded in with both fists, punching Michel in the throat and then, gripping him by the lapels of his regimental pyjamas, flinging him to the floor. He plunged on top of the fallen figure, but Michel, despite the anger which was dissipating all his fighting skill, managed to get his knees up, and divert the full force of the diving aristocrat's arrival. For a few moments the two of them scrambled about in the dust and gloom until Roland managed to get an arm-lock on Michel's throat, but the force of this hold, designed to quell and calm, had the reverse effect, and drove Michel to greater rage. He squeezed his fingers behind Roland's arm, pulled it forward, and bit it as hard as he could. At this, Roland let out the only cry of their encounter, relaxing his grip at the same time. Michel spun around and unleashed a whirlwind of fists and blows. The great majority of these fell wildly and uselessly, hurting only the aggressor's hands, but suddenly, as if from nowhere, a great arching right-handed punch caught Roland full on the cheek, and sent him spinning. He appeared to fall back for two or three steps on his feet, but they were barely on the ground. His legs gave from under him, and he fell on to the seat of his trousers, seeming to skid across the uneven floor, his feet in the air, his back somehow still preposterously upright.

Michel remembered for the rest of his short life that Roland's eyes were open, and that he had a look of tremendous surprise on his face, as though nothing so amazing had ever, or would ever again, happen to him. Caught in this posture, he shot out over the top of the trap door, and then with a clatter as his back, hands and ankles all came in contact with its edge, he fell through. Michel said later that he felt as though Roland had been poised above the opening for seconds, as though in suspension and awaiting a reprieve. Then there was the terrible crash of Roland's fall below, out of sight, and a shout, half-scream, from Philip, who was still in the yard.

Jeannette was first to the trap door, her hand to her throat, her face white. Michel was on his knees behind her, sobbing.

'Oh dear god,' she said. 'You've killed him.'

Still Sunday   *Late morning*

Well, I did get my breakfast, but I didn't get any further with Philip's manuscript, because no sooner had I settled down with it in the garden than Beatrix turned up. Rather tentative, to begin with, she apologized for disturbing me. I said it didn't matter, which wasn't true, and that I was glad to see her, which was. Initially I thought how well she was looking, pretty steady on her legs, not too washed out. It was a nice sunny morning, though the clouds came up later and we had some more rain, but at least briefly it felt and smelt like summer. And Beatrix fitted in with this. She'd put on a long Laura Ashley dress with blue flowers and a lace collar, but, I have to say, it didn't really suit her, though I doubt that she wore clothes like that often enough to be aware of the fact. In the old days she used to have a line in astonishingly short skirts and little rib tops, or hipster shorts with a leather belt, and tight trousers with flares and tassles in combination with knee boots, and headscarves tied close the way women wear them in Russia and Yugoslavia. She plopped herself down on the bench seat by the garden table, opposite where I was sitting on the brick patio. From there she guessed my thoughts.

'No, not really me, is it?' She fingered the material at the hem. 'I was going to reform a few years ago, and did a raid on London. Part of a new image.' She gave a grim little smile. 'It hasn't had much use.'

I didn't like either to agree or to disagree with her judgement. She had been so fragile every time I'd seen her that any sort of

113

handling, even with words, seemed likely to break pieces off. I covered up by offering her something, tea or coffee.

'Yes, thanks,' she said. 'Coffee'd be nice.' She didn't seem to mean it, however. 'You're busy, though, aren't you? And I'm in the way. I'm just a nuisance. I should . . .'

'No, it's OK, Beatrix, really. I do have things to do, but they can wait. Stay, do. I'll get some coffee.'

Which I did, and maybe she started to relax a bit then. Hard to know, though, because her hand trembled so much when she tried to lift her coffee cup by the handle that she had to give up, and only managed to drink from it by planting her elbows firmly on the table and cradling the cup in both hands. It was watching her do this that made me realize that actually she wasn't looking well at all. Quite apart from the trembling, she was unable to sit still, a perpetual crossing and uncrossing of legs, squirming and sliding on the garden seat. 'I don't go visiting much, round here,' she contributed, apropos of nothing and as though, in drawing attention to the rarity of it, she needed to alert me to its reasons. 'No call for it, somehow.' She turned her head as she spoke, moving it from side to side as though groping for something, like someone who spots the tail or wing or shadow of an animal, bird or object disappearing round a corner, or flitting across a window, just too late to be seen, and too fast for the image to clarify. At the same time her eyes kept up a steady sluggish movement, as though it cost her a great effort to do this but she dared not stop.

'It's nice here,' she said. Perhaps she had been seeing the garden after all, and not chasing shadows. She swivelled her body, and looked around her more deliberately. 'Whose place is it again?' she asked. I told her. 'I ought to get something like this,' she said. 'Mine's too big, don't you think?'

I had no answer to this. It all seemed like automatic talking. I tried to slide from one topic to another. 'You'd need a bigger place for visitors, I expect. Don't you have family who come down from time to time? Are your parents still alive?' I nattered on like this for a bit, covering my embarrassment. Somehow, despite our earlier encounters, the full extent of Beatrix's wreckage was only fully apparent to me now. Perhaps it was her being away from her own territory, where she fitted in, belonged as she was. Here on your patio, Felix, it was like meeting a camel in the Cornmarket, or a penguin on the Kowloon ferry. She was suddenly and completely out of place, so one saw her with different eyes.

'Parents?' she said eventually, stopping my prattle. The word seemed to imply to her some freakish natural feature – a boulder balanced on its point, or a three-legged dog. 'Haven't thought about them for a while.' She sniffed, and had another attempt at her coffee. 'My dad was a doctor in Stoke-on-Trent, but he got struck off for doing abortions. This was when I was about three – in the mid fifties – and my mum divorced him. Well, he went to prison for a while, and we went to live in Macclesfield. I was fat as a child. My stepfather was a grocer, and used to call me his "half a lard". Prick. He never liked me and it was mutual when I was growing up. It's funny about Dad – I often think of this – if he'd waited, what, ten or twelve years, you know, been respectable and everything, he could have made a fortune out of it. Once it was legal.' She lapsed into silence, perhaps over the irony of this misfortune. 'Anyway, they're all dead now,' she said. This fact, or at any rate the iteration of it, may have acted as a spur, however, because she perked up, and chased after them again, though in no obviously particular order. Her conversation reminded me of her kitchen.

'Sainsbury's or someone forced him out of business in the seventies and he got a job cleaning buses at the depot. Do you know, once, when I went back to see Mum because she was sick and I'd been away on tour or whatnot, all he could talk about was how the Tory Club hadn't asked for his resignation, and what good people they were to have him there still, "One of us, eh Gregory?, in misfortune as in joy", and more crap the same like that while my mother was upstairs fit to croak.' She gathered the voluminous skirt of her dress about her, pulling herself together. 'Which she did shortly after. I was with her when she died. She was in the hospital, but they couldn't do nothing for her. All she said was, "Don't make a mess of it like me, Bea. It's the only one you've got."' She gave another sniff. 'It's the family motto. I should have had it carved on her gravestone. Except she was cremated, of course. We had to cancel two big gigs in the States so's I could be with Mum, but I'm glad we did.'

All this was said quite slowly, with long silences between the, what were they?, not sentences, really. Just observations. Things viewed from a great distance through binoculars, all the surrounding detail and distraction removed.

'Did you lose touch with your father?'

'Dr Stapleton? No, course not. Well, actually, yes, for quite a long time – till I was about fifteen. But then I went to see him, you know, without letting on to Mum or Gregory. That's what they still called him in the Potts. Dr Stapleton. Decent people, they are. His name was Rufus, but they wouldn't have that. Dr Stapleton.' She gave another of her wry smiles. 'He hadn't moved, you know. Still lived in Church Road, opposite the graveyard. The only little patch of green in miles of Pot Banks and slag heaps, and just round the corner from a bit of canal bank where the boys and girls'd go to screw on Saturday night. My customers, he said. No good looking for Church Road now, though. They stuck a motorway ramp through it. Dad had a housekeeper called Moira – funny dart of a thing with peroxide hair and a quick tongue. He told me once that as a girl, during the war, she'd been on the game, and that he sort of saved her in the late forties, when the Yanks and the Poles and that had gone, and she was down on her luck. I suppose she'd been one of his clients too. Anyway, she went to live at number twenty-six, which was his surgery in those days, and was where he went to live when he came out of Stafford, and acted as his receptionist until after he was struck off. Why am I telling you all this?'

'Is it connected with Sim?'

'You a mind reader?' She scowled and pulled a face, but it might as well have been a smile because the mention of Sim brought such warmth into her voice. 'Yes, it is, I suppose. Dad, Rufus, Dr Stapleton the good, let Moira rent out a couple of rooms at the top of the house, and when I started visiting in the late sixties one of the tenants – oh how grand, but it was nothing like that: two sticks of crummy furniture and a threadbare carpet in the cold and damp, with a gas meter to soak up your silver – there was Sim, my golden boy. He said he was doing a course in industrial design at a college in Hanley, but he could have said he was a toddy man or a Southend eel smoker for all I cared what he actually did. It was who he was that mattered. And anyway he wasn't actually studying industrial design or anything else, for that matter. He was playing in a band. And that's how I got started. Him and me. Sim and Bix.' A reflection that brought her to a stop.

I went in to fetch some more coffee, but when I came out with it a minute later the sun had gone in, and Beatrix said she was cold. She looked it, and was shivering, so I suggested that we go indoors, and I must have thrown Philip's manuscript a glance or something because she mimed a question at it, and when I nodded – 'Please' – she gathered it all up and brought it into the kitchen with her. She spilled it on to the table, making a mess.

'Sorry,' she said, pulling the sheets together. 'Clumsy, aren't I? Don't seem to have any coordination these days.' She picked a page out of the others, then held it well away from her – those specs, again – and read, '"A silence settled, so dense that Philip could feel it, and he woke up to its touch." That's nice. I like that. What is this? A novel? Who's this Philip?'

I took the page from her and returned it to the pile on the table, pushing and prodding it together. 'I haven't reached that part yet. Yes, it is nice. Lots of it is anyway. But I haven't finished it. It's meant to be autobiography. Philip was my husband. I found it among his things.'

'Is he . . .?'

'Dead? Yes. Six months ago. In a car accident.'

'That's bad. I'm sorry. Was he a writer?'

'Um. Yes, I suppose he was, though I never thought of him like that. He taught philosophy.'

'The meaning of life.'

'No. Philosophers don't do the meaning of life any more. They do the meaning of words.'

'Must be easier.'

'To listen to them you wouldn't think so.'

We drank our coffee in silence, while outside it began to rain once more. Despite her anxious twitching and constant movement, Beatrix was quite easy to be with, which I liked.

'I haven't been much of a reader,' she said after a while. 'Missed a lot, I suppose. I tried one of those, what's his name, Jeffrey Archer ones. But I couldn't get on with it. I kept thinking that he must believe people are really stupid . . .'

'The characters he creates?'

'No, no. The readers. His audience, or whatever you call them. When we wrote our songs, me and Sim, we never did that. We never patronized anybody. I reckon ordinary people are pretty complicated, really, but they don't know how to say the things they feel. Old Jeffrey A. didn't seem to me to think much of . . .'

'He sells a lot of books.'

'Wall's sell a lot of pork sausages, but that doesn't mean people like them. They're cheap, and they don't have many alternatives. A lot of life's like that for people.'

'There are lots of books to choose from.'

'Not if you haven't been shown how to read. I wasn't. And nobody else at my school was either. Sim said it was normal, and I think he was right. Of course, Sim was different, but then his parents were Jews, and they're not like us, eh? They were musical and had lots of books, though his dad did just shoe repairing and stuff, you know, belts and bags, and his mum, Jessie, was a barmaid. Sim could play the violin, you know. Serious. He really could. He learned when he was a boy – had lessons – and he always took his violin with him wherever we went on the road. He loved it. He used to tune the guys' guitars, and show them how to do harmonics. All the progressions were his. People used to think he was the dumb one because he was just the drummer, but he was the music, really, and he wrote all the tunes for our lyrics, he made it all happen. We'd have been nothing without Sim. Specially me. He taught me everything about microphones, how to hold one and use it, and how to hear yourself through all the noise and stuff, and how to sing – "Pitch is a good word. Find it and throw it." That's what he said – and how to hold a note and then just let it fade off so it seems like it'll last for ever. That Rod, who was so upfront and smart-arse, and went round telling everyone he was the man – well, he could riff a line if he was blind or stoned, but he wasn't what you'd call musical. The girls all fell for him but he had bad breath.

'Why am I telling you all this? I haven't seen Rod for donkeys – wouldn't want to – and Sim's been gone, well, he's been gone a long time . . .'

'He died, didn't he, in Italy? Somewhere like that? I remember . . .'

'Sicily. Yes, it was all over the papers. He had a 750 Ducati. We both did. One each – his and hers. We went out one day, and going over the top – they have these marvellous mountain roads there, great on a bike – Sim came off. Flipped. You know. Back wheel went, tried to straighten up. Ping. Gone. Near a little place called Troina. I was following behind and I knew he'd gone as soon as he left the saddle. His angle was all wrong.' She went silent again, but I don't think she was repressing anything more that she might have said, or trying to think of something to add to the story as she'd told it. That was it. She gave a sigh and went on fidgeting in her seat while I said something conventional and probably tiresome like, 'You must have missed him a lot', or 'So shocking those sorts of accidents, aren't they? Over in the blink of an eye and everything's changed', but I honestly can't remember. What I do recall is the atmosphere that settled in her silence, its palpable, heaving presence, the way the sound of heavy breathing in a dark room can suggest the presence of a large grubby animal of uncertain species and temper. This was a place of darkness and fear, but suddenly Beatrix snapped out of it.

'That telegram I sent. You know, on Friday, when you and me met for the first time up there in the ditch. That was to Johan. He's threatening to come, but I told him not to bother. I don't want to see him. And I'm not going to see him. And I told him to F-off. Well, actually I didn't because you're not allowed to in a telegram, though if you wrote it in Basque or something I don't know how they'd know. But anyway . . .'

'Is he giving you a lot of trouble?'

'Yeah, a bit. Though I haven't seen him for six months or so. But he's got some new hair-brained scheme he wants me to sign up for, I don't know, and he sends me stuff all the time, letters, and forms to sign, and God knows what. I don't open them any more. Throw them away.' She waved her thin arms over the table. 'The river's a good place. I think of Johan's plans floating all the way out to sea.' The thought may have cheered her up because she suddenly changed tack. 'It's funny, isn't it? Your Philip and my Sim both being killed on the road. Sort of makes us a pair, really. Highway widows. Do you mind?'

'Mind? Why should I . . .?'

'Oh, some people would. Death's like that. When someone has a death, someone close, it's theirs, and they don't want to share it. I noticed this with Sim. No one could have him in death except me. It was mine. His death belonged to me. He was my golden boy, my lover. I was there when he did it, when it happened, and no one . . . Well. I wasn't very nice to people. His parents . . .'

'Was this when Johan . . .?

'Came in? Yes, sort of. He'd been our road manager for a while, but we'd never been close, and Sim and me had just decided to give up, you know, retire. Sim was thirty, and had other things he wanted to do, musical things, and we were both

120

fed up with the touring and the creeps. Then, when he was killed, along with all the other people who surfaced and clustered there was Johan, still making the arrangements, booking the hall, clearing the way. He took care of things. And I was a mess.'

'His takeover bid.'

'In a way. But I have to be fair about this. In the beginning Johan was really good to me. I didn't know if I was on my bum or my knees, and he just, well, he was there for me. And eventually everyone else drifted away. Too much booze and mayhem, I suppose. I wasn't very nice to people . . .'

'You said that.'

'It's true. And it was only later that the full Johan revealed himself. Canal rat sod of a bastard that he is.' Suddenly Beatrix stood up. 'Anyway,' she said, hitching her blue flowers around her and stepping carefully from behind the table, as though conscious that one false move or missed step would tip her straight on to the tiled floor, 'I thought I ought to explain. Would you like to come up to . . .?' Her voice trailed off and she looked around the kitchen, tugging with her fingers at a thread on the sleeve of her dress.

'I've got these things I must do,' I replied.

'Yeah. Well, it's such a mess isn't it? Thanks for the coffee.' She went to the door and pulled it open with a lurch. Outside the rain had almost stopped and there were patches of blue in a chequered sky. She produced a rather good husky American voice and said: 'Come up and see me some time.' So I said I would and walked with her up the steps to the gate, from where I watched her stumble off up the road, past the metal fences round the private gravelled gardens of your neighbours, and the tall yew hedges, and the old dilapidated sign saying '*Chaussée déformée*' that no one has bothered to take down.

Then I went back to Philip and his 'Portrait'.

121

A new era started at nine o'clock the next morning, when Yvette Delachêne presided briefly over a sombre breakfast.

'As of today,' she said, eyeing them round the scrubbed kitchen table, 'there are going to be some changes. And they can start now and be continued after breakfast. Berthe, you will go for a good walk in the fresh air where Philip, I'm sure, will be glad to accompany you. Marin, Alphonse will have the car out in half an hour to drive you to the village where Dr Coutance will do that foot up for you properly. Danielle, you will please come to see me in the living room. The rest of you will have a quiet morning keeping out of trouble. I want to hear nothing more from any of you until lunch.' She swept from the room, and Mamette began serving coffee.

The scene was composed of what Philip's mother would have called 'a gathering of unrepentant sinners'. Roland had survived what he later called 'unassisted powered flight' mainly because the loft ladder, which had snapped into three pieces, broke his fall. He was bruised and shaken, but the more spectacular of his wounds came from Michel's assault, and consisted of a split lip that barely concealed the gap from a missing tooth, a large brown bruise on his cheekbone, and a long graze down one temple. The tooth marks on his forearm he kept out of sight.

Berthe, whom no one could remember ever having been so quiet before, was a sort of green colour, and wouldn't look anyone in the eye.

Marin hobbled about painfully on one foot.

Mireille hid behind dark glasses from which, above and below the right lens, there spread the ugly purple stain of a black eye.

Jeannette, wearing thick stockings to conceal the bruises on her shin, had been banished to the guest rooms, where she stripped and remade beds.

Michel's knuckles were rather like Jeannette's shin, but

122

harder to hide. His conscience was bruised too, and his anger, which persisted, made him sullen.

Only Danielle and Philip were not physically wounded, but they were exchanging such highly charged glances of accusation that even Roland, who was more than usually employed in the contemplation of his own circumstances, was aware of the tension between them.

'Oh dear,' said Philip, a decent interval after Yvette had withdrawn. 'Not quite what we intended, I think.'

'Which was?' said Danielle, her olive-black eyes aflame.

'Well, not quite the same as you, at any rate. That's obvious enough.'

'Shut up, you two,' said Mireille.

'Why should they?' said Marin. 'I think it's about time someone . . .'

'Because it's my bloody kitchen, that's why,' snapped Mireille. 'And I want my breakfast in peace.'

'Well, perhaps you should take it somewhere else, then,' said Danielle, tartly, heaping jam on to a piece of toasted bread, 'and not be so childish. If Philip feels aggrieved about something, I think we should be told. Come on, Philip, surely you can tell your friends.'

'Bovary,' Philip muttered under his breath.

'I don't think we quite caught that,' said Roland. 'Would you mind repeating?'

'Oh do belt up, all of you,' said Berthe in a weak voice. 'You have no idea how dreadful you all sound from here.'

'Well, we didn't prepare the morning after the night before with quite your enthusiasm, did we?' said Marin.

'I suppose that's true,' Berthe replied, very subdued. 'But I believed I could trust you, Matelot, old friend.'

'That's rather my point too,' said Philip, looking daggers at Danielle, who glared back at him over her toast without flinching.

'You're the one who's always giving us the crap about

123

individual freedom,' she said. 'The obligation to choose, the need to make our actions compatible with the projects we have chosen. Now it seems this only applies to you. When anyone else does it, all of a sudden the philosophical universe moves over a degree or ten, and it's all "Do as I want" not "Do as you think". Bourgeois hypocrite!'

Clamour spread across the table, guffaws engulfing demands that Danielle and Philip stop their argument. Philip tried to make himself heard through this hubbub.

'There was supposed,' he shouted, 'to be some moral basis for the chosen action. Not just whim. Not just the gratification of desire.'

Philip immediately wished that he hadn't used exactly these words. This was because the chorus of demands for him and Danielle to stop suddenly fell silent just before he had finished, with the effect that the one word 'desire', spoken very loudly, rang round the kitchen like a call to arms. He fell back into his seat, on fire with defiance, and poured scalding-hot coffee down his throat. This made him splutter and cough uncontrollably.

'Come on,' said Madeleine, thumping him on the back. 'Let's be good boys and go for our walk before you choke to death on whatever it is.'

Philip threw her a dark glance, but she didn't see it. He got obediently to his feet, tossed a jacket over his shoulder, and went out into the yard, where Madeleine joined him. She pulled on an oilskin as they went out on to the road. It was raining very gently, Scotch mist, and the trees, suddenly autumnal, seemed to be bending low to the ground, wet, tired, sap on the ebb.

The two walked along side by side for a kilometre or so in silence, Philip angular and dismal, his jacket collar turned up above his thin shoulders, Madeleine big and powerful beside him, her feet stamping the asphalt as she threw back her broad shoulders and resolutely hung her pale face and deep-set eye sockets out in the bleak Sunday weather to heal. Eventually she broke the silence.

'Bad scene?'

Philip didn't reply directly. 'Don't you remember anything?'

'Not much, no. I remember some sort of a shindig over a bottle that somebody wanted to take away from me. And DD told me I was evil sick. Did I disgrace myself?'

Philip shrugged, but without the Gallic emphasis. A pathetic English gesture. 'You disgraced everybody.'

'Oh good. A successful party.'

'No, seriously. You belted Mireille in the eye, tried to knock my head off, vomited on anyone who came near, and then passed out. Lots of fun for all of us.' He lapsed back into his silence, which Madeleine, perhaps impressed with her crimes, did not dare to break.

'But that was only the half of it, really,' he continued, eventually. 'Michel came back from some midnight ramble or the other and for no reason at all just about killed Roland, which brought the grown-ups running. They found Roland looking like Nelson at Trafalgar, surrounded by broken spars. Once they'd got him into bed Patrick said he needed something, cotton wool, I think, and Jeannette said there was some in Marin's room, so Yvette barged in and found Danielle in bed with him, your friend and mine, the theatrical sailor. She went through the roof. On the way down she asked for an explanation of why Marin was bleeding all over her sheets, why her daughter had a black eye, and why you were asleep in the old salon smelling like last week's fish market. You have to admit, it didn't look too good.'

Madeleine laughed. 'Sounds bloody marvellous to me.'

'It would.'

'And I suppose you're all wet-eyed and gut-twisted about DD and Marin the good.'

Philip's scowl went a slightly darker shade of black, and he aimed a kick, as he walked, at a pebble lying in the road. 'There was something else,' he said at length. 'Do you remember anything you said last night?'

'I recall having a few hard things to say about God. But I suppose you're going to tell me that I insulted somebody important. Did I?'

'No,' said Philip. 'Never mind.' And the two of them went on in silence together, large drops of rain, which accumulated on the browning leaves above them, occasionally plopping on their shoulders and heads. Berthe put her arm through his, which Philip found oddly comforting. After a little while they had to move over to one side of the road when a car came up behind them. It was Alphonse driving Marin to the village doctor. He slowed to a crawl as he came by, lowering his window. Later Philip remembered the swishing of the windscreen wipers. Le Matelot was lying in the back, his wounded foot up on a cushion. Alphonse offered them a lift, which Philip declined. 'Berthe still telling you sweet nothings?' shouted Marin, as the car picked up speed away from where they stood.

Marin's words, left on the wind of the departing vehicle, had a curious effect, creating palpable tension. Philip and Madeleine might pretend to ignore it for the rest of the hour, while they made a circuit of the watery lanes, but in that case they both knew that it would grow, and appear to them ever afterwards as a sort of moral cowardice. Eventually it was Madeleine who spoke.

'Did I,' she asked, with a rare display of caution, 'in my barbaric way, declare some sort of interest? Last night?'

'Yes, I'm afraid you did.'

'I'm sorry.'

'Why?'

'Why sorry, or why the interest?'

'Why sorry?'

'You're not interested in me, probably don't even like me. It's an imposition.'

126

'Less of an imposition than trying to knock someone's head off with a beer bottle.'

'I'm sorry about that too.'

'It doesn't matter.'

'It does. But not as much as the other thing. Look, I really *am* sorry. Not sorry about telling you, because God awful as it is, it's true. But sorry about telling you when I was rotten drunk, instead of just simply sometime, as something just, I don't know, just to give you, as a present or something, to say there, that's for you and I don't want anything back. Like now, for instance. Now's a good time. Except it's too late because it got spoiled last night, so that my, well, loving you, is all mixed up now with other things that get in the way.'

'Like what?'

'Like being dead drunk, and being sick everywhere, and thumping anyone within range. You know. Oh dear, I am sorry.'

'Don't keep saying that.'

'Saying what?'

'You're sorry.'

'Do I?'

'Yes.'

'Sorry.'

'Christ.'

'Anyway, why shouldn't I say it if it's true?' Madeleine stopped her pounding stride at this point, and stood, hangdog, in the middle of the lane. Philip, a few steps ahead because of her stopping suddenly, turned to look at her. She was staring at her feet. He reached out to lay a hand on each of her shoulders, and she lifted her head to look at him.

'It's probably me that should be sorry. I worked out yesterday that it's neither necessary nor desirable to be liked by everyone. What I should have seen was that neither was it possible to decide who should love whom, or by how much. Just through being we force responses, and we can't always know what they're for, or how far they might go. You frightened me a lot last night, physically and emotionally. I hadn't asked for your love, and didn't like the way it was declared. Later I suppose I realized I was just embarrassed for not having noticed first . . .'

'So's you could have one of your clever answers ready.'

'That sort of thing. Now I think it's all right again. Can we be friends?' He gave Berthe a wan smile.

'Is that what you really want?'

'Yes.'

'Well, the answer's no. N. O. No, we can't be friends. And I never want to see you again after today.'

'But I! . . .'

'Balls, England.' Madeleine set off again, brushing his hands from her shoulders, and marching past him. He scurried to catch up. 'I don't want your bloody friendship. Fucking intellectuals. You're all the same. Here I am talking about my feelings, and all you can do is blather about abstractions, interpreting the social fucking fabric, or whatever the latest fashionable crap is.' She stopped again as suddenly as she had started, and turned on him. 'You don't really think I'm real, do you?' she shouted, digging him in the chest with her fingers. 'You think I'm clockwork. Wind her up and she'll make you laugh. Well, listen to me, Mr Heavy Brain. I don't ever want to see you again. I hate you. And if I do see you again, I swear I'll throw every fucking beer bottle in France at your oversized head in the sincere hope of knocking it clean off your measly little shoulders. So fuck off. And leave me in peace.'

Madeleine resumed her march, and Philip made no attempt to follow. He was belittled and bruised, astonished at the surprising and surely unreasonable reversals of her views. One moment sorry, placid and somehow helpless, the next full of spleen and indignation, as though I'd done something to her. It's not my fault. He turned his back on the figure disappearing into the fine misty rain, and started to walk back slowly along the way that they had come.

After a few hundred metres he reached a shrine, the usual Madonna figure above a little rock at the foot of which a tiny stream trickled into a ditch. Alongside was a shelter with a single wooden seat from which to contemplate the Holy Mother. Philip ducked under the wooden eaves and sat down out of the rain. He remembered his jealousy, and the stab of pain that passed through him with the memory really was, he realized, physical. It was the place where emotions and anatomy came together, he thought, and his whole being seemed to be concentrated there, electrified and paralysed. How could she do that to me? While I was still here, still loved her, still wanted her? He groaned, recalling Saturday afternoon, how Danielle had laughed, kissed him on the mouth, moved under him on the grass as they made love. The thought brought on an erection, and he had to shift his position to accommodate it. Then to go off to bed with that awful bloke Marin, for all the world as though I didn't exist, or we hadn't just been sitting in the yard, holding hands, looking at the moon.

If this is the new era, he thought, then I don't like it much, and it doesn't seem all that keen on me. In this mood his misery expanded to fill the space that adults generously set aside for self-pity, and then the tears which he had thought appropriate to his circumstances all morning at last spilled from his eyes. He wept at the betrayal of his passion, at the failure of his love, and at the damage to his pride. He wept for the one big thing that he thought he had done, which was to lay himself open to this sorrow by risking love instead of staying remote, independent, invulnerable. And he wept for the one small thing that he thought he had done, which was to love without being loved truly in return. Above all, however, he wept not for anything that he had done, and not for anything that had been done to him, but simply for himself:

for what he had been, what he was becoming, and what he was now, at this place by the roadside – beleaguered and isolated, loving wrongly and wronged in love, more knowledgeable than ever before and yet utterly confused.

A little while later, still damp about the cheeks but seeing clearly enough, Philip heard the sound of a car. He ducked out of the shrine in time to spot Alphonse coming towards him, and waved for the car to stop. The chauffeur held the door open for him and he clambered in. Marin had, apparently, been taken to hospital in town to get stitched up properly. Something about needing an instrument they'd only got in the theatre. Philip made no comment, and they drove to the windmill in silence. It was still raining.

It didn't take Philip long to find Danielle. She was sitting by the fire in the living room, mending a hole in a grey woollen stocking. He went to stand by the hearth, but Danielle didn't look up, and he didn't speak. After a while he smelt wet clothing, and then noticed that his jacket and trousers were steaming. He turned the jacket collar down and ran his fingers roughly across his scalp, trying to imitate the effect of a comb in his soggy hair. He felt very scruffy all of a sudden. Danielle looked up.

'You smell,' she said.

'Sorry to give offence.'

'Are you?' She spoke pointedly, her voice hard. Philip made no effort to pick up the sarcasm and play it back. He felt cold and tired.

'Look here,' he said. 'I thought you'd like to know that Marin's been shipped off to the local hospital. Doctor said he could fix the gash up better there.' Danielle appeared to ignore this. 'Just thought you'd like to know.' She pushed her sewing out on one knee, and put her head back to examine it critically.

'Well, by returns,' she said, 'you ought to know that while you were out Mireille coaxed your friend Roland into

130

explaining last night's shindig with Michel, and she was not amused. First she told me all about it half an hour ago, and then she went off to see her mother, saying something about getting servants fired and Roland and you out of her house before the end of the morning.' She started sewing again. 'And her mother, I can report, is not in a very good mood.'

Philip sat down on the rug and took off his shoes and socks. Steam rose from him in clouds.

'I wonder if I'm harming the Sisley,' he said. Danielle went on sewing. Philip desperately wanted to talk to her, but couldn't think of how to get started. So he leaned back on his hands on the rug and went on steaming before the fire, allowing his mind to wander. Danielle interrupted him just as he was wondering whether Turkish baths were called Turkish because they really were, or whether it was something like Dutch courage, or Irish stew, or French letters, more a sort of cultural . . .

'Yvette and Patrick are not very pleased with us.'

'You don't say.'

'I did try to explain everything to Yvette, but she couldn't see it.'

'I'd have thought that in your case she'd already seen all there was to see. After all, there you both were . . .'

'Philip, that's unfair, and it's not true.'

'Well, you were in bed with Marin, and . . .'

'But not the way you think.' She threw her sewing aside and glared at him, but he looked away, refusing to meet her eyes. His heart was racing. He watched the smoke and sparks going up the chimney. 'Yes, we were in the same bed. Yes, it was a single bed. Yes, we were cuddling. And yes, until you lot came crashing up the stairs with our bruised aristocrat, we had been asleep together. But that's all. Absolutely all.'

Philip stretched his legs out and looked at the steaming corduroy. 'But *why* were you in bed with him. I'd have thought . . .'

131

'You'd have thought what, Mr England? That it's wrong to comfort a friend who's in pain? That it's not allowed to cuddle people who are sad and lonely? You and old Yvette Delachêne would make a good couple. She thinks exactly like you do. Good little girls should be tucked up safely in their own beds at night, and they should go for nice polite walks with their boyfriends in the afternoon. And no hanky-panky or I'll tell your mother . . .'

'Just let me finish, will you?' said Philip, still not looking at Danielle. 'What I was going to say was that I'd have thought you'd not feel particularly inclined to climb into bed with Mr Lonelyhearts just because he asked you to on our very last night together, and after, well, you know, after this afternoon, and how happy we were.' And he stopped here, though his intonation gave no indication of the end of a sentence. Philip couldn't see how any of this was answerable, so there didn't seem much point in going on. And anyway, he thought, Danielle and I had already agreed that we wouldn't try to sleep together at the windmill for fear of what might happen if we got caught. He added the postscript. 'And after our agreement I find you doing it with someone else. It makes the agreement look pretty cynical, I must say – in some lights anyway.'

'All the wrong ones, then. I've told you the truth. If you can't accept it for what it is, then you're no better than Yvette, who keeps wanting to know, incidentally, why everyone was in pyjamas.'

'And not just those of us who were in bed,' said Philip.

'Yes,' said Danielle defiantly.

Philip wondered how much longer this could go on. Slightly to his surprise he found that his taste for the drama of ruined love and the harvest of betrayal was limited, and was being replaced by mere feelings of acute discomfort. Part of him was dry, but other parts were still cold and sodden. And underneath, along the insides of his legs, his clothes clung to him, damp and irritating. He sniffed at this experimentally, and found it attractively repulsive. He began to think about medieval castles, and the discomforts of life before the industrial revolution. He turned himself round on the rug. His jealousy was still there – occasionally he checked to make sure – but it seemed difficult to keep it in the foreground all the time, and he felt somehow purged. Not that he had become indifferent. It was just that it had stopped being a matter of injustice, or even bad luck, over which one might be entitled to weep, and had become a matter of pride. Danielle reached out and touched him on the shoulder. He shook her away irritably, and gave her a black look.

'How am I supposed to feel about all this?' he asked rhetorically. 'I break off a heart-to-heart with my girlfriend in the middle of the night so that she can go and help someone who's had an accident, and before you can say jack rabbit she's jumped into bed with him, and I'm in the cold and dark wondering where she's got to. Fine bloody way to spend my last Saturday night in France.'

Danielle looked sullen, her eyes puffy. 'I'm sorry,' she said eventually, her voice rising several tones, and the first tears beginning to break slowly from her eyes. 'I'm sorry. If I'd known you'd take it this way, and not believe . . .'

'You mean, if I'd never found out.'

'That isn't what I mean,' wailed Danielle. 'I was going to tell you. I wasn't even going to stay with Marin for more than a minute or two. Just to get him calm. I wanted to come back to you. But somehow I was so tired, and . . .'

'So tired! So tired! And that just after you'd told me to wait because you were coming back.'

'But I didn't say that.'

'Yes you did.'

'No I didn't.'

'Oh don't be so damned silly. Would I have still been mucking about down there in the yard if I hadn't thought you were coming back? I distinctly remember. You said you'd taken the piece of glass out of Marin's foot and that you were just going to see him up the stairs.'

'I said no such thing. We never said anything to each other.'

'But we did, we did. And anyway it's not just what's said. There's other ways of being understood, for goodness' sake. It was the way you spoke, your manner, everything. Some affection, when one minute you're promising to come and rejoin your lover, and the next you're in bed with someone else.'

'It wasn't like that.'

'Then what the hell was it like? You tell me. After all, you should know.'

After this Danielle broke down in such a flood of tears that conversation was impossible. Philip gazed at her brutally. Folded double on the sofa, her face buried in her hands, forearms resting on her knees, Danielle rocked backwards and forwards with grief. 'You don't understand. It's not fair,' she sobbed, over and over again, a sort of litany that made Philip angrier than ever.

'Not understand?' he cried, with mock but convincing incredulity. 'Not understand? Christ almighty, it's all too bloody obvious for words, and she says I don't understand. What the hell do you take me for? I understand only too well. I'm the boy you took on for the summer, but the summer's over now, and the game's up. There's a long, cold winter ahead, and many an empty bed between here and the fun of another summer. So now you're off. Somebody a bit more dependable. Someone who'll be around when he's needed.' Philip's hectoring died away here. He got to his feet and walked up and down the rug before the fire. 'What a marvellous way to say goodbye to me,' he added, pretending to a wretchedness that he wasn't now sure he could really feel. 'I'd have thought you might have been able to wait another couple of days.'

Danielle had fished out a handkerchief to sob on: 'How could you? How could you say those things? How could you?'

'Because it's all true, that's how.'

'But it's not,' she howled. 'And if you really loved me, you'd understand, and know that what I'm telling you is the truth, and that there's nothing between me and Marin, nothing at all, nothing . . .'

'Then why the hell were you in bed with him? Does going to bed with someone mean nothing in France?'

Philip felt a dreadful combination of triumph and shame. He turned away and went to the mantelpiece, leaning on it with the heel of one hand, and lowering his head to look directly into the quietening fire. Neither of them spoke as the sounds of Danielle's suffering faltered to an occasional snuffle.

'Oh Philip,' she said eventually, 'what are we going to do?' He shook his head as if in irritation. 'Please say something. I can't bear it when you close up.'

There was no response. He just stared stonily into the fire, completely walled in now. He appeared to be lost in thought, but he wasn't having any thoughts at all. His mind was empty and brittle at the shell, while his body was a vessel washed by conflicting emotions, all of them dark. First among them were the waters of hatred: hatred for Danielle, which was of course his love for her rearranged; hatred for Marin, his tormentor, hatred for everyone who had conspired to produce his misery at this place at this time, when he might have been anywhere else in the world; and hatred for himself, for what he had just done, at how he had done it, and for what he had become.

After hatred there was the tide of remorse that flowed against it. This began with remorse for himself, for his suffering, for his misery, for the failure of others to understand his intentions. But there was also remorse for the things he had said, and the way that he had said them.

Then there was bitterness, which scoffed at remorse, and in which he saw himself as a passive victim of treachery. He felt particular bitterness at the idea of forgiveness, the more so as this emotion also welled inside him, rising and falling more or less in time with the sobs and pleas that came up from the sofa.

And in the midst of them all, from the currents and under-tows of this emotional sea, there rose slowly two tall pillars of sentiment, the sheer strength and force of which compelled attention. The first of these was fear. By bullying Danielle into submission to his will he had divorced himself from all human contact, and gained entry to the territory of isolation. It was a desert, and it appalled him. And alongside fear was the other tall pillar, the great column of sexual desire.

Out of this reverie Philip eventually heard Danielle speaking to him again, this time close at hand. 'Philip, please,' she said. She touched him on the back. He straightened and turned to her. She looked frightful. Her face was blotchy, red and white, and her eyes puffed up like a snake's. In his own way, however, he looked no better to her: pale, grim, his expression a dead mirror. 'Please, Philip,' she said again, and reached up with her arms to enfold his neck and pull his head down on her shoulder. He submitted to this manoeuvre, glad for the moment not to be looked in the face, and his whole body relieved by contact. 'Oh Philip,' she said, sobbing against him with her body, and whispering into his ear. 'You must believe me. Please believe me. My poor dear boy. My England. I love only you. You are everything.'

'I know,' he said. 'I know. I'm sorry.' He put his arms around her, pulling her close, putting her warm body against his own, and feeling wonderfully at peace all of a sudden, as though purged again, so that ordinary everyday feelings of welfare, ease and painlessness were marvellously, literally, sensational.

'I'm sorry about the smell.'

'Is that all?' gurgled Danielle.

'You know what I mean.' He squeezed her at the waist, ran his hands up and down her slim back from shoulders to hips. Danielle gave a little noise of contentment and snuggled closer in his embrace. It was true. She did know what Philip meant.

136

And she knew too that this was the moment of painful commitment. She wanted Philip to tell her about his love in every way that he knew, beginning with this near-silent embrace, and the caress of his hands on her back. She had become completely careless. She did not care about the future, bleak as it would certainly be once Philip had left. She did not care about their row, or the misunderstanding, or about Yvette and the trouble she'd be in with her mother when she got home. She didn't care about Marin, poor fellow, or the mess they'd got in together. She lived only for this warmth, the tenderness of this immediate love, and her own unspoken hope.

Philip understood that this was how Danielle felt. In the endeavour to endorse and reciprocate he pushed her shoulders away slightly so that he could kiss her on the mouth. Danielle bypassed all preliminaries, and opened her mouth wide to his. They rocked backwards and forwards before the fire, Philip steaming from the seat of his trousers. The great pillar of sexual desire towered over its companion fear, which temporarily shrank on to a distant shore. Philip felt Danielle yielding her whole body to him. She closed her eyes and threw back her head, arching her spine, relaxing her knees, pulling him deeper and deeper. He reached with his hand for the hem of her dress, felt the gloss of silk in her stockings, the firm curve of her leg. Then she straightened so that his hand came up, cradling the thigh. He pulled the skirt up to her waist and slipped his hand inside her panties.

Danielle had just lifted her leg to caress the side of his thigh with her knee when the door opened, and in walked Yvette Delachêne.

—

Philip, Roland and Michel sat under the awning on the village railway station, waiting for the train. It was five minutes to midday, and the countryside was still hidden in the fragrant

137

and soft moisture of a misty drizzle. Michel sat on one bench, his legs thrust out in front of him, his hands in his pockets, his neck sunk deep into the collar of his reefer jacket. A cigarette hung limp and unlit from the corner of his mouth. Twenty metres away Philip and Roland sat side by side on another bench. No one spoke.

The final half-hour of their stay at the windmill, during which matters had evolved with what Philip later described as 'unsurprising swiftness', had been very disagreeable, an experience leaving each of them with unhappy recollections. Yvette had arrived in the doorway of her own living room not long after she had finished smoothing her daughter's ruffled feathers. She had, however, persuaded Mireille that the proper role of a good hostess was to accept the eccentric behaviour of one's guests once they had been invited, but also to strive to invite only those whose behaviour might be counted upon to be cooperative and sociable. 'Everyone makes mistakes,' she said, 'but a good hostess strives to minimize them.'

On the medical front, Marin was now in good hands. Madeleine would soon feel better. Mireille, Roland and Michel had unpleasant, but ultimately superficial wounds, which time would heal. On the moral front, no real harm had, she thought, come to Danielle, whose account of her presence in Marin's bed was probably true. Yvette had decided that although this was an issue on which it would be prudent to preserve a decent severity, she wouldn't now, after all, report the incident to Danielle's mother. As far as she was concerned the matter was closed.

It was in this state – reasonable good humour, coupled with a sense of once more being in command of affairs – that Yvette had gone to her kitchen to supervise preparations for lunch. From there she had seen England arrive back from his walk looking fairly bedraggled, and realized, perhaps from the droop of his shoulders, that in all the pandemonium of the middle of the night, Philip had been the one person who was thoroughly

138

blameless. He had even managed a sort of dignity, daft as he looked in those dreadful pyjamas. Here, then, since Philip was disappearing in the direction of the living room, was a perfect opportunity for her to reopen relations with Danielle. Once Danielle had been perhaps a little comforted by the diversion which Philip's conversation might provide – and one had to admit he spoke well – she would herself join them, dispel the gloom, enjoy herself, and do her duty as a hostess by putting England at ease, and poor, sad Danielle back in a happy frame of mind.

These sentiments of good fellowship could hardly have been expected to survive the spectacle which greeted her as she entered the room, and in the ruinous wake of the tidal wave of her wrath, Philip, Roland and Michel were all ordered to return to Paris on the next available train. This turned out to be the 12.15 slow stopper, due to arrive in Paris at four o'clock. They sat waiting for it with rather different feelings.

Michel, who refused to look at, let alone speak to, the other two, was torn between bitterness and frustration: bitterness at being expelled for brawling, as Patrick put it, when he had done no more than honour required; frustration at being unable to see or to talk to Jeannette before his departure. Immobile in the mist, he scowled across the deserted tracks at the deserted platform opposite.

Philip was feeling extremely unhappy. It wasn't the being caught in the act, slight as it seemed to him that the act was. Nor was it embarrassment at Yvette's sharing, so to speak, in a vignette of the absurd. The antic must have looked grotesque, but he had been the sort of child who was always being caught in what adults defined as grotesque postures, and one more addition to a lifetime's accumulated total didn't worry him all that much. He wasn't even much troubled by the vaguely distant feelings of anger that he felt, at having betrayed himself into exactly the all-too-readily possible behaviour that he had wanted to avoid. His unhappiness was more progressive, in anticipation of the reception which he knew would await him first on arrival in Paris, and subsequently in London. Yvette may not have spoken to him about his behaviour, but she had certainly spoken to Madame Beaumanière about it on the telephone when ringing to announce their premature departure. Philip did not much fancy the idea of a Beaumanière roused.

Neither did Roland. His face bore, in addition to the more prominent physical disfigurement, a look of profound hopelessness. Here was one of those situations in which no amount of explanation could dissipate parental displeasure. Touching up the servants; fighting with Michel (and incompetently); attending midnight pyjama parties: these things were custommade to drive older Beaumanières to an orgy of recrimination likely to spill over into pretty well every other area of life. 'What am I to do with you?' he could hear his father saying. 'What am I to do? I ask myself. You are lazy at school. You are rude to your mother at home. She is amazed at the things that you do, yet can't seem to talk to you. You are frivolous with money. You smoke to excess. You are arrogant with the servants. And you choose your friends, if these escapades are anything to go by, from the most debauched elements of what your countrymen, for reasons that escape me entirely, are pleased to call French society. I spend a fortune to keep you in school and provide you with opportunities commensurate with your obligations, and this is how you thank me. A fine thing. And no, you can't apologize to your mother. It must wait until tomorrow. She has gone to bed, she is so utterly distressed. And you will do likewise straight after supper. As for you, Leroux, young man . . .' Further mental preparation eluded Roland at this point.

'I'm afraid you're in trouble, old chap,' he said.

'Could be,' said Philip, laughing nervously.

'My father will do one of his acts, and then he's sure to get on the telephone to your people in England. There'll be a welcoming vendetta all the way from Dover, I shouldn't wonder.'

Philip was too glum to reply. The thought of his father groping for the occasional word of French down the telephone, while Roland's father outlined the full extent of the scandal which had ruined him and tainted the good name of Beaumanière, was too painful. Even more so the thought of the abject apology that would flow from his father's lips, and the effect this would have on the head of the Beaumanière household. It would confirm him in his long-held view that the world was going to wrack and ruin, that the English were in the vanguard of this unnecessary development, and that his own son and heir, through various unfortunate connections, was a willing participant in it.

Everything, it occurred to Philip, was suddenly at risk. His love for Danielle, with its confusing elements of lust and jealousy, wild good humour and fear of loneliness – this was surely at risk. Her mother would never let it continue, not after the report she was certain to get from Yvette. Yvette, after all, had now formed the view that Danielle was a nymphomaniac, and Patrick had not exactly helped by contributing to this judgement the feeling that he'd had the previous night at dinner – movements of her eyes and feet, that sort of thing – that tended to support it. Even writing to her was going to be difficult. All the grown-ups would be sure to close ranks to keep him out. And if their love was going to be killed off like this, it might be as well to acknowledge the death sooner rather than later. Perhaps the whole of the immediate past was dead too, he thought. The mill, the Delachêne household, la Grande Berthe, Marin: perhaps he'd never see any of them again. Michel is already showing every sign of having decided that I don't exist. The main feature of the summer at Tréveneuc, which was the beautiful complexity and confident happiness of the group they had known as *les gosses*, seemed suddenly to have died. Death is the right analogy, he thought.

And since it can't be revived, then it can only be buried. Or cremated.

The future didn't look all that lively either. Roland's dad would probably be pretty frosty while giving Roland a lambasting. Philip knew from experience that this was what other people's parents did when they were furious with you too, but felt that the right to exemplary discipline was not exactly theirs. He would be in the dog house while a proper reception was prepared for him in London. He sighed at the thought of returning to his homeland. His mother would go into maternal shock, and have a migraine for a week. His father would do one of his pained perplexity acts, including 'If I had had your opportunities, goodness me . . .' type statements, interspersed with bursts of deliberate and controlled anger oiled by, indeed running on, a lexicon of all the weakest swear words in the English language. Philip knew only too well that these oscillations between perplexity and anger, and the changes in vocal timbre and volume which accompanied them, were largely associated with the degree to which his father did or did not care, at any particular moment in the proceedings, how much the neighbours could hear. He groaned inwardly at the thought that the social advantages to be derived from the opportunity to employ the Beaumanière name at full volume would not be lost on his father. It was not, after all, every night of the week that even minor members of the French aristocracy telephoned to coordinate parental retribution in the dark deserts of the London suburbs.

And there would be nothing to be said in defence, let alone mitigation. He had learned by painful experience that to speak was to open further channels for paternal exploration. Silence could at least help to keep things to a minimum. Containment was the key to crises of this kind. After the storm of the first night's confrontation, there would be an awkward morning composed of barked instructions over a silent breakfast, followed by the blessed relief of school. Even so, this immediate future looked as bleak as the immediate past. History, the continuity of people, things and forces, seemed to Philip to have been expunged. With it, hope had also died.

He was roused from these thoughts by the whistle and snort of the train as it crept into the station and came to a halt, wheezing noisily. The station-master came out on to the platform and put on his cap. Nobody got off. Since it was a Sunday there was no mail and no freight to be busied with. The three young men clambered aboard. Michel went into a compartment and shut the door behind him. Philip and Roland selected another compartment and sat down face to face by the window. They both looked out. The station-master moved his hands from his hips and put them behind his back, and in response the train gasped and hissed into creaking motion, and drew slowly out of the station. The wheels and rails began to assert the familiar rhythmic pattern, but the pace was slow, and Philip and Roland didn't need to speak to acknowledge to one another that four hours of the slow stopper was going to be as dismal a way to spend a Sunday afternoon as could be imagined. Philip looked out of the window and concentrated on nothing. Roland stretched out on the bench seat, folded his arms across his chest, and appeared to fall asleep.

The countryside rolled past, wet, bleak and silent beyond the rumbling of the train. The mist was a veil preventing a view, so that the train seemed to be travelling slowly down a diaphanous tunnel, the boundaries of which were real, but could not be precisely located. At the edges, trees, hedgerows, occasional farmhouses were blurred, ghostly shadows that sometimes seemed to advance towards the foreground of the tunnel before then once again drawing back to become smudges against the grey backdrop of rain, mist and sky. There was no evidence of an horizon somewhere beyond the deceptions of this landscape, no point at which the solidity of earth, the events of nature, or the facts of human residence in it, could be said to be separate, identifiably distinct from the insubstantial expanses of the air and sky. The spaces above had the same texture, the same quality, the same colour as the spaces below, as though there were a mirror magically suspended six metres above the ground which, following the contours perfectly, signalled the dissolution of both earth and sky.

Almost nothing moved in this strange mirrored tunnel. Occasional cows stood motionless in the fields. Once or twice there might have been glimpses of a crow flapping from one branch to another. Everywhere among the silent trees bundles of mistletoe hung, threatening and sadistic. There were no people to be seen, no farmers herding stock, no scouts huddled round a fire or strung out on a hike, no cars at crossings, no bikes on the deserted lanes that followed the railway from time to time before suddenly and inexplicably swerving away into a distance whose existence could only be assumed, not verified.

Every now and then there was a station where the train would stop. Each new station seemed to be just like the last. No people, no activity, just a small cluster of flat buildings pulled together by an iron roof with a brick platform glistening wet amid the monotony of a cinder surround. A tub or two of geraniums, a row of barred windows, a couple of empty benches, a ticket-office door that looked as though it would bang in the wind. Each halt posed an alternative, a route that could be taken, a choice that might be made, a future to be denied or asserted. Each stop was, thus, an invitation to an act of faith, with no guidance on the utility of reason or the purpose of rationality. Philip thought about the alternatives. He didn't really have any idea where he was in the complicated geography of France. He had simply come down on a train with the others, and now got on one to go back again. He couldn't even remember whether the stop where he'd boarded the train just after midday had a name or not. He certainly hadn't looked for one. What if he should just get off the train here, at this next unknown halt? Michel, next door, wouldn't know. Roland, asleep, was unlikely to notice. The grey and infinite tunnel of the world outside the carriage window contained nothing of which he could be certain – just one more little station like the last one, one more wayside halt identical to the ones yet to come. All he had to do was to stand up, pull down his grip from the rack above his head, slide through the door and jump down to the platform. With his collar turned up he would stride into the veil, passing out of this tunnel, with its rails already set, where both the journey and the destination were preordained, and, worse, effortless, and set off down a different tunnel, one that had been chosen, affirmed.

The thought grew in Philip's mind. Why not? There was nothing really to go on for. The future was in ruins. Or soon would be. It had been mined in advance, and all the mines were set to explode. There were no real practical difficulties that he could see. He spoke the language, and could begin by looking for a job on a farm. A dry barn would do to sleep in for a start. School was hateful, parents incomprehensible, the Beaumanière connection finished. Danielle he would never see again.

Philip felt the satisfaction that flows from dreaming of the punishment that sudden absence can inflict on our enemies. The panic that would seize Patrick and Yvette Delachêne, the guilt of the Beaumanières, the shame of his parents. A particular stigma attached itself to couples whose children ran away, never to return. A stigma that settled on them after the first shock, after the initial sympathy and sharing of the neighbours. The train heaved and puffed again, and clanked forward, rattling its couplings. Station gave way to countryside once more. The grey, wet, misty tunnel of the known world encircled the row of grey-green carriages as they clattered in single file, like a line of coffins, down the track.

Eventually they came to a bigger station, where Roland

woke and sat up, scratching his head. Here was a town, its grandeur emphasized by the single track splitting into four. They pulled in to a side platform, and further up the train a number of doors opened. A few people got off and scattered. Philip saw Michel get down and saunter into a kiosk, emerging a few moments later with a carton of drink. He climbed back on to the train without looking to right or left. While they waited, two express trains thundered through, and in the dull silence that followed their passing the swirling mist rearranged its veil, closing off whatever remote possibilities the hurtling speedsters might have aroused.

'Anything you want?' Roland asked.

Philip declined, chewing at his lower lip for a while. 'Actually,' he said, 'I was thinking about getting off. Doing a bunk. Thought I might make a fresh start.'

'What on earth for?'

'Seemed like a good idea. After all, there's not much to go back for, is there? We're already in the stew.'

'Fat lot of good that would do, though,' said Roland. 'My father'd have every policeman in France looking for us by midnight tonight, and once they'd found us the future wouldn't look any brighter. Anyway, Beaumanières aren't allowed to run away.'

There were a couple of bumps and the train edged forward again, snaking round the end of the platform to rejoin the track. They went past some dismal housing, grey stonework with peeling plaster, walls of fading advertisements, maroon and yellow, *Quinquina, Dubo, Dubon, Champigneulles, Sobriété, Santé*. Crazy slate roofs that surely leaked, slanting windows and shutters, balconies that looked out on the rubble that collects around railway yards and sidings. There were no suburbs to this town. They were soon back in the slippery countryside.

What I really need to be is dead, thought Philip. Not really dead dead. Just apparently dead. Now what if this train were

146

in a terrific smash-up, one of those express trains coming down the track and knocking us for six? I survive, thrown clear, unharmed. But the rolling stock is so terribly crushed that, after attempts at a search, the crumpled boxwood and concertina'd iron of the carriage are simply designated a grave, sacred and revered. Mother weeps over the few remains from my grip. White with grief, the Leroux, Beaumanières and Delachênes gather for the memorial service. Danielle reads the lesson. She is very beautiful in a black crepe dress. She weeps, but her eyes do not puff up. I creep away among the hedges and the mist, an escapee, a tragic figure, it's true, but confident too, poised, ready for a new life. I make for Bordeaux, the dockyards, to be a deckhand for the Far East. The Pacific. Gauguin. Stevenson.

The train settled into a long stretch where it bumped along steadily, the countryside flowing past as though on the surface of a broad river, like driftwood. Philip fell even further into abstractions. The great benefit of being apparently dead was instantaneous release from the prison of necessity, but it also had some gratifying side-effects that worked to warm his unhappiness. What a lesson it would teach them! If they hadn't chucked us out early, we'd have been on a different train. They'd never get over it, my dying unwanted. She'd always say she loved me, and be their permanent accusation. He saw himself at the funeral, in a chapel to one side, watching the ghostly proceedings through the rings of Gothic pillars, hearing the stifled sobs, cold and diffuse, amid the autumnal damp. Notre-Dame? Chartres? Amiens perhaps, with all the other accidental English dead. This was powerful imagery. Observing it, words decayed in his mind, and without them he sank into a shallow sleep, his chin riding awkwardly on his chest to the rhythm of the train, his neck slowly developing a painful crick, the full order of service still incomplete.

The train pressed on, passing through a long and dismal forest before at last emerging on to the plains that surround

Paris. The weather did not improve, but the train showed signs of being more business-like. Its rural visiting service was accomplished. The suburbs could look after themselves. It rattled along at what would have seemed a reckless speed an hour or so earlier, and took audible pleasure at going through a number of peaceful stations at a smart spank. Then, crossing by bridge into the central area of the city, it came to a dead halt in a cutting, the sky somewhere invisible above, the little train suddenly dormant among the half-dozen sets of tracks that lay imprisoned between high concrete walls. A silence settled, so dense that Philip could feel it, and he woke up to its touch.

'Where are we?' he asked, looking at his watch, rubbing and stretching his neck.

'Just about there,' said Roland. 'Probably just outside the station.'

'What are we going to do?'

'What do you mean?'

'Well, I thought it might make sense to have a joint strategy. You know, say the same things, give the same account of what happened. You know what parents are like. Divide and rule.'

Roland shook his head over this. 'You don't understand, England, old chap. There isn't anything we can do or say to stop this one. It isn't going to matter how we explain things. They're already absolutely certain that they know what happened, and they won't want to hear our version. Even if we were allowed to tell them, they wouldn't believe us. And even if they knew our version was true, they wouldn't admit it, probably not even to themselves, and certainly not to us. I've been through this routine before. And anyway, I still haven't heard what it was you and Danielle were up to.' He grinned, though reluctantly, because his cut lip hurt when it was stretched. 'Something carnal, I hope.' Philip grinned back at him humourlessly. 'Oh dear, oh dear, oh dear,' sighed Roland.

148

'What with me first, then you, we are certainly in the unconditional shit.'

'Do you think you'll be seeing Mireille again?'

Roland gave one of his category-A expressive shrugs. 'Shouldn't imagine so,' he said. '*She* wouldn't speak to me after breakfast, her mother wouldn't speak to me after your run-in with her, and her father wouldn't speak to me as we left. Not cause for optimism. Anyway,' he went on after a pause, 'what's done is done. No use worrying over it. Since none of it can be undone, we may as well get on with the next thing on the agenda. And these things always blow over eventually.'

Philip said nothing. He couldn't yet imagine that it would all 'blow over'. Some people would forget about it, of course. He didn't expect the events of the past twenty-four hours to result in permanent domestic crisis. But he certainly wouldn't forget, and the past not being over, but now being a part of him in the way that memory gathers things together, meant that it could not readily be discounted. Like the bedrock of mourning when the evidence for bereavement is insubstantial, as when a soldier's wife is widowed by telegram. How can it really be true, all that loss, the suffering, the grief, all the unutterable loneliness, when the only evidence for it is a little piece of paper, a few smudges of typewriter ink in the hands of an embarrassed messenger? And does it become any more true when they deliver his effects: a silver necklet and charm, a watch and wallet, a photo of you, a few coins in a battered leather purse? Later there will be a monument, a little white stone cross in a walled field somewhere over the sea. But even so, where can he be?

There are many ways of being left, and many ways of leaving – Philip could see that. So, in a sense, could Roland. But some points of departure are qualitatively different from all the others because they are located on cleared ground. Everything that stood there before has been felled, possibly by fire, and

149

the newly scorched earth awaits the imprint of a new future, the planting of seeds, the growth of a new crop. For a moment, in the silence of the railway cutting, Philip sensed that he was standing on this ground. The past was dead. The present by consequence was barren. The future, though it might belong to him, was inscrutable, and would take some organizing.

After these thoughts the train gave a snort and jolted into movement, making the two friends look up at each other. They smiled.

'Courage,' said Roland.

They chugged into the station, the long platform unrolling beside them, the train creaking and complaining to its last hissing sigh.

—

Philip met Danielle the following afternoon in the Place Saint-Sulpice, and they went for a last walk together. He had been tentative when he rang in the morning, afraid that she might not answer the phone, or that she might be cold (blaming him for her disgrace), or, worst of all, that he might get her mother. In the event Danielle was delighted. Yes, she said, her mother hadn't been too pleased, but what was she to expect? She hadn't exactly qualified for the *médaille de la Résistance*. Anyway, what the hell, she was grown up enough for it not to matter.

When they met a few hours later, the moods were reversed. Philip relaxed and confident; Danielle tense and nervous. Neither could explain why.

'You managed to get away all right?' he asked.

'Of course. Mother's at work all day.'

'I meant, from the windmill. Yesterday.'

'Patrick drove us all up in the afternoon. Except for Marin. They kept him in hospital overnight.'

'Oh,' said Philip. He didn't want to know about Marin,

whose existence he was trying, unsuccessfully, to forget. They walked away from the Place Saint-Sulpice and drifted up the Rue Bonaparte towards the Luxembourg Gardens.

'Is that all you can say?' asked Danielle.

'What? Oh, sorry. Miles away. Poor old Marin. Anyway, I'm glad you got back all right.'

'Actually, it was a lousy trip,' said Danielle, suddenly reaching to take hold of his hand, and nestling it in both of hers in front of her as she walked. 'Mireille lectured us just about all the way on Roland's character, which is vile, corrupt and decadent. In-between-whiles Patrick gave us his version of the French class system. And Yvette, whenever she turned round to look at us – happily not often – gave off the most frightful scowls.'

'What about Berthe?'

'Oh she's all right. She'll survive. I don't think you'll be hearing from her in a hurry, though. Perhaps never again.'

They crossed the Rue Vaugirard in silence, and went into the gardens by the gate near the chess players. The trees, browning at the edges, were advancing into autumn. Children were at school, families at home at lunch, workmen at their break, the chairs and benches awaited the afternoon occupants, empty, serene, dignified beneath the statues. The gardens were almost completely empty. Philip and Danielle walked south first to look at the statue of Massenet, which Philip thought funny, and then they went east, to the fountain and the boating pond. They walked round this several times, crunching the gravel. There were more people here, loitering, some eating sandwiches.

'Americans,' said Philip. 'Inhaling the culture. It makes them feel civilized.'

'And what does it do for you?' asked Danielle. Philip looked at her in surprise. 'Well, you're one too. An outsider, I mean. You don't belong here either, do you?'

'What do you mean, I don't belong here?'

'Well, it's true. This isn't your society. You're a pretend Frenchman. A sort of advanced version of the holiday tripper.'

'That's very unfair,' said Philip, suddenly feeling badly wounded.

Danielle gave his hand a squeeze. 'Oh come on, England, cheer up. Can't you take a joke any more?'

'If that was a joke, I hope I never hear you get serious on the subject.'

'Well, you said yourself you were only here for the holidays.'

'When did I say that?'

'Yesterday. When we had our row.'

Philip gave a deep, moderately theatrical sigh, as if to say, 'You're surely not going to bring all that up again, are you?', but after a pause he spoke, looking down at his feet.

'Listen,' he said. 'I'm sorry about yesterday. I've told you that already. I didn't mean to hurt you, or to say, you know, any of those things. But, well, it was all such a – I don't know, finding you and le Matelot together like that. And I was tired as hell.'

'You still find Marin a threat, don't you?'

'Yes, I suppose I do.'

'Silly old thing.'

'No, it isn't silly. I think if, you know, yesterday Yvette hadn't come in, and we'd gone on somehow, made love again, everything would have been different today. I don't know how. But she did come in. And instead of getting closer to you for my last weekend in France, I was shown the door. Now it's all got bigger again somehow, so that it isn't over, and I, oh I don't know . . . I don't know what I think, really.'

'We could still make love this afternoon,' said Danielle, stopping her walk and looking up into his eyes with a tiny smile playing around the corners of her thin lips.

'Where?' said Philip. And then, without waiting for a reply: 'In the shrubs behind the Medici fountain? That'd look good in the papers, wouldn't it? French girl's virtue shed among lilacs. Hangdog Englishman accused. Friend's mother reports nymphomaniac tendencies. Christ!'

Danielle said, 'Why do you always imagine love-making interrupted? I've noticed it in you before. And anyway, I did not have in mind a public fornication in the Luxembourg Gardens, as you know very well. You can come back to my place. Mother's at the bar all afternoon.'

Philip shook his head slowly. 'No,' he said simply. 'Come on, let's sit down over here.'

They deposited themselves in a couple of iron chairs, their backs towards the Palace, facing in the direction of the distant Observatory. Philip tilted his chair on to its back legs. Like Michel, he thought.

'Do you think we are at all well suited?' asked Danielle.

'To what?'

'Oh don't be awkward. You know what I mean.'

'Yes, of course we are. Why do you ask?'

'Because sometimes you seem so wrapped up in your own concerns, your own idea of what's right or what's possible, that I feel as though you aren't really aware of me at all.'

'I don't understand.'

'Well, like your going away . . .'

'Tomorrow.'

'Yes, tomorrow. Back to London. You seem to think about it wholly in terms of your leaving me, of being lonely without me because you have to go, of my being somehow simply the damaging cause of your experience.'

'Whereas you see it completely differently.'

'Oh don't be sarcastic, Philip, please. I do want to understand what's happening to us. And yes, as it happens, I can see it from your point of view too, how awful it will be for you to go back to your school, and your parents, and for us to be apart. But I can also see it from my position. And it's very painful for me to watch you go off, knowing I mightn't see you again for almost a year. Another country is no place to keep the man you love.' Philip said nothing, so she pressed on. 'Being left behind is very hard. Travelling, new places, even when you know them well, means a kind of new beginning. But staying put, the same people, the same dreary routines, even the good things like the same friends, they are colder, harsher, emptier without you. This is what I learned when I was in the Alps in August. I missed you a lot, but I didn't need to write to you to say so because being away was like having you with me. Seeing something new, something I'd never seen before, I always found myself mentally discussing it with you, as though you really were there. I know it sounds silly. I haven't thought about this sort of thing before. But the point is that when you go away I shall miss you terribly, even more than you will miss me. And I don't think you really understand this.'

'And that's why you ask me if I think we're suited to each other? Because you think I don't know how you feel?'

'I don't know. I don't want to be morbid, not on our last afternoon. Let's go somewhere we . . .'

Philip brushed this aside. 'No, I don't want to go anywhere. I think you're wrong about travel, about leaving, going away. Or maybe not wrong about that, but wrong to say that it's all the same whether the departure is for somewhere new or for somewhere like home, somewhere that defines the past. Going home for me is not to go forward, it's to go back, so it's a kind of retreat, a sort of surrender. Ignominious and unconditional.'

'Oh come on,' said Danielle cheerfully. 'Things aren't that bad. There's English weather and English cooking to look forward to.' She danced her eyes at him, but he didn't respond. 'And I might be able to come and see you.'

These words, said lightly enough, but with quiet determination, brought Philip to life. He set his chair down on its four legs and turned to look at Danielle.

'Are you serious?'

'Why not? I'm old enough to catch trains too, you know.'

'But how?'

'How do you think? Really, England, you are hopeless sometimes. I'll get a job and save some money, and then I'll take a holiday and come and see you. I could even do it before Christmas.'

'But where would you stay?'

'Do you want me to come?'

'Of course I do. But there are practical difficulties. You couldn't come and stay at my place. After what's happened this weekend we'll probably have to keep you secret from my parents altogether.'

'Well, at a hotel, I suppose.'

'Christ!' said Philip, the full enormity of what Danielle was proposing beginning to settle on him.

'Actually, I had another idea as well,' Danielle went on, laying her hand gently on his wrist as she spoke. 'I thought I might see if I could find some sort of a job in London. You know, looking after children or something. And sign up for a language course. Then I could stay several months, perhaps a year, and we'd be together the whole time. I could practise my English on you.' Philip pretended to shudder at this. 'Would you like that?'

'Like it?' said Philip. 'Like it? Do you realize what you're saying?'

'Of course I do,' she replied, laughing. 'You think I'd come up with a suggestion like this on the spur of the moment? Without thinking about it very carefully in advance?' She thought Philip's sudden tongue-tied surprise very amusing. 'What's so big about the English Channel that you're amazed at my thinking of crossing it?'

'No one goes to England to live,' said Philip, putting on a look of mock horror, and gesticulating with his arms. 'You go to England to die. The fog closes in on you, and you are asphyxiated.'

'Phooee,' said Danielle. 'You just like to be mordant about it because it's where you're from, but I bet it's no different from France, really. Anyway, what matters is that it's where you're going to be, so that's where I want to be too.'

'All right, then,' said Philip, getting up out of his chair and starting to circle Danielle slowly, waving his arms in crude imitation of what he imagined an Oriental dance might be like. 'Not a fog, but a serpent.' He widened his eyes, as if to hypnotize her. 'It tempts you as it hisses into your orchard; it wraps its deliciously repulsive skin around you, and then it squeezes, gently at first, looking for a grip, but then harder and harder as it finds one, until finally you are wrapped in an unbreakable embrace, all the breath is forced out of you, your bones are cracked and crushed, your flesh pulped, and you become a corpse, indistinguishable – in the eyes of what passes for an English gourmet – from suet pudding.' Here he broke into a straight lecturing style, a Pathé News commentator perhaps. 'A local delicacy, much eaten in the better class of school, where it is impregnated with raisins, and is known colloquially as "spotted dick". This is at its most colourful when covered with a lumpy substance known among the indigenous tribes as custard and when the two are served, very slightly chilled, after a first course of cold mutton fat and greens. Is this' – and Philip returned to his arm-waving imitations – 'the kind of future you imagined for yourself? A lump of suet pudding on a cracked school plate to tempt the palate of some snobby, toffee-nosed urchin whose senses have already been dulled by the weather and his parents, and who has nothing to look forward to but a lifetime of bad dinners and Protestant church services? Ah, woman. Not only are you shameless, but you are senseless too.'

Danielle couldn't answer this for laughter, which made Philip laugh too. The lunch hour was just about over, and more people were coming into the gardens, some of them watching with mildly suspicious curiosity, one eye on their children, the strange ritual being performed by these two young people. Neither Philip nor Danielle noticed.

'And all you do is laugh,' sighed Philip, sitting down again. 'I try to warn you, but you find it funny. No one ever believes the truth, or even recognizes what the truth is, until they see it, hear it, touch it, or say it for themselves.' He was still smiling, and he edged his chair round in the gravel so that she could see him better. 'Are you serious, though? About coming, I mean?'

'Of course I am. Would I say so if I wasn't?'

'Ah, then there is life after death.'

Philip put out his hand and she took it, caressed it in her own. They sat thus, comfortable, silent, together, for some minutes, but as the time went by Philip's spirits sank once more, the tempo slowed, he felt tired again, and miserable too.

'I'm glad it makes you happy,' said Danielle.

Philip didn't reply, and in the silence created by his failure to speak he realized that he was not happy at all. Danielle's proposal had filled him with darkness. He couldn't understand why. He thought about the autumn and winter ahead, the shape of the immediate future as he imagined it in his head. Anything to do with time had a graphic disposition for Philip, as though on a map, and he saw the months of October, November, December, January, February and March running away from him in a downhill line that curved sharply to the right around the tenth of December, snaked back left and right again before and after Christmas, and then curved away still to the right, and gently uphill again towards the spring. The unbroken line of this winter future was black, as though drawn with a soft lead pencil, and the landscape surrounding it was a featureless and uniform grey. He realized that it gave him a perverse pleasure to look at this design. It was an old friend, and he felt about it as a carpenter feels about a good workbench, or a religious man about a well-made pew. It fitted him, it was comfortable, and it made the tasks that had to be done that much simpler. He could board this line at one end tomorrow, and simply be carried along on it. Each day would succeed the one before, each date would be in its allocated place, every week, every month would fulfil its promise. There would be holidays here and here, examinations at this spot, a Sunday morning in bed at this one. There would be school debates on Friday evenings, class parties on Saturday nights, and history essays to be prepared for Monday mornings. The past would accumulate behind the line like a colourful valley seen from the edge of a wood, full of light, because down this pasture the steady bright beacon of his other life, his French life, himself as other, would still be shining.

The idea of mixing the two lives together was a dangerous prospect. The union filled him with dread. But it also perplexed him terribly because he was sure now, more sure than he had ever been of anything before, that the sentiment he felt for Danielle was the true sentiment of love. He wanted her terribly, and in wanting her for himself he could feel all the pent-up jealousy that he held for other men, real, potential and imagined, who also wanted her now, or might yet want her in the future, and the mere thought of being thwarted in this intense desire to possess and to keep, to shield and to hide what he felt was unquestionably his, made him long to take her away, to have her with him, never to let her out of his sight. But he wanted all of this somehow in another place, or rather, as he now realized, he wanted it with himself as another imaginary self, and not as himself as he really was, or looked like he was becoming. What he wanted was the curving line of his pencilled future exactly as it had, until a few minutes ago, promised him that it would be, full of the delicious misery and unhappiness of being alone, separated from the woman he was said to love, slightly aloof from his contemporaries in the mysteries of his continental being. Here was a self that he coveted.

'How happy I am,' said Danielle.

Philip didn't really hear her, although he gave her arm a squeeze as if he had. What he did hear was an insistent whispering as of conversations not yet born, exchanges that were coupled to, although not synchronized with, imagined scenes of various kinds in which another and more romantic Philip made his first theatrical appearances. Philip the withdrawn, admitting to insomnia when questioned about his pallor; Philip the melancholic, prowling the corners of the great hall during the last stages of the school Christmas dance, turning away invitations from the belles of the sixth to take them in his arms; Philip the inconsolable, his collar turned up against the wind, hands thrust deep in his pockets, mooching through the snow in the local park on a Saturday afternoon, observed, though unbeknown to him, by the new young English teacher, who would want to help and protect him; Philip the fiery wit, quick as silver, deadly as mercury, doyen of the debating society, carrying all in the audience before him, smouldering, unknowable and remote, brilliant and unpredictable. 'They say he's in love with a beautiful French countess . . .'; 'He has had TB, you know, twice . . .' He walks home alone in the rain from a party, the water sticking his trouser legs to his knees, his shoes leaking at the toes. 'She offered him a lift, so Smalls says, but he refused. She's crazy about him . . .' He disappears for a week in the Christmas holidays, walks across the Fells in a bitter wind under a bright but short-lived sun, returning to school more distant, more silent than ever. 'I heard he'd been with her in Monaco . . .'; 'Her people have a chateau in Burgundy . . .'; 'He won't look at salad without garlic . . .'

'Aren't you happy too?'

'Mmm?' said Philip, shaking his head and blinking comically, as if coming out of a dream. 'Oh yes, of course. Look, I think we should go.'

He stood up, and Danielle stood up beside him. She put her

hand through his arm and they walked among the trees, Philip dragging his feet through the leaves to make a rustling sound. Neither of them spoke. It is all falsehood, Philip was thinking. We are brought up to be ready for the parts we're to play, but what if we refuse the parts that are assigned to us? What if we should just want to be ourselves? And how does anybody tell, anyway? Is there any visible difference between being oneself and acting some other part altogether? And who's to know the difference? And how do you know who your real self is anyway?

Just to get to know one thing, and to know it so well that it can be the basis of a perhaps small, perhaps insignificant, but none the less authentic act, is so incredibly difficult.

Together, Philip and Danielle walked away from the gardens, through the tall wrought-iron gates, back down the Rue Bonaparte, and into the Place where they had met earlier. Near the fountain, with its bishops and lions, Philip stopped, and Danielle turned to face him. The two tall unequal towers of Saint-Sulpice rose behind him, like an image from the day before, when desire had triumphed.

'I'm sorry, Danielle,' he said. 'But I think it would probably be for the best if we didn't see one another again.'

The words lay between them like an ocean, into which Danielle began to cry, quietly but insistently.

'I knew you were going to say that,' she said. 'I had a sudden intuition.' She pulled a handkerchief out of her sleeve and blew her nose. 'Will you write to me?' Philip looked at the ground and, without speaking, shook his head a couple of times tersely, as though shuddering. 'Then can I write to you?'

'I think you'd best not,' he said.

'Philip, please,' said Danielle, putting her hands on his waist, rocking his body backwards and forwards slightly, trying to get his eyes to look at hers. 'Don't, Philip, please. Don't just leave me.'

'I must,' he said.

160

'But why?'

'Because I must.' Philip took her hands from his waist, one cluster of frail fingers in each of his, and lowered them to her side. He looked into her face, aching with the sorrow of it. 'Please, Danielle. I'm sorry. But I must go. And so must you.'

He stepped back half a pace. Danielle moved towards him, offering to kiss his cheek, but Philip pulled his head away abruptly, then looked once more at her face before turning and walking away. She watched him for a moment, and then she ran across the paving stones and the cobbles, up the steep steps under the high portico with its massive pillars, and in through the open door of the church. There, in the sanctified darkness, sobbing breathlessly at first, she wept.

Philip, when he reached the corner, turned to look back, but Danielle had disappeared. The Place behind him was deserted.

———————

Still the same Sunday　　　　　　　*Very late, nearly Monday*

I'm exhausted, and just want to topple into bed, but I have to finish writing to you. After Beatrix left this morning I found myself feeling melancholy, which is rare for me. I think I decided – the morning is so long ago now that it seems like another life, and I'm finding it hard to remember how things were arranged in the former set-up – anyway, what I seem to recall is deciding that sadness stemmed from frustration, and that what I'd really been wanting to do all along was read the rest of Philip's manuscript, and not sit listening to Beatrix giving a schematic account of life, love and betrayal in Tin Pan Alley. I needed my space too, as we say. I put it like this, a bit nakedly, because I'm feeling ashamed now, and have my head in my hands. Almost literally. I'm so tired I'm sitting here at your desk with my head propped up on one hand, scrawling illegibly with the other. You'll just have to forgive the mess. God knows, I need forgiveness.

Not from Philip, however. At least I don't think so. I settled back into 'The Portrait of a Philosopher' and read the rest of it at a go. And I was profoundly affected by it. He was there, all of him, making a mess of things in ways one would never have imagined possible. Some bits of it were quite alarming for me – you'll probably guess which bits when you read it – because it was like finding him again in some sort of adjacent dimension, where you have never been but where everything bears an uncanny resemblance to the way they were somewhere else. And right in the middle of it there's Philip, still wanting reasons for doing things, and still believing that when he's found them they can justify what he does. And then, most remarkable of all, ten years later – well almost – if he did write it in 1980 he'd have been twenty-four, which is as far removed from sixteen and a half as seventy is from thirty-five – having the integrity to sit down and write about it, exactly as it was, with all the pain and uncertainty restored.

My immediate reaction to it, as I turned the final page, was a huff of tiredness. Coming immediately after Beatrix and all her troubles, it was like accumulated stress, one thing in one sphere of life adding to something in another sphere to produce over-load. Too much. I'd been reading it at the kitchen table, so I made myself a sandwich and took it up to your study, and lay on the couch. The sun had come back after the morning rain, and the light coming in was being filtered through steam coming off the trees and the lawn. Food helped and the melancholia dispersed, and I began to see how funny it all was, really. 'The Portrait', I mean. Not just the jokes, and the coincidences, and the wicked portraits of all the grown-ups, though they are funny, and capture Philip's view of things extremely well. But more the intrinsic humour in how seriously we all take ourselves in adolescence, how intense it all is, how earnestly we expect that our choices will matter and make a difference. I got quite excited thinking about this, partly because of Philip, of course, and the sort of person that I'd known him to be, but also because it suddenly seemed relevant to Beatrix and her circumstances.

Perhaps, I thought, what had happened in her case was that she'd gone on being an adolescent. This wasn't a criticism, even then, before the rest of what happened this afternoon. Staying young as she did was a terrific benefit, both to her and to others. But when it ran out she was – this was how I thought of it at the time – too old to grow up. Like those bonsai trees, or bound feet, and isn't there something in genetic theory about evolutionary routes so that once you've gone one way you can't go back? It all just seemed to fit Beatrix's case. And I had been a bit selfish in the morning, afraid to give her advice, and basically getting her to go away so that I could get on with 'The Portrait'. And all she really wanted was company. She'd as good as said so herself.

So I decided to make a social call, and I'm very glad that I did. But, even so, I could have been quicker about it. I had a bath first, spent some time deciding what to wear, and then spent more time locking up the house and picking a few flowers from your garden to take with me. It was late afternoon by this time, though there was still some heat in the sun, the sky clear and light, rather white.

When I got to 'Favelas' I found Beatrix sitting outside, but not in a chair or anything. She was actually more or less lying in a puddle, her back propped up against the wall next to the door into the kitchen. She looked such a frightful colour, chalk-white where her face wasn't smeared with dirt, that I initially thought she was dead, that somebody had killed her, but then she moved a hand as I ran across the garden to her.

'Wanted,' she said. 'Oh fuck', and she waved her fingers as though she was trying to shake them off into a bed of weeds nearby. 'River. Wanted water. Swan river.'

I crouched beside her, all the excitement about Philip's manuscript gone. She was still wearing the Laura Ashley dress, muddied now, and saturated from the puddle she was half-sitting, half-lying in. Somehow she raised her hand again and got a grip on the lapel of my raincoat, pulling me down and closer.

There was no strength in the pull, but the grip in her fingers looked tight because they were white, drained of blood.

'Fucking Johan. Help me, Alice, will you? River. River will help. Water away Johan.' And more of the same, very disconnected, but terribly agitated. I think she wanted me to help her get to the river bank. Then she drifted off into mumbles that I couldn't follow, and I was able to prise her fingers off my coat.

I went into the kitchen. One of the stove elements was on, glowing bright red, and there was a terrible stench of vomit. My first thought was that I'd better get her into bed, so I went upstairs to see the lie of the land. Upstairs was a worse mess than down. Clothes all over the floor, no curtains anywhere, three bedrooms all equally in a shambles, and the largest of them almost indescribably awful. This must have been where she'd slept most recently. There were a lot of empty vodka bottles. When I turned back a filthy cover I found that the bed had been fouled, perhaps days ago. She'd been sick on the floor and on top of the bedside cabinet next to the door, but this must have been a while ago too because it was dry. There were flies everywhere.

I obviously couldn't bring her up here. Even lying in a puddle of rainwater she was better off where she was. So I took a couple of crumpled blankets and a cushion from a *chaise longue* under the window and went downstairs again. Beatrix was where I'd left her, and didn't look capable of going anywhere soon. I tried the phone, but of course it was disconnected, as she'd said. So I stretched a blanket out on a dry area of paving in a sunny corner and then, well, dragged Beatrix, since I couldn't lift her, on to the blanket. She was groaning like a wild animal, and kept saying something indistinguishable about 'him' – Johan presumably – and money, and Sim. I don't know. It was pathetic, but dreadful too, and some of the time I wanted to throw up myself. Once I'd got her there I rolled the blanket round her, then covered her with the second blanket, and put the cushion under her head. Then I wiped her face with a wet tea-cloth, and

164

while I was doing this she looked at me briefly, really looked, you know, quite suddenly focusing from whatever terrible dark place it was she had gone to, and croaked, 'Help me, Alice. Please. I don't want to be . . .' But before I could say anything even a bit reassuring, she had gone again, back into her raving coma. I honestly thought she was dying. I said I'd be back as soon as I could, but I don't think she heard.

I haven't run so far or so fast in a long time, but even so it must have taken me ten or fifteen minutes to get to Madame Jeanne. Thank God they were in. Micheline has a little Peugeot, and after ringing her hospital for an ambulance she drove her mother and me back to the house.

Micheline and Jeanne were just wonderful. No other word for it. Micheline went to work on Beatrix, taking her pulse, temperature, blood pressure; then cleaning her up, asking for hot water, sweet tea, a clean nightie or shirt 'if possible'. (It wasn't, but I found something usable.) I scurried about doing her bidding, glad not to have to take decisions. Madame Jeanne, meanwhile, went into the kitchen, and in the space of about ten minutes had cleared an area covering about a quarter of the room; disinfected it with mop and pail; cleared, cleaned and remade the couch; and been to the cellar to find bottled water which she put on the stove to boil. The three of us then managed to carry Beatrix in from the pavings to the couch, though she howled the whole way, making me shudder. It was so unearthly and awful. Once we'd got her there I said I'd fetch the tea.

'The tea's for you and Mum,' said Micheline, who had started rubbing Beatrix's hands and arms with tremendous speed. You could hear the friction. 'A little boiled water for her for dehydration, though she probably won't keep it down. Nothing else.'

I did as I was told, feeling foolish. You know how one does when a real professional's at work. You just realize instantly how little you know about some things that are fundamental, and how incompetent and dependent you are in a crisis. Micheline was just so admirable.

'Is she going to be all right?' I asked, though I was probably pretty hard to hear through the noises Beatrix was making.

'I hope so. But her pulse is irregular, her temperature is low, and her blood pressure is poor. Also she's in terrible pain, so there's an element of shock.' She was still rubbing like mad, and her mother had joined in, working on Beatrix's legs.

'What is it, though? Food poisoning? Drugs? Or just drink?'

'*Just* drink?' Micheline gave me a look that said, 'Where have you been?', or 'Where do you come from?', but then she tempered it with a smile and relaxed a bit, sitting back for a moment. 'I'm sorry. A little bit of stress. And I'm the one who's supposed to know how to stay calm.' She went back to her massaging. Beatrix had stopped howling, but was muttering incomprehensibly. 'I would say she has serious liver malfunction,' Micheline went on. 'Possibly pancreatitis. She's very distended here' – and she moved her hand, without touching, over Beatrix's belly – 'which is one sign. Another is the number of empty bottles in the fireplace over there. Sufficient to keep a regiment of the Russian army going for a while, I'd say. If I'm right, then, most of the chemistry governing her digestive and circulatory systems is in serious crisis. She needs an intravenous painkiller, a saline drip, a strong sedative, a lot of luck, and all our prayers for the next thirty-six hours or so. And I hope that ambulance gets here soon because at least they'll have the painkiller and the saline drip.' Then she redoubled her efforts at massage. A lot of this was definitely over-my-head French at the time, but I got it sorted out later when Madame Jeanne and I had a talk.

I felt even more helpless after this. I'd never even heard of pancreatitis. But I thought that if Beatrix was going to hospital, she'd need a few things, at least a toothbrush and a hairbrush. However, when I went upstairs again to look, it was quite hopeless. It was only then that I realized and fully grasped the extent of the appalling degradation of Beatrix's way of life. That this lively, talented, entertaining woman, who had seemed just a few years ago to have everything anyone could want, should have sunk to this . . . I took my tea and went out into the ruined garden and sat down on a mossy sundial that was standing at a crazy angle on the river bank. It was sunny, and I had a little cry. As with Micheline, the stress, I suppose. But also some more tears for Philip, whose manuscript I'd just read (though it seemed an age ago), and for myself because I'd lost him, because I loved him so much, and because when he died the light in my life went out. Yet I don't feel that I've ever been able to mourn for him properly. Does everyone feel this, do you think?

He came into my life, quite by accident really, and all of a sudden our stories were bound together. Do you know what I mean?

I might have become seriously maudlin here because the ambulance took an hour to reach us, but Micheline sent me up to the road to watch for it and guide it in when it came, and the act of doing something useful, if marginal, cleared away the clouds. And Beatrix did survive until the ambulance came, though she was pretty comatose by the time the paramedics got to work on her, and she was out completely once they'd given her a shot. I offered to go with her in the ambulance, but Micheline said that she had planned to drive back to Orléans in the afternoon anyway, and she'd follow the ambulance and make sure that Beatrix was checked in properly. In any case, there was nothing anybody would be able to do for a day or so. 'If she survives the night,' Micheline said, 'she'll probably be OK. But there's no medicine for this kind of thing. She'll have to change her way of life.' We agreed that I'd look in at the hospital first thing in the morning, just before she went on duty at eight o'clock, and she'd tell me how Beatrix was doing. She gave me directions on how to find it.

Then they were gone. Madame Jeanne and I walked back to the house together, not saying much. For some foolish reason I felt that Beatrix was my responsibility, and I tried to apologize for her, to say how grateful I was for everything that she and Micheline had done. Madame Jeanne was very matter-of-fact and told me not to be silly. We went into the kitchen and sat down for a little while at the table, and drank another cup of tea together while I got her to explain to me more slowly all the things that Micheline had been saying while we were at 'Favelas'. That photograph of Philip, the one I was telling you about, was still in the kitchen. I'd propped it up against the little box containing his ashes, and they were together on top of the dresser. I realized that Madame Jeanne must have seen it, and just for a moment I thought she was going to ask if this was my son. But instead, in a kind of roundabout way, being very careful – she really was thinking about my feelings – she asked about Philip, explaining that you had told her about me, and why I was coming here, and adding that she was very sorry. She was too. I could tell. 'It is terrible to lose a husband,' she said.

So I told her a bit about Philip, that he'd been a philosopher, and the work he'd done, and how he'd been killed in a stupid accident. And then she asked me something very interesting, something along the lines of 'Was he very difficult to live with?' I was surprised at this.

'Difficult? Why?'

'Philosophy,' she said. 'I know very little, really. I had to leave school when I was young, and I haven't studied much, or been anywhere in particular, but I always assumed that philosophy must be so difficult that the people who did it, who, what do we say?, think for a living, must be hard to be with. Is that him?' And she picked up the photograph.

'A long time ago. Before I knew him. I found it in one . . .'

And, do you know, she started to cry. Sitting there, as though I was her oldest friend and she had come to share my grief. Now that really *is* empathy. I went round the table and gave her a hug. She said she was sorry – you know how people do when they cry but think it's inappropriate – and said she supposed it was the strain of dealing with Madame Beatrix. And so we talked

168

about 'Favelas,' and the awful mess that some people make of their lives.

After a while, when she left, she turned to me at the door and said, 'You know, I have lived here in the Sologne all my life. People come and say it's boring. Nothing ever happens. But I believe in miracles.' So perhaps Beatrix will be all right.

But she had set me thinking about Philip once again.

Hard philosophical ideas never distressed him at all, never made him 'difficult' in the way Madame Jeanne probably meant. It was 'pop sociology' of the Sunday colour-supplement sort that used to upset him far more, just about as much as 'recalcitrant objects,' in fact. He particularly despised assertions about twentieth-century originality: an age unlike any other; a world remade by science and rationality; a time of intellectual, technological and medical progress and innovation that was enabling us to slip the noose of history and necessity. That sort of stuff. I remember his laughter over something he had read by Anthony Burgess, that the story of the twentieth century resided in its three major discoveries: the human unconscious, the possibility of extra-terrestrial colonization, and the salvation of human society through world socialism. He took to calling Burgess 'Poppycock,' and used to ask Amelia Righoffer (that colleague of yours – the one who writes about literature in pre-Columbian Latin America) to invite Burgess to a guest night at the Court 'so we can have some fun'.

What Philip thought was that the twentieth century was really a dull age, living and feeding off its nineteenth-century inheritance, and, like a playboy beneficiary of a surprise will, spending its inheritance profligately on wars, techno-baubles, psychoanalytic chicanery, and all the temporary pleasures of sensationalism. Its very excitements made it vapid and unoriginal.

He believed that our age was really being made by the traditional forces of religion, power and art. But for us, the religion was Darwinism, the power economics, and the art – unnoticed

169

in the firework displays of the debased culture of satellites, sport, celluloid and sex – the long, unfinished traditions of literature, music, painting and architecture. No one could escape these forces. They shaped us, then held us in their grip.

This sort of thing must make him sound intolerant, but actually he was a very tolerant person – at least, he was tolerant of the weaknesses and misjudgements of ordinary people, with whom he sympathized. I think this was because he believed that they were trapped, and could see no way out. The people whom he despised were the intellectuals who, in his terms, had sold out to contemporary nonsense. And chief among these were the prophets of post-modernism. He detested post-modernism in every form, from music to psychoanalysis. We heard something truly ghastly at a piano recital once – one of those concerts where that Italian pianist Panini plays only contemporary music, and sort of beats up the piano as he goes along. Philip said afterwards that it had all the intellectual content of the score to *Valley of the Dolls*, only without the music.

Philip could be very funny about this sort of thing because he had the twin gifts of irony and mimicry. He used to do deadly imitations of Amelia R. 'The post-modern world is beyond belief if you'll allow, as you must, the pun, don't you think, Philip?' And he'd have that curly Canadian accent of hers off to a tee. 'We're all recursives now. Symbiosis of thought, and its immediate negation in the active imagination, make commitment impossible. All loyalty is disloyal. All honesty untrue. We live by the word, and the word divorces us from itself, makes us castaways. It accounts for our all feeling marooned, don't you agree, Philip?'

Sometimes, when we had Moser to dinner, if he was feeling a bit down, he'd beg Philip to 'do Righoffer'. 'Just give me thirty seconds of Amelia, and then I'll go quietly.' 'There's no such thing as authority in criticism or justice,' Philip would respond. 'All views of the world are equally valid because we have at last learned what science has been trying to teach us, but has forgotten itself, that everything is created by the mind that perceives it, and so everything and nothing is true.'

Philip used to say that Amelia was deceiving herself, because if he had said to her that his own ideas, which completely repudiated theirs, were equally valid with Lacan or Foucault or de Man or whoever, she'd have been incensed. They were right. And he was wrong. At Christmas, a year or so ago, he sent her a copy, very beautifully packaged, of Martin Gilbert's book on the Holocaust. He marked various passages with little stickers, and invited her to let him know how and in what ways the various points of view expressed at these places were equally true or valid. Her only response was to thank him for his 'little joke'. Philip used to say that fanatics find it impossible to believe that those who disagree with them may be serious people. And of course this was exactly the sort of opinion that made him unpopular, or got him into trouble. Paradoxically, it also led to people saying about him that he wasn't tolerant, when of course it was he who was the tolerant one.

He made things worse for himself, however, because he couldn't resist a joke. He knew very well that what serious intellectuals of the round-spectacled, staring-eyed, postmodern-ist persuasion dislike most of all is to be made fun of. So he set out to do it. Did you ever hear his party piece about contemporary writers? He worked it up for me and Moser and Vita, but I know he did it once in the S CR at the Court and caused an awful stink. Perhaps you were there. It was set in an imaginary literary tavern he called 'The Best Cellar', supposedly located in a revolving room on the next-to-top level of a City skyscraper. 'A cellar on top of a skyscraper,' he would begin, in his Righoffer literary criticism voice, 'is a contradiction appropriate to the millennial imagination.' The Cellar was populated with thinly veiled portraits of successful best-selling writers and intellectuals, whom he would release 'like the hounds of the Scruton Hunt' into conversation. Some of this he didn't even have to invent, because these characters already live mainly in the pages of the

171

literary periodicals and the fashionable magazines, and he would just have strings of quotations 'to allow them to be funny about themselves'. Of course some of these characters were his college colleagues, whom he particularly enjoyed bating. The Best Cellar didn't just have writers, however. There were also barmen and waitresses who were the publishers, editors and agents, dispensing small favours to feed the vanity of the writers. The Cellar's owners made all the money, but no one knew who they were because they had forsaken the earth, and lived entirely in aeroplanes. One floor up, right at the top of the skyscraper, was the 'Studio Restaurant and Grill' where the film-makers went, and where all the writers secretly longed to be. Once in a while a film magnate would go slumming in the Best Cellar, allow the writers to buy him or her a drink, and then lure one or two of them back to the Grill, where they would be abused and robbed of their talent. The writers so afflicted would enjoy this. And so on.

I think *The Greatest Sorrow* is a sort of tragic counterpart to the extended joke of the Best Cellar. Though it reads like a documentary, it is really a novel. Even though some of us are apparently in it, it's a work of the imagination, and not a non-fiction document. Some details in it are simply wrong, like his muddled description of my sisters. And many aspects of it are really private jokes: like Philip's calling Blount Bros 'Scorpion'. 'Ah, the venomous arachnid of finance capital,' he used to say.

And of course Gradle doesn't exist. I think there may have been a Gradle at his grammar school, a boy with a reputation for being nosey, or a know-all, or a crawler, or something. Philip used to use the word to name people whose attitude he didn't like. He knew a lot of Gradles.

But I can't go on. I'm dog-tired, and I'll have to make a very early start tomorrow. Micheline rang an hour or so ago with the detailed arrangements. I'll just gather all this together now and sort it out. My bits have got so mixed up with Philip's. Then after I've been in to the hospital and seen how Beatrix is,

I can go on to Orléans, photocopy 'The Portrait', and then mail it off to you along with this, what is it?, letter?, account rendered?, imitation journal *à la Philip*? Well, at least it's got your *Chronicle* piece off my plate. Air freight, I think. Philip's too important to entrust to mere mail, and of course I'm dying to find out what you think of the MS. Dear Felix, it comes with my love and heartfelt thanks. A.

2

The Worst Five Weeks

The infamous gaudy was on the evening of the last Thursday of Michaelmas term, just five days after Moser died. Philip's behaviour at it, from the various accounts that I subsequently heard and read, including his own less than complete confession in *The Greatest Sorrow*, was clearly little short of appalling. Knowing this, I should hardly have been surprised that the immediate aftermath was unpleasant. Philip was completely out of things, of course. Felix told me that he thought Philip had drunk the better part of three, perhaps four, bottles of wine, so there was nothing to be done with him but get him to bed. He slept for a long time, woke up with a dreadful hangover, came down for tea in the morning, and then went back to bed with the aspirins. He didn't have much to say for himself.

Meanwhile the phone was ringing. Felix was first, asking after Philip, and giving advance warning of what might follow: 'various disagreeable stews on the hob'. In the circumstances, this was very helpful. I thought of putting on the answering machine and just going to earth, but it reminded me too much of disgraced politicians, so I decided against. Better to start the way we intended to go on. And anyway, the college was bound to want some cooperation, and Philip would have to face the music at some stage.

Sir Philip was next to ring. He gave me a fairly full catalogue of the bad news, beginning with 'an edited version, for your ears only', of what Philip had actually done at the gaudy. Rudeness as only Philip knew how; lack of hospitality; drunkenness; fighting. Apparently Jesty wanted a prosecution for assault, and said he was going to lay charges. Campbell-Quaid and that awful man Preggett, the minister, were less enthusiastic about criminal charges ('though they have perhaps at least as much justification as Jesty', according to Sir Philip), mainly, I think, because Preggett already had enough troubles in the public eye, what with divorcing his wife, being a bit too close to Aitken, that sort of thing, and with the election coming on would rather let matters drop. Both of them, though, were breathing fire about the difficulties they might cause in other ways. Righoffer thought the college should expect Philip's resignation out of solidarity with someone called Dr Spekeleiner, whom Philip had insulted. Monica Summerton, that screech owl of a junior minister who's since lost her seat, wanted a formal, written apology from governing body and a new evening gown. Actually almost everybody wanted an apology. And now the press had got wind of things, and already been on the phone. Sir Philip said he 'would hold the line' as best he could, but 'damage limitation was the best we might hope for at this early stage'. He asked me 'to keep Philip in the background as far as possible'. He would call again later.

Then there were calls from the *Guardian*, the *Sun*, the *Mail*, the *Telegraph*, and three of Philip's colleagues, one hostile, one perplexed and one gleeful: Hosking in Social Admin. 'Marvellous,' he said. 'Marvellous, marvellous, marvellous. Couldn't have been done in a more deserving cause. Marvellous. We're all delighted.' And more of the same. The *Telegraph* were the worst because someone, and they wouldn't name their source, had given them an 'exclusive' account of what happened, and they kept pressing me for corroboration or denial. Daft stuff, though. We get courses on media handling at the bank, and eventually they tired of my stonewalling. After that, Hugo Rawlinson, the chairman of Blount Bros, rang, but in this instance wearing one of his other hats – loyal adviser to Harcourt College. He was kindness itself, and told me not to worry. He'd been at the gaudy, seen most of what happened, and was staying on in college for a day or two to lend a hand. 'See if we can't tidy matters up, mmm?' In his view, the best thing was for Philip and me to stay in the wings. Also, had I ever heard of a chap called Peter Khan? Dr Peter Khan. 'A wise man.' Which I hadn't.

Sir Philip rang back at midday to say that he thought matters 'might be rather clearer', and that he hoped to have at least 'solution headings' in an hour or two. In the meantime, did I think I could get Philip into some sort of therapy? 'If he was in counselling, it would help,' he said. 'And everyone is conscious of what a blow to him Moser's death has been. There are grounds in this sort of thing.' Rawlinson came on the line and mentioned Khan again. He'd talked to him, he said, and Khan thought I might drop round and see him about coming to an arrangement for Philip.

Philip turned up in the kitchen at this point, looking regretful and very seedy. He didn't want to talk, he said. I gave him a boiled egg, and went off to see Dr Kahn. This was useful. He'd already heard from Hugo Rawlinson – 'an old friend' – and sat me down opposite him at his desk. I was impressed with his manner straight away: thoughtful, non-judgemental. He even seemed actually to be listening to what I said, something I've rarely encountered in the British medical professions. He said he was generally happy to help University people, and from what little he'd heard he imagined that Dr Leroux was suffering rather badly, and was certainly in need of help. I was relieved to hear this. Everyone else was so aggrieved, so full of the wrongs that had been done to them, the suffering *they* had undergone. And God knows, I knew what it could be like. I lived with Philip, after all. But here at last was someone whose automatic reaction was that Philip was ill, and that, as with any acute illness, he was probably in pain – fearful and suffering. He would see Philip today, this evening, if that suited. I asked him if there was anything that I could do, but he just shrugged and gave me a smile that wasn't a smile. 'I know next to nothing at the moment, and without talking to your husband I couldn't offer an opinion, or advice. These things take time. But don't be discouraged. These sorts of events, the illnesses of which they're an expression, are really a lot more common than we perhaps realize. And they can be cured, or at any rate helped and mitigated until such time as they go away. So don't despair. We shall see.' Philip was to see him at 6.30 that evening. This was the meeting that Philip described in his journal the next day, and after which he stopped writing it. I've no idea why.

At home in Cranham Street I found Felix trying to get Philip to answer the door, so I let him in, and we met Philip coming down the stairs. He'd been in his study, writing. Felix was very nice, gentle and kind as always, but it was obvious that Philip didn't want him to stay, so he handed over the little parcel from Moser's rooms, wished us luck, and went on his way. Philip still wouldn't, or couldn't, talk, and shut himself in his study again until it was time to go and see Khan. I walked round with him, and left him there.

I don't know what I expected from Philip's first meeting with Khan, but what I got at first was one of his silences. He said nothing, and gave nothing away in his expression either. We had some supper at the small table in the living room, and he picked his way through a little food, looking dejected and defeated. When I cleared away the plates, he laid his head on his arms on the table. When I tried to comfort him, putting my arms round his shoulders and saying a few things about how the gaudy didn't matter, and it was Moser we must think about for a while, mourn him properly so that we could face things without him, and so on, Philip just remained as he was, head down, unmoving and unresponsive. I felt as if I might as well not have been there. I went to clear up the kitchen, and when I came back Philip had gone. I found him in his study, looking through his CD collection and muttering to himself, just names, I think – Turgenev, Brahms, something like Viek, Joachim – not much else. Philip had always been an intense person. Now he seemed to be turning into someone else, someone strange to me.

So began one of the worst parts – if not *the* worst part – of a terrible time. Philip was inconsolable. He retreated into an inner world that was far away, and impossible to reach. I didn't even know where he was emotionally, most of the time. He slept very little, and ate very little, and did very little. A deep inertia had set in, and it was as if he was locked inside it, impenetrable. I found this rather frightening. Sometimes I would discover him just looking at me, when I woke up for instance, or perhaps when I was busy with something in my study or in the kitchen. I'd look up to find him standing in the doorway, or propped up in bed beside me on his elbow, just watching, unblinking and unmoving. It wasn't staring exactly. It was a troubled and deeply troubling gaze that seemed to linger, and then pass right through. I thought it was creepy.

'Why are you looking at me like that?'

'I'm trying to understand you.'

'There's nothing to understand. It's just me.'

And he would give a little wry smile, as if to say that there were so many complicated things encompassed in my 'nothing to understand' that it didn't make sense for him even to begin to explain.

'Tell me, Philip,' I'd say, imploring really. But he'd just pull a face, shake his head, and turn away. This was what was so frightening. Was he going mad? Later, when I'd read more, I also found these scenes menacing. There was so much pent-up energy in Philip's remoteness, and so much irrationality in his jealousy, that I began to wonder whether he was still the person I had once known, the man I'd fallen in love with.

On the Monday there was Moser's funeral. Philip saw Peter Kahn in the morning, and was calm enough when we went to the crematorium at two o'clock. It was a horrible day, cold and bleak, everywhere awash in slush, the surviving snow dirty, the wind chilling. Philip didn't want to have to talk to anybody, so we deliberately arrived last. Felix had kept us a couple of seats at the back. There were a lot of people, the chapel place packed, more standing outside. Philip sat with his hands clenched in front of him and shivered continually. Just as things were about to start, there was a commotion, which I didn't understand at the time, though I think Philip may have done because he knew some of the people who were involved. Anyway, it turned out that Moser's older brother, who normally didn't have anything to do with the family at all, had turned up unexpectedly and was demanding to be allowed to conduct the service. Apparently he was some sort of a religious person, though Philip didn't think he had ever been ordained, and he was claiming that Moser – Ger, he kept calling him – wanted him 'to say the obsequies and beseech for his soul'. Moser's sister, Belinda, who was sitting in the front with Sir Philip, tried to get her brother to sit and be quiet, and a rather unpleasant squabble broke out in which the brother, whose name turned out to be Arthur, and who was very stubborn, made a number of unpleasant references that caused the disturbance to spread across several rows of seats. Eventually Kirkup, the Dean, and one of the physicists, Donald Povey, who's actually a devout Christian, and would have been very upset by this sort of thing, pulled the chap aside, and said or did enough to silence him.

Once under way the proceedings didn't last long – perhaps forty minutes or so. Some of it was a bit banal, and I felt Philip stiffen at one point when someone was spilling platitudes about Moser's popularity. But when there was some music – one of Vita's recordings of some pieces by Debussy – Philip at last let go, bowed his head, and cried very quietly on to his hands. Afterwards he wanted to get away immediately, so we didn't talk to anyone, and when we got home he went into his study and shut the door.

In the evening I tried to get him to talk, and I succeeded. But in a way, certainly so at the time, I wish I hadn't. I thought it would be good for him to talk about Moser, to empty out some of the grief that he was feeling. Well, that we both were, actually. Perhaps one way to achieve this was in the context of his sessions of therapy. So when he came through to the kitchen just before dinner, I asked him whether he'd talked to Peter Kahn about Moser.

'Why do you ask?'

'Well, I suppose I thought it might be a good idea if you did. Talk to someone. I . . .'

'I don't think this is fair,' he said, glowering. And then he really started in on me. I can't begin to remember what he said exactly, it was such a nightmare, but the words flowed from him, gushed from him. He'd been cast, he said. He was officially now a depressive, labelled and pinned, part of the socio-medical taxonomy. Not ordinary any more, not normal, not even just talented, or bright, or even – God forbid – a philosopher, but a patient, named and numbered bi-modal 2. Perhaps he was even a bi-modal 1. That hadn't been decided yet. It was sometimes difficult to isolate each family within a species, but the experts were working on it, and soon they'd have him tucked neatly away in his category. Did I even begin to understand, to grasp, to imagine, let alone fully comprehend, what a catastrophe this was for him? What it meant? Then he would tell me. It amounted to total defeat. Capitulation. Unconditional surrender. All his life he had struggled with this or that problem, necessity, require-ments of one kind or another, the need to do this, fulfil that, complete the other. Such freedom as he had, he had secured by will-power. Now his will-power was exhausted. He was crushed. And the scale of his fall could be measured by the fact that he was now in the hands of 'a shrink'.

'You shouldn't call Dr Kahn . . .'

'Me! Me, of all people! I know, I know, I know' – raising a finger – 'I mustn't be sceptical. No bringing to bear on another man's discipline the same standards of inference, argument and proof we require of our own. And anyway, I agreed to go. I'm part of the decision. And I'll keep my promise. I'll play my part. But just give me this last little bit of my self-respect and indepen-dence by not now also wanting to be in the consulting room with me and Kahn, to know what happens between us, what I say, what we talk about, whether he's got the first idea which way is up. This may be the last place left to me. I didn't choose it. I still don't really want it. But, even so, you want to know what's happening there. Well, I'll tell you this. I don't lie on his bloody couch. I sit in a chair.' He stopped here, breathing heavily. For some reason I remember his breathing very clearly. Then he added, very quietly, 'And it isn't fair.'

I don't know that Philip was angry exactly when he said all this. But he was very forceful, and left me feeling demolished. I was only trying to help, and it had never occurred to me to want to know what he was doing with Kahn, or what he was saying to him, or asking of him. I suppose I assumed that he was doing what people are expected to do when they see a psychiatrist: talking about his childhood, his parents, his relationships.

'I just thought it might help to talk about Moser.'

'What is there to say? He's dead.'

'But he was your friend. He . . .'

'Just stop, Alice. Please just stop. Stop. I can't talk about it. I can't bear it.' And he put his head down on his arms at the kitchen table and shut his eyes, still breathing heavily, trembling and shuddering occasionally. I tried to put my arms around him, but he didn't respond. It was as if, with his words, he had shoved me outside, and then blotted me out by closing himself up entirely.

They say that when you live with someone who is ill like this you should carry on as normal. Be cheerful, stay on top, keep the world in focus. In this way you encourage the patient to come back to reality himself. This advice is far easier to give than it is to take, especially when the view of reality, like Philip's, seems potentially explosive. There were times when I began to think that I needed psychiatric help myself.

Over the next two weeks he seemed to spend more and more time with his head in his arms. Did it bring him relief, or was it just an expression of his despair? I don't know. But, paradoxically, one effect of his outburst about Kahn was that it did, eventually, seem to break the logjam of his silence, and he did start, slowly at first, but progressively over the ensuing ten days, to communicate more. Perhaps it was just the result of talking *to* Kahn rather than *about* him. But at any rate he did become a bit more communicative, and started to talk: about his childhood and the very first things that he remembered; about his parents and their treatment of him, as well as their relationship with each other; about school teachers and various incidents – many of them funny in a convoluted sort of way, though generally accompanied by Philip's disclaimers: 'Always assuming that that's what it was really like', and 'These sorts of things are cobbled together out of shreds and fag-ends of memory, some of them not even mine, so it's hard to take them seriously', and 'Even if that's how I remember it, it may not be true', and 'There's no centre to anything any more.'

This development – his talking again – gave me some hope. He was seeing Kahn four times a week, and after his fourth or fifth session Kahn started him on an antidepressant. This certainly helped him to get some sleep, but he would wake up shaking violently, as though having spasms in the arms and legs, and he complained that the drug left him feeling stunned and slow-witted, 'like a mild – if that's possible – state of catatonia'. But its most obvious effect from my point of view, and Philip agreed with this, because we talked about it, was that it seemed to return him, in however limited a sense, to the real world of other people and their concerns.

This was just as well, because I still had my own life to lead, including my job, which brings with it the sort of work that is seldom easy, even when you have a secure and happy home life to get back to at the end of the day. I think Hugo Rawlinson sensed this. That first weekend after the gaudy he rang me several times 'just to keep in touch'. He confided to me that his wife had been through one of these 'episodes', as he called it, when their third and last child, a daughter, left home to go up to university. He understood the strain of living with, and trying to help, someone who at least initially, and for a while, seems impossible to help, has given way to the egotism of suffering, and is somehow out of reach. He didn't want to interfere, but he had had an idea that might help to make a practical contribution. As part of repositioning Blount Bros in the emerging global economy, the bank was providing more and more financial services for governments and government agencies –

particularly in the developing world and the former Soviet Union, where they were a bit short on these sorts of skills. Everywhere he went in the world – and Hugo travels an enormous amount – he kept coming across something called, he thought, social choice theory, which seemed to be influencing the way governments decided on policy. He wanted to know more. What was it? Did it make sense? He was a pragmatist himself, bankers had to be, and was suspicious of people who thought to govern any institution – from tennis club to government – according to theory. But this one seemed to be everywhere, Chicago to Osaka, and he wanted to know about it. Why didn't I take a month or so off from the office and write him a paper on the subject? Tell him what to think.

'What about the research department? Won't they . . .?'

'Oh don't worry about Bissett and his merry men. Estimable fellows in their way, but I need something I can digest without Greek mathematics. No doubt we need those sorts of people, no doubt at all, but on public policy they're about as interesting as a milk churn. What do you say?'

So of course I agreed, though I knew he was really just throwing me a lifeline. If it hadn't been for Philip's illness, it's not something Hugo would have asked me to do.

'Is it an illness?' Philip asked me.

'Yes, it is. And you *will* get better.' But he ignored the second part of this, shaking his head.

'I think it's who I am. I hate this, turning personality into pathology, manipulating who people are for the sake of social tranquillity. I have always been like this, it's me. Oh I know, previously I could get myself "under control", as we so nicely put it, whereas now I don't want to, or not all that much, at any rate. But no one bothers to ask why that is. Why am I more prepared to let myself show, to be who I really am? I'll tell you. It's because most of the time I don't really believe in this illness stuff. I have terrible thoughts and fantasies, accusations to make, and suspicions too. But there's nothing intrinsically wrong with them. Many of them are not nice, but then much of life, from Bosnia to Cambodia via Treblinka, Tasmania and Armenia, is not nice. Like everyone else I assume that people, even those close to me, among whom I count myself, are untruthful, not just in the sense that they tell lies, but also in pretending to values and beliefs that they do not have, and emotions that they do not feel. I know that this is normal, so it's hard to understand why the act of pointing it out should be symptomatic of illness. It's no more than what everyone thinks, but doesn't dare to say. It's the psychological equivalent of people who blow the whistle on corruption in large institutions. They are the first to suffer, and are never rewarded.'

And he went on to say something very interesting about the gaudy. I can't quote his exact words because I can't now remember them, but basically he agreed that he'd behaved badly, and done some terrible things that he now regretted. But the fact was, he said, the occasion was fatuous, the participants posturing ninnies or hypocrites. He didn't feel guilty about them. What he did feel guilty about was the one thing that everybody who heard it remarked on, afterwards, as evidence of his decency: a few observations that he had made by way of a speech, during dessert, in farewell of Maurice Singleton, the Bursar, who was about to retire. Philip said that he made these remarks, and proposed a toast, when he had actually been thinking about something else altogether, and that he'd done it to conceal the turmoil of his real feelings. He said he thought that most civility was probably like this: hypocrisy and insincerity to conceal the self in some way. And now he was feeling great remorse about it, and would be tempted to go to Maurice and apologize if it weren't for the fact that saying something along the lines of, 'Look, Maurice, I'm sorry. I owe you an apology. All those things I said about a long and happy retirement and so on, well, I didn't mean them at all really, and I sincerely regret having said them', would only compound the offence. 'Almost all authentic acts are like this,' he said. 'They heap unkindness on to others from a misplaced desire for purity of the self. And this is itself usually a fantasy, a dramatic projection of the self on to a façade of the imagination.'

When I asked him if he thought, then, that all sincerity was possibly makeshift, perhaps untrue, he said he hadn't been talking about sincerity, though it was true that people often confused it with authenticity. But it was possible to make an inauthentic act in a quite sincere way, as with his toast to Maurice, or to do something authentic without any sincerity whatsoever. 'Most obviously, having sex with someone. But most politics are probably like this too.'

Once he had started on his SSRIs (there's a whole new nether world of books that I read about diseases of the mind, but it's not one I care to re-enter here) and the newspapers had stopped ringing up, things were a bit more normal. Only a bit, however. Some of Philip's problem – and it's hard to believe that I only really saw all the detail of this after I had read his journal – expressed itself in jealousy. But it was an odd sort of jealousy, and not something that I ever really understood. It was some sort of fundamental insecurity that stood apart from intellect and learning, and was untouched by his rational self, or even by cognitive things, like what he knew and believed about the rest of the world. It flew right in the face of just about all his other aspects. For instance, Philip was one of the very few men I've known, perhaps the only one, who really, genuinely believed in equality for women. One of his quips used to be that the only sure proof of equality in the workplace would be when there were as many incompetent and stupid women in positions of power and authority as there were men. And, without liking the implications of this all that much – typical Leroux scepticism about people – I think he was right. Yet, despite this commitment, he somehow couldn't accept my love for him for what it was, and tormented both himself (mainly) and me (second) with anxieties about infidelity.

In part this was mixed up with his dislike and mistrust of men in general. Philip really didn't like men much at all. 'Rough, hard, smelly and violent,' he used to say. 'When not just corrupt.' He couldn't understand what any woman found attractive, let alone enticing, in any man. 'They, we, are so profoundly unattractive.' Then he'd ask me what I thought. Are men attractive? Which ones? What makes a man attractive? Why?

I always found these questions nearly impossible to answer. Apart from a few utterly trivial preferences that presumably differ from one woman to another – height, slim hips, eye colour – the only things that I could think of were intelligence and a sense of humour. It's very important for a woman that a man can make her laugh. These qualities sound so inconsequential that it's hard to imagine why people do become so intimately and often permanently involved, even enthralled, with each other. Philip said that if that's all it took, then women would do better to listen to the radio. 'Plenty of blokes there to make you laugh, and no danger of anything worse.' He developed a theory that what actually happened to a woman when she fell for a man was stimulated by a chemical secretion in the brain, and that this biochemical event was to the world of practical social life what the cusp was in catastrophe theory. I think he had been greatly influenced by Michael Thompson's wonderful book, *Rubbish Theory*, which he often talked about. A woman could know a man for weeks, months, years, any length of time, without feeling the slightest desire for sexual intimacy, and then suddenly, perhaps even against all her other and surely better instincts, it would become the single most important objective in her life, and 'zap, or pow, or, as I prefer it, splat,' he would say, she was taking him to her bed. Men knew this by instinct, he would add, and so always kept an eye open. He didn't believe that men had any real sense of morality at all, and thought that, unless inhibited by institutions, they were inclined to help themselves to whatever came along.

This would have been all very well, so to speak – how easily, thinking about him, I fall into his syntax! – if it hadn't been for the fear that these generalities were specifically directed at me. And I think he truly was tormented by this. When I was away on business sometimes – not always: the occasions seemed to be quite arbitrary – he would live in agonies of jealous fear. And these jealousies were a significant part of these worst five weeks of my life.

Somehow he had formed the idea that I was having an affair with Alan Pendry, a colleague with whom I have to travel from time to time. Alan is a nice man, and it's true that I like him far more than I like most of my male colleagues. He comes from Australia but, apart from the usual chauvinism about sport, is quite unlike the ocker image that his compatriots enjoy promoting. No MCP strutting. None of that 'Pauline Hanson's only saying what most white Australians think' stuff. (Actually, he told me that what characterizes her supporters is that they don't think at all.) Travelling with him for work is a pleasure because he respects other people's space, their silences as well as their opinions, their need for independence as well as occasional help. If we have to work late on a report or something, he always manages to rustle up some coffee just when you need it. He invariably travels with a portable CD player and a little pair of speakers, and it can be bliss sometimes, after a day dragging yourself round a tropical coffee plantation, or ferry- and taxi-jumping in Hong Kong, just to kick off your shoes, shut your eyes, and bathe in the sounds of Joan Sutherland.

Alan used to be the bank's point man on show business, sport and popular entertainment, and he managed a number of big takeovers in the film and music industries a few years ago. But when this area started to grow very rapidly in the early 90s he asked for a change, and came to join the Economic Development Projects Bureau. To be honest, I don't think he much liked the new hot-shot 'players' – as they *will* call themselves – who were being brought in on the leisure and entertainment side, and anyway he was thinking of going back to Sydney in a few years, and believed that some Third World experience would stand him in better stead for the move. Merchant banking is a bit like the intelligence service. We don't like to say it too explicitly, but espionage is part of what we do. 'The top end of the information industry,' Hugo says. We keep an eye on people, collect information about them and their businesses, keep records of who's rising, what's selling, which companies are badly managed, or too highly geared, or not doing enough risk analysis. We try to know about the economic environment as well, but to be truthful we're not as good at that as we perhaps ought to be. What we're really good at is knowing about personalities. If a merchant banker tells you he'll find out about something, well he probably will, at least a bit. But if he promises to find out about some*one*, then he certainly will, and probably more than you thought possible.

Perhaps all this is irrelevant, but the point is that when you work very closely with someone in this sort of environment, where secrecy matters, and you have to share confidences about other people and their businesses, you come to know them rather well. Even so, I do perhaps know more about Alan and his life than is usual in a place like Blount Bros, and I think this did unnerve Philip quite a lot. Then something very important happened. It's difficult to know when to place it exactly because, although I found out about it during these awful weeks after the gaudy, it had actually occurred some time before – perhaps six months before – and was, I imagine, one cause, though unknown to me, of much that then unfolded.

We had had a pretty uncomfortable evening, I think exactly a week after the gaudy. Philip was gloomy and untalkative. For some reason he'd got into the practice of playing his CDs, chamber music mainly, in his study, very quietly, but with the door open. The sounds of this – his study was off the landing, halfway up the stairs – were never quite properly audible, but always and everywhere present like someone whispering, or singing or complaining or something, only at the other end of the

191

garden. Despite being indecipherable, the noise was detectable all over the house, so that it was irritating, and sometimes, when I was trying to work on my paper, pretty well intolerable. It was going when we had supper, and I asked him if we couldn't either turn it up or turn it off, or shut the study door. Anything rather than this uncertain sort of brushing sound. Philip wasn't very receptive, but eventually he went off to silence the machine, muttering about 'domestic tyranny' or some such, but in a tone of voice that implied a joke. When he did this you were never really sure whether he was genuinely fed up with you or not. However, he was pretty scratchy for the rest of the evening, and went to bed more gloomy than ever.

It was just about midnight, and I was on the point of coming to bed myself, actually in my nightie, when the phone rang and, like a fool, instead of pushing the answer button, I picked up the receiver. It was Alan calling from the other side of the world to tell me that he'd managed to sign up on the terms for a really big loan that we'd been working on together, on and off, for months. He was elated – one always gets a bit of a high at these times – and wanted to tell me about it. Perhaps I should have put him off and got into bed, but at the time I was so pleased to hear a friendly voice just being cheerful – it was so difficult and miserable with Philip – that I sank on to my dressing-table stool and just let him talk. I don't remember contributing much. Maybe that was a problem too, because when it was over, and Philip said, 'Who was that?', I realized that for some reason I was actually feeling guilty. 'Just a colleague about a loan.'

'Ah,' said Philip, sitting up in bed. 'Gradle number one, presumably. Funny time to ring. Does he like to catch you in your nightdress?'

'He's in Sydney. It's breakfast-time there. He just got in from Jakarta . . .'

'Lonely without you . . .'

'He did say he was sorry to call so late. And he sent you his regards. I do wish you could . . .'

'There's something I never told you.' This came like a stone through the window. 'Something about Gradle.'

'I do wish you wouldn't call him that. His name is Pendry, and I don't see why you can't call him Alan. It's his name, after all. And what is it?'

Philip went silent. In the half-light of the bedside lamps he looked desperately bleak, his eyes hollowed out to mere holes. He cleared his throat, and drew his knees up to his chin, his arms round the shins. I remember thinking how like the foetal position it was, a tiny physical echo of his need for security. Then he talked. But he wouldn't look at me as he did so.

'This happened quite a few months ago. July. You were away somewhere, Malaysia or Uzbekistan, I don't remember. You've been away so much this year. Some nice person at the bank – well, it was written on bank notepaper anyway – sent me an anonymous letter about you. About us. Red Biro. Spider's scrawl. It said, though not in so many words, that you and Gradle Pendry were having an affair. Embracing warmly in his office, up late making harmonious music together, holding hands in some park or other. Nasty too.'

'They what?'

'I'm serious. It happened. Never more so.'

'When was this? Where is it? Why didn't you tell me?' I was feeling so angry that for a moment I failed to notice Philip's misery. He had put his head down on his knees and was sobbing. I went and sat by him on the bed, and through his tears he talked.

'I didn't know what to do with it, about it, for a day or two. I was lost, I think. But I still had some of my rationality, my will-power, then, and I tried to be still, and to reason. If it, the letter, was untrue, then paying any attention to it at all was like giving it credence, handing a victory to malice. On the other hand, if it was true, and I brought it up with you, then you might just draw a deep breath and say something like: "I wouldn't ever have chosen for you to find out in this way, but yes, we do have a problem. What are we going to do about it?" And I realized that I couldn't face that. It took me to the brink, just thinking it. And after all, it was just possible that (a) it was true, and (b) it would pass, and, if I said and did nothing, (c) it would blow away altogether.'

And in the end that was the decision he took. He destroyed the letter and turned his back on it.

I can see him doing this. He used to have terrific strength of mind, even seemed sometimes to make things happen simply by concentrating on them. He could use whatever was to hand to distract himself from some desire, or to impose a discipline on his own behaviour, and this time, by his account, he did it through Herzen.

The poisonous letter came at a time when Philip had finished his research, and written the first half of the biography – up to the point where Herzen arrives in London in 1852. There were two parts still to write: the London years, and the final years from 1864 to the end of his life, when Herzen was back in continental Europe. It was the London years that were the problem. Philip felt that he had lost sympathy for his subject; was nervous at dealing with a time and a place already so well occupied by historians; and sensed himself inadequate for the task of combining the analysis of Herzen's writings with the contextual material that is essential to the description of a life. He was particularly uncertain about how to treat Herzen's affair with Natalie Ogarev – matrimony without marriage – and the betrayal of his oldest and closest friend Nicholas. 'Somewhere,' he said, 'amid the complicated geography of 1850s London, and the grammar of the Russian language – fully inflected, devious about time and number, with completion in place of perfection', Herzen was evading him. 'Ducking and weaving, a figure in flight across the no-man's land of historical biography.'

Philip said he had been in this state for two months, throughout Trinity term, and knew that he was in deep difficulty. He didn't usually suffer from writer's block, a concept that he didn't really understand. Occasionally he had what he called 'writer's reluctance', which was, he said, a product or consequence of implicit perfectionism. You didn't want to start writing because the act of committing some words to paper began the process of exclusion, whereby all the other possible words and phrases, the whole universe of lexical possibilities, were shut out, pushed aside into silence. This time things were different, however. Herzen had gone dry on him. Or him on Herzen. He was close to abandoning the project.

I realize now that it is almost impossible for me to understand the scale of the disaster that this represented for Philip. He had worked on Herzen for twelve years, perhaps a quarter of his working life. He had learned Russian specifically so that he could research and write this book. To give it up now would have been a terrible surrender to an only half-understood deficiency. The poisonous letter came just in time, because in a complicated way it gave Philip a compelling reason to return to his Herzen biography, and immerse himself in it. In fact, the expression he used was 'to wall' himself inside it. To shut out the rest of the world and to live elsewhere. He put aside moral scruple and intellectual fear, and tore back into the work, writing the last two parts, another ten chapters, over 80,000 words, in the three months of the summer.

I have to confess that I missed something here. I was terribly busy at work, having to travel a lot. Philip and I had already decided that we wouldn't take a summer holiday. Philip's working hard was not something new. On the surface, domestic life might well have appeared to be quite normal, or at any rate normal for us. In fact, and in retrospect, everything was different. Philip got up at five a.m. and came back to bed at midnight, barely able to sleep when he did. He wrote all morning and revised all afternoon, often missing out lunch. At night he worked on what he called 'the machinery' – footnotes, references, bibliography, the plan for an index. He was driven, and couldn't stop. When I read the manuscript later, in October, it was his finest writing – experimental and conservative together, the extended implementation of a radical view, not just of Alexander Herzen but of the business of biography. But the toll on him must have been terrible. He seemed fanatical sometimes, obsessed all of the time, sometimes surly and curt, but sometimes expressive of a, well, manic (it is the right word) joy. Also he was pretty filthy: his hair uncut, often not shaving for days on end. He didn't shower too often, and he wasn't eating enough, losing weight. His study was a nest of papers, filing boxes spewing their contents everywhere, every surface covered three, four, five deep in open books, journals, dictionaries, filing cards and dirty plates and mugs. No one was allowed in. Dust, balls of fluff, overflowing waste-paper baskets. It must have been a nightmare he was going through. Normally Philip was so tidy, his desk just so, pens in this drawer, reference books on that shelf, everything very neat.

The last was the worst. By September he had finished an advanced draft. In the few weeks remaining before term started he revised it completely twice, checked and reorganized the footnotes, and sent selected chapters to various people for comment. When this was done Michaelmas term was starting, and he flung himself back into college and teaching.

I don't think, I can't remember, that we made love at this time, throughout all these months. Not once. And the terrible thing is, or at least it is terrible to me now, that I have no recollection of its having mattered. Philip was a man on a mission, and I had let him go without even noticing. I am ashamed of it now.

Philip said – he was still sitting in bed, his legs drawn up to his chin, though the tears had dried on his cheeks – that he realized the very night that Moser died that it hadn't worked. He had written the book, and it was the best thing he had done, perhaps the best he could do. But it still wasn't good enough. And instead of saving him, it had destroyed him. He was only his will, and his will was now dead. He didn't know how to live like other people, naturally, ordinarily, just being himself, and being

196

accepted or rejected for what he was, because he didn't believe that he was anyone other than his acts, and his acts had all been acts of the will, and now he had none left. He said, 'I am dead, really. And so I have lost you after all.'

'You don't really believe it, do you? The stuff in the letter?'

He shrugged. 'Does it matter what I believe?'

'Of course it matters.'

But he didn't answer. He just lay back on the pillow and turned on his side. 'I hate Gradle,' he said. 'He is physically degenerate, intellectually dishonest and morally unsound.' But this was a quotation, or misquotation, from a film Philip had seen as a schoolboy, which he used to quote for fun, and which had become if not a joke then a familiar between us. Like 'I'm a gorilla. They're big, but good!', which came from the same film. Philip often joked like this when he was at his lowest. It was heartbreaking for me.

The days and nights after the revelation about the letter were terrible. Philip couldn't leave it alone, but he couldn't refer to it rationally either. Its accusations had become his, and the feelings of betrayal (or fear of betrayal) that he didn't want to have – and which he had used Herzen to exclude – could no longer be kept at bay. All this was made worse, as he said to me one evening, by the persistent thought 'in my calmer moments' that it would have been quite understandable if I had formed a relationship with someone else, given how badly he had behaved. Frankly, this was hard to disagree with. Yet even when I tried to console him about it, and to say that it didn't matter, that the past was over and there was nothing that either of us could do about it, only the future mattered, he just got more upset.

Partly, I think this may have had something to do with denial, or rather the lack of it. Mine, not his. I made up my mind, as soon as he started to tell me about the poisonous letter, that I wasn't going to be drawn into this. It was disgusting – and I have an idea who might have written it – and I wasn't going to allow it to dictate the course of events. I didn't have to answer it, and

I wasn't going to. Something – this wasn't a rational thing – told me that it wouldn't make any difference anyway. These sorts of things only turn into shoving contests. Did you? No. You'd tell me, wouldn't you? Of course I would. Then wasn't there something? I've already told you. But you haven't. That there wasn't. And so on. Back and forth, without resolution. This is, I think, because these sorts of things are not about events, or facts, or even, in the last analysis, about trust. Or not much anyway. Philip had simply lost all of his self-confidence, and he wasn't going to find it again by coaxing unnecessary assurances out of me. I loved him very much, and this was a test my love didn't have to take. Or pass. I put my foot down about this.

Slowly, over the next week or so, Philip became more distant. Perhaps I mean more strange. Or more of a stranger. I would hear him whispering in the night, though I could never make out whether he was talking to me or to himself, or to himself about me. Sometimes I thought I heard him speaking Alan's name. At other times I knew he was lying awake in the dark, silent and unmoving, breathing evenly as though he were asleep, but with his eyes wide open, and all of his senses alert. If I put an arm round him, he'd be unresponsive, then move slightly, in imitation of a sleeper being disturbed but without waking. When I woke in the morning I'd invariably find him facing me, on his side, staring at me, like an inquisitor trying to extract a confession by hypnosis. This was the worst thing of all, and always left me feeling afraid. Undermined and vulnerable. I badly needed someone I could talk to about it, and felt isolated and alone in Oxford.

He coupled this unnerving silent observation with a sort of progressive withdrawal, spending longer and longer hours in his study, sometimes talking on the phone (mainly to Felix, I think), sometimes reading to the sound of music from his CD player, and at least some of the time writing. This may sound normal enough, but it wasn't really. For one thing, his reading became quite undisciplined, which was most unusual for Philip. He wouldn't go into the Court or the Bodleian. Instead he took to using other libraries, the city one, and the humanities library at the Taylor, where he would go in the middle of the day, when the streets were crowded, buttoned up in his long overcoat, with a scarf wound round his mouth and chin and an old trilby pulled down on his forehead. The stacks of books he brought home ranged from volumes of nineteenth-century correspondence to textbooks on behavioural psychology, from aesthetics to geography, and from German nineteenth-century novels to technical manuals on singing. This was odd, but even odder was the feeling that I got that he wasn't really reading them. He was somehow just plunging into them, as though they were a pool in which he wanted to submerge himself. Also he kept changing them. No sooner was a load brought home than it was being returned. Back and forth he went to the library, carrying the books in an old Habitat carrier bag, returning one lot and bringing home another. In all the time that I had known him Philip was never a particularly fast reader. He was a dogged one. Something he started, he finished. So it was inconceivable that he could possibly have been reading all the books that he so earnestly fetched and carried every day. I may be wrong about this because Philip never really liked me going into his study, so it's hard to confirm, but on the few occasions when I did get a look in, because he'd left the door open, or I was calling him to lunch or something, he'd be surrounded by open books, little yellow sticky tabs poking out of them at all angles, and Philip in the middle of them all, scribbling in a big notebook. I asked him several times what he was up to, but 'just an idea I had', was all he would say in reply.

None of this seemed very healthy to me. I asked him if it was something Dr Kahn knew about, but at the sound of the name Philip turned on me with such a withering glare that I knew there was going to be nothing gained down that street. In its place I tried to coax him along by talking about my own work, the survey paper on social choice theory. 'The surveillance paper' is what Philip called it. 'A convenient way of keeping me under observation.' I tried to argue. 'It's all right,' he said, interrupting. 'Everyone's agreed, even me, that I'm sick. And you have to keep an eye on the sick. All the medical texts say so. I don't disagree. And anyway' – wan smile – 'it's nice to have you at home. We haven't done much of this, just living together, for a very long time.' This was true, and it was nice that he said it. But it was hard to know how much he meant it.

It was at about the same time as this exchange – perhaps even the same afternoon – that Mummy rang and suggested that we go to Suffolk for Christmas. She and Daddy had originally planned to stay in London, but talking it over the night before they had decided that country would be nicer, and after ringing Constance and Viola to see how they were placed, she thought it would be fun for us all to get together. There were one or two complications with Vi and a skiing trip, and the usual mutterings from Beastly Robin about 'the office', and *Bagehot's* not sleeping just because the West wanted to give itself indigestion, but apparently it was workable. I must say I felt a great surge of gratitude for this suggestion. Mummy and Daddy had read the bits in the newspapers about the gaudy, and rang up with offers of support and so on during the immediate aftermath, so I'd had to tell them at least something about Philip's condition and the subsequent events. His going to Kahn, etc. Mainly, I think I'd been able to leave them with the impression that Philip's difficulties arose pretty exclusively from Moser's death, that he was completely distraught and inconsolable about it, but that there seemed every chance that he'd be out of the wood pretty soon. Now they seemed to think that a family Christmas was just the kind of thing to get Philip back on an even keel, while also giving me a break. When I raised it with Philip he didn't seem to mind. He just gave a shrug of acquiescence, perhaps noticing how the idea had lifted my own spirits. After all, it was ages since Tanny, Vi and I had all been together, and although neither Philip nor I was particularly fond of the farm, there was fresh air, and walking, and my nieces and nephew, that almost tangible quietness of the countryside, and the chance to get Philip out of his study and into some company. He'd become such a recluse. We drove over on the Sunday before Christmas, and stayed for a week.

Clarke Hall – it was originally called Locke's Manor, but Daddy renamed it, for some reason, when he bought it in 1970 – is a few miles from Lavenham, lost (as Philip always said that *he* used to be) in a maze of tiny lanes off the Stambury road, and just outside the village of Benfield St George. We never lived there, even when I was a girl. Daddy ran it as a working farm for almost twenty years, putting in a manager, and taking advantage of efficiency gains and, after 1972 – which was what he really had in mind when he bought it, I think – Euro-subsidies. It had probably made him a lot of money. However, in 1988, when Mr Dyer bought a place of his own, Daddy sold him the stock, let the pasture to his neighbours, ploughed in the arable, and started to plant trees. He said he wanted a forest as a long-term investment and a park for his retirement – 'rather shorter!' He took to encouraging bird life and releasing butterflies. The farmhouse, parts of which were built by Huguenot refugees, and dated from 1685, had been considerably extended and rebuilt over the years: much enlarged in the late eighteenth century, scarred with embellishments in the 1880s, improved with electricity and monumental central heating in 1922, and then completely modernized and redecorated in 1979. Mummy put Philip and me in the turret room, which is green and restful, and has lovely views across the garden towards the river, which curls around us and is flanked, like a trail, seen from the turret, by coppices and clumps of hawthorn and blackberry. The tower gives the feeling of being a bit apart from the rest of the house, so with the exception of the rooks, which are noisy in the mornings, offers a sort of refuge.

For the first two days we were more or less on our own. Daddy had business in London and couldn't get away until Christmas

Eve; Tanny and Robin the same; and Vi had taken the girls skiing somewhere for a week, so they wouldn't arrive until Christmas morning. Mummy was there, of course, but terrifically busy with shopping and preparations. Mummy had always rather liked Philip. She used to ask him questions about philosophy – the moral sort mainly: what *should* one think about euthanasia? Are there *really* any good arguments for eating meat? That sort of thing – and when he was in a good mood Philip used to pull her leg, pretending that she was Scottish (she came from just outside Carlisle, and one grandparent was from Aberdeen). He introduced her to someone in Oxford once as 'indicative of a completely unanticipated social development, a Scotch intellectual renaissance'. They used to laugh together a lot. This time, however, she seemed wary of Philip, and looked for an opportunity, early on, to draw me aside for 'a good natter'.

I wasn't having any of this. One of Philip's great anxieties was that he might have become a subject of speculative talk; the sort of head-shaking, tut-tutting, 'what-is-the-matter-with-Leroux' type chat that's a staple of Oxford life. Perhaps any life. He knew he couldn't do it, but he would have liked to draw a blanket over the whole affair, making it, and him, invisible. The best thing for me to do was, I thought, to help in so far as I could, so that with the exception of Hugo Rawlinson and Felix, of course, I hadn't discussed Philip with anyone. And I certainly wasn't going to start with Mummy, whose idea of how to keep a secret is to share it with her twenty closest friends. This put a little bit of a wedge between us.

'He's been under a lot of strain, Mummy, but he's all right, really. Nothing that a bit of rest won't cure. And he'll get some sabbatical now, I shouldn't wonder, a term off, so I'm sure it'll all come right.' I knew this wasn't going to work. These are the sorts of comments that switch Mummy's antennae on, and have her, like a radar dish, sweeping the drawing-room horizons for remote intimations of trouble. Still, there was nothing to be done about that, and at least she'd put us in the turret, where we could be out of the way. For the first day or two Philip and Mummy, when they were together, which wasn't much, coexisted in a state of mild tension: silence occasionally punctuated by politenesses.

Philip didn't seem to mind, and initially gave every sign of being content. The first night he slept better, and on each of the first two days went out for long walks. This was unusual behaviour by Philip's standards, and drew 'Good to see Clarke's being put to good use' and 'You'll be needing your overcoat' type remarks from Mummy. Frankly, it was a bit unusual to see Philip 'making good use of Clarke's'. In the past he had always regarded it as a bit dull. He called Lavenham 'theme-park England', and said Suffolk as a whole was indicative of English middle-class values: 'a landscape of brown sherry and suet pudding'. You could always hear Moser in Philip when he talked about things through food.

'You should come in the summer,' Mummy said to him once, 'when all the flowers are out. The hay-making. The trees so green.'

'Oh, you mean in the rain,' said Philip. 'Constable, Adrian Bell, A. P. Hartley, Windsor soup and cold trifle.'

'Hartley is Norfolk, dear,' said Mummy.

Anyway, these two days were an oasis. Apart from a little present-shopping with Mummy, I was able to get on with my work, and when he wasn't out walking, Philip was deep in his books. I can't remember which, but he'd brought a cartonload over with us from Oxford. This went on until the Tuesday evening, Christmas Eve, when Tanny and Robin and their boy James, who's thirteen, arrived together with Daddy.

It's at times like this that I wish I could write. I mean, really write, like Philip, or like the women whose novels I enjoy when I get the time – Margaret Drabble, Isabel Allende, people like that – but I haven't got the talent. Philip said you just had to learn, and self-taught was the only way. It was a technical skill, and as with any other technical skill, you acquired it by work and self-discipline. Well, maybe. But it has always seemed like a talent to me. Just dropped on you, or given. And I don't have it. The writing skills that I do have are known in the banking, business and government circles where I work as 'drafting'. I've always been good at this. It consists mainly of making complicated but generally banal ideas comprehensible, come alive even, and it's a talent much sought after by the power-hungry, all those men who clamber to the top of institutions and pride themselves on their all-round skills. They can't 'draft' themselves – God forbid – but they need associates who do. This is one explanation for the glass ceiling. Women who are as good as men at everything else *and* who can prove it by drafting the documents, papers, reports, opinions, aide-mémoires, minutes, agreements, understandings, accords, all the paper paraphernalia of money, trade and transactions, never get promoted above the middle rank because their talents are too valuable for the men who do. And by a superbly ironic reversal, the very talents that these men exploit in women in order to get ahead then also serve as the subtle critical denigration that prevents women being promoted. 'Is she any good?' 'Well, she's very good at drafting.'

I expect Robin would call this drafting. Tanny's husband Robin, Robin David, is a senior editor – actually, one of the three deputy editors. They divide the world between them, and he's the Americas – on *Bagehot's*, the glossy weekly of economic analysis and current affairs which likes to think of, and present, itself as the cutting edge of liberal and rational intelligence in world affairs. And, in micro, Robin is *Bagehot's* on legs, a classic Manchester Liberal to the tips of his tiny pink fingers. He's a small man, smart and crisp, with the refreshing perkiness behind which small men sometimes conceal their envy. I have never really understood why Tanny took up with him, because although he has a quick intelligence, you never get the impression that it will be put to the service of anything more serious than self-advancement, or more important than the scheming which is a necessary part of it. At *Bagehot's* he's always called by his initials, R. D. Philip used to call him Laing, partly because of the initials, and partly because, as Philip used to say, 'he's a drunkard – though in his case the libation is power, not alcohol – and because of his tendency to corrupt through the alchemy of words, by which boring and untruthful things are made to seem enticing and right.'

I think this may have been how Tanny was drawn to him. He certainly knows he has this power – perhaps she's his proof of it – because he's smug in the same way that *Bagehot's* is smug, with that sort of manipulative charm which people sense perfectly well to be manipulative, but to which they nevertheless succumb. It's so self-assured, and it seems so clever. And it is never more evident than when he talks about economics. There is no morality superior to the market. No judgement better than the bottom line. No reference grander than wealth. If it is privately owned, it must be as good as it can be. If it's in the public sector, it must be inefficient, unproductive and corrupt. This outlook spills over into his politics. Mrs Thatcher's weakness was timidity. President Reagan's failings those of his advisers. On President Bush's involvement in Iran–Contra, he would quote a Supreme Court Justice, met at a Washington dinner: 'Oh' – wave of the hand, dismissing irrelevant testimony – 'you mean that little perjury thang.' Philip said, 'Too-clever-by-halfery is Robin's *modus vivendi*', and once asked him if he realized that *Bagehot's* might be in danger of losing its readership. 'After all, there's no issue left on which its "take" – as you say – can't be accurately predicted in advance. Instead of the mag, all we really need is a little card, like those ones restaurant-goers carry to tell them what to think of this or that wine vintage. Then when any issue comes up, say at a dinner party, I could snatch a quick look at my card and know what to say.'

Hardly surprisingly, Robin didn't much like Philip. But he didn't much mind him either, because on his check-list of liberal assumptions there's one that says you meet all kinds of people in life, and lots of them are losers. The important thing to remember is never to let losers run anything that really matters. Universities don't really matter, though, as he liked to point out to Philip: 'If we' – Robin always uses the plural personal pronoun. He assumes that other people agree, or soon will do, or, if they don't, will be made irrelevant by all the ones who do – 'could get them into the private sector, they'd be a damn sight better than they are now.'

Philip, who never did have a general theory about the nature of other people, or how to treat them, used once upon a time to regard Robin as a joke, and when he was in a good mood he would egg him on. But in recent years, as people like Robin have taken over the world, or at any rate have persuaded themselves that they have, the joke has faded. And its fading ('a symbol of certain truths', Philip called it) has coincided with Robin getting fat, so that he has gone from lean to tubby more or less in unison with the growth of stock markets, heads and egos. His fingers are still thin, though. 'It's a warning of some sort,' said Philip.

To tell the truth, I don't much like Robin either, and never found him either funny or amusing, even when he was being goaded into enormities by Philip. For one thing, he wouldn't notice, because he's too sure of himself, too cocky. 'It's worse than that,' Philip said. 'He's quite unprincipled, and with a theory to justify it.' But this was a bit too strong. Robin really has only half a theory, which is what makes him insecure, and which in turn accounts for his assertiveness and presumption. As with most opinion-givers, certainly on *Bagehot's*, his economics are thin. In fact, Robin has no training in economics at all, and has merely learned how to manipulate its vocabulary. This is the ideology of our day and age. '*Bagehot's* is the bugler for the legions of prejudice' is how Philip put it.

Having said which, Robin is Tanny's husband, which must mean something, because Tanny is a decent person – thoughtful and kind, with generous instincts and a mind of her own. Philip thought that perhaps Robin had been intelligent enough as a boy but had grown into the stupidity of expedience as he grew older – 'many people do' – and that he'd met Tanny before the worst of it had happened. Certainly when he was with the *Sunday Times*, though he could be painfully trendy, he wasn't a mindless born-again economist. Anyway, putting all that aside, Tanny never seems to be either tired or critical of him. 'It's the money,' Philip said, just before we went down to Christmas Eve dinner. 'Money's a terrific aphrodisiac.'

The whole dinner might have been a disaster. Philip was keeping himself on such a tremendously short leash that I could just about hear it creak. He had rung Kahn in the afternoon, and, though I don't know what they said, I do know that Philip was now taking the maximum dose of whatever antidepressant he was on (Zoloft?). With the wisdom of hindsight, it would have been better altogether if Philip had pleaded a headache and stayed in bed. Anyway, at first everything went off nicely enough. Carol singers came round for half an hour at seven o'clock; aperitifs in the library till eight; then dinner, with Tan and Daddy swapping London shopping stories, which was quite amusing. Tan can be nicely tart, and Daddy encourages her. The problems came when James, who's at the Brewster Academy in Dorset, said he'd got a project to do over the Christmas vacation, which was to find out why the Soviet Union had collapsed. Robin simply leaped into the space created by this opening, proprietor of both the answer and the boy.

'Communism doesn't work,' he said. 'That's the full answer.' Looking round the table, eyes finally settling on his wife. 'Not much of a project. Are you sure we shouldn't take him away from Brewster, Con?'

James looked crestfallen.

'I think it may also have had something to do with politics, religion and morality,' said Daddy, pursing his lips the way he does, and looking over the top of his spectacles at his grandson.

'Not much in that, I'm afraid, Dads,' said Robin. I could feel Philip squirm beside me. 'Popular view with politicians, priests, probably philosophers too' – quick grin at Philip – 'but useless as an analysis. Reds couldn't compete. That's it. Full stop. QED. The state's useless at picking winners. Once the US got tough after twerp Carter and said come on, then, compete, show us what you're made of, pouff, all-fall-down. Just a house of cards. End of story.'

James didn't seem to have understood much of this and was looking at his father with his mouth open. Tanny tousled his hair. 'Tell Mr Forster that your daddy swears this is the truth.'

Then Philip said, very quietly, and looking at James with a friendly smile, 'You could try mentioning Slav culture, and the weight of institutions and history. Historically the Russians have always had difficulty reconciling government institutions with cultural . . .'

'Pastry decoration,' said Robin, coming in over the top. An unfortunate habit. Philip's squirm stiffened, and I put my hand on his thigh. If he blew up now, Christmas might not happen at all. 'This chicken definitely preceded the egg,' Robin was saying. 'A few years of the fresh breezes of capitalism and you'll find the Russians have sloughed off their so-called historic problems and joined the rest of us having life instead of fantasies. They don't have a choice, you see. The reason they're still in a mess is because they think they do. But they don't. They'll have to come to their senses.'

'Also,' said Philip, trying hard to pretend that Robin's interruption hadn't happened, and failing fairly comprehensively in the attempt, 'also you might mention Willy Brandt's *Ostpolitik* as a counter to Cold War bullying; the futility of trying to establish an empire among disparate proud and intractable people such as Afghans and Poles; the geopolitical consequences of the Second World War, and . . .'

'Uncle Philip – I must tell you this, James,' said Robin, running a hand through his own fashionably well-cut, greying, curly hair as he did so, and grinning at the same time, 'uncle Philip doesn't live in the real world, like us. So he finds it hard . . .'

'Give me a hand with these, Philip, there's a love,' said Mummy, indicating the dirty plates that she'd stacked beside her, picking up the vegetable bowls, and heading for the kitchen.

' . . . to see the wood for the trees. The point about private enterprise is its discipline. It rewards and punishes for success or failure . . .'

Philip left the room.

' . . . and it's completely impartial. The hidden hand . . .'

'I think you'd better lay off, Rob,' said Tanny. 'It's Christmas Eve.'

'Is there a better time for the welcome truth?'

Philip didn't return to the table. Mummy covered for him by saying that he'd cut his hand rather badly, 'silly boy', and gone upstairs to find a plaster, and perhaps I'd better go and make sure he was all right. He hadn't, of course. Cut his hand, that is. He was in the tower, the lights off, looking through the windows into the blackness. I imagined him seething inside.

'I won't come down again tonight,' he said. 'I can't bear it. I'm sorry.'

I put my arms round him from behind, but he didn't respond. There was no answering pressure on my hands or wrists. 'But you see what I mean,' he said. 'I am right about people. But we're not allowed to say so, are we?' Later, it occurred to me that this was the moment when we started, finally, to lose him. But I'm not sure of this now.

The next morning things should have improved. Vi and Christopher were to arrive with Emma and Harriet, and Philip had always really liked Vi, who's musical. And he got on well with the girls – 'my sort of nieces', as he called them. Also, of course, it was Christmas Day, and there'd be presents after breakfast, and champagne before lunch, and a walk across the fields to Benfield St George before it got dark in the afternoon. I remember thinking, as I went down to make us some morning tea – pretty early because Philip had, I think, slept only briefly during the night – that if this was anything like previous occasions, then in the evening Daddy and Mummy would play board games with Emma and Harriet; Christopher and Vi, Tan and I would play bridge; Robin and James watch videos; and Philip read a book. A good distribution of simple things. With a log fire, quiet conversation, mince pies. These sorts of thoughts still gave me a warm, hugging-myself feeling.

But for some reason things never went well. And it started with the Christmas mail. In the two weeks before Christmas, Philip and I had both received a ton of letters and cards, but neither of us had opened them. Philip, shut in his study, or slumped at the table with me, had barely seemed to notice them. I decided fairly early on that it would be for the best to hold them back and get Philip away to more neutral territory before opening them. You know what people's end-of-year letters can be like. I remember once, after reading a particularly self-congratulatory one about brilliant successes of children, hugely enjoyable trouble-free holidays, incredibly fulfilling career moves, and sensitive appreciation of the nicer points of ageing parents, that Philip described them as 'the world according to Disney'. A fanciful report on the possibilities of the previous year, and not much to do with real life.

When I got back to bed with the tea, I pulled all this mass of mail out for us to read. And it all went wrong more or less right away. A thickish-looking white envelope addressed to me, in handwriting I didn't recognize, turned out to contain a card from Alan and his wife Valerie, along with a slim volume of poems by an Australian writer Alan had talked to me about once or twice. He had put a little inscription about friendship on the title page. Philip was reading some improbably long end-of-year letter of his own while I was opening this, but I sensed him noticing, watching, and my half-baked attempt to shove the thing aside, get it out of sight under the duvet or somewhere, only made things worse.

'Your faithful friend, I suppose,' said Philip.

So I passed him the card. 'You see, it's from Valerie too, and that must be her handwriting on the envelope because it's new to me' – which I realized immediately was probably a mistake. 'Unlike his,' I could almost hear him saying. He flicked through the book.

'"Where the scent of her still lies in the sand/Though dissipated since in rock/Pools, seaweed slime, and the hand/Maiden strokes of the sea." Very nice.' And he slapped it shut and gave it back to me. 'A memento?'

'Philip, it's Christmas. He's a colleague. It's a little gift. Can't you see it's harmless?'

'To whom?'

He was pretty white in the face, peaky and sharp, but after a moment of what may have been reflection, he went back to reading his letter. Actually there were several of these, long ones, mainly, I think, from his academic friends in various places – Stanford, Geneva, Paris – and he seemed absorbed, so best left alone. It's hard to tell now whether I should have done or said something more. But Philip was very quiet, and didn't refer to the book again. He seemed distracted about something else, so that it was as if the incident hadn't occurred, and in these sorts of situations I had long ago learned that it was best to let things lie. Later I tucked the book away in my briefcase, the Christmas card with it, and let it go. This was a mistake, I suppose, because Philip never forgot these things, really, and would brood on them, allowing them to sprout and shoot – the awful, colossal blossoming of his imagination. And the warning signs were there. His alienation from the family group, his sense of himself as isolated, the attractions – he had spoken of these since he started seeing Kahn – of darkness, blackness, what he called 'the security of oblivion'. He told me once, 'What people don't realize about depressive illness, perhaps because of its name, and the implication that it carries of sadness, is how deeply enjoyable it is. Perverse, of course, masochistic even, perhaps, but a wonderfully secure anchor in a supremely well-ordered world. No one who

211

has never been there can ever understand this. And I *mean* those negatives!'

I don't now believe that he could really have meant what he was saying about the enjoyment of depression. I have learned that it is terrible and tragic, and that Philip was desperate to find a way out. He clung to it partly because of its wicked internal logic, and partly because of the brain chemistry that sustained it. But it wasn't enjoyable: it was unavoidable in the same way that hell is unavoidable for the damned. And after the horrid incident with Beastly Robin the previous night, and now this, Philip just withdrew into it even further. He had next to nothing to say, and his descent into silence was easy to conceal amid the noisy chatter of family life on Christmas morning.

We dressed Philip's hand with a fake, or at any rate unnecessary, bandage, and went through the day's routines. Philip managed reasonably graceful expressions of gratitude for the customary presents. Mummy has an unfortunate, peculiar weakness for the most dismal line in Scottish tartan scarves, and Philip's collection of these woeful objects was duly increased by one. Philip said later that he would give it to his colleague Jesty as a New Year peace offering. 'He'll like it. It's his kind of style.' And I think he meant it too, because there was no humour in the way he spoke.

To be honest, as the day wore on, Philip just grew more and more preoccupied. He wasn't drinking because of the antidepressants, so that wasn't the problem. But he wasn't eating much either. His appetite had deserted him again, and he just picked at his food, keeping to himself. The joke in his cracker he gave to James to read for him. His paper hat soon went down on the floor. When we went for our walk, I took his arm and tried to talk to him, but he was monosyllabic, keeping his eyes on his feet.

'Is there something new the matter?' He shook his head, looking fearfully grim. 'Is there something I can do?' A tiny counterfeit smile, and another shake of the head. 'I want to help.'

'I've got help. I've had help. It's not in my control. Nothing ever has been. Everything's just a set of variations on a theme. My theme, your theme. There are various keys, major and minor; inversions and reversals; colour and tempo; phrasing and modulation; harmonic exploration; counterpoint, polyphony and atonality. All that. But the theme is always there, and it always returns to the foreground. Inescapable. It is who we are: who I am. Eventually, we come to recognize it. To know our fate, or destiny. I see this now. It's the present I've had for Christmas.'

Something like that, as best I remember. It was hard for me to understand. But then Philip often had been.

In the evening Vi and Christopher and the girls got out their instruments and played for us. First a setting for trio, that Vi had done, of one of Vivaldi's string concertos, which was very pretty. Vi is still a wonderful violinist. Though she gave up concert ambitions long ago, she plays a lot in various groups in London, and she has done wonders with the girls on viola and cello. Christopher, to be honest, isn't quite up to them at the piano, but he's the first to admit it, and he stressed it quite adamantly on Christmas night when introducing the other piece they played. 'We've been practising this for you for ages you see' – pushing his glasses up, adjusting the piano stool, squinting at the score – 'but with the girls all away last week we may be rusty, and also the piano part's a bit out of my class. Well, a lot actually. But anyway, here it is.' And they played Brahms's First Piano Quartet. I suppose it was a bit beyond him – 'A lot,' said Philip. 'Especially the Zingarese cadenza, which he wisely cut short' – but the others played beautifully, and I'm sure that Philip appreciated it, really. Near the start he had tears in his eyes.

Over the next two days, until Vi and Co. left on the Saturday, we had lots more music, Bach and Telemann, but Philip had gone back to his reading and scribbling, and seemed to have made a calculated and complete withdrawal.

We went home on the Sunday. Philip wouldn't drive. Along

the way I tried to prattle on as much as I could about this and that, my work – Hugo Rawlinson wanted the paper by 6 January, which is when I was to start back at the office – the family, and Philip's parents, whom we were to drop in on in London on the way through. Nothing touched him, however, and it was such hard work that in the end I was silent too. Nothing changed when we reached his parents. Doris had prepared tea for us. 'Tea like childhood,' said Philip, surveying a table loaded with cold ham and salad, beetroot and cucumber, tinned salmon and fresh celery stalks, fruit cake and jam tarts, mince pies and sponge cake. 'Cups of tea with everything. How nice. How nostalgic. Reminds me of welcomes when I was a schoolboy, coming home from France.'

'What a nice thought,' said Doris. 'Thank you, dear.'

Stanley chattered on about 'Major's lack of spark' – which surprised him, for some reason. Philip ate barely a mouthful, and slipped away after half an hour or so. Later I found him sitting on the bed in what used to be his bedroom, the yellow candlewick bedcover spreading like a commentary around him.

'Are you all right?'

'You're always asking me if I'm all right. Of course I'm not. That's been decided. The question is, how wrong am I?'

'I'm sorry.'

'Don't be. You see that wardrobe over there?' He nodded towards a big, tall, dark brown wooden thing that looked as though it might have come out of a Welsh manse. 'Looks impressive, doesn't it? Solid. Oak and all that.' He got up and went over to it, getting hold of the key that stuck out of the wardrobe lock. 'Well, it's not.' He gave a jerk, and the whole piece tilted towards him on its base, threatening to topple over, until he put up his hand and pushed it back, so that it rocked against the wall, and then swayed back and forth a few times on the carpet before settling to be still again. 'Its solidity is fake. It's made of balsa or some such. I always hated it. It's a metaphor, really.'

We left shortly after this. It was the last time he saw his parents. Or they him.

I thought he might pick up a bit the next day, when we were back in Oxford and he started seeing Kahn again. And so it seemed, for the few days until the New Year drifted by in apparently companionable peace. Frankly I was glad of this, given the state of my work. Then we spent New Year's Eve with Felix. Felix lives on his own in a house on Southmoor Road with a garden that backs on to the canal. Each year in the spring, a couple of swans return to build their nest at the bottom of his lawn on the canal bank, and he has had to put in a stout wire fence to keep them out of his vegetable patch and flower beds. He likes to say – I've no idea if it's true – that half a century ago Iris Murdoch used to live in this house, and would paddle up and down the canal in a canoe to visit her neighbours. One of these, at least for a while, was a peculiar writer called Julian Maclaren-Ross – himself apparently the original for some literary figure or the other in a famous novel of the period. Apparently Maclaren-Ross had formed an obsessive but hopeless passion for Sonja Orwell (the widow of George) and spent his days either in penning her rococo love letters in a tiny copperplate hand, or in sobbing out his romantic despair to anyone who would buy him a drink and listen to his monologue. 'Not many takers after a while,' said Felix.

'Julian' – Felix often speaks of public or quasi-public figures using their first names, as though he knows them personally. He has a small, high-pitched voice, with what used to be called a BBC accent (though it's actually how my parents and their circle talk) so that when he starts a sentence with a first name it takes on great emphasis – 'Julian has persuaded me – because I knew him slightly when I was a young man, though he's long since dead. He had a fatal heart attack from a surfeit of beef fat, to which he was addicted – Julian, or at least his reputation, has persuaded me that the world is ready for a new *Brief Lives*, and I have been at work on one.'

215

He slipped away to one of the numerous rooms that he uses as a study. His house is oddly constructed, each floor being half a floor with a short flight of stairs joining it to the next, and Felix has a study on each of the four half-floors. He does different things in each one. Tax, bills, personal correspondence in the basement. Eighteenth-century studies ground-floor back. Lectures, thesis supervision, pupils, examinations, first-floor front. Other scholarship, book reviewing, memoirs and poetry, top-floor back. *New Brief Lives* must have been top-floor back because he was some time away.

'Here,' he said, eventually returning to us – ground-floor front: his living room – 'this might add a bit more fizz to the champagne.' And then he read us two of his pieces, both of them hilarious and wonderful, and, in the nature of things, quite unbelievable yet absolutely true. One was about a professor of astrophysics in Gresham called Madgewycke whose wife, Carmen, was a well-known, perhaps even famous, expert on sexual matters. 'They had no children, but she published various books with agreeable titles, such as *Better Orgasm. A Handbook* and *Clitoral Amusements*. The marriage of star-gazer to sex guru provoked various Oxford jokes of a literary character. People would say, for instance,' Felix read, adjusting his bow tie and drawing on a cheroot, 'we all of us are looking at the stars, but some of us are lying in the gutter. In the fullness of time, and with the growth of commercial interest and technological innovation, Carmen was persuaded to produce video films about her subject for the larger and possibly non-literate segment of her audience. Professor Madgewycke was widely believed to star, as it were, in these productions, but since, despite the enlarged portrayal of various physical features and attributes of a private character, faces and other distinguishing marks were (so I am told) never shown, Madgewycke was able to brush aside inquiry by quoting Maurice Bowra's dictum: "I don't know about you, old chap, but I'm known around Oxford by my face." The Master of Gresham in those days, Maurice Feiner, would sometimes introduce Madgewycke to visitors at High Table by saying, "Professor Madgewycke specializes in black holes, and other pleasing features of the universe."'

This sort of malicious piquancy was one of the things, perhaps the principal one, that Philip loved in Felix, and I know that he relaxed on New Year's Eve, was more himself – or his old self, of younger years. It was an extremely cold night, but even so Felix insisted on taking us out into the garden and down to the canal as midnight approached. The water had frozen, the air was stone dry, and the sky studded with stars above Port Meadow. In the distance, a freight train rumbled along. Felix had a coke brazier going under his pear tree, and had roasted some chestnuts over it on a grill, so that as the hour and the month turned, and this new year began, we were warming our fingers by the hot fire, and drinking a toddy that Felix had concocted in such a way that it tasted the same to all of us, though Philip's was unspiked. We exchanged kisses under the cold, beautiful sky, and I remember Philip looking at me with great tenderness. I also remember thinking that I was determined to be more strong-minded in future, especially with respect to Philip. Partly because of this, perhaps, there was a real sense of a new beginning in the air. At the time, I believed that Philip shared it.

The very next day, however, quite a lot of this progress – mine certainly, perhaps Philip's too – was lost when the Master dropped round 'for a chat'. Sir Philip was at his affable best, genuinely friendly in so far as it's possible to describe any of the ordered, precise, rehearsed actions of the Master as genuine. And his expressed concern for Philip was certainly real. He didn't want anything in particular, he said. 'Just to see how we're coming along, and to wish you both the best of good health and happiness with the New Year.' He took 'a little coffee' and explained how he thought he would now have no difficulty in securing a term's leave for Philip. 'Opinion has matured with time, of course. And the faculty is being helpful. Also Conrad Jesty has come round to the common point of view. He is a good

217

fellow at heart, you know, Philip. At heart.' And he tapped the arm of his chair with the flat of his right hand. 'Registering the beat of good fellowship', as Philip described it later. The Master was only with us for about half an hour, but it was more than long enough for me to see Philip starting to slide away again. The drift, or whatever it was, was just about visible in the tones of Sir Philip's conversational manner.

As soon as he had gone – 'having, I hope, reassured you both' – I got Philip out for a walk across the Meadow. We kept up a good pace all the way to Wolvercote and back, but the damage had been done, and when we got home to Cranham Street Philip returned to his study, and went on with whatever preoccupation was consuming him. In the absence of any alternative, I went back to my economics.

A day or so later, presumably on the Friday, at any rate certainly before the end of the week, I went to see Peter Kahn because I badly wanted to get his advice. The trouble was, of course, that I was going to have to start back to work in London the following Monday, and I was worried at the effects on Philip of my being away all day. Was it even really safe to leave him alone so much, and so soon? Kahn was reassuring. Without going into details, he said he thought Philip was showing good signs of stability. Not much progress or improvement yet, it had to be said, but these were early days. And stability, well, that was a lot to be grateful for so early on in treatment. 'The music,' he said, 'is doing him a lot of good, and should be encouraged.' Clearly, or perhaps only presumably, Philip and Kahn had been discussing music, but in what context, and for what ends, I had then, and have now, no idea.

There's a real problem here. The confidentiality of the consulting room is a terrible impediment for primary carers. I was the one looking after Philip for a hundred and sixty-four hours a week, when I had to manage his moods, remember his medication, try to talk and jolly him along, be sympathetic, find common ground to discuss problems, and all the rest of it. Throughout most of this time he was silent, or uninterested, or bitterly estranged, or lost in his own concerns, or paralysed with misery and despair. Peter Kahn saw him for just four hours a week, during which – at least as I imagine it – Philip talked constantly, so that Kahn knew far more about him and his condition than I did. But, despite this, or perhaps because of it, Kahn wasn't able to help me to cope better with my far more difficult task by telling me even a little of what he knew. Nor could he, or would he, explain to me why this was. He just gave a shrug, and lifted his arms as though helpless. 'It's in the nature of the doctor–patient model' was the closest he would come.

I suppose a lot of what Philip talked about was me and our relationship. Kahn will have a pretty funny idea of what I'm like if so. Still, it must come, or go, with the job: filtering the evidence. No doubt a lot of what they're trained to do, and paid for doing, is not just learning how to listen, but how to sift, discount and interpret.

'Have you any idea at all how I feel?' I asked Philip, during the weekend. He looked at me very quizzically, as though I was trying to speak under water, the sound so distorted as to be unintelligible.

'How you *feel*?'

'Yes. My feelings. About you, and how you are, the way you treat me.'

'Well, you're being very nice to me. Looking after me. And I do know how difficult it must be, has been. I suppose you must feel very tired and demoralized.'

'Not at all.' Long Philippic silence. 'Well?'

'Well what?'

'Can't you guess?'

'You're pregnant.'

'Philip, do be serious. This is important. I'm worried about you, and I'm anxious about having to go back to work, being at the office all day, knowing that you're here on your own. I do so want you to understand how important you are, not just to me, but to all the people who depend on you and love you, like Felix, and your parents, and your pupils, and so many of your colleagues. We all just want you to get well again . . .'

'I expect I'll . . .'

' . . . and be your normal self.'

' . . . be all right. Normal, did you say? Normal? I thought the whole point of all this was the general conviction that I'm not, and that I've got to be psyched back into my box.'

'You hurt people, Philip.'

'I know. I'm sorry. I wouldn't have thumped Jesty if I hadn't been drunk, and he hadn't said those disgraceful things. And the rest – Campbell-Quaid and Preggett going in the fountain – that really was an accident. A real mis . . .'

'I didn't mean physically. What I meant was you hurt their feelings.'

'But that's not my fault . . .'

'Yes, it is . . .'

'No it's not. I don't even know what these feelings are that I'm supposed to be hurting. And anyway, if the evidence of life is anything to go by, everyone differs in his feelings. Yes, yes, all right. Hers too. Tell something, a joke say, to one person, he can't understand it. Tell the self-same joke to someone else, he gets terribly upset. Tell it to a third and he laughs. "How do you feel?" has become the common daft question of contemporary life, insulting when not vacuous, and yet everyone seems to think it should be taken seriously. Turn on the TV, open a newspaper, read a review. Everywhere you turn there's some impertinent opinionated nitwit telling me how he feels. Not what he thinks, but how he feels. As if he knew! As if I could understand it if he did! As if I should care! You. Can't. Know. Other. People's. Feelings. Full stop.'

'But Philip, you could try to imagine them.'

'What? Imagine? Why?'

'Because we're here, us others. And we're important too. And we aren't just products created by your sensory perceptions, any more than you are one created by ours.'

'Let me get this right. You exist in the real word, yet you want me to *imagine* you. Really, Alice. These contradictions are absurd.'

'Maybe. But as you yourself like to say, looked at from some angles, life itself is absurd. None the less, it remains true: the world, and the lives we lead in it, are not a game that philosophers play. It is a real place, and we are real people. It's true, as you so often say, that we can't know what other people's feelings are. Not in the sense of proving them anyway. But this doesn't mean that we shouldn't try, as best we can, to imagine them, and to give our own imagination some sort of benefit of the doubt when we do. Isn't this what we mean by the utility of experience? So when we say, for instance, "I know how much he is suffering", this is really just a shorthand for something along the lines of, "I know from my own experience, and the experience of others as reported to me, that such and such events can cause great anguish, and from the set of his face and the nature of his speech, it is plain that he too is suffering real pain. How I do sympathize."'

'He might just be an actor.'

'Or he could be you, Philip.'

Which brought him to a stop at last, so that he looked away, and then put his head down on the table, like all the other times.

Had this made a difference? At the time I remember thinking that it had, because on the Sunday, reading the newspaper at breakfast, Philip suddenly asked me if I'd like to go to a concert. This was a surprise, and made me very pleased, because apart from his brief visits to the library Philip had shown no inclination to go out at all, as though he had a horror of other people and the places where they congregate. He had seen an advertisement, he said, for a Brahms evening at the Barbican – the violin concerto in the first half, and a German requiem after the interval. If I liked, we could stay at the flat afterwards, and do something together in London the next day. I was so delighted at this proposal that I even suggested getting the tickets on the Monday.

Sometimes, if things are booked up, I can still get tickets through the bank.

'I've already got them, actually,' Philip said. 'Did it yesterday in the High, after going to the library.' He was hiding behind the newspaper, but he put it down at this point. 'I know you've been worrying about me, what with going back to work and the pressures, and so on. I thought it would be nice for us to have something to look forward to at the end of the week. That it might help, somehow.' He gave one of his little smiles, wry and self-deprecating. 'I shall be all right, while you're away . . .'

And so he seemed to be. He started cooking again, which he hadn't done for a while, and had a meal ready for us when I came home in the evenings. On the Monday, after we'd eaten, he suggested that we walk round to the Gardeners Arms in North Parade for a drink, and then he asked me all about the office, my work, what it had been like going back after a break, and what was new. He even managed to talk about Alan, asking after him, and how our various joint projects had been going without me. 'New Year resolution,' he said, when I looked surprised.

The next night I asked him about the music we were to hear on the Friday evening. He knew so much more about music than I do, and Brahms was a favourite composer for some reason. He didn't seem to want to talk at first, but he warmed up after a bit, and told me about Joachim, a violinist whose friendship had been important to Brahms. How Joachim, though he was only two years older than Brahms, had long been an established virtuoso performer by the time the two of them first met in 1853, when Brahms was twenty. Joachim invited the unknown pianist and composer to visit him at Göttingen, where he was concert master and soloist at the Hanoverian court of King George. Their friendship flourished in their music, and much of what Brahms was to write for the violin over the course of most of his life was written if not for Joachim, then with Joachim's talents in mind. At the beginning, though Brahms was incredibly handsome, he was shy and withdrawn, needing guidance. And it was through

222

Joachim, that summer and autumn, that Brahms was introduced to Robert and Clara Schumann. 'Out of their patronage and admiration, his career flourished.'

'The preparation of a life in music,' or some such, I said.

But Philip said, 'I don't think so. I think he was struggling for the freedoms of his own space, not the constrictions of dependence.' I think that was what he said. He was speaking very quietly and wasn't always easy to hear, but I didn't like to ask him to speak up because it might have put him off, and once he lapsed back into silence he could be difficult to coax out of it again. I especially liked a story that he told about the Schumanns, who foresaw the brilliance of Brahms's later career. They sat up to all hours listening to him play. Clara – that was Schumann's wife – was a wonderful performer by Philip's account, the product, like so many great musicians, of an obsessive parent. 'Clara was like an icon to Brahms,' Philip said. 'A sort of prefigured ornament in his imagination, though real enough in other respects. A model for life, though it was the life of the mind, not of the flesh.'

The next two evenings, the Wednesday and Thursday, I have searched my memory for, but can barely recall at all. Only one thing stands out as unusual, and it happened just before we went to bed on the Thursday night – the last time we were together. We didn't make love. We hadn't done that this whole time. But just after we turned out the light Philip started talking about Herzen. This was very strange, really, because ever since the events at the college gaudy, and then what he told me about that poisonous anonymous letter, Philip hadn't mentioned Herzen at all. The book was finished, of course, and Felix had arranged to pack up the manuscript and send it off to Mullens in London. But Philip seemed to have put it completely out of his mind. I assumed at the time that this was because he thought it was over and done with, and so of no further interest.

'It's funny the weight we attach to things,' he said, out of the dark. 'Part of being a good scholar, a big part of being a good

an, I shouldn't wonder, consists in not allowing events
:ts to seem or look ordinary or unimportant. You have
how to fasten on to them, allow them to be neutral, so that
you can then assign them the appropriate weight. And I've been
thinking recently of something about Herzen. You know – well,
of course you do because you've read the manuscript, and it
comes close enough to the beginning – that Herzen was illegit-
imate. His father never married his mother, and it was her on
whom Alexander depended. When I wrote the book, I just
accepted this. It was common enough in tsarist Russia. And it's
common enough today for most people to think little of it. But
should I have done? Just accepted it, I mean? Perhaps it meant
something really important, especially to Herzen himself. Something on which I should have reflected a great deal more. But
I didn't. And I missed it. Just completely missed it. Don't you
think that's strange? It has taught me something about history
and memory: that people who try to redefine themselves by
rearranging the past create an intolerable future. This is because
the will is useless for shaping life, which just flows on regardless.
Everyone finds this out eventually, but some people are unable
to accept it, and become deranged with struggle; while most of
the others, once they make the discovery, just give up and
vegetate.'

'Is there an alternative?'

'Perhaps,' he said. But he didn't say anything more, and we
just went off to sleep, though I was sure that he hadn't finished,
and that I was hearing about something to which he would
return. Later, when we, Felix and I, found the manuscript of *The
Greatest Sorrow*, and I had read it through a couple of times, I
remembered what he said that night about Herzen's being a
bastard. And the interesting thing is that it must have been true
– not the fact of Herzen's illegitimacy – of course that was true –
but what Philip said about never really thinking about it enough.
Because in *The Greatest Sorrow* the fact is never mentioned, and
yet *The Greatest Sorrow* is Philip's account of his obsession, and if

he had really internalized this fact in the same way that he had clearly internalized so many of the others, then it would surely have been there. And not once, but several times.

The Friday was the worst day of the worst time, but like all terrible things it can be told very quickly. Philip was to have met me at the flat at six. We were going to have a snack at the Barbican café before the concert at eight. I sat and waited, and he never came. Worry and anxiety turned to fear by seven-thirty, and I rang Dr Kahn and various other people without learning anything. Half an hour later the Master rang to say that he had been contacted by the police with news of an accident on the motorway, in which Philip had apparently been involved, and that Philip had been taken to a hospital in Reading. He gave me an emergency services number to ring. When I called, and explained who I was, they asked if I could go to the hospital immediately. 'Dr Leroux has severe injuries, and his condition is giving cause for concern' was the formula they used. I took a taxi, and we were at the hospital in ninety minutes or so. When I got there Philip was dead. The police asked me to identify him, which I did. While I was doing this, Felix arrived, and later he took me back to Oxford, gave me a sedative, and let me sleep at his house. The next day, before all the things started to happen that happen when someone has died, Felix held my hand and said, 'He's safe now. And not in pain any more: *frei aber einsam.*'

I'm not really sure why he said this.

3

Sympathy in Choice

I

I went away to Clémont because I was afraid of forgetting, and wanted to write things down. Writing's not in my blood. I've never kept a diary. I always believed that the past was a dead place, really, something, or somewhere, that we couldn't do anything to so wasn't worth worrying about. But Philip's last days were so difficult, and as I thought about them in the months after he died, I could feel them changing, becoming more slippery, the big and the little things adjusting themselves in the light perhaps of what people said to me, or wrote to me, or as a result of some chance event, like finding myself in a particular spot where I had once been with Philip, and sensing suddenly the sound or the aroma of him – his presence anyway – and realizing how his return like this, the function of another part of my memory, involuntary and surprising, kept nudging the past into a wholly different arrangement. A sort of reordering of experience that I found very unnerving. I thought that if I could just write it down, at least the sequence of events, where we were, what we did, how he looked, then I would have secured something, and made it safe for myself to remember.

Is this a special, or at any rate peculiar, response to the big events in life? Since getting back to London nearly two months ago I've been gripped by the desire to write more, even about things that were nothing to do with Philip. I felt that I wanted to recall my childhood and remember my parents as they were when I was little, to register the small torments of sisters and school, the troubles of first encounters with sex. Simple things too, like being ill as a child and having to stay in bed, but not so ill that you couldn't read and enjoy being coddled, and fed hot lemon-barley water with milk-chocolate-coated digestive biscuits, and watching the bedside-lamp shadows make faces and animals and adventures on the wallpaper by the dressing table. Perhaps it's the run-up to forty that makes us want to do this. I've heard people say so.

Anyway, all sorts of things had to be changed when I did get back to London, so I had to put writing aside for a while. I wasn't going to go back to the Barbican flat. I hated it, and put it on the market. This meant I had to get organized to move my stuff down to the house in Oxford, and once I began doing that I realized that I ought to make a start on sorting and disposing of Philip's things. Someone said this is the worst part of bereavement, and I can believe them. I decided I wasn't going to go and live in Oxford, though. I didn't know where I was going to live in the long term, but initially I needed somewhere big enough for Beatrix to come and stay without our being under each other's feet. And I also wanted somewhere out of the City – prying eyes and jealous gossip. The result was that when Mummy told me that she and Daddy were going to go to Suffolk for the whole summer I asked if I could come and live here, in the flat in Ambrosden Avenue, while they were away. It's nice here, lots of reminders of when I was young. And the cathedral, with its mock Italian campanile on the other side of the road, sort of looming down through the long living-room windows, is perfect company given the muddled state my mind has been in ever since those last few days in France. Daddy was seventy in the spring, and has decided to retire, to run down his business interests. I think he and Mummy would like it if I bought this place. Perhaps I will. Philip had quite a big life insurance policy, but I haven't decided what I ought to do with that money yet.

Beatrix arrived last week from Northampton, where she had spent five weeks in an addiction and rehab clinic – a really good one that Alan knew about, where she ended up quite enjoying herself. I went to meet her off the train when she'd finished there. She said the best bit had been group therapy sessions, when everyone had to tell their story, and explain how they'd become addicted. She said it gave her quite a kick to be performing again, especially as the other patients – for the most part advertising executives, Surrey housewives, merchant navy officers – quickly realized that she was a star, and started treating her like one. 'Time capsule,' she said. 'But without the juice. Nice.' We had agreed weeks ago, before I left Orléans, that she would move in with me while she found her bearings and waited for her affairs to get sorted out. It was years since she'd last lived in England, and she didn't seem to have any friends or relations left.

Almost as soon as she arrived she showed every sign of liking it here. Almost on her first day, coming home from the office, I found her sitting on the pavement in the square, in front of the cathedral, chatting away to a couple of the down-and-outs who doss down there. She told Alan one of them's a poet. I think Alan really liked Beatrix too. 'Drawing power,' he said. 'Very magnetic.' But this was before she started bringing Poge Brewster, who's some sort of promoter in the East End, that she met in Northampton, back to the flat. I think I could do without Poge – 'You're looking peeky today, darling. No oats in your sack last night?' isn't my way of saying good morning – but that's another story that I haven't sorted out yet.

Anyway, Beatrix did really well in the hospital in Orléans, and in the end only had to stay there for a fortnight, but I must say that when I went in to see her at the beginning, I didn't think she was ever going to recover. The first time I went she was still in a coma, and I just sat there and looked at her for a few minutes. The next time I went, the Wednesday, I suppose it was, she was awake but barely conscious. Or perhaps I should say conscious but barely awake. She had Johan on her mind, though. In retrospect this was hardly surprising. She would have been agitated if she hadn't been sedated. She was muttering about a Johan van Voorhous, or some such, anyway. Micheline dropped by while I was there, very starched and proper in her uniform, and beckoned me out into the corridor. She had sat with Beatrix for half an hour the previous evening, she said, before going home. And Beatrix, half awake, half out of it, had rambled on about Johan (she thought the name was van Voorhuis) the

231

entire time she was there. Nothing coherent, but a lot of fear and anxiety. Perhaps, she said, this Johan is a cause of Beatrix's troubles, and did I know anything about him? Could I find anything out? This was pretty difficult for me because Micheline doesn't speak much English, and my French is pretty half-baked when it comes to anything specialized or complicated, but I tried to tell her, as best I could, what little I knew. That Johan was her agent, or some such, perhaps also a former lover, and that he seemed to spell trouble in her life. Beatrix had said that he was supposed to be turning up at Clémont soon. Micheline said that she had already picked this up from Beatrix's ramblings the night before. She had had a word with the doctor in charge of the case – who would want to talk to me herself in due course – and she had agreed with Micheline that Beatrix should be shielded from this Johan at least for the time being. The ward staff and administrative personnel had been instructed not to let anyone in to see Beatrix without my prior approval. She hoped I didn't mind taking the responsibility, but it wasn't something any of the hospital staff could authorize on their own.

When I got home to Clémont Alan rang up, and I suddenly felt a great surge of relief, joy almost. It was such a pleasure to hear a familiar, friendly voice. His news was good, or at any rate amusing. Hugo Rawlinson had been made a life peer, and we would all now have to call him Lord Sawsdyke. I think I shall call him 'My Baron' or 'Your Baron-ness'. Alan said that Blair's boys expected him to help vote the House of Lords out of existence, but opinion in the bank thought this either overly optimistic or just plain funny. Hugo's brilliant at persuading people that he thinks as they do while quietly keeping his own counsel. We laughed about this, and Alan asked how 'the scribe' was getting on. He knew I was going to Clémont to write. Remembering his former incarnation as restructuring expert to the music industry, I told him about Beatrix. 'Have you ever heard of someone called Johan van Voorhuis?' I was going to try to spell it for him, but he jumped in before I could start.

'J. V. Squared? Good God, is he involved in this?'

'Well I hope . . .'

'J. Vee Vee is to rock music what the Mafia is to Gazprom. The Americans tried to have him extradited from Holland a few years ago – fraud, tax evasion – stuff like that, but someone in the Justice Department made a mess of the application, and it failed on a technicality. The last I heard he was wanted, mainly civil suits, but some criminal too, in five or six countries. If this Beatrix of yours is mixed up with him, then she really has got trouble. Say again, who is she?'

'It's not who she is really. It's who she was.' And I told him about Nix, and Johan becoming her agent, or manager or whatever, after the group broke up. Alan said he'd look into it if I'd like him to, and that was exactly what I wanted to hear.

Boswell – now this was an interesting discovery – Boswell was on a twenty-three-hour clock. Never known a cat like him. Madame Jeanne said that he must be fed every day at six o'clock, but one day at the weekend he was miaowing so plaintively at five that I fed him then. The next day he was back at four. The day after that at three. This was when I called a halt and told him he'd have to wait until six. He listened to this information with his customary bland indifference, went on miaowing for twenty minutes or so, and then gave up and slipped away again. For a day or two I wondered how he'd been coping, but he came back on to the six o'clock schedule, and stopped badgering me any earlier. Then quite early on the Friday morning he came into the kitchen with a dead rat. Miaowing with pleasure, almost crowing in fact, he laid it down on the kitchen floor, and then sat beside it, suddenly disengaged, cleaning himself. The rat was bedraggled, mangy and dilapidated, with a long tail that looked as though it might have been made from little elasticated metal rings. It gazed at me from its dead eye with what I imagined was world-weary cynicism, no trace of the panic and terror that must have beset its final moments. 'In a way, and on balance, I'm glad to be out of this,' it said. My own feelings were rather more direct. I hate rats, alive or dead.

I was just contemplating this repulsive scene, wondering how I was going to get the rat out of the kitchen, and where I would take it when I did, when there was a skidding of tyres on gravel, the slam of a car door, and the patter of feet outside. A man, *the* man, I knew who it was instantly, stepped sharply into the sun-lit doorway. Tall, muscular, fair, thin ponytail from the base not the top of his head. Without pausing or knocking or anything he crossed straight to the kitchen table where I was sitting. Bigger now, taller, clean-shaven, weighty, he whipped off his dark glasses and leaned down towards me, both hands on the table. Good manicure, three rings, one with a diamond. Bad taste.

This is where I fluffed my lines. What I should have said was: 'Please excuse me for a moment. A rat just came in and I want to get rid of it.' But one only ever thinks of these things afterwards. Unless you're a JV2 type, of course, in which case it's how you got where you are today.

'Hi,' he said, giving me his full-frontal face-in-mine treatment. Open, sunny, just a tad fat. 'You must be a collector. In addition to this dead one on the floor, have you got my Bix here? She's not at home, and they said in the shop you were hanging out with her.' He spoke English in that fluently colloquial Dutch way that I usually associate with football players and Euro-politicians.

I still didn't get my lines right. Just thinking about it now, weeks later, and in the safety of red-brick Victoria, shaped balconies, double-glazing and net curtains, makes me run hot and ashamed – or at any rate fiercely disturbed, my pulse racing with the recollection. At the very least I should have asked him whether he didn't normally knock before bursting into people's homes. Or alternatively, would he mind doing me a favour – so good to meet a man with a sense of timing – and put this dead rat out for me? You'll find a dustpan in the corner over there. Or even the good old English stand-by, often employed by my mother,

234

getting to one's feet, offering to shake hands: 'Do forgive me. I don't think we've been introduced. You are . . . ?' And raising the eyebrows – or just one of them, if you're Mummy – while simulating a smile that says, 'How cold I feel! Did you know that when I get cold I bite?' I don't suppose that any of these would have made the slightest difference to Johan, but at least they would have made thinking about this incident afterwards less humiliating for me.

'Beatrix? Beatrix Stapleton? Are you . . . ?'

'Johan. Yes. Her only friend. You know who I am. She tells everyone what a wonderful person I am, and how well I look after her.' He leaned forward a little more, shoving his face closer. Very even, expensive teeth. Half a dozen white hairs in his nostrils. 'Where is she?' Somehow he compelled a reply.

'She was taken ill. I found her. Very ill. Seriously ill. She's in intensive care and the hospital said no one . . . '

'Which hospital?'

' . . . is allowed in.'

'They'll let me in. Which hospital?'

'It's not my . . . '

'Business. No. How annoying of you.' He straightened up, folded his sunglasses and put them away in an inner pocket of his jacket. Black cashmere, very good cut. Armani T-shirt under. Fastidious the way he closed the glasses case, tucked it away. 'You must not interfere in things you do not understand. Bix has been difficult always, but I know what she wants and I take care of her.' He looked at the dead rat at his feet, then bent down and picked it up. Not by the tail. Not with a brush and pan. Not with kitchen towel, or tissue, or newspaper. Just picked it up so that it lay across his hand, black and grey and dead. 'You see?' He held it out to me briefly across the table, then walked to the door and hurled it into the shrubs. 'It's not difficult.' He went to rinse his hands at the sink. 'All management is the same, really. You just have to be prepared to deal with disagreeable things occasionally.' He dried his hands on a tea-towel, coming back to me at the table where I felt just about paralysed, or at any rate hypnotized by his sheer, brute force. 'You, for instance,' he went on, in what I realized later was a complete reversal of the truth. 'You are being very disagreeable. But I don't suppose it's deliberate. You wish to take Bix's side. She is what you English – you are English, aren't you? Your number-plates are English – she is what you English call a waif, is that right? And you feel for her. You feel her pain, as we say now. And you want to help. Above all, you think that you can help her to escape. Perhaps you think you are in a fairy story. There is a princess, and a wicked uncle, and a strange house with ghosts and evil spirits, and you are the knight that has come to her rescue. Well, allow me please to tell you something interesting. This is indeed a fairy story, but the parts are not as you imagine them. The haunted house does not contain a princess but a witch who can change her form, and who casts a spell on unwary travellers. They are enchanted. They become captivated. They lose their reason. And their will to resist.' He pulled a chair out from under the table and sat down opposite me, leaning forward again to stare into my face. 'Miss? It is Miss, isn't it?'

I told him my name.

'Well, Alicia, let me tell you some things you don't know. Bix and I go back a long way, back to when she was down and finished, her career a ruin, her world shattered. If there is a knight in shining armour here, then it's me. I saved her, rescued her, looked after her, and made her a new life.' He gave a sigh, spread his hands palms up on the table. Pink and white, too fat, they made me shiver. Suddenly, however, the menace was gone, replaced with a disarming intimacy, the most remarkable charm.

'She's not easy to help, you know, Bix. Not easy. She has these demons – you will have observed – no doubt they explain her return to hospital. Oh yes' – and he interrupted with a raised hand before I could speak. 'This is not the first time. In Amsterdam, in Lausanne, once in Bali. Terrible time we had there. We have been in this situation before. She is a silly girl, careless with her health, her money, her safety and welfare. But what is one to do? I try my best, but she's a grown woman. It's her life. She makes her own decisions. I do my best because she does have to be looked after, but I can't mop up behind her every minute of the day. I'm sure you've been a help to her, and you're not the first I've had to thank, believe me. And I'm grateful to you. But you must understand that I know her, far better than anyone else, in fact. I know what she needs. And I know how to take care of her.'

He stopped and flashed me a beautiful smile, slipping a slim gold case from his jacket pocket and offering me a cigarette. 'Do you?' I shook my head.

'And I'd really rather you didn't either, if you don't mind.'

'Of course not.' He put the case on the table, between us.

'Bix and I have been together for a long time now,' he said, confiding, almost intimate. It was quite uncanny. 'After Sim died – I expect she's told you about that. Yes, yes. You don't have to say a word. But what she won't have told you is how badly she crashed off the rails. She went completely to pieces. You won't believe . . .'

'She told me.'

Johan stopped here and looked at me, seeing me properly perhaps for the first time.

'That's unusual,' he said. 'I'm impressed.'

'And that you saved her from herself. And how you cared for her. And how she depended on you.'

'So you *do* understand.'

'Yes, I think I . . .'

'So you can help me after all. Just tell me where she's been taken, and then I can make the appropriate arrangements.' He smiled. 'And I could use a cup of tea, if you have one?'

The great thing about charm, even when superficial, or blatantly counterfeit, is that it helps to put people at their ease. Johan succeeded in this, and I was able to start functioning again, thinking even. I got up and put on the kettle, rummaged in a cupboard for some tea. Johan swung his chair around and sat astride it, his hands on the back, watching me at the kitchen counter. It reminded me of some business types I'd met. A developer in Hong Kong who could turn charm on and off like a light switch, and with much the same effect, drenching everyone with light, or plunging you into the dark. It's a part of the repertoire of manipulative people. I once had to go to a breakfast meeting in Zurich with some senior executives of the big three Swiss banks. Breakfast business meetings are bad enough at the best of times, but these suits had remodelled it as torture. One flattered while another wound the rack, and the third just examined you as though you were a curiosity, a specimen to be looked at idly while he picked his teeth. They kept this up for the best part of an hour, occasionally exchanging parts, and then got up and left. 'Thank you, Miss Leighton,' said the one who shook hands, making sure that he got my name wrong with deliberate precision. 'That was most interesting.' Which it was in a way. Well, so was this. But the funny thing was, I think Johan really did care about Beatrix in a way. And he really was worried about her. 'Well, he would be, wouldn't he?' was what Alan said, later on. But I think that deep down, at least at the beginning, it was more than that. Somehow they had been drawn to each other.

'Have you come for a holiday, Mr . . .?'

'Van Voorhuis. Johan van Voorhuis. But please call me Yo. I used to tell Bix that she could call me Yo-Yo, because she had me on a string, and I always came when she pulled.' He shook his head, smiling. Ah, the good memories of better and simpler times. 'But no, not holidays this time. Strictly work. Which is why it is most important that I see Bix, if only for a moment. There are some papers that she must sign. There are good things for her happening, and I am here to help.'

I kept my back to him, getting mugs down from the cupboard, searching for some teabags that I remembered were particularly repulsive, and so might do nicely for this occasion. I found them:

238

blackcurrant with mint. 'An infusion to delight the senses.'
'Beatrix still has business interests, does she?'

'Some.' A pause. The good manager, the best of agents, a man of prudence. 'Copyrights. That sort of thing. Complicated.'

'Ah.' Pouring boiling water. 'I don't suppose I'd understand.'

He gave me a tolerant smile, accepting and excusing my inadequacy for what it was: the sort of thing you'd expect from a dummy. But they teach useful things in the corporate seminar world these days. 'Techniques of negotiation. How to secure the contract you need, the way you want it.' Step one: at the beginning conceal the extent of your knowledge, the scope of your expertise. I passed him the mug, the teabag still in it. He sniffed over it. 'I think you'll like it,' I said. 'It's different. Quite unusual. I always think it suits people like us.' Step two: assert identity of interests, common tastes. 'More adventurous.' Our mutual superiority to all the littler, unadventurous people. 'I'm glad to hear it's only work that brings you down, though. Poor Beatrix isn't in any state for a holiday, or socializing or anything, so if you'd come for a break, and to be with her, it'd be quite wasted. Work, on the other hand, signatures and things, well, they *can* always wait, can't they?' I drank some tea, not the same as his, and gave him one of Philip's pliant, complacent smiles. 'Since you're her agent, and so naturally want to look after her interests, perhaps the best thing would be to give her a day or two to pull through this crisis – she really is seriously ill, you know. I thought she was going to die. It was terrible. And after a bit give me a ring from, where was it? Amsterdam? And I can give you a progress report, and prepare the way for you to come back. That way you won't be wasting your time.' Step three: never reject the unacceptable out of hand, but find a method for putting it on hold. Then go rapidly to step four: put up some practical proposals that have confidence-building elements (you can trust me) plus a preliminary timetable (we can settle this at a mutually agreed time).

Johan van Voorhuis, unfortunately, had not been to business

school, and took little interest in techniques of negotiation. He swept his cigarette case into his pocket, got up and went to the door, and flung the contents of his mug out on to the brick forecourt.

'That muck,' he said, 'is more than enough for me. And I have better things to do with my time than listen to your crap.'

Madame Jeanne arrived at this point. Johan was blocking her entrance, so she gave him a quizzical, inquisitive look. He answered this by sticking the empty mug in her hand and brushing past her, out into the sunlight. Then he turned and looked at me, straight through Madame Jeanne as though she wasn't there.

'This is a stupid little village,' he said. A man alone, reflecting on life's funny little curiosities as he gets out his sunglasses and gives them a polish. 'Full of gossip. I'll find out where Beatrix is, no problem, and I will see her today or tomorrow, and be back in Amsterdam before the weekend is over.' He gave a gesture with his arm. 'Motorways,' he said. 'Very convenient.' As though they had been constructed specifically for his benefit. He smiled broadly in the midsummer sun, then fitted the sunglasses over his nose, behind his ears, cut the smile, and relaxed his face into its normal fat, intolerant sneer. 'And I don't need *your* help. So fuck you.' And then he was gone.

'Well,' said Madame Jeanne, or something similar, because she was speaking French, of course. 'I understood nothing but the last words, and they are not nice, I think. I learned them once. Mr van Voorhuis is not a good man.'

'You know him.'

'Everyone here knows him. André at the *auberge* thinks he is very clever, with his BMW and everything, but I used to see him with Madame Beatrix – he doesn't come much these days – and he was mean and unkind.' She pulled a face. 'Not a good man.' She washed the mug at the sink, and set it to dry in the rack. 'If I had known he was here, I wouldn't have come. He makes me feel' – she laid her hand on her breast – 'boum, boum, agitated.

Just seeing him does this to me.' She dipped into her shopping bag and came up with a piece of paper.

'I wanted to give you this.' It was a map of Orléans, one small district circled, with an enlargement of this part on the back. 'François made these on his computer. So clever, these young people today.' She gave a sigh. 'The hotel for the wedding reception tomorrow is here' – she pointed to an area of narrow streets near the cathedral. 'And this' – and she handed me a stiff envelope, my name on it in italic script – 'is the invitation, which we should have given to you before. You must forgive us. So much to remember.' And then she hurried away, *à demain*ing up the steps, and not forgetting, as she went, to clear away the teabag that Johan had thrown out.

I put the formal invitation with its lists of names up on the dresser, next to the photo of juvenile Philip looking lost. I only thought of this later, but it was so detailed, sharp and precise that it stood as a kind of antithesis to him. An ordered world, where people belonged and stood in a hierarchy of family rela-tionships, one to another, established and particular. Madame Morisot – Madame Jeanne herself; le colonel Morisot, *officier de la Légion d'honneur*, presumably Micheline's grandfather or an uncle; a Monsieur et Madame Hugues Bazard (whom I worked out must be the parents of François, Micheline's fiancé); and then half a dozen or so more Bazards, including a *curé* and a *professeur*, along with a Madame Mirbel, whom I later learned to be François's maternal grandmother. Eleven a.m. it announced, Église Saint-Aignan, and afterwards, from twelve-thirty p.m. onwards, at the Hôtel Aurelianis, Cloître Saint-Aignan.

I locked up and drove into Orléans the long way round, via country roads through Isdes and Sully, and then along the right bank of the Loire, past the abbey at Saint-Benoît, the river behind it glinting in the summer sun, everything in the countryside and villages gleaming and golden and tranquil. In Orléans in the early afternoon I went hunting for a wedding present, and eventually, in an antique shop on the Rue Royale, I found something that looked and felt right. It was a porcelain figure of two young people dancing. The shopkeeper, a rather intense man with narrow shoulders and such a bony chest that his jacket swung on him as though he was a coat-hanger – odd how we retain these details about some people – was very helpful and informative. The figure was early nineteenth century, and made in Orléans. He was very proud of this, and I got a lecture on the history of the local porcelain trade. The couple depicted – they were about sixteen centimetres high – looked wonderfully mobile and happy, his arm around her waist, she leaning away from him, her straw hat, perhaps in the very second of falling, making a halo round her radiant face. The intense thin man packaged it beautifully for me as a present.

A bit further down the street was a little clothes shop with the rather wonderful name of Valentine Visconti, where the proprietor – one of those superbly turned-out fashionable French women who might be aged anything from thirty to sixty – helped me select a dress and a hat. Thinking back, I don't think I really did the selecting at all, because although she showed me a lot of different dresses and outfits, all this was somehow preliminary to her eventually saying: '*Ah. Eh bien,*' as though she'd just thought of something that had previously eluded her. '*Peut-être, et après tout, c'est bien ça.*' And she produced a little cream silk dress, sashed at the waist, high-necked and long-sleeved, but deliciously light and cool, and with little *taches* and pools of crimson and gold that glowed and flared from the skirt as I walked or turned in it. She had a wide-brimmed hat to match. 'And your husband must give you a little spray to wear here,' she said, indicating a spot below the left shoulder. 'Freesias, yellow and gold, with little streaks of this red.'

'*C'est parfait,*' she said when I gave her my credit card, but she wasn't referring to the money. And she was right: it was. Then I got a coffee in the Place du Martroi, bought a big bunch of early summer flowers, walked back to where I'd parked on the boulevard, and drove south across the river to visit Beatrix.

I think it was then, though it may have been later, that I realized that most of this Friday of pottering and rambling – though it's true, I did have to get something to wear, and to buy Micheline and François a present – was really Johan avoidance. There was a sort of malevolent force in him, an animal ugliness that communicated itself and that he was aware of, and exploited. It was very unsettling, and I felt very unsettled.

I told Beatrix this when I eventually reached her bedside at about four o'clock. She was looking quite a lot better than the day before. Not sitting up yet, but the IV was gone from her arm, and there was focus back in her eyes, some strength in her voice.

'I knew he'd turn up,' she said. 'What a bloody awful cock-up.'

'You really don't want to see him, Beatrix.'

'I might have to.'

'But why? He's nothing but trouble, and . . .'

'He's my manager, my agent, whatever, and I have to do what he says. I'm a silly cow and I signed a contract years ago that means he, well, basically, that he owns me. And if he tells me . . .'

'That's not possible. Contract law . . .'

' . . . to do something, I have to do it.'

' . . . contains provisions prohibiting unfair . . .'

'And he wants my signature.'

'What for?'

'I don't know. Does it matter? It's just words.'

'We've got to get our words right.'

She gave me a wan smile. 'Yeah. Well, that's true, I suppose.' She shook her head from side to side on the pillow and held out her hand for me to hold. 'Christ, I could use a drink.' I squeezed her hand a little bit, trying to be comforting. 'And a snort.' Then she gave me another limp smile. 'It's all right. I know what's what. Gonna stop, aren't I? It's all got something to do with a new album, this signature wot's-it. Well, not a new album exactly. Just an old one really, re-con-fig-ured, as we say in the business. *Nix's Nuggets. Biggest Hits: The Collector's Edition.*

243

That sort of touch. Three CDS boxed, snappy photos from the glory days, a few paras on life after fame – "Happiness by the banks of the Sauldre" – peace in a new life after strife, great songs, wonderful memories for all the fans who loved Nix then and love us still. God bless you all. Wallow, wallow, wallow.' Beatrix made an effort to sit up at this point, but gave up as soon as she'd begun. 'Christ, I'm weak. Bloody baby. You know I wrote most of those numbers? "Dead Embers", "Sand Shoe Run", "Cry Baby's Broadside", "Fold Me Away, I'm Finished". All those. I was bloody brilliant in those days, full of ideas, thought it'd go on for ever. Load of crap, of course.' She lay back on the pillow, a couple of tears edging out of her eyes. 'Now it's down to me and that creep Johan, my signatures and his monthly handouts.'

'Why didn't you, don't you, just walk away? Leave?'

'I don't have anywhere to go. And it's all Johan's, you see – the house and everything. He gives me my royalties once a month – bugger all these days, of course. Can't even pay the phone bill half the time. Oh, and he keeps me in booze and the other stuff, which is something. Or was. Going to give up now, aren't I? He says I should be grateful.'

Beatrix talked on in this vein for quite some time: details of places and concerts, discs and presentations, songs and contracts, television appearances, stadiums, plane trips, laughs (as she called them) and moments of fear. Much of the detail I can't now remember, but this hardly seems to matter. The main, perhaps the only, point was that it all sounded very messy. She tired after a time, and dozed off, so I went out into the corridor and rang Alan. He sounded relieved.

'Thank God it's you, Alice. I've been trying to call you since yesterday afternoon, but your mobile's been switched off. Don't you ever listen to your messages? Are you all right?'

'Yes, but I've met your J. V. Squared, and he's not nice. Were you worried?'

'Rather, a bit, yes. Well, all right, very. And Vee-Vee's not

244

mine, thank you very much, but he ought to go to someone who'd take care of him for good. Now I've got the dirt you wanted. I was going to say information, but it is just dirt. Apparently J. V. 's got Beatrix Stapleton skewered on a full-rights contract of his own devising. He's probably been milking her for all she's worth, which would be a lot, though it's impossible to know how much without disclosure of his accounts and tax returns, and frankly they're unlikely to be reliable. I wouldn't care to be in her shoes one little bit. His latest project is a big retrospective album – all the hits plus previously unreleased studio takes – of the Nix numbers that Stapleton wrote, plus all her solo releases of songs she wrote herself. He's bought up the performance rights of the two former Nix band members who're still alive. Apparently Bix Nix already gets Sim Nix's share because he died intestate, and Vee-Vee successfully brought a case, on Bix's behalf naturally, that she was entitled to his estate as his common-law wife. They were a pair apparently.

'This new release is due out in October/November, worldwide, aimed at the Christmas market. Trade, radio and TV advertising space is already booked. That's why all this was relatively easy to find out. Vee-Vee's making it a direct mail-order sale, from P. O. Box addresses here and there. The one for Europe's in Geneva, but there's another one in Mexico, and one in Jakarta. Others too probably. The set won't be available in the shops. Greedy, I guess. Doesn't want the retailers getting their percentage. He doesn't need them anyway, because everyone knows the music already, it's all vintage classic stuff. Nix twenty years after the bust-up. All that. Max Strögssen, who follows entertainment stocks for Gagnons Frères in Brussels, told me the industry thinks Vee-Vee will move two million units worldwide at £24 a pop, which on an estimated sixty-five per cent margin should net him around thirty-one million pounds. Nice work if you can get it. Strögssen doesn't know what Stapleton's share will be. If any.'

'He was here this morning trying to see her.'

'I'd do the same if she was my goose.'

'No, Alan, seriously. He still needs her signature on something, though I don't know what.'

'Well, if I was her I'd hang fire and go get myself a good lawyer.'

'I agree, but where's she going to find one at this short notice? She's in hospital and can't be moved, probably not for weeks, and Johan's a real scumbag. You should have seen him this morning. He's an ugly customer, a bully, very menacing. I don't just not like him, I think he's dangerous. And he's wound up about this signature business. The hospital has instructions not to let him in, but he's manipulative, and can turn on the charm when it suits. If you ask me, he's mad, but other people don't always see things the same way . . .'

'OK, OK, points registered. Let me see if I can come up with a lawyer who'll act. Shouldn't be too hard, given the amounts of money involved. And I'll dig a bit more into J. V. Squared as well. But don't hold your breath. It's late on a Friday afternoon one week before half of France goes on holiday. And *please* leave your phone on.'

Which I promised to do, and then went back to Beatrix. She was being plumped and tucked and tidied by a very energetic nurse, who gave a scowl as I came in, pointed at her watch, and said that visiting hours expired in five minutes.

Beatrix was awake again and said, 'I've made such a mess of everything.' So I told her about Alan, and what he had suggested she do. She shook her head. 'It's never going to work. Johan's my lawyer, or at any rate he's got a lawyer who used to do my stuff. And I can't do anything from here, can I? And Johan'll come in any time now, you just see. He said he would. And then what am I going to do?'

'You must try to be positive, Beatrix,' I said, not feeling it myself in the least. 'Believe me, I know a bit about these things – contracts, business deals, property rights and so on. It's all part of what I do in my work. Contracts can sometimes be overturned.

And in any event you are entitled to an audit of the accounts to ensure that you're not being cheated. According to my colleague, who knows his way around, your Johan has a bad reputation, possibly for fraud, certainly for sharp practice. If we can come up with the right kind of lawyer . . .'

'Why are you doing all this for me? I hardly know you. You came down here on holiday, that's all.'

I couldn't answer this question. I still can't answer it now, nearly two months later. It was just something that drew me in. 'I don't know,' I said. 'But it's all right. I don't mind. And we will sort it all out.'

'That's what I thought, years ago, when I came here originally.'

'What was that?'

'That I'd sort everything out. You know, make a new start. I was going to get away from Johan, cut down on the drink, give up shit and everything. I was going to reinvent myself. Isn't that what people go to France to do?'

The nurse came back then and asked me to leave, which I was reluctant to do, though I wasn't sure what I'd have said if I had stayed any longer. I bent over the bed and gave Beatrix a kiss, and she gave me back a bleak little smile, a bit tearful again.

'Now is it all right with you if I try to find you a decent lawyer, someone you can at least explain everything to?' She gave a nod. 'I can't promise, but I'll do my best. And I'll come in again in the morning to make sure you're being good.'

'Neat,' she said.

II

I didn't want to go home to Clémont. Johan was somewhere about, and I really didn't want to see him again. But I had promised to feed Boswell – Madame Jeanne was staying in town with Micheline overnight – and at least part of me, the stubborn part, was not going to be intimidated by Johan. So I drove back to Clémont by the more direct route, via Tigy, the early evening air warm, and full of butterflies and insects. Quite a lot of traffic too. The end of the working day in Orléans coupled with the arrival of the first of the weekend visitors. It was hard not to think of Philip. Had he been driven this way too, along this same road, under these same trees? He wrote about the French countryside in the autumn, season of mists and rain, but it wasn't hard to envisage him somewhere like this at other times. That hillside, for instance, where he has Michel go at night with the serving girl, her village below them in the dark, the river winding invisibly among the trees in the valley. Things like that in Philip, so beautifully evoked, gave the lie, I thought, to his idea that it is impossible for any of us to know how others feel. He did it as the rest of us do, by an extension of the self, an act of imaginative transformation. It is what makes us human: not that we always have the same feelings at the same times, and about the same things, but the knowledge that we *can*, and the fact that we can apply this knowledge. It made me very sad, this thinking once again about Philip, and especially thinking of him as he was when he was perhaps wrong about something. 'In error', as he would say. He used to get so defensive and irritable. As though his being wrong, and then stubborn about it, was a fault in me. That was how it felt, anyway. Typical woman, blaming myself. And then I'd have to find a way to wheedle him out of the silence, which he would draw round him like a cloak.

I approached the house very cautiously, but there was no sign of Johan. Just Boswell, very patiently waiting for food, and rubbing himself against my legs as we went into the kitchen together. It was such a beautiful evening, one of those lovely times that make you feel restless, they do me anyway, and make me feel that I must go somewhere, just lose myself in it. So after feeding Boswell I locked up again and drove down the country lanes, keeping the sun on my right so that I knew I was heading south, and not worrying too much about where I might end up. Eventually I came to a little town called Henrichemont, which I couldn't resist because it sounded like a banker's pun. It didn't take long to locate a decent-looking restaurant, and I tucked myself away at a corner table next to an open window, and settled down to enjoy the solitude and the food. The quiet pleasures of a French provincial town on a warm summer's evening.

This didn't last all that long, I'm afraid, and I fear that I eventually made myself deeply unpopular because I got three longish phone calls in a row on the mobile, and there was quite a lot of huffing and puffing from adjacent tables, head-shaking about '*Américaines*', and so forth. A pity because, like my neighbours, I would far rather have turned the thing off, drunk my half-bottle in tranquillity, and just let my mind wander. After all, I had now done all the things I'd come down here to do. Unwound and relaxed; sorted Philip's papers; written the piece that Felix wanted; and written down my own memories of those terrible weeks before Philip's death. All this stuff was now off my back. Tomorrow was Micheline's wedding. On Sunday I'd be seeing Roland and Florence Beaumanière. With any luck, Alan would come up with a lawyer for Beatrix and I'd be able to leave her in safe hands. Then two or three more days being lazy, a little bit of sight-seeing here and there, and then back to London before every road in France got gummed up with traffic at the end of the week. That's how I was anticipating it anyway.

The first call was from someone called Plessis, whom I later came to know as Bertrand. He said he was a partner in the Paris law firm Astrophel, and he understood that I was acting for someone who might need their services. I was to learn a lot more about Astrophel in due course. It's a law firm set up by an American of French Jewish extraction, whose parents fled to the States in the thirties, and brought him up there. After a successful legal career in New York, he came back to live in Paris in the early seventies, setting up Astrophel, a partnership that mainly handles clients from the entertainment industries. 'Film stars mostly,' Bertrand told us, Beatrix and me, over dinner a week or so ago, when he was over in London to discuss her affairs. 'Contract work and so on. It gets dressed up a bit these days. And there's all the new law on intellectual property rights and so on. And the end of the Cold War has made a difference to our business. But actually not a great deal has changed. It's contracts, rights, agreements. Line by line stuff. It's fun, though, because the people are fun. Paris is a major centre for this kind of work.'

But this is to run ahead. On the phone Bertrand said he'd had a call from my colleague in Blount Bros, and perhaps I would care to explain the problem to him. He understood that matters might be urgent. I did as he asked, but if I was worried that he might need persuading, or that he'd insist that it could all wait until Monday morning, it was unnecessary worry. As soon as I mentioned the name Johan van Voorhuis the atmosphere changed. Can atmosphere change in a telephone conversation? I sound like Philip. It certainly seemed to me that it could. Bertrand said he and a colleague would drive down to Orléans first thing in the morning, that he would call me *en route* to let me know an arrival time, and that he'd expect to see me early, at the hospital, 'if that will be convenient'. When I told him that I was worried that Johan might try to get in to see Beatrix despite my expressly forbidding it, he said he would ring the hospital, explain that he was acting for Mademoiselle Stapleton, and that any questions regarding her treatment, welfare or visitors should be referred to him. In the meantime he would make it clear that no one should have access to her, and that he would be there himself first thing in the morning.

Shortly after this, Alan rang. Had I heard from someone called Plessis? and so on. Alan was on a train going to Brighton because he'd agreed to take part in a university seminar on the Asian economic miracle. He didn't want to do it, but His Baron-ness kept twisting his arm. 'I wish you were coming to it too.' Hugo has this obsession that the Asian economies are on the brink of a financial crash, and keeps insisting that those of us who work there should pay more attention to what the academic Cassandras are saying. 'I'm only doing this for you, you know,' Alan said. 'And thinking of which, any further sign of J. V. Squared?' I told him where I was – 'enrichment' – and he laughed.

'Well, just be ready to see him tomorrow.'

'Oh God, really? I honestly don't . . .'

'Plessis's bound to want to see Vee-Vee sometime. He may even be setting it up. In any event, I think you should be prepared for it, but ringside this time. Not inside the ropes. Call me and let me know what happens.'

And if this was merely the history of what remained to be done to redeem Beatrix Stapleton, I would leave Alan's phone call there, sparse but informative, friendly but detached. But of course it's not just about Beatrix, who's a pretext possibly. No, that's not right. An extra. An unexpected diversion in other stories altogether. Except that you can't slice life up into this one story and that one story. You can't tease them apart. And anyway, Alan wasn't detached about all this. And neither was I. And there was so much else for us to talk about.

The result was that by the time we had stopped talking I was still looking at a largely uneaten dinner. And I still hadn't made much progress with it when the phone rang again. This time it was Mummy. When was I thinking of coming back? Would I come up to the farm? Where was I going to live? How was the Sauldre valley?

So I told her my plans, and then added a little bit about Beatrix.

'How interesting,' said Mummy. 'What a coincidence. I was just reading about her in the paper . . .'

'Really?'

'Yes. One of the Sundays' feature things. Last weekend. There was a big spread about her, and what a success she's made of her life since her band, or whatever, broke up. It said there'd been a history of drugs and, oh, you know, all the usual things, too much sex and so on, but that she'd put it all behind her. It said she lived somewhere in France. How lucky for you to fall right . . .'

'A success?'

'Yes, that's right. The aftermath of fame, that sort of thing. I don't usually read these things, pop music doesn't appeal to me, as you know, but there was a big photograph of this extravagantly beautiful young woman – that certainly caught my eye – and then something about successful adjustment to changing circumstances. It was well written. It drew me in, rather. I'll find it and keep it for you. It said she'd become a bit of a recluse, wouldn't give interviews, and that she had planted a huge herb garden at her house in France, where she practised transcendental meditation, and sometimes rode an old motorbike around the country lanes.'

'It's only got one wheel.'

'I'm sorry, dear, you'll have . . .'

'The bike. One wheel. Her manager removed the other one. Frightened she'd kill herself before she laid him another egg.'

'I don't really follow.'

'There's to be a big new release of her recordings . . .'

'Yes, it said that. Mid November. "A defining moment" – I do so dislike that silly expression – in the history of contemporary music. An act of retrieval, I think it said.'

'It's Voorhuis, her manager. Setting things up. He's planning to make a killing.' And I explained to her the distance that separated the public relations of commerce from the dross and despair of experience. Well, I didn't mean it to come out on paper like that, but I'll leave it because it's true, though you only seem to discover it when it happens to someone you know. Like those horrible accounts of Philip and the gaudy. And now it was poor Beatrix, with a fake portrait of her hung up for public scrutiny just like a royal princess in a PR honeymoon with public life. What Johan has destroyed he will put back together for public consumption, and the newspapers will supply the superglue. This was the mood – and the fact is, Philip, that I remember the feelings really, really well – in which I went home to bed in Clémont.

III

What happened next was sherbet. I got up early on the Saturday morning and dressed for the wedding, so was feeling really smart and confident, the way you do in a new outfit that is just right. I was almost into the southern outskirts of Orléans, approaching this time on the Vierzon road – Felix's quick route – before Plessis rang to say that he and his companion were well south of Paris, and expected to be at the hospital at nine. Would I meet them at reception? We were expected.

I was in good time and had half an hour to spare, so went to reception and settled down in the waiting area behind a newspaper because I must have looked pretty out of place. The hospital was crowded, which was a bit surprising on a midsummer Saturday morning. Delivery people coming and going; a queue at the information counter; quite a lot of bored people waiting, like me, I supposed, for permission to visit, or for information, or something; officials and a few uniformed hospital staff chatting in the corners, or as they passed through the swing doors that led off the reception area in different directions. The waiting area wasn't terribly comfortable. Vinyl and tubular steel chairs, SIDA ads on the walls, *familles nombreuses* advice posters. Two men asleep in the corner, who looked as though they might have been there all night, were the only items to detract from an atmosphere of brisk, noisy activity.

Into this – my heart skipped a beat, then speeded up as I saw him – came Johan van Voorhuis. Smart this morning in a light-weight summer suit and polished shoes, with a polka-dot tie and a slim, dark brown leather briefcase. Another man was with him, shorter and bulkier, bald, with one of those thick, bushy, black 'I'm still young and virile' moustaches. They crossed to the reception counter where Vee-Vee extruded his charm, like toothpaste, all over a quite attractive young woman who was manning (as we have to say) the desk. She laughed at something he said, took off her glasses and ran her fingers through her hair, to one side, just above the ear. Then she leaned forward to talk more intimately, indicating as she did so the *Renseignements* queue. I could see Vee-Vee reply, but my view was from behind, and I had to imagine the language of his facial expressions, the skill of his 'you'll understand my difficulties' approach, and the seductiveness of his words. The young woman laughed again and picked up a telephone, spoke briefly to someone, then asked Vee-Vee a question, covering the mouthpiece. He gave her a business card, and she read from it into the telephone, nodding and smiling. Then she pointed, my heart sinking, at the waiting area, clearly inviting him to use it. Moustache turned to look, but Vee-Vee never took his eyes off the young woman. He put his briefcase on the counter, opened it, and removed something. From where I was sitting I could see it was a boxed set of CDs, which he opened, passed to her, taking out the pamphlet as he did so, and unfolding it to show her the pictures. I could see the receptionist's eyes widening, little winks and flashes of gold from Vee-Vee's cuff-links, smiles from Moustache as Vee-Vee said something clever and the three of them shared a confidence. Vee-Vee made gestures indicating that she should keep the box set. She set it to one side on the counter, in full view, as if to say, 'This is mine. This gentleman gave it to me. But it's not a bribe. This is all above board.' She picked up the phone and dialled again. More chat and body language, after which she handed Vee-Vee the phone. He turned slightly to one side and I could see him in profile: quite a lot of animation when he was speaking, a gentle, versatile smile to give his voice the tones of warmth, confidence and plausibility, hand movements for emphasis without threat. A very good performance, at the end of which much gratitude. He handed back the phone, and there was more chat across the counter, though my view of this was impeded by a queue that was building up behind Moustache, and also by the general bustle of the whole reception area, which by this time was considerable.

However, after a minute or two the receptionist indicated a door to one side which was swinging open to admit a rather harassed-looking man in a suit that was far smarter than he was, and which would surely soon be far too formal for such a glorious hot Saturday summer morning. He greeted Vee-Vee with a look that said I *do* understand your problem, and they shook hands as he guided him and Moustache towards the swing doors at the top of the reception area.

They did not make very much progress, however. First of all a very smart and slightly plump man with wavy chestnut-brown hair cut fashionably long, though he must have been in his mid forties or thereabouts, came through the front door accompanied by a petite young woman carrying one of those big document cases that airline pilots use. This turned out, fairly soon afterwards, to be Bertrand Plessis and his assistant, Marie-Laure Rivet. Simultaneously, a woman in the middle of the reception area, who was wearing a tiny scrap of a miniskirt, and one of those T-shirt tops that stop above the midriff, giving a shelf-like effect to the breasts and revealing substantial areas of brown skin and possibility, suddenly gave a sharp, high-pitched yelp, a bit like a dog being wounded – short, quite painful to hear, and the focus, briefly, of attention. All heads turned. So did she, spinning on the high heel of a fashionable summer slingback, and, without pausing in the single movement of this spin, she struck Johan van Voorhuis on the cheek with the flat palm of her right hand. The slap was everything a satisfying slap should be. Crisp, clear, resonant. The woman then poured out a stream of what I suppose was invective, though I understood not a word of it. Johan's face turned a brilliant red. An ugly-looking man in shorts and tennis shoes, apparently with the woman, said something along the lines of '*espèce de cochon*' and grabbed Johan by the throat. Moustache tried to get between them. The woman wailed. The harassed man in the elegant suit stepped back from the spotlight of affairs. Some parts of the crowd in reception fell back, making space. Other parts closed in, turning Vee-Vee and Moustache into what looked like the central players in the middle of a rolling maul in a rugby match. Vee-Vee tried to lash out at the woman who had struck him, but missed. Then he contented himself with wrestling Ugly's hand from his throat, and delivering a very firm, straight punch to the man's face. Ugly fell backwards and collapsed on to the floor, shielding his eye with his hand. Miniskirt went dramatically to her knees by his head, begging Ugly to tell her that he was all right. There were oohs and ahs, and a shriek or two, from the twenty or so witnesses of this sudden explosion.

Then the two men in the corner who might have been asleep materialized in front of Vee-Vee and Moustache flashing police badges. Moustache started to say something about being a lawyer, but one policeman had him handcuffed to Vee-Vee, and Vee-Vee handcuffed to a third uniformed officer, who had emerged as if from nowhere, before his legal explanations had gone anywhere much at all. 'Yeah, yeah. And I'm a cosmonaut' was what I thought I heard the first policeman say.

I dropped my newspaper and stood up at this point, whereupon Vee-Vee spotted me and immediately started shouting and swearing in English, 'You bitch. This is a put-up. You wait till I get . . .', but the police were bustling him out of the building, and loading him into a police van parked by the steps. His words, however, were an informal introduction for Plessis, who came over and shook hands, and introduced me to his assistant. Plessis looked at his watch.

'Well,' he said. 'Mr van Voorhuis was punctual, but now he doesn't seem able to keep our appointment.' He grinned. We were joined by the harassed man in the gorgeous suit, who turned out to be the hospital director, less harassed now. Ugly didn't seem to be too badly hurt, and he and Miniskirt were talking to one of the detectives who had broken up the squabble, and then dispatched Vee-Vee and his lawyer to what I assumed would be the gendarmerie. Going down to the gendarmerie in handcuffs suddenly reminded me of Philip. The other detective came over to us.

'Bertold,' or something like that, he said, showing an ID card, shaking hands. '*Préfecture. PJ.* Extraordinary business. Came over here to interview a drug addict who's just come round from an overdose about his tax affairs. Then this happens. Complete coincidence. Amazing. Dutch creep.' Then he laughed. 'That was a vice squad officer he touched up too. Then belted her colleague. Very bad judgement!' He winked. It was wonderfully shameless. 'Didier Thibaudat – here's his card.' He gave it to Plessis. 'You're Plessis, right? Thibaudat's my *patron, juge d'instruction*, he'd like you to drop by and see him around eleven this morning. This'll just be a holding charge on Voorhuis – is that how you pronounce it? But it'll tie him down for a month or so while we open a dossier on him.'

'A month!' I exclaimed. Eyes wide, I imagine.

'Assaulting two police officers. Resisting arrest. Causing an affray. Lots of witnesses.' He shook his head, like a man bewildered at the astonishing stupidity of his fellow man. 'If it turns out he's a foreigner, then we'll have to check his papers, make some inquiries in his home country, ask through Interpol if anyone else is interested. It's all going to take a while.'

'This is France,' said Plessis, with that first indicator of legal pedantry that always augurs well for a client in trouble. 'If the *juge d'instruction* isn't satisfied that the suspect won't abscond, he can keep him inside during the investigation. And there'll be a lot to investigate, eh Marie-Laure?' And Marie-Laure indicated, with a small movement of her very large briefcase, that this was, regrettably, indeed true.

The three of us went up for coffee to the director's office, where Plessis explained the plot. 'Not too many difficulties,' he said. 'After I talked to you last night I got hold of Edmond Baudet. He's the prefect for this *département*. He and I were at Sciences-Po together years ago. Then I went into law and he went to ENA, on to the *ministère des Finances*, and then up the ladder. We kept in touch a bit, the way one does. I explained the situation to him, with particular emphasis on van Voorhuis's reputation for irregularities in his financial dealings, tax arrangements, and so on. Baudet had never heard of him, of course, but he agreed with me that this wasn't the sort of visitor he wanted to have running free on his patch. He suggested I set up a meeting and then tell this man' – he tapped the business card – 'Didier Thibaudat. Let him know where and when, and his people would, I think he said, sweep van Voorhuis off the streets.'

The hospital director seemed anxious about time, and anyway his phone wouldn't stop ringing, so we thanked him for his trouble and left him to his various harassments. 'Always happy to oblige the *préfecture*,' he said. Then I took Plessis and Marie-Laure Rivet up to meet Beatrix. She seemed a bit livelier than she'd been the day before, and we would have had more tears (of gratitude this time, once we told her of Vee-Vee's whereabouts) if I hadn't been running seriously short of time by now. I left her in the company of her new lawyers.

Outside in the summer sun my car had turned into a furnace, and the traffic was heavy going into town. The bridge across the Loire was completely bottled up, and it took forty minutes for me to get across the river and then find somewhere to park. By the time I had threaded my way on foot down past the cathedral and into the narrow streets north of Saint-Aignan I was running seriously late. It was well past eleven when I finally went through the church door. Then I discovered that Saint-Aignan was absolutely packed with people, and I had to push through quite a crowd of other latecomers just inside the door, and almost fight my way to get to the back of the church, where there were still a few seats. I was so far back, and the light through the stained-glass windows was so limited (though so beautiful) that I couldn't really see, let alone understand, much of what was going on. And in any case I was hot and sweaty, and had a lot running through my mind from the events of the morning, so I was quite happy just to sit back in the delicious cool gloom of the church, and allow what was left of the ceremony to wash over me.

Afterwards, outside in the square, I felt awkward and out of place. There seemed to be about three hundred people present, and I didn't know any of them. Members of the wedding party were being busily arranged for photographs at the door of the church, but apart from Micheline there didn't seem to be anyone I recognized. Even Madame Jeanne wasn't visible. I knew none of the people in the huge crowd of well-wishers and onlookers, and anyway they were all in groups or couples, and not looking for anyone to talk to. I felt very alone in this setting, the way one often can at formal gatherings. I had just begun to wonder whether coming hadn't been a mistake, and whether perhaps I should just slip away, when there was a gentle tap on my shoulder, and I turned round to find myself being addressed by a tall man with receding hair. He was in morning dress, carrying a top hat.

'Madame Leroux, how very glad I am that you were able to be with us.' I blinked. Was this – he shook my hand – someone I knew? Then I realized. Of course, Beaumanière, Roland Beaumanière. 'I'm so sorry. I didn't recognize you for a moment. You're so handsome . . .'

'Well, thank you.'

'I mean. In morning dress. You . . .'

He grinned. 'It is true. I am not normally handsome, but morning dress counterfeits the condition to perfection.'

I sighed. Probably blushed. 'Can we start this again? I'm sorry. You surprised me. I was actually just thinking that I should leave. And now here you are. And looking very distinguished. I didn't expect to see you here.' I shook his hand again. 'Yes. I am Alice

Crighton, Philip's widow. We were going to meet tomorrow. I was expecting you to ring.'

'Please don't leave. I am so glad you are here. When you wrote to say that you would be in Clémont, I thought that perhaps you might have one of the houses that Jeanne Morisot looks after in the village. So I asked her, and she told me that this was so. It was at my suggestion that she and Micheline invited you to this wedding today.'

'Your suggestion!'

'Yes. But look, come with me. We would like it very much if you could be in one of the photographs. Please.' And he drew me with him through the crowd to the church door, and eventually I stood in place, just behind Madame Jeanne, for a group photograph that included all the members of both the Bazard and Morisot families, plus Roland and Florence Beaumanière, and me. About forty people altogether. I have the picture in front of me now as I am writing this, and I see, with a little flush of satisfaction, that without Valentine Visconti I would have been the only woman in the picture without a hat.

The next half-hour or so was very slow-moving and rather confused. Many more photographs had to be taken. Roland was busy marshalling people, politely organizing, efficiently keeping things moving. Florence Beaumanière was almost as busy, but in between giving and taking suggestions, lining up children, exchanging greetings, and helping to straighten collars, retie cravates, and reattach button-hole carnations and hip posies, she found enough time to explain that Jeanne Morisot had once known the Beaumanière family at their house near Viglain, and that Roland's father and mother had been Micheline's godparents. So this was a family occasion for her and Roland, the more especially so because, her own husband having died many years ago, Madame Morisot had asked Roland to give the bride away.

This was more or less all that I was destined to understand for much of the rest of the day. Eventually, at the nearby Hôtel Aurelianis, something like a hundred and fifty guests sat down to a sumptuous meal. Here I found myself seated at a table with the harassed man in the wonderful suit. Appropriately dressed! Of course, Micheline's fiancé, husband now, was a surgeon at the hospital. The director was a colleague. More, as I found out, a friend. And half the other guests likewise: nurses and physicians, orderlies and technicians, laboratory assistants and physiotherapists. They were a noisy crew, and it was a lively occasion. Also at our table were a couple of Roland's business friends, one of whom was a banker with what had once been Rothschild's, and he not only reminisced about the days when there were still banking families, but gossiped amiably about common acquaintances. There was some material here to amuse Alan when I got home.

At the end of the meal Roland proposed the toast to the bride and groom, and spoke very movingly of his parents' attachment to Micheline, and how delighted they would have been to be present today. His only regret at giving the speech was that, had he not done so, it would have been because his father was giving it, and everyone here would have greatly preferred that. He told some amusing stories about Micheline as a girl and young woman, and of the pride that her whole family – not *including* the Beaumanières, but *beginning* with them – took in her achievements and accomplishments. Then he had lots to say about her bridegroom, François, his talents and skills, his joy in his bride, the future happiness of them both. We drank their health, then sang them a song – though my part in that was negligible, since all of this was quite new to me.

After that, and rather to my surprise, though apparently no one else's, Micheline spoke. This was superb, though my French let me down, and I could understand very little. She edged into her speech with thanks to Roland and Florence, and then to all the guests who had been so kind and considerate. It had not been easy to persuade all of them, Monsieur Blanco, for instance (this turned out to be the hospital director), and she launched, or perhaps lapsed is better in his case, into a brilliant imitation of him – his air of harassment, the movement of his hands, his constant quest for the right word that always lay just beyond his grasp. Everybody roared and cheered, the director among them. Micheline said that Monsieur Blanco had eventually persuaded her mother that François would make a good husband – and there was an imitation of Madame Jeanne that almost stopped the show. Then she moved on to people I didn't know, mainly her colleagues, then some former schoolfriends. She was very funny – or must have been, because the assembly was repeatedly swept by gusts of laughter – though I don't believe she ever told a joke. It was all done with turns of phrase, wicked little pauses between observations, sudden darts of wit. She had no written speech. Not even notes. She just stood up and performed. And then she ended with some very moving tributes to her mother, and to Roland and Florence, then to François and his parents, and last of all to the colonel Morisot, whose name I remembered from the invitation. He was clearly the old gent sitting a couple of places along from her, and she talked about his wisdom and his generosity, and how much she loved him. Everyone cheered her to the rafters when she finished, and they were quite right. She was splendid.

Later there was dancing, and once more I was going to slip away but was saved by Roland, who sought me out again, and brought me to a table on a terrace overlooking the hotel garden. He sat down with me for a few minutes to introduce me to the colonel. At last I understood. Colonel Morisot was the father of Michel, and Michel was '*le Militaire*', the third of the triumvirate that had also included Roland and Philip. And of course Madame Jeanne – or Jeannette, as I had learned at table was the name by which Roland and Florence knew her – was the girl whom Michel had married all those years ago, before he went to his death in Beirut. The Jeannette of Philip's 'Portrait'. The colonel was very warm and mellow, and talked about the times, years before, in the late sixties and early seventies, when Philip had been a boy, and he and Roland had come visiting to the Morisot apartment in Vincennes. And he told me stories about the young Philip that I had never heard before, and he reconciled me, as I thought, to the idea that Philip had not died in loneliness and misery, because there had been so much laughter and happiness in his young life, and the colonel could not believe that Philip – '*ce clairvoyant*', as he called him – would not always have carried these things with him, even to his death.

Later, after I had said my thanks to Madame Jeanne, and we had exchanged a few words about '*le professeur*', I went to find Roland to say goodbye. He asked me, very warmly, to come to lunch the next day at their house, 'La Forge', near Viglain. And he gave me directions for how to find it.

IV

I drove over to 'La Forge' on Sunday morning, following Roland's instructions to go via Isdes and then take the back road to Viglain. The sun was already hot at ten o'clock, and the place-names, the trees hanging in the heat and the dappling effect of light and shadow across the windscreen, all stirred vague recollections and reminiscences, my own and perhaps not my own. The house, as Roland had said, was not hard to find, well signposted, though set far back from the road among trees, and approached along a cobbled way. Eventually, after a kilometre or so, the drive opened out into a parking area with a couple of garages. A big estate car stood under the trees, its windows rolled down. A cluster of stone buildings with steeply pitched roofs was visible on the far side of a brook. I walked over the little curved footbridge, crossed a wide lawn, and walked through an open archway that gave on to a brick courtyard. Roland was sitting at a small round iron table, smoking a cigarette, and talking to a couple of labradors that were lying sprawled at his feet in the sun. He stood up as soon as I appeared. The buildings almost completely enclosed the yard, their walls studded here and there with doors and windows. There was no sign of Florence.

'Beautiful,' I said, stopping to admire, and indicating the buildings, the trees rising above the rooftops, the intense blue of the sky. 'What a setting!'

Roland gave one of those deprecating little movements of the lips as he came towards me, pursing and relaxing them so quickly that it was made and gone almost unseen.

'We would come here more often if we could,' he said, embracing me with pecks to both cheeks. 'Florence is busy for perhaps half an hour more, so I thought we might take a walk. Such a beautiful morning.' I had been rehearsing one or two things to say in French, but Roland's English really was so stunningly good that I decided to put them away. Perhaps I would get them out again later, if need be, with Florence. I complimented him on it. 'Did Philip never tell you that I worked in Canada for a few years, back in the mid eighties?' I said not. 'Yes, in Ottawa, where they put their government so that it is not in anyone's way.' He smiled. 'I had to work mainly in English, but Florence and the children escaped by speaking that execrable guttural argot that the *Québécois* will insist on calling French.'

'You didn't acquire a Canadian accent in your English.'

'It is impossible for a Frenchman to copy. But it is useful. In trying to sound Canadian a Frenchman can get an English accent.'

Roland clicked his tongue at the dogs, and they hauled themselves lazily upright, blinked a few times, and then padded across, tails wagging, to sniff and assess.

'They are ten years old now – we got them when we came home from Canada – and that is quite old for such dogs. They have trouble with their hips.'

We had crossed to a gate in a corner of the yard while Roland was saying this, and he opened it and let us through into a small garden, flowerbeds to one side, herbs and vegetables to another, a lawn in between. 'Madame Belvoir's kingdom,' he said. 'She is not here on Sundays. She goes to her son in the village.'

We joined a path that climbed through woodland, the ground soft beneath our feet, the two dogs running among the shrubs and saplings beneath the trees, snuffling and probing, disappearing and then emerging into view again to check on our presence and progress, one front paw raised, head forward, tail rising and still.

'You have a word for that in English, don't you?'

'Pointing.'

'Mmm. I should remember. You enjoyed our little party yesterday?'

'Very much. It was a privilege to be invited. And a wonderful surprise to find you and Florence there.' He gave another little facial movement of deprecation, this time a smile.

'I should have realized, it was foolish of me not to, when you first wrote with your address in Clémont, that you might be staying in one of the houses that Jeannette looks after. It's the kind of coincidence that crops up in life, don't you think?'

'You call her Jeannette?'

'Yes, ever since we were young. I expect you know her as Madame Morisot or something similar . . .'

'Madame Jeanne.'

'There. But she has always been Jeannette to us. We are very proud of Micheline, whom we think of almost as one of our own children. Come. I want to show you something.' We forged on up the hill until the path curved back from the east towards the south, and we came out of the wood at the top of a long sloping field that fell away in front of us, one side of a shallow valley. To our right was a dry-stone wall, perhaps a metre or so high. Along its base, stretching to the edge of the field, were clusters of wild flowers, patterns of hot and soft colours on the grey and khaki carpet of the earth. The field itself was planted with vines. Roland stepped into the nearest aisle and walked along, me following, the dogs grunting at his heels. He stopped now and then to hold

265

up a leaf for inspection, or to put his hand under a cluster of the tiny green fruit that were more like seeds, the grapes not yet bulked up around them. The sun blazed down. You could almost hear the vines growing, tendrils and stems crawling forward along the supports from post to post.

'What do you think?'

'Is it new?'

'Fifth year. Perhaps the first potable vintage. If this weather settles, it might even be memorable.'

'What sort of grapes?'

'Just sauvignon. They do well further south, but not normally in these parts. The Sologne is poor soil for agriculture. But I always had a feeling about this slope, that it might be different. So I had an analysis carried out. It was quite encouraging. Even so, we're a bit far from the river. Would you buy a Domaine de la Forge?'

'Not a Château Beaumanière?'

'Tut, tut.' He shook his head, and crouched down to run his fingers through the earth. 'It's only a little sauvignon. Domaine is quite grand enough.' He stood up and we walked on, Roland warming to his project. 'If this goes well, and the wine's the way I hope it will be, it could turn out to be a good investment, as well as a hobby. You know I had a dream about this piece of land. I was going to make a really distinctive sauvignon blanc, almost green, full of melon flavours, do you know what I mean? And then I was going to persuade the Brasserie Balzar in Paris to take it for their private label. Do you know the Balzar? Did Philip never take you there?' He outlined a rectangle with his hands: 'Cuvée Balzar. Sauvignon de la Loire. Domaine de la Forge. Côte de Chasne. Propriétaire Roland Beaumanière, Domaine de la Forge, Viglain, Loire.' He dropped his hands and gave a shrug. 'Michel, Philip and I used to meet at the Balzar. Then I heard a rumour the other day that they might sell up to some chain or the other. I'm not going to offer my wine to the Café Mickey. They can drink Algerian anti-freeze.'

266

I didn't understand much of this, and said so.

'Being robbed of one's past, I suppose,' he said, 'when you want it to be preserved as it really was. You know we used to meet at this place the Balzar. It's by the Sorbonne, on the corner of the Rue des Écoles, almost opposite the Musée de Cluny. You'd think, in a central location like that, students, millions of tourists, it would have been ruined years ago. But somehow it had survived. The same decor, same waiters, same clientele, the sense of space in a confined area, mirrors, bustle, hubbub – is that right? You say hubbub for that undertow of happy conversation? And the same menu. The Balzar was a fixed point for us. It was where we met when we were three. It was where Philip and I went after Michel was killed. We used to say it was where we'd go, old and widowed – forgive me – to celebrate our eightieth birthdays.' He sighed, ducking under the vines, crossing a couple of aisles, and then turned uphill again to walk back towards the wood. We were both perspiring in the sun, the dogs slinking about in the shade beneath us. 'And now, instead of our private rendez-vous, and me supplying it with the best sauvignon outside the Sancerre, Michel and Philip are gone, and the devil of commercial profit is going to turn my memories into a fast-food outlet.'

At the top of the hill, back under the trees, we turned to look south again, across the tops of the vines.

'That over there' – and I pointed – 'is that Villemême?'

Roland nodded, dabbing at his high, balding forehead with a handkerchief. 'Yes. Funny little place. It's where your Madame Jeanne, our Jeannette, came from originally,' he said. And, clicking his fingers to rouse the dogs from where they had flopped down panting in the grass, he turned away from the vineyard and the view, and we went back into the wood, and once more followed the little slowly curving path that took us down to the house.

As we walked along I asked him about Philip's parents, their home in Finchley, whether he'd ever visited and so on. 'Oh yes,' he said. 'Several times. It was an exchange at the beginning, a school thing, and if you signed on you couldn't escape.'

'It must have seemed very, what shall I say?, very different.'

'Why do you say that?'

'Philip used to say he felt it was hollow. Inauthentic. He only ever really felt at home when he was with you in France.'

Roland laughed. 'Philip's parents were always very kind to me. At the start I wouldn't eat anything, and couldn't speak any English, and thought everything was strange, but Philip worried more about this than I did. He was embarrassed, I think. So he thought I didn't eat because the food was not good, but it was just different. Everything was different. I learned eventually. It was interesting.'

'Did you go often?'

'Several times, yes. At least twice. I forget exactly when. When we began this, you know, we were only thirteen . . .'

Florence was bringing coffee out to the courtyard table as we arrived, and together she and Roland chatted to me about the house, its origins, and the things that they had done to improve it: new roofing, new bathrooms, bricks for cobblestones in the yard, a barn made into guest accommodation over a playroom. 'Children,' said Florence, raising her eyebrows, and giving out one of those sighs that signals maternal cares.

'You have some . . .?'

'Oh yes. Four . . .'

'And there would have been more if Florence had . . .'

'The oldest is eighteen and the youngest twelve. They are not here this weekend . . .'

'A wedding,' said Roland, 'was definitely second best to a weekend at home with their parents away. We are going to the south next week, so they preferred a last weekend in Paris with their friends.'

'Do you?'

'Yes please.'

Florence smiled and passed me the sugar. 'Really, I meant do you have children also?' Roland was shaking his head at her. No doubt this was something he had already told her about Philip, and she had forgotten. It didn't matter. Something else had occurred to me, perhaps as a result of their mentioning the barn.

'Did this place once belong to a film director? And was it once a windmill, rather than a forge?'

'A film director?' echoed Roland. 'Heavens no. It's been in my family since the mid thirties, when my grandfather bought it for next to nothing. It was rather derelict because no one had actually lived here, or used it as a forge, since the end of the First World War. It's true that there did need to be windmills in this part of France. It is very flat here, and the rivers are sluggish. But this never was one. Why do you ask?'

'Something Philip wrote. A place he wrote about. I suppose this wasn't it, but somehow it might have been.'

'He came here often enough.'

'Really?'

'Oh yes, from the time of his very first visit to France. It was at Easter, and we always came to the Forge at Easter. For three years after that he came here a lot, so it was somewhere he knew well. Did he never tell you?'

I shook my head. Philip had told me about Brittany, and about the south, and about his visits to Paris, but I'm sure he never even mentioned this part of the country, this house and its setting. Roland had gone on talking while I was thinking about this, wondering what it meant.

'Yes, in a way this was the part of France that Philip knew best. We had bikes in those days and used to ride all over the place. Up to Tigy, or over to Gien. When we went farther afield – down to Châtillon or to Sancerre – then we'd set off in the morning, and my parents would drive down in the afternoon and we'd meet somewhere for a meal, and then put the bikes up on the car to drive home in the evening.'

'Did you say that you rode your bikes to Sancerre?'

'Yes. Why not? You sound surprised. It isn't all that far . . .'

'Philip said once – this was in something else that he wrote, quite recently, not long before he died – actually it's going to be published soon – he said that when he came to France with a friend of his in the summer of, it must have been, ooh, 1975, when he was nineteen, he met a man who came from the Sancerre, and that at the time he had no idea where this was.'

'Really,' said Roland. Then he fell silent for a while, as though absorbing the information, adapting something to it. 'In fact, he knew it well,' he said eventually. 'There used to be a shop that sold particularly good ice-creams, which we were both fond of. Or maybe they just seemed very good after a hot bike ride.'

Florence left us at this point, clearing the coffee cups away on a tray and going off, she said, to do something about lunch. I was now feeling really quite perplexed, puzzled and immensely curious, and also a little bit excited, as though something was about to happen. These feelings, strong at the time, I can still recollect now, though they were offset to some extent by a sensation not of fear exactly, but of a sort of frightening anxiety. Was this deception on Philip's part? Or forgetfulness? Or something physical, like a part of his brain not functioning properly – one comes across stories of these sorts of things from time to time, and it's certainly true that Philip was not at all well during his last six months of life. Or was there something that he wanted to conceal, to bury, something that it might be better not to dig up? Roland got up, and went to sit in the shade, under the awning of a swing cot, from which a cat darted away as he sat down. The dogs had disappeared.

'This, um, business of your coming here, to Clémont, I mean, was that, er, how can I put this?, was it, is it, um, deliberate?'

'Well, I'm certainly not here by accident . . .'

'I'm sorry. Let me, you don't mind my asking, I hope, Philip and I . . .' And he lapsed for a few seconds into silence, apparently scrutinizing his hands. I thought suddenly of that little ebony-handled manicure device, Philip's account of Roland's fastidiousness as a seventeen-year-old. I wanted very badly to help him over whatever difficulty it was that he was encountering, but I didn't know how to do it, so kept quiet. He started talking again eventually.

'It just seems such a coincidence. I remember saying to you at Philip's funeral that it would be nice to meet you again. I think I even said that we probably had quite a lot to talk about in one way or another. We had both known Philip so well, yet separately. He never brought us together. I suppose what I imagined was that one day you and I might have lunch, either in Paris or in London when my business interests bring me there, which they do once in a while. And then I was delighted to get your letter saying you were going to be in Clémont, so close to us here, and at exactly the time that we had another engagement – well, Micheline's wedding, of course – and so were bound to be here too. You will agree, this was rather surprising.'

'Well, it is a coincidence, yes. Coincident with you and Florence owning this house, which I didn't know about, in the same part of the country. Coincident with its being somewhere that Philip came, as a boy, before I knew him, and about which he had never told me. Yes, a complete coincidence. But rather nice, don't you think?'

Roland gave a warm smile, and spread his hands. 'Perhaps, like me,' he said, 'you can almost see him still, over there, climbing up into the barn where we used to, how do you say it, lark about?' I looked where he indicated, but the old barn doors now existed only in outline, and what had once been, I imagined, vaguely derelict, or at any rate messy, just as he had described it in 'The Portrait', was now pointed masonry, stained wood doors, polished brass fittings. It was all so very different, I thought, from what it once must have been.

'I came to Clémont because – well, for a number of reasons, really – but mainly because a man called Felix Cunningham, who was a colleague of Philip's at Oxford, and a good friend to both of us – actually you met him at Philip's funeral, in January

271

– he has a little house there, a country place where he likes to come in the summer to write. He said I could have it for a couple of weeks. Madame Jeanne, whom it then turns out you knew, keeps an eye on the house for him when he's not there. She feeds his cat, clears the mailbox, makes sure the place is secure, that sort of thing. When he's going to come down, she opens the place up for him, airs it, makes up the bed, gets the fridge going again . . .'

'She makes quite a living at it,' said Roland. 'These little country places, within three or four hours' driving distance of Paris, are all dead, really – or at any rate, they're not what they were. They keep going on the strength of weekend second-home owners – lawyers, doctors, professors, accountants. They bought up these places in the seventies and eighties. It's what's kept the rural economy going, really, in this part of France, because they employ masons, roofers, gardeners and so on, and they support the local shop-owners. Your Madame Jeanne, she looks after half a dozen places for people while they're away, and then cleans and so on for them when they're in residence. She took it up six years ago, when Micheline went off to nursing school. Until then, and this is why we know her so well, she used to live here. She was our housekeeper.'

Mystery solved, I thought, and felt quite relieved. Roland had moved on, however, and seemed launched on a much longer story.

'Jeannette, Madame Jeanne, came to work for us when she was twelve. That sounds terrible. Actually, of course, she didn't come to work for us then, but she did come to live here. She was a local girl, Jeannette Martin, whose father ran off when she was three. This was in 1958, so she's exactly the same age as me. There's a story about her father, though whether it's true or not I don't know. It's said that he was mixed up in some popular rural political organization or the other, one of those awful peasant things, Poujade or whatever, and that during the crisis of 1958, when the old Republic collapsed and de Gaulle came back, this fellow answered whatever call he got, and went up to Paris thinking he was going to man some barricade or the other. My father told me that at the time it looked as though there might be a civil war, but it all blew over, the new regime settled in, and everything returned to normal. With one exception, however. Jeannette's father never came back. One story was that he'd met a woman in some part of Paris who ran a café or a cheap lodging house or something, and that he moved in with her. Anyway, whatever the truth, he certainly abandoned Villemême, and his wife and daughter with it. Jeannette's mother scratched some sort of living for the next ten years, but in 1968, I suppose still a comparatively young woman, she died, and Jeannette was going to be put into an orphanage in Orléans.

'Street disturbances again.' Roland lit a cigarette. 'The history of France. This was in May, and we had come down here after the events broke out to wait for them to blow over.'

'Blow over? There was very nearly a revolution . . .'

'No, no. There was never any danger of that. All the sensible people did what we did. I remember it all very clearly. My father took me fishing, and told me it was all a lot of noise, and that it was one of the oddities of French culture that a people so good at cooking and loving and living combined these things with the most astonishingly cruel self-deception about politics. He was right too. It's still true. Anyway, our being at Viglain was the big coincidence, because without the *événements* we wouldn't have been here, and so my mother wouldn't have learned about Jeannette. She did learn about her, however: through the local priest, who was making the arrangements. She was touched by the story, and suggested to the priest that it would be better for Jeannette to come to us and spend the rest of the summer here at "La Forge", where she would have young people her own age, and also still be near the village, which was her home, and where she knew everyone. So this was agreed, and she moved in.

'She was shy and very awkward, and had had very little education, though she could read and write. But she was adept

273

and observant, and my mother quickly saw that she was very intelligent, though not in any trained kind of way. I think we – that is me and my brother and sister, who are both younger than I am – underestimated, or more probably had no real idea of, what it was like to grow up poor in the fifties and sixties in a tiny cottage in a small village tucked out of sight in the heart of the French countryside. You know, even in the early sixties the peasants round here still wore smocks and clogs, and the children had no shoes. Jeannette had never had a radio at home. No telephone. Of course, no television. She told us later that her mother cooked on a very primitive wood-fired stove, and that they fetched water in a bucket from the village pump.

'When she first arrived, my mother put her in that room there' – and he pointed above the archway through which I had come earlier, where an oblong window looked down on the courtyard. 'But we found out after a week or so that she couldn't, or wouldn't, stay up there, and had actually been sleeping in the barn, where there was hay, and where Madame Métrard, who was our housekeeper then, kept chickens. And it was Madame Métrard . . .'

'Was this the person you used to call Mamette?'

'Yes, that's right. So Philip had talked to you about this.'

'No, no. But he wrote a piece, quite a long piece, a while ago now. I found it among his college papers, not among the things he kept at home. I thought at first it was autobiography, but from what you're saying it sounds as though it may be several different things condensed together. Anyway, there's a house-keeper in it called Mamette, and a girl who helps her in the kitchen called Jeannette.'

'Well, that certainly sounds like us. It was Mamette who was the first to see what was wanted, really. Instead of leaving Jeannette to tag along with the rest of us, where she didn't understand what was going on, and was lonely and sad, she took Jeannette into the kitchen to help her. Jeannette liked it there. Mamette was good with her, and knew how to draw her out.

Eventually she became much more talkative and lively, and after several years, I think, very happy. But this is to run ahead. At first I think she was just badly in need of security, and it was Mamette who had the sense to see that she, and the routines of the kitchen and the house, could provide it for her.

'Something then happened. I'm not quite sure what. The local priest who was nominally in charge of Jeannette's case went away, or was moved, or died or something. No one was paying much attention to detail in the summer of 1968, because all the talk was about grand topics like History, and the State, and Hegemonic Forces.' Roland laughed, stubbing out his cigarette. 'Jeannette's case disappeared from official view. The social services were poorly developed then, and never made much impact in the provinces anyway. Public attention in those days, where it was interested in social issues at all, was focused on factory workers, or on the *pieds noirs* who'd returned from Algeria. One little orphan girl on the edge of the Sologne was easily lost either in the tumult, or among the neglect. In any event, my mother had grown fond of her, Mamette deeply attached and protective, and my father, as was usually the case, only too ready to indulge the women in the household. So she stayed . . .'

'Never went to the orphanage?'

'No. She went to school, of course, in Viglain, at least for a couple of years. But never to the orphanage. She just became a part of the family.'

'Really?'

Roland looked at me, perhaps a tiny bit severely, and then began to rock the hanging cot very gently, backwards and forwards, with his heels. It made a little creaking sound. I must have sounded critical, and regretted it. But perhaps it was how I was feeling. I don't now remember.

'You don't believe me,' he said. 'Well, in a way, perhaps you are right. But, you know, there are many ways of being a part of something, and Jeannette's way of being part of us – certainly at the beginning – was to watch and to help. Nobody asked or

275

told her to do this. It was just her way of being. We have to respect each other's ways of being. Philip used to say that, I remember. And Jeannette was happy helping Mamette – I'm certain of this: indeed she came to love her very much – and I think she was frightened of the possibility of being sent away, and she was deeply attached to my mother and completely in awe of my father. She would have done anything for my mother, who was a fountain of good advice for a girl of that age, and took her in hand. Little things: how to stand, how to sit, how to dress, where to put her hands, when to say thank you, whom to kiss, when to remain silent. And all the big things too: sex education, I'm sure, though of course my brother and I weren't part of that. And what was honourable in a girl. And how to deal with the problem of men. Jeannette was a godsend for my mother, really, because Danielle, that's my sister . . .'

'Danielle was your sister?'

'Well, yes. Still is. Er, shouldn't she be? Is there something wrong with that?'

'Philip had a girlfriend here in France called Danielle. At that time. He said he did anyway.'

'Oh I don't think so. Leastways – is that the right expression? – not my sister. Danielle was far too scatterbrained for Philip. He barely took any notice of her at all. She lives in America now.' He said this in a tone that implied an explanation. 'No, no, I knew all about Philip's love life, just as he knew all about mine, and it certainly didn't include Danielle. Where was I?'

'Your mother being good with girls and their etiquette.'

'Oh yes. Well, all I was going to say was that I think mother was glad of Jeannette, who listened to her at a time when Danielle wouldn't be bothered with what mother called "the essentials" and what Danielle called "all that old-fashioned stuff". Danielle got away with it because she was my father's favourite, and he spoiled her. She could be wickedly funny in a crude kind of way. You know, shocking people with outrageous statements, quoting obscenities from things like *Zazie dans le métro* or *La*

Guerre des boutons, and swearing loudly in the middle of some polite social occasion or the other. It could be funny to some outsiders, but it was a bit of a trial to the rest of us. Especially my mother. I think Jeannette was a great comfort to her.'

Roland fell silent having said this. He seemed for a moment a little like someone in a maze who has reached a junction, and can go either left or right, but has no obvious reason for choosing one rather than the other, so just sits down and does nothing but rest for a while. I remember thinking, looking at him, how much I liked him despite myself. In all sorts of ways he stood for things that I'm against – elitism, the benefits of being well-connected, effortless money and the comforts it buys, the privileges of the French *haute bourgeoisie* – the *École Polytechnique*, country houses, mothers who never think further than the *Figaro* magazine. But I could also see why Philip had liked him so much. He wasn't thoughtful, but he had the kind of understanding that ran on reliable tracks, that went where it intended, and that generally wanted to do the right thing even when it knew this was impossible.

'Why have you been telling me all this?' I asked.

Florence came out at this point and asked us to come in for lunch. Roland stood up.

'I thought you asked.'

'No, though I am interested.'

'Perhaps just to pass the time before lunch.' He grinned. 'And to conceal the fact that, very rudely, I was failing to offer you an aperitif. Will you?' I said no, and we went into the house.

This was deliciously cool after the midsummer sun. Brick walls and tiled floors in the corridor. Wooden boards, damask curtains, Persian carpets, oil paintings in the dining room. Irish table linen, English silverware, Italian pottery, Swedish glasses. 'The new Europe,' I said.

He smiled assent. 'But nothing German. A family tradition. We did have some German pieces once, so I was told. Some officers, quite senior, I think, lived here during the war, and when they cleared out in a hurry in the summer of forty-four, they left various things behind.' He sat down at his place at the head of the table, speaking slowly and deliberately. 'My grandfather burnt them all.' Then he smiled: 'Seems silly now, doesn't it?'

Florence came in with a superb spinach soufflé, and we ate that, and some salad and cheese and fruit, and drank water, and chatted about our work and acquaintances. We must have talked about Philip some more, though I can't now remember in what context. Perhaps about his work, the two books that he wrote, his approach to philosophy. But never mind about that, because the important thing is that after lunch we all helped to clear the table, and so went through into the kitchen together. And this room simply convinced me that 'On the Edge' (which is perhaps, and after all, the better title for it) really did contain a portrait of, or at any rate descriptions of, this house. That really the windmill was 'La Forge'. Here was the door directly on to the yard, with what had once been the barn diagonally opposite; a pantry off to the rear, with high shelves, beams with great hooks for hanging things, and a sloping skylight. To one side of the door, under a window, was a deep ceramic sink, of the sort for washing vegetables. Along the right-hand wall, on the other side of which I was later to learn that there was a sitting room with a huge fireplace, was a big coal-fired kitchen range and oven. In the centre of the room stood a large square antique oak table, where we sat down to drink coffee. The sun was still high over-head, sunlight spilling in through the open door across the ochre-coloured tiles. The dogs had reappeared, and were lying, snoring, by the dresser, their heads propped up against it at improbable angles. Neither Roland nor Florence seemed aware of the snores. Roland took his chair over by the door, where he could smoke a cigarette and blow the smoke out into the open air.

'I was glad you were able to talk to Colonel Morisot at the wedding breakfast,' said Roland. 'Or rather, I was glad that you didn't seem to mind my taking you to meet him. When I told him you were there, he literally commanded an introduction. Did you enjoy talking to him?'

'Very much. He told me some very amusing stories about Philip.'

'Yes, well, Philip and I were often at the Morisot apartment when we were still schoolboys. And both the colonel and his wife, Madame Adèle, liked Philip a lot. For some reason, I suppose because he was a foreigner and a guest, Philip was allowed to get away with all sorts of things that I would never have dared to do. One thing I remember very well: if we went there for lunch, as we did sometimes, Philip would end the meal by rolling and folding his napkin so that it ressembled a flower on its stem, and then he would tell the colonel's wife that she was a wonderful hostess, that he adored her, and with his hand on his heart would put the napkin-flower into her water glass. She thought this was delightful, and would give peals of laughter and tell the colonel that he would have to fight a duel to defend his honour, or hers.'

'Yes, he told me that story, and some others too, about going to the races in the park at Vincennes, and visits to the chateaux in the Marne valley. One at Champ, where Philip fell in the fountain, and everyone thought it was deliberate . . .'

'It was.'

' . . . and another one where there was a wedding party being photographed, and the bride was chewing gum. So Philip marched up to her, in the middle of all these people clustered on the steps in front of this terribly grand palace, and, pretending to be the photographer's assistant, told her that she absolutely had to stop chewing now this minute, or they – the photographer and his assistant – would leave, refusing to do the job. And anyway, what sort of impression did she think she was making? She was getting married, not attending a baseball game. Had she no sense of occasion? And then he marched down again, and stood behind the photographer, nodding and pointing, and giving directions.

'It was just wonderful. The colonel was so charming. Well, the whole occasion was. Really, I've had ten quite extraordinary days here.'

'Did he say anything about Jeannette and Michel – how difficult it had been at the beginning?'

'Not a word. But he's terribly proud of Micheline, and I thought it was very nice the fuss she made of him. Michel and Jeannette must have been very young, though, when they married.'

Roland smiled and flapped his left hand as though it needed cooling. 'It was all very difficult for everyone.' He flicked his cigarette out into the yard and leaned back on his chair, putting his hands behind his head. 'Though you wouldn't know it now, thank goodness. The colonel is widowed, lives on his own, and it's Micheline who travels up and down to Vincennes at the weekends to make sure he's all right. He calls her "Bibiche". Yet years ago, when Michel said he intended to marry Jeannette, the colonel was speechless, and Adèle, well, words can't describe, really. Actually at the time she reminded me of an old English joke that Philip taught me, and I used it at a reception somewhere – the British embassy, I think – to rather good effect. "Madame Morisot and this marriage?" I said. "Of course she does not approve. Indeed, she is beside herself with unhappiness, and a less attractive couple it is difficult to imagine."'

I laughed aloud at this myself. The authentic Philip voice, transferred to a Frenchman. Roland talked on. 'The wedding was a rather tense affair. Easter 1978. All sorts of things had come together. Mamette wanted to retire, so Jeannette had agreed to stay on as sole housekeeper for us here. Michel had graduated from Saint-Cyr the previous summer, served nine months with a tank regiment, and just learned that he was to be posted to the Lebanon. This was a military attaché job in the embassy in Beirut, and there was something not very nice about it. Michel wouldn't say – I expect it was state secret stuff – but I know he wasn't looking forward to going all that much. Just a week or so before he was due to leave he asked Jeannette to marry him. She agreed, the ceremony was held at the *mairie* in Viglain on the Thursday, the day before Easter, and he left for Beirut the next day.'

'And never came back.'

Roland nodded. He unclasped his hands from behind his head and twisted his fingers together, stretching them away from him until they all cracked very gently. He was sombre and distant, lost somewhere. These three, I thought, Roland, Michel and Philip, had really imposed themselves somehow. In a way that most of us never do. The loyalty was almost tangible.

'My father was one of the witnesses. If they'd had time for a church service, he would have given her away. After the ceremony there was a reception in this house. My mother and Danielle prepared it here, in this kitchen. I came up from Toulouse, where I was with Aerospatiale in those days. The colonel and Adèle did come to the ceremony, because military etiquette and social custom required it. But they refused to come to the reception, and Adèle never forgave my parents for, as she put it, "harbouring this disgraceful union".'

'They must have been very much in love.'

'Michel was quite sure,' Roland went on, 'that he was going to die in the Middle East. He didn't expect to see any of us again. He told me, before he left for Paris that evening, which was the last time I saw him, that he thought someone ought to have his pension.'

I may have been being stupid up to this point, but this remark changed everything, like a landscape falling into place when you adjust the focus on binoculars. 'You mean he married her . . .?'

'Love?' Roland shook his head. 'A lot of affection. He cared for her very much, and she had always liked him. And of course she wanted Micheline to have him as a father. So there were oceans of sympathy. A lot of generosity. But there was no church wedding, and, to my knowledge, their marriage was never consummated.'

'But it *had* been. Micheline must have been three or four years old by . . .'

Roland was still shaking his head. 'Forgive me,' he said, 'but Jeannette was in love with our friend Philip. Always had been, I think. Probably always will be. She was certainly devastated when I broke the news to her of his death. And Micheline, before you even start to guess the obvious, is Philip's daughter.'

Being told this made me light as air. I felt I might float away. I couldn't speak. I had become ethereal, sailing through a thick sky on the wind of Roland's words.

'It started at Easter 1971. Easters, summers, Christmases, our lives were lived by the pattern of the holidays. We came down here for a few days, and Philip was with us. He was fifteen, am I right? The weather was unusually fine, and one day we decided to ride our bikes down to Sancerre. It was me and Philip, Danielle and Jeannette. I don't know what had happened to Christian, that's my little brother. Perhaps he'd gone to camp or something. He learned to sail, which I never did, really. Anyway, he wasn't with us. Perhaps everything would have been different if he had been. Along the way my sister got a puncture, and I stayed behind to help mend it while Philip and Jeannette went on ahead. I thought we'd catch them up, but something went wrong and slowed us down, I don't really remember now, and eventually we were so far behind that we just fell back on the contingency plan, which was to meet at the usual rendez-vous with my father, on the edge of town, in the early evening.

'All of this went off apparently normally, but when we came back to "La Forge" in the summer it soon became clear to me that something was going on between Philip and Jeannette. The usual sorts of adolescent signs, obvious to us now we're grown up: blushing and sweating; getting excitable, then morose; all those things. I pulled Philip's leg about this – that's another term Philip taught me: peculiar when you think about it – and eventually he confided in me. It had all started in Sancerre at Easter, up at the top of the town, looking down over the river. I don't know the details, of course, one never does, but clearly it was first love. I imagine that she kissed him, and that it was the first time for both of them, and that it was, like all such first tender exchanges, begun in trembling hesitation, experienced in surprise and excitement, and reflected on in delight so intense that it breeds disbelief, and makes us wonder if this can really be true.

'I had guessed, of course, but Philip was ready enough to tell me because it was just bursting out of him, and anyway he needed my help. He wanted to spend as much time as possible with Jeannette, but he didn't want my parents to know. He was afraid that if they found out they would report it to his own parents in London, and that would put an end to everything, and not just his affair with Jeannette. As it happens this was relatively easy to do – keeping it from my parents – because my father had just then bought some land in the Midi, on which he was going to build a house, and both he and my mother were preoccupied with this project, which took them away a lot of the time. When they weren't here Mamette was left in charge. We were all fifteen or sixteen and there wasn't much supervision. Jeannette went on helping in the kitchen and around the house, but otherwise she came with us on our excursions, and she and Philip would sometimes just slip away together, especially in the evenings – walks in the woods, that sort of thing. I think it was all pretty innocent. Philip was still very young, and Jeannette, though she was a year older than Philip, and already quite grown up, and certainly very beautiful, was shy and reserved.

'All this was changed a year later. Philip was much more mature when we got together in Brittany in July. I remember because there was some horsing around with a group of people we met there, art students for the most part, a bit reckless and disorganized. One of them had a terrific crush on Philip, and tried to impress him by being daring. He dealt with this by ignoring her, which made her all the more desperate and extreme. Philip used to do good imitations of her. My mother was very critical

ese young people, but she loved Philip's imitations. After
tany Philip and I had to go to a family wedding in Reims,
one of those terrible occasions when distant cousins make a
nuisance of themselves, and unbearable aunts comment on how
tall you're getting, and what a striking resemblance you bear to
Aunt Agathe, and so on. One of my cousins, a rather nice girl
we used to call Marie-O, from my mother's side, the Lascombes
– a Bordeaux tribe – just about threw herself at Philip during the
reception, but he didn't take the slightest notice. I mention these
things because they showed, I think, that Philip was already very
attractive to girls, but that it didn't affect him. He wasn't much
interested. Somehow he could just sort of handle it. Perhaps he
even thought it was a bit peculiar.

'After that, along with Michel, we came on down here. Once
again my parents were away, mainly in the south. The house
there was just about finished, but they were painting and fur-
nishing, and my father was laying out a garden. We stayed here
for the whole month of August. Philip and Jeannette were now
hopelessly in love. "She lives in his shadow, and he finds himself
there in her reflection." That was something Michel said, and I
have remembered it all these years. Michel and I were in awe of
both of them. And we were quite sure – this is probably why we
thought they were gods – that they had become lovers. A tender
topic, of course, because both Michel and I, despite the usual
adolescent bravado and posturing, were hopelessly slow and
clumsy with girls, and despaired of ever actually finding out
what sex, and all that side of things, was like. Anyway, they
were together for the whole of August, and I think we believed
that it would carry on. We had to go back to Paris at the beginning
of September, but I'm certain that Philip and Jeannette parted
just as they had been reunited, very much in love.

'Philip had somehow persuaded both my parents and his to
let him stay on in France for the month of September. I can't
now remember the pretext, though there must have been one
– some pressure-cooker course at the Alliance Française, some-

thing like that. Something he certainly didn't need. While he did this, and I was back in school, we both worked on my parents to persuade them to take us all down to "La Forge" for one last weekend at the end of the month. Actually this wasn't hard to do. Even though we had Mamette as resident housekeeper, my mother was addicted to the ritual of closing up the house after the summer season – a ritual of which she had been deprived by being in the Midi. Also, in those days my father had an eight-millimetre movie camera, which he was actually rather good with, taking films of his travels and so on. He'd put together several reels showing the building of the new house, right from when he first bought the land to the stocking of the cellar, and he wanted us all to see this. "La Forge" was a good place to do it. So he invited various friends and relations to make up a house party, and we all came down for the last weekend in September.

'The autumn was well advanced, and it was, I remember, wet and cold, so it was pretty unpleasant to do anything out of doors. We came by car on the Friday, and the various guests trickled in on Saturday morning. There were a couple of my father's business partners and their wives, and Marie-O Lascombe, who had just started at ENA, so was living in Paris, and the Bosanquet family, cousins of my father, who in those days lived in Tours. They had a boy, Bruno, who was about our age, Bruno Bosanquet, who of course got called "Bé-Bé", which he didn't like. We didn't like him either. He was nervy and irritable, but quite good-looking, and vain. Philip dreamed up a silly slogan about him which went "*Qu'il est bête, le beau inquiet*", and the three of us used to chant this in unison. He hated it. He's a journalist now.

'The whole weekend was a disaster for us – that's me, Philip and Michel – because we never seemed to be able to get away on our own. Michel rather liked Marie-O, but she was a few years older than us, and anyway all she'd do was follow Philip around looking tragic. All Philip wanted was to be alone with Jeannette, which was just about impossible. And Bruno had decided that Jeannette, whom he mistook, understandably enough, I suppose, for a domestic servant, was fair game. I think now that it might have been funny: we were just teenagers after all, trying desperately to be grown up. But at the time it was agony, and it all came to a head late on the Saturday night, when my parents and the other grown-ups had at long last gone to bed.

'The details were hard to collect afterwards because various things happened in different places, but basically Bruno made some sort of clumsy pass at Jeannette, which Philip witnessed. Philip got into a jealous rage, and he and Bruno had a fight. I suppose now, thinking back, that there was more noise than terror in this, but they both ended up with a black eye, and Bruno had a split lip too, which bled like the devil. Meanwhile, and elsewhere, Marie-O had had far too much to drink, been sick, and then been put to bed by Michel. As a friendly gesture, and just to comfort her, Michel climbed into bed with her for a few minutes to give her a cuddle and warm her up. Unfortunately, however, he fell asleep. When the parents came running to find out what all the racket was about, they found Bruno and Philip doing battlefield imitations, Jeannette looking all-too-stunningly inappropriate in a white cotton nightie covered in bloodstains, Michel sound asleep in Marie-O's innocent arms, and me clearly not in charge of anything, least of all my guests. This was, still is, a grave dereliction in the Beaumanière household.

'We were all in disgrace, of course. Michel was sent home the next morning by train. My mother rang Philip's father in London to explain why he would be returning home "disfigured", and apologized for this in a way that made it quite clear that she did not feel the slightest bit apologetic because it was the product of the boy's own reckless bad behaviour. Happily my mother couldn't speak English, and Philip reckoned his father would have understood less that twenty per cent of this. Marie-O got a lecture from my father on the correct deportment of *Énarques*. I had to endure various fairly familiar tortures. "Bé-Bé" was made a great fuss of, and had to have some stitches in his lip. But I could see what he couldn't: that my mother's concern for him was her idea of being a good hostess, and that actually she felt nothing but contempt for any man who would, one, make sexual advances to a household servant, and two, mistake Jeannette for a household servant. He was doomed, and never set foot in the house again. On the other hand, I think my mother, for all her apparent displeasure, was secretly very pleased with Philip, because he had defended Jeannette's honour. But she couldn't say so at the time because fighting was a breach of good manners, and Bruno was family. And of course she knew nothing of their love affair.

'We went back to Paris that evening, and I was in school all day on the Monday. But I met Philip, who was going to be leaving the next day, in the Balzar in the late afternoon. I was astonished to learn from him that he had just spent several hours with Jeannette, mainly walking in the Luxembourg Gardens. This really was amazing because she had never been to Paris before. Never been out of the Sologne, in fact. I could hardly believe it. Philip was looking terrible, pinched and deeply unhappy. When I asked him why, he told me that he and Jeannette were finished, and that he didn't expect to see her again. I remember saying to him, "But you love her!", and his replying that yes, he did. But then he went on to say a lot of things that I didn't really understand at the time, and so have probably not remembered very well – that he didn't want to be that person, the one who loved Jeannette. That he despised him, and that she should too. That he wanted space, but that he didn't know where, or what for, and she might make it impossible for him to find it. That he had a horror of ending up in a suburban villa somewhere. That he had to escape, but that his first idea of her – that she would help him to do it – might turn out to be a trap. He was ashamed, he said, and couldn't understand, given his mixture of feelings and thoughts, why he couldn't stop loving her. He supposed there were just some objects in life that one loved, but which it was better to do without.

'Then he said one thing which was rather peculiar, but which I've always remembered because it puzzled me terribly at the time. Still does, in fact. "I think," he said, "that a lot of life is going to be like this. We will know what might be true, but our being there will prevent it." The next day he went back to London.

'We saw a lot more of each other over the next couple of years, until he went to Oxford, but he never came back here to "La Forge", and he never mentioned Jeannette, and, in a sense, as I eventually came to see, things were never ever again the same between us. It was as if in finishing with Jeannette he somehow also finished not so much with us as with himself. He cut himself adrift from the person he had been, and became someone else.

'Funnily enough, his mother said something similar to me about him at the funeral. She said, poor Philip, he'd been such a happy boy, so lively and funny and fun to be with, and then something seemed to happen to him in his teens, and he changed into someone she couldn't understand. I pretended to some conventional view or the other, philosophers being difficult and so on, but actually I knew exactly what she meant.' Here he fell silent for a moment, and gave Florence a rueful smile. She had been sitting very quietly at the table, concentrating on his face, and I noticed now the look of deep concern that seemed to suffuse her whole body. And it was through her, or my suddenly seeing this in her, that I realized that Roland was feeling very emotional, and was close to tears.

'Sometimes when I come here,' he said, indicating with his arm out through the door into the sunlight and the courtyard, 'I think I can still feel his presence, like a ghost. All that laughter, and his cleverness, and his jokes, and the happiness, and the way he used to, well, glow, really. And Jeannette watching him with those blue, faithful eyes. And my parents completely unaware. And our world, his and mine and Michel's, safe and separate and bound to last for ever.'

Roland may have been overcome at this point, because he

covered up by getting out a cigarette and going out into the yard to light it. He stood with his back to us, a line of deep shadow creeping towards him from the west side of the building. I could see his shoulders rising and falling with the deep breaths he was taking, his head thrown back to look up at the sky and the treetops rising above the roofs as he blew streams of cigarette smoke up into the air. In the silence of his going out Florence said, in her fractured English, 'This is a thing I think we do not understand perhaps enough. Women, that is. That men too have friends, other men, and feel very much for them.'

I agreed with her. It's a feature of the modern world. We women have created a myth that it's only we who are capable of these kinds of friendships, that something similar among and between men is mawkish and silly, so that a lot of men have been fooled into thinking that it's so, that it isn't manly to have or to express the feelings of intimacy or affection or delicate understanding that they might have with other men. So they shy away from it. And their lives are poorer as a result. There was a lot of sorrow in the way that Florence said what she did. And when Roland came in again a few minutes later she changed the subject by saying to him, in French, something like, 'I think Alice would like to hear about Jeannette and Micheline now. You have been very tantalizing.' He gave me a very beautiful smile, and went to rinse his fingers at the sink, to sprinkle water on his face. 'Of course you would,' he said, drying himself, then blowing his nose. 'Forgive me.

'Micheline. Now I didn't learn about Micheline for several years. Like Philip, I didn't come down here to "La Forge" after that summer. For one thing we started going to the Midi. Also, as I realized later, we didn't come down here precisely because of Jeannette and the baby, and my mother's decision, initially at any rate, to conceal it from us. Danielle in particular, I imagine. So I didn't learn about Micheline until my father told me "everything you need to know", as he put it, when I turned twenty-one. He did it in the context of informing me that he intended to make "La Forge" over to me on my twenty-fifth birthday. And before you start thinking that it was a bit quaint that I should learn about Jeannette's baby as part of a family property transaction, let me reassure you that the truth was far better than that, really. My parents cared for Jeannette, and were determined to protect and look after her, and this was my father's way of letting me know that when "La Forge" became mine, it carried with it certain obligations, and I was to take them seriously.

'What happened apparently was that Mamette, in a great state of agitation, made one of her rare appearances in Paris some time in December of that year, 1972, and broke the news to my parents that Jeannette was pregnant. My mother went straight back with her to Viglain. Jeannette told her that it had happened in October, but she absolutely refused to say who the father was. Mamette had her suspicions – a boy from the village who'd been employed to turn over the vegetable patch for winter planting – but Jeannette sneered at this, and by all accounts my father did too, when he heard about it. My mother, who was very religious, becoming increasingly so in those days, thought that she was going to have to dissuade Jeannette from having an abortion. She needn't have worried, however. Jeannette was quite deter-mined to have the baby. What Jeannette was worried about, and she told me this herself much later on, was that my mother would insist that she have the baby adopted. But she needn't have worried either. My mother believed very firmly in the principle that, wherever possible, a mother should raise her own children. My mother wasn't pleased, of course. Jeannette had demonstrated a regrettable lack of judgement. I'm sure that's how she would have described it, once the initial shock had worn off. But, on the other hand, to be a bit ungenerous, at least it had happened to Jeannette and not to Danielle, who must have been a constant worry during these years. Also, I think my mother rather admired Jeannette's pride in refusing to discuss the paternity. Also her stoicism in accepting what had happened, her obvious truthfulness in saying that it wouldn't ever happen again, and her remorse at the trouble she was causing.

'In the event, I doubt that she caused much trouble at all. Mamette will have clucked round her like a maternal hen, and it wasn't as if there was a shortage of space at "La Forge", or of money at the bank. My father shrugged it off, probably happy, in his own way, to indulge another female member of the family. When Micheline was born he readily agreed to be her godfather, and as the years went by he played this role with ever-greater pleasure. It would have made him very happy to be at the wedding yesterday.

'I first met Micheline in the summer of 1976, when she was three, indeed not long after my father had told me about her. Curiosity, no doubt. Michel came down with me, and I think we both knew, as soon as we saw her, that she was Philip's child. Jeannette got us to swear that we would never tell anyone, and once we had done that she told us the parts of the story that we had never been told, or hadn't been able to piece together for ourselves.

'She and Philip had made love together only once, she said. It had happened on that dreadful weekend, on the Friday night, after the rest of us had gone to bed, and before the guests arrived on the Saturday morning. She had taken him up to the valley field – where we were this morning, though there was no vineyard there then, just pasture, and the lights of the village far away on the other side of the valley. He had been very tender. She said he made her feel complete. Conventional, I know, but true for her.

'After this came the awful events of the Saturday night and Sunday morning, and our departure on the Sunday evening. Together, these things had made it impossible for her even to talk to Philip again. And he was leaving for England, and wouldn't be back for a year. She couldn't face the thought of this without their having some sort of understanding, so on the Monday morning she made an excuse to Mamette, and walked into

Viglain. There she caught the bus to Sully, the local train to Orléans, and thence to Paris. On arrival she rang our house and got Philip. He went to find her at the station, and then took her to the Left Bank, where they walked as far as the Luxembourg Gardens. Then she told him all the things that she had been burning to say, why she had come to Paris to see him: that if he wanted, whatever he wanted, then she would do anything to go on being near him.

'He seemed very happy, and she was very happy too. They had something to eat on the street, and he went with her back to the station and helped her to find her train. "Then out of nowhere," as she said, he became grim and cold and distant, like someone struggling for something he feels he must have but does not really want. He wouldn't kiss her. He wouldn't let her touch him. He just said that he thought they should part and never see each other again. And then he walked away. And she never did see him again. But she was convinced that he still loved her. And the following June, twenty-four years ago yesterday, she had his child.'

'Does she know?'

'Who, Micheline?'

'Yes.'

'No.'

'Did Philip?'

'I'm sure he didn't. This was the whole point. Jeannette discovered that she was pregnant three weeks or so later. She realized that if she so much as hinted at the responsibility being his, then he would accept it. But he had broken with her irrevocably. And to undo the breach was impossible. She made up her mind that he was not to know, and events conspired to help in ensuring that it was so. I am absolutely certain that Michel and I were the only people who knew. And she didn't tell us. We guessed it. I don't know whether this was very mature of Michel and me, or very juvenile, but it's one or the other, there's no in between. We felt a strong sense of responsibility towards

Jeannette and Micheline because Philip was one of us, part of us if you like. There was a "one for all, all for one" quality about this friendship, and other people might laugh at it, but it mattered to us. Jeannette was doing the honourable thing. Philip hadn't been dishonourable. He didn't know about the baby. In some obscure way I felt that, in breaking off with Jeannette when he still loved her so much, he was trying to protect her from himself, from a side of himself that he didn't like. I kept remembering him saying that he felt ashamed. And that remark of his about knowing the truth, but preventing it by his presence. So we decided to keep their secret, but to sort of watch over it. Michel's decision to ask Jeannette to marry him was definitely a part of this, and Jeannette understood it for what it was. As did I.

'I did write and tell Philip that Michel had married, but this was only after Michel's funeral. I told him that Michel had married in a hurry "for obvious reasons" just before going to the Lebanon, and that he had left a widow and a little girl. Philip wrote to the colonel and Adèle Morisot. He must have assumed that he didn't know who the widow was. Poor old Adèle was completely devastated by Michel's death, and just withered. She died within a couple of years.'

'And Philip never learned anything else about this young woman, his daughter?'

'I don't think so. I never told him, and I'm certain that Jeannette didn't. Philip and I didn't write letters to each other. A note occasionally, if we were expecting to visit, but even then usually we'd ring. As you know we used to send you both our annual Christmas letter, with all the family news, and the last one did have something in it about Micheline and François planning a summer wedding, but he wouldn't have known who this was a reference to. Funnily enough, I did plan once to tell Philip that it was Jeannette whom Michel had married. I thought I could do that without his knowing that the child was his, and not Michel's. As usual we arranged to meet at the Balzar, this would have been maybe eighteen months or so after Michel was killed, but in the event I didn't tell him. We actually talked a great deal about you on that occasion. I think you had recently met, and he was feeling very pleased with life.'

Florence had gone out of the kitchen shortly before this, and she returned now, fastening on her wristwatch. A signal perhaps, because Roland stood up and said he was sorry, there was so much still to talk about, but they had to be on their way. It was late afternoon, and the entrances to Paris got very jammed up on Sunday evenings, and they needed to make a start. I offered to wash up, but they said to leave it. Madame Belvoir would look after it in the morning. They locked up the house, and the three of us walked out to our cars together, through the archway, across the lawn and the little hump-backed bridge.

'I would love to come here again,' I said.

'Well, you must,' said Florence.

'And we will taste the wine,' said Roland. 'See if Philip would have approved.'

'What about Micheline?'

'I'm sure she would take a glass, in mod . . .'

'I meant . . .'

'I realize. I was imitating Philip. He used to do that, didn't he? Deliberately answer the wrong question.'

I laughed. 'He used to say all questions were interesting, and the supposedly obvious ones often the most interesting.'

We stopped alongside our cars, and Florence opened the back door of their station wagon for the two dogs to jump in. They flopped down, backs up against the rear seats.

'How much of the story does she know?'

'I discussed this with Jeannette after Michel was killed,' said Roland. 'Micheline believes that Michel was her legitimate father. Indeed, that she was named after him. And that her father and mother were unable to marry initially because of the hostility they knew it would incur from his parents. She believes that they concealed her existence from them until the spring of 1978, when they decided that they would get married in the teeth of his parents' opposition because of his Beirut posting. She remembers the wedding. She was nearly five years old after all. Colonel Morisot was reconciled to Jeannette and Micheline after Adèle died. He is her grandfather. She believes in him just as he believes in her.'

'Did you tell Madame Jeanne, Jeannette, that you were going to tell me the truth about all this?'

'No, I didn't. I have explained all this to you because I owe it to Philip, who was my friend. But apart from Florence here, you are the only person I have told. My own children don't know, and never will. I expect you to keep it in confidence.'

I agreed, and went to shake hands. Roland ignored this gesture and enfolded me in an embrace. When he did so, I could feel the emotion still running in him. Then Florence took both my hands in hers and kissed me on both cheeks, and we said goodbye. 'Come back for the wine,' Roland called out, as he put his car in gear and started forward. 'You will see!' I followed them down the driveway, and when we reached the Viglain road, we turned, with waves and smiles, in opposite directions.

I drove back to Clémont, but didn't stay long: just long enough to feed Boswell and change my shoes. Then I drove back to 'La Forge' – in the evening sun now, a delicious warmth in the air, fragrant with grass and wild flowers, and the smells of woodland. I parked once again by the stream, and then walked back the way that I had gone with Roland in the morning, through the gate, across the garden into the wood, then up the hill through the trees to the vineyard. This time, however, I didn't go down among the vines, but turned to my right, and followed the line of trees until I found what I remembered: the dry-stone wall, rather more than waist-high, which divided the woodland trees from the field. From here, in the days before the vines were planted, you would have had a clear, uninterrupted view of the valley, and, on its far side, of the little hamlet of Villemême. At the base of the wall, for as far as one could see, were the wild flowers and grasses that I remembered from the morning: clover and dandelion, cowslip and buttercup, periwinkle, poppies and foxgloves. Here, half among the vines and half among the wild flowers, I scattered Philip's ashes. Dust where his past had been lived, and his future had been made.

V

I decided not to stay on any longer in Clémont. I packed as soon as I got back to the house, loaded up the car, and left Madame Jeanne a note saying that I'd been called back to London on urgent business. Apologies. Thanks. I would write again from England. (Which I did and sent her a present, and subsequently heard more both of her, and Micheline and François, from Felix, who went down for two months in mid July.) Then I drove in to Orléans and booked myself into a central hotel. I went to see Beatrix in the morning: sitting up, very cheerful, expecting a visit from Bertrand Plessis. It was just a week since I had found her almost unconscious, lying in a puddle. We had a quick talk about detox alternatives, and I invited her to come and stay with me in London. She gave me a long, long hug. In the space of eleven days I seemed to have found more kindred spirits to cling to than I had in all the previous eleven years.

Back in England I devoted the rest of the week to moving into the Victoria flat, and ferrying things from the Barbican to Oxford. Then I started back at the bank. It was three weeks after this, when I went down to Cranham Street with one or two last bits and pieces of furniture, that I began going through Philip's correspondence files in his study there. I was planning to weed them, to make space in the cabinet for some of my own papers from London. I didn't get far. In the second folder, the Bs, was a file of end-of-year letters from the Beaumanières. As I was flicking through them, my eye fell upon this paragraph at the end of their most recent message, from the previous December:

296

And already there are family pleasures and joys to anticipate in the year ahead. It was with immense pleasure that we learned, just a few weeks ago, that our goddaughter Micheline Morisot, Jeannette's daughter, is to marry her friend and fiancé François Bazard, next midsummer's day, which is also her 24th birthday. An occasion of great happiness made doubly . . .

And on the floor of Philip's study, on my knees at his filing cabinet, I saw him once again sitting upright in bed on Christmas morning, the mail scattered around us. There was Alan's little volume of Australian verse, my anxiety to conceal it, the combination of distress and excitement that I thought I could see in his face and hear in his voice. And without my knowing, the ground of the past shifting. And simultaneously, like a flood of words all released at once, I recalled what he had said later that day as we walked across the fields to Benfield. How life was a set of variations on a theme. So that perhaps I understood at the end what Philip's theme was: how for some reason he was unable to accept the love that we brought him; how his encounters with it so overwhelmed him that he turned it aside, rejected it, and then had to bear all that emptiness and isolation. And how constant this theme had been, through all the variations played upon it by time, circumstance and memory.